Lifeblood

J. CHANNING

LIFEBLOOD

Red Team Ink
DBA of Zealot Solutions, Idaho LLC
9480 W. River Beach Lane
Garden City, ID 83714
Copyright © 2024 by Red Team Ink

All rights reserved. Without limiting the rights under the copyright reserved above, no part of this publication may be reproduced, stored in, or introduced into a retrieval system, or transmitted in any form or by any means (electronic, mechanical, photocopying, recording, or otherwise) without prior written permission.

This is a work of fiction. Names, characters, businesses, places, events and incidents are either the products of the author's imagination or used in a fictitious manner. Any resemblance to actual persons, living or dead, or actual events is purely coincidental.

For permission requests or information about discounts for special bulk purchases please contact: redteamink@gmail.com. Substantial discounts on bulk orders are available to corporations, professional associations, and small businesses.

Printed in The United States of America

ISBNs: print: 979-8-3303-4858-9 || electronic: 979-8-3303-4859-6

Title: Lifeblood

Description: First Edition

Editing, proofreading, formatting, and cover concept by Donna Lane

CONTENTS

1	Fallout	1
2	Inge's Tale	19
3	The Resistance	49
4	Sam's Story	71
5	Somewhen Else	101
6	Roots	155
7	Hollywoodland	183
8	Festivities	243
9	Bombshells	259
10	Forever	309
	About the Author	355

| 1 |

Fallout

Der Dom, Bavaria, December 25, 1943, 0207h

Columns of fire swept the control panels, curling red-hot across the debris-strewn floor near where Yanis had landed. Someone dragged him toward the curtain of blue light, but before they could force their way through the smoke and screams and mayhem, the mountain lurched suddenly. A sequence of drumbeats boomed through the rock, as though a stampeding beast might soon add itself to their enemies. Instead, the shaking intensified and Yanis would always remember that the mountain, seemingly tired of these endless human commotions in its bowels, began to *growl*. He was pulled by his shirt collar, then harder still by the very skin of his shoulder, into the strange there-but-not-there blue of the curtain. Then, just as he thought they were safe, ten earthquakes began all at once, from within the rock *above* them.

The attacking SS unit paused, worried that the abused stone fabric of the mine would split asunder and crush them under numberless tons of rock. Most had looked up, though an assault team was continuing its advance on the control panels. Two of the console's metal legs had collapsed, and the panels, with their sensitive dials, were being warped by tongues of flame from underneath. A trooper reached the console and braved the flames to grab at the levers and dials. After such horrendous losses, he risked death rather than let these brazen enemies slip away; he hoped to stall and confuse them, even as Yanis' team sheltered within the time device itself.

"Let's go!" someone was yelling, a man who was in pain. They could see the struggling trooper, his ambition finally exceeding his grasp as his uniform caught fire. He wheeled away, screaming, only one awful noise among a dozen.

But around them, within the placid, hazy marine blue of the chamber, there was only a chorus of demands from everyone who still had enough breath. As the descending curtain of dirt and rubble began to enclose the ship, there were screams for Yanis to *do something*, to *get them out*, get them OUT, *now. Now. NOW...*

***

Unknown Location, Unknown Date

For two seconds, there was nothing but a sound deep in Yanis' skull, intense and obscuring, as though he had fingers in his ears and his jaw clenched. Then, he saw that the light had changed. The terrible orange glow of SS *Flammenwerfer*, which had ferociously lit *Der Dom*, was gone. He looked around, searching for the approaching Nazi death squads. Surely, they'd found a way to follow them to … wherever this was.

Then everything lurched and he felt the ground drop from under him. Sick to his stomach with sudden vertigo, he hadn't even time to shout in complaint before the movement ceased with a firm, resolute bump. Outside, he heard trees being split apart, loud and close, as though a huge lumberjack were at work.

The walls of the compartment were yielding their blue color. As they gradually became transparent in all three hundred sixty degrees, Yanis was able to confirm his first suspicions.

"We've moved!"

And as he peered through the clearing haze, detached still from his own senses by the horrors of the mine, he found they could see outside the ship.

"This isn't the mountain. We've definitely moved!"

There were trees, illuminated by soft sunlight. It could have been a spring morning, fine and fresh.

We escaped the mine. And we're not dead. Best news all day.

A face appeared before him, streaked with sweat and dirt. "Talk to me, Yanis."

"Huh?"

The sound in his ears was receding only slowly; as his hearing began to clear, he found he was musing to himself.

Earthquakes that come from above, and tinnitus which rings low, like a church bell. This is one crazy ride.

The voice tried to follow him, but he raised a hand and took a quick turn around the chamber. "It's translucent, like a curtain made from some kind of ..." He turned again, suddenly, but the perspective was consistent. "It can't be a projection, surely." He wandered the circumference of the chamber, loathe to touch the invisible drapes, and soon found that he'd circled back to where he started.

And remembered that he'd forgotten to check on Jillian.

Way to show some chivalry, Romeo.

"Jillian!" he breathed. "Are you ..."

She was sitting upright, hugging her knees, too shocked to speak. Unbound, her long, brown hair was a mat of disorder, and she was pale, almost shivering. Yanis crouched down next to her and held her close, oblivious to anything but her, even in such an ignominious moment. Her hair smelled of cordite, and of the cloying, awful naphtha which fueled the *Flammenwerfer,* and her green uniform shirt, three sizes too large, was torn and stained with grime and sweat. They sat quietly, watching the others adjusting to their new situation. "I'm okay," she said finally, sounding exhausted. "Yanis, where are we?"

But once more, Yanis was called to attention by the soldier's urgent, mud-streaked face. "I need a situation report." It was Captain Keller, one of only two NATO soldiers still with them, and the most senior man still in fighting condition.

"A situation report, right," Yanis said. "We're in the woods," he felt confident enough to say.

"Or," Jillian qualified, "it *looks like* we're in the woods."

All Keller wanted was some simple answers. "Are we still in Bavaria?" Like the others, he looked like hell, with singed hair and a range of cuts and scrapes on his exposed skin.

"Sorry, Captain, I'll need a little time to figure out the rest." Yanis brushed down his shirt, which had been awaiting the opportunity and simply fell into ragged pieces. Unconcerned, he paced with Jillian over to the others. "This is as grim as it gets, but we have to see who survived," he said to her.

"Yeah." She quickly tore a length of fabric from Yanis' old shirt and used it to tie back her hair. "Salon perfection."

The group looked bedraggled, burned, and pitifully, tragically small. An area about the size of a basketball court, black-floored and cool, surrounded by a panoramic woodland view, held every survivor from Operation Asphodel. All of them were wounded, including the assault's erstwhile leader, Sergeant Jim Thompson, and a single French NATO soldier, Clavel, whose lungs still gurgled from the effects of tabun gas.

Somehow, four Royal Marines from 1944 had made it through, though Marine Stewart had an awful leg wound and could not stand. Five of the 82nd Airborne troops had also survived, but they seemed in worse shape still. Two knelt by the side of another, trying in vain to coax him back to consciousness, while the other pair remained immobile on their improvised stretchers, either shot or gassed, Yanis couldn't tell.

In total, Yanis found, their forces had dwindled to a handful, with only Sergeant Jenkins, Harry Entwhistle, and perhaps five of the others capable of combat.

"My God, Yanis," gasped Jillian. It was scarcely believable. "Five *thousand* parachuted in, but ..."

"Not now," he said, reaching for her. "Just ... breathe with me, okay?" It was all he could think of, and all he wanted. A silent minute together, in each other's arms, when they could stop everything else and just be grateful.

Because, for all the confusion and death, Jillian had *survived*. He thanked God, as sincerely as he ever had. If he'd lost her, and been forced to solve this deadly puzzle alone ...

Snap out of it. First, figure things out. Then wallow in the indulgent pain of 'might-have-been.'

"So," asked Jillian, replacing the torn fabric with a ponytail holder which had miraculously survived in her uniform pants pocket, "what's the word, Professor Miller?"

"No idea," Yanis said. "There are gonna be plenty of questions we can't answer for a while, so let's prioritize a bit."

"Best that we start with the where and the when," recommended Jillian. "Those are the critical data points right now."

"Well, we're definitely not in Kansas anymore. Doesn't look like southern Germany, either." It was a deciduous forest, quiet and deep, seemingly miles from anywhere.

"Did you expect we'd change location, as well as chronology?" Jillian was asking him as they toured the edge of the compartment together.

"It had crossed my mind, but we didn't know enough to say." He renewed his fascination for the ship's capacity to transform itself. "No obvious seams. It's like a projection, but the perspective's completely convincing—"

"I mean, I figured we'd still be under the mountain," Jillian was trying to tell him, "but that we'd jump to another time, maybe before the Germans found the machine."

A delightful puzzle though the projection was, Yanis tried to focus; she was right about the key data points. "The control panels were in the middle," he reminded her with a shudder, "of being incinerated, so your guess is as good as mine."

Although the critical panels hadn't been visible from their hazy, blue chamber, Yanis had a distinct memory of troopers approaching the consoles, and flames all around them.

If they had been destroyed...

"But they worked well enough to get us here," she said.

"I'll be sure to include that in my online review of *Der Dom* on NaziMountainAdventures.com. 'Amenities remained open and available, even when they were on fire.'"

Of the consoles themselves, of course, there was no sign. As far as he could tell, the chamber had separated from the remainder of the ship.

Which completely wrecked any notion of traveling onward. "Got to feel like the ship knew it had to bail out. Like it knew the roof was gonna cave in."

"Another very useful feature of the design," she said. "Well, I suppose it felt this was the best place to bring us." She had to accept the other aspect, too, one which loomed large. "Or maybe the best *time* to bring us to."

He shook his head hard, as if to clear it. "You're giving agency to a *spacecraft?*" Yanis asked. "You think it analyzed our situation and decided to help us?"

"Yep," she said. "Know how I'm so sure?" She pointed toward the exhausted, bloodied knot of soldiers. "Thompson was the third-last to be dragged in, before Clavel and you. We set Jim on the other side, away from the curtain, in case any fire came through."

Looking around, Yanis couldn't see the sergeant. "Yeah, I think I remember. So?"

"So now," she said, pivoting right and pointing to a recessed area of the floor, "he's, well, in this thing, here."

"This is new," Yanis saw at once. The whole floor was covered in a thick, flat, coal-black coating, somewhat like rubber, except for one area. In a space just large enough to park a family car, it had reorganized itself into an orange, two-tier bay, about two meters deep. In the top 'bunk,' behind a transparent film, was Jim Thompson. The lower was empty.

"That's a little unnerving," said Yanis. "Looks like the ship can change or reassign materials at will. But what's it for?" He peered into the recessed, orange bay and saw a familiar shape. "Wait, is that Jim, down there?" Together, he and Jillian looked, then others came to confirm the find. It was Thompson, and he was breathing.

Sergeant Jenkins heard Thompson's name mixed with gasps of surprise, and instantly ran across the compartment. "Is he alive?" Then, like everyone else when they first encountered the self-formed medical bays, he asked, "What the hell's he doing down *there?*"

The bay seemed custom-built for an injured human. Jim's head was supported with a white cradle made from slender, interlaced fibers. A black mouthpiece was settled between his teeth, and though Jenkins guessed it was to protect his tongue if he had a seizure, it was in fact an oxygen tube. The black valve moved slightly with each breath, apparently helping the air into his lungs.

"I've got to hand it to the ship's medical staff," Yanis tried to joke, "whoever and wherever they are." It seemed quite simply miraculous; the sergeant had been brought both sixty feet across the room, and simultaneously, back from the brink.

"He's able to breathe?" Jenkins marveled. "After the gas attack, I thought we'd lost him."

"No lie," Yanis said, head down, pained by the memory. "That stuff, the gas," he shuddered, "was just ..."

Before Yanis looked back toward them, Jillian had reached under the orange film and put her hand on Jim's.

"Whoa! We don't know that's safe!"

She gave him a look, one which was becoming habitual. It meant, 'Why don't you think I can handle stuff?' Jillian assessed the sergeant, albeit inexpertly, to have good vital signs. "He's warm, but not feverish."

A figure joined them, and it took Yanis a moment to recognize Harry Entwhistle. "Harry, thank God," Yanis exclaimed, "I thought you were—"

"Having m'self a cuppa in the mess?" quipped the dusty, exhausted Scot.

"Well, erm ..." Yanis could only say.

"Dead?" was Entwhistle's second try.

"Yeah."

"Happy to disabuse you, old chap." He reached instinctively for a top jacket pocket which was both torn to smithereens, and depressingly devoid of cigarettes. "Hell's tits," he observed, worried. "Anyone got a gasper? Anyone?" Moments later, Yanis heard him canvasing the wounded. "Just one, old boy, cross my heart I'll pay you back double."

With Jim Thompson's hand still clasped in her own, Jillian watched the men slowly coming to terms with their new surroundings. "We've been here twenty whole minutes," Yanis said, "and no one's come to attack us, yet."

"Bloody good thing, too," said Entwhistle. "If a ten-point buck wandered into view, I don't think I'd have anything to shoot it with." In other words, Yanis knew, although they had beaten the odds, they could easily be beaten by any stroke of bad luck. It was time to take stock and understand their situation.

Jillian stayed with Jim and kept an eye on the three unconscious survivors—two Airborne men, and a Royal Marine. The remaining Airborne joined the little meeting, their heads bowed. One muttered to the others that their platoon-mate, Cuthbertson, had just died. "Better way for it," Entwhistle told him compassionately. "The laddy couldn'e breathe, poor sod."

All the remainder were 'walking wounded,' and they gathered to hear Entwhistle sum things up.

"Righto," Harry said. He'd miraculously found cigarettes from somewhere. "Hello, everybody."

"Hey, Harry," replied a cluster of tired voices.

"Our esteemed German colleague from NATO," he pronounced the still-unfamiliar acronym *nah-tow*, "is the senior officer, but Captain Keller, I understand you wanted to do something formally?" There was a quick discussion, confirming details already agreed. "Yes, alright. It's been decided that I should take nominal military command of the operation." There were no objections; Entwhistle had been a tower of calm competence during each stage of their mission at *Der Dom*. In the end, once he'd had a chance to explain what in God's name a 'Company Quartermaster Sergeant Major' might be, the Americans concluded that he was outranked only by Thompson, the wounded, scared Frenchman, Lieutenant Clavel, and Captain Keller.

"Can I say, before we begin, how relieved I am to see every last one of you? Even the ugly ones," he added. "I literally thought I'd be the last fucker standing. I mean, the last *man* standing," he said with a courteous nod to Jillian, "but then our NATO friends and the lady policeman here, well, they performed bleedin' *miracles*, isn't that the truth?"

Whistles and some tired applause were her reward. From his pole-and-canvas stretcher, Lt. Clavel raised an exhausted hand, but the young Frenchman was too tired even to smile.

"And then somehow, we're here," Entwhistle found. "Professor Miller," he began, generating more applause, "is there any new information on that question?"

Yanis summed up what they knew. "We're on Earth."

The biggest of the Royal Marines, Corporal Osborne, felt it was time for a joke. "Thank *fuck* for that!" he exclaimed. "I'm still wanted by the Martian police after last time!"

"Anything else, Professor?" asked Harry hopefully.

"Um. We're in the woods."

Once Jenkins burst out laughing, the others couldn't help it. "Well done, professor," the young sergeant chuckled. "Now I know how it feels to work with Sherlock Holmes."

"Do they pay you actual *money* at that fancy college of yours?" came another jibe, this time in a British accent.

Miller found a little more patience, but his reserves of this—and absolutely everything else—were nearing their red lines. "Deciduous trees," he announced. "That tells us we weren't flung a long way into the past."

"What's he mean?" another of the Marines asked. "I'm crap at history, but I'm pretty sure they had *trees*, even 'way back' in the 1930s."

There was an unnerving twang from one of the few cords keeping Yanis tethered to the ground. "What gave you the impression," he asked the younger man, "that we've only traveled a handful of years?"

The Marine, Corporal Hyde, looked a bit uncertain but replied, "Well, that SS chap, Koch, or whatever his name was, he zipped forward seventy years. So, I thought that was, you know, like a limit, or something. Otherwise, why wouldn't he go way, way further into the future, and take advantage of all the—"

"Shut up," Yanis said.

"Oi, now I don't know how you're used to doing things," growled Hyde.

"I said, shut up," Yanis repeated. "And listen."

"Please," Harry Entwhistle added for him. "If you wouldn't mind, corporal."

"Alright," Hyde sniffed, "you're the professor. Let's have it."

"Picture," Yanis began, "a handsome, blond dude. Now picture him dropping out of the sky one Thursday afternoon in the thirty-fifth century and announcing that he's a Nazi from 1943." He looked around, making sure the whole group was with him; if they were underestimating the power of this spacecraft, he'd quickly set them right. "How far do you think he'd get, huh? Keck needed a shit-ton of money, lots of introductions, arrangements for secret meetings, you name it. After a few generations, there'd be no hope of sustaining a large, active group of Nazi sympathizers." He explained for a moment, describing Keck's resources as an 'ecosystem' but some tired eyes were glazing over.

"Fair enough, Professor, but that still doesn't tell us *where* or *when* we are, does it? Unless you've got some other fancy theories you want to try?" Hyde asked.

"It's not a theory, but it's a possibility," he said, "that we've been sent into a different timeline."

Jillian worked it out. "Still 1943, but someone *else's* 1943. Not the one you all started in."

"Someone catch my brain, please," Entwhistle said, "if it falls out of my ears again."

Osborne stood. "We could try going outside," the corporal suggested. "Have a look around. See what's what, you know?"

Jillian clapped her hands and rubbed them together. "Excellent, Corporal Osborne. We'll have a gander. Well done volunteering to lead the way."

***

There were plenty of theories to go around, enough for each person in the chamber. In the end, Jenkins and Keller decided there was no point in delaying, and that they should prepare to leave. "For one thing," the German explained, "many of us need medical attention. It might be available here."

Confronted by a thousand equally plausible outcomes, Yanis turned to humor. "Alright, I'm taking bets," he declared. "I got odds of seven-to-two, says we're in the second millennium, but the *first* millennium is at twelve-to-one, so grab it while it's hot."

Jenkins weighed these up. "Nah, what else?"

"Sixteen-to-one says the whole thing is a massive computer simulation. That's my theory."

"How's that go, then?" Entwhistle asked.

"In theory, if we walk out there," Yanis claimed, "we'll all march face-first into the outer wall of the gaming chamber, and some audience of aliens will laugh at us."

"Will we win any points for doing that?" Jillian asked rhetorically. She was keeping up with the discussion but as short on data as everyone else.

"Maybe it's like *The Truman Show*," Keller offered. "Out there, beyond the shell, there's just a whole bunch of camera people and producers. Right now, they're in ecstasy because confusion and misery are so very *good* for television."

Yanis had adopted a cross-legged position on the floor, but now he rose purposefully. "You have to be *alive* to be confused and miserable. I'll take those two over the alternative." He began probing the outer wall of the chamber with his fingertips. The screen was permeable, but not at every location. Yanis calculated there were 'hardened' bands within the screen, placed roughly every thirty degrees around the circle. These areas remained transparent but resisted physical pressure; Jenkins' hand sunk half an inch, but then the material seemed to firm up and rebuff him. "Exit only," the sergeant decided. "Let's try farther along."

In the end, it was almost too simple; once they found the right place, they just eased into the wall as though it were a vertical sleeping bag, and suddenly they were through and outside. Yanis was delighted to see a sturdy, metal ramp emerge to lead them down to the ground, around three meters below.

The forest's air hit them immediately, and all at once. "Oh, crikey, *that's* more like it," Entwhistle enthused, taking in deep gusts to cleanse his silted, irritated lungs. "Almost as good as a cigarette, after a long while without."

The dry leaves underfoot made a crunch almost like snow, but the air was that of a late spring morning in New England. With each step into the blanket of dry leaves, the group offended the forest's deep silence, but the chance to stretch and breathe in open space—and in near-solitude, for the first time in weeks—was irresistible.

"Stay within sight of someone at all times," Entwhistle reminded them. "If I understood Miller, it could be dinosaurs from the right, or courtly knights from the left. Let's keep our eyes open."

It was only minutes before someone spotted a deer, darting away into the birch wood. "You mean, a huge spacecraft landing in The Forest of Silence didn't scare them away?" Jillian asked.

Two men were dispatched to trap it, though with its pursuers exhausted from battle, the creature had a head start. The others wandered around the wood in a dazed, relieved kind of bemusement.

"Without any buildings to clue us in," Osborne commented to his squad mates, "this could be anywhere."

"Deer are familiar and reassuring," Yanis said. "They're Earth creatures."

Jillian said, "Thought we'd already decided we're on Earth."

"The game's designers *want* us to believe that," Yanis hypothesized mischievously, "but what's actually true?"

She slapped his backside. "Things are already complicated. No need to go all Stephen Hawking on this group."

"Yeah. Simplest explanations are usually the best, anyway." He paused, spotting another angle for his burgeoning business as a bookmaker. "I'm taking dollars, euros, or pounds sterling. Eight-to-one, this whole thing is a collective dream, and we're all asleep in *Der Dom* after Christmas dinner."

Another slap from behind. "Stop it."

"Sorry."

"I know you're freaked out, but there's no need to spread it around. These guys want straightforward answers."

He shrugged, then rubbed his eyes, causing an oily smear around each one. "I ain't got any right now. And I won't until we find a way through."

For its part, the spacecraft remained very discreet. Its outer wall, a geometric circle, curving away on either side, shimmered very slightly as it impersonated the background landscape. The effect was convincing enough to have an observer doubting their eyes. The outer membrane of the compartment—or ship, or whatever it truly was—allowed members of the team to come and go, but only through the single hatchway with its steep, metallic ramp. The gradient added to the difficulties of transporting the wounded, but everyone pitched in; no one could think of a reason to confine them in the eerie quiet of the chamber.

Informally, their team meeting resumed. The most able of the walking wounded and Jillian took a knee in a circle, and quickly agreed on several things.

"Right. Osborne, please have your Royal Marines scout a half-mile in each direction," Entwhistle requested, "then come straight back. Everybody else, it looks like we're nearing sunset, so let's get a fire going, eh?"

"That's a point," Jillian said. "What about food?"

Had they been limited to the provisions each individual brought they'd have starved in days.

"Ah, yes. Fortunately, some bright spark planned for this eventuality," Entwhistle said proudly, "and we shan't be forced to navigate a long, dangerous stretch of Shit Creek." The food stored in the blue chamber would keep them alive for five or six days. "We've water for twenty days, maybe more. There must be a river near here, and it seems there's wild game in the woods."

"Doesn't sound too bad a life, now you describe it," Jenkins decided. "Take some hikes in the woods, do a spot of hunting. Only thing missing would be the girl to warm my hearth."

"If you've finished imagining your perfect rural life," Keller snapped, "I'd like to find out where the fuck we are." He brandished a flat-screen device which had apparently angered him. "I'm still not getting an up-link," he said, tapping the screen.

"A what's-that-now?" Jenkins asked.

"There's no satellite feed."

"No feed?" Jenkins asked. "Why? What does it eat?"

"No, I mean, either the network is down, or we're still a long way from where Clavel and I started."

A long pause. "Eh?"

Watching Keller try to explain GPS to Jenkins was to observe a strange collision of mindsets, one from each side of the millennial boundary. To Keller, the idea of an orbital communications facility, flying two hundred *miles* up, was routine, but Jenkins instinctively rubbished it.

"You've got a telephone," he said, piecing together the parts which made sense, "which can talk to outer space? Oh, sure, and I got the biggest schlong in Long Island."

"Well," Keller said huffily, "it's a bit difficult to show you *now*. But these devices guide all our military operations in the twenty-first century."

Jenkins didn't care for this. "Sounds like cheating. You ain't even gotta look around for the enemy, just send up one of these UPS things …"

"GPS," Keller tried, but there wasn't much point.

"… and zap him from outer space. No finesse to it," Jenkins decided. "Where's the *craft* of soldiering, eh?"

"Speaking of craft," Jillian said, "has anyone here learned how to sail?"

Exaggerating for effect, Osborne scrutinized the wood in both directions before asking, "Did I miss something, and we're in a fuckin' boat, now?"

"I think she must have hit her head in the mine," Yanis explained, and went to poke some fun at her until, withered by a single glance, he stopped.

"I need someone with a good working knowledge of the constellations," she explained patiently. "And maybe planets. For navigation, you know."

"I'm clueless about that stuff," Keller admitted.

"We're not," PFC Irwin told them. "Back at Ringway, they taught us the constellations, so we'd have something to do during night jumps, instead of just hanging there. Would have been quite nice, too, excepting it was so *cold.*"

"Son," Jillian said, her patience wearing dangerously thin, "all I need is for you to lay on your back once the stars come out and shout if you see anything familiar. *Capisce?*"

"Roger that, ma'am."

"Where are the others?"

Osborne had taken two Marines on a circular patrol of their landing site, while Jenkins used his slender Airborne manpower to look for fruit-bearing trees, or more signs of game. Anyone who could walk was collecting firewood, or daubing specific trees with camo paint, to act as distance markers. "If we have to defend this place, the trees will really screw up our depth perception," Keller warned. "Most of all, I wanted to set up an OP, maybe two, but we just don't have the people." Leaving a handful of men out in the chilly night, watching for other humans—who might not yet even have evolved to walk the earth—all while their colleagues slept in a warm spacecraft, seemed unfair anyway.

Tasks were delegated. Jillian alternated between their improvised sick bay—in reality, a group of stretchers arrayed in the area around Thompson's still-inscrutable bunk bed—and whatever Yanis was doing at that moment. "I'm looking for clues, inside the spacecraft, as to where we are." He had only a little help and didn't know what he was looking for. "Some sign that we've traveled. A new panel or a set of dials, recessed somewhere in the floor, like those orange beds." He was trying all manner of gestures, stepping this way and that, stroking the exterior fabric in geometrical patterns. "There must be a way for the ship to talk to us."

If there was, it eluded him. Osborne's Marines returned just before dark, relieved to have found the elusive, shimmering chamber in the failing light. "Birch, larch, and ash. We saw squirrels and birds, but no signs of habitation or people."

"Damn." He'd hoped for some sign, even just an old ruin, or a building seen in the distance, but the woods here were deep. "That'll do for tonight, yeah? Everyone's pretty done-in."

Someone would take watch, and it wouldn't be him, so Yanis did as the others were doing and found a quiet patch to call his own. He had a basic field poncho, and a moth-eaten blanket which had made it through the fires of *Der Dom*, but they served more than well enough.

Even when Yanis found out, as Jillian slid in beside him, soot-covered and exhausted, that he was expected to share.

| 2 |
Inge's Tale

Bonehouse headquarters, 85 miles SW of Argentina-Paraguay border, 1945

From her overlook, she saw 'Taschner' emerge from his hut just after 0800. His was the largest of the residential structures by far; six or eight of the U-99X crewmen would have found it less cramped than their submarine. Modeled after a Swiss chalet, albeit a diminutive version for a single occupant, his quarters were crafted with just a hint of Alpine elegance. It was entirely typical of 'Taschner' to demand the best of *everything*. Even in a place like this.

The self-appointed *Commandant* stretched and lit a cigarette. Then she watched him begin his usual breakfast-time walk toward the mess hall. Taschner had aged somewhat on the voyage, with new hints of grey at his temples, but he was always immaculately turned-out, as if neatness carried its own authority. As he strode across the large open area at the center of the camp—a parade ground, an open-air church, or a movie theater, depending on needs—Taschner seemed at once the master of his domain, yet also somehow disappointed.

She'd noticed the shifts in his demeanor during the weeks of careful, silent observation. It didn't take a psychology degree; Taschner would fly off the handle at the slightest thing, berating crewmen and locals alike. His anger seemed to come in waves, timed roughly with results and reports from his subordinates. If Neumann and the others could muster a few days' good news in a row, they knew Taschner would calm down and maybe share a joke with them, or break out one of his widely–rumored, secret crates of schnapps. But on his worst days, all restraint left him, and it seemed the entire calamity of Germany's 'defeat' (as Taschner would always call it) could be blamed on one cowering crewman. She knew all too well that submariners had limits; in fact, she'd enjoyed testing and exploiting them. But in his red-faced tirades, Taschner was shattering the crew's hard-built but fragile morale. To do more, and to carry out the severe punishments he so frequently threatened, would be tantamount to inviting mutiny.

In fact, the situation was becoming dangerous. Her sources from inside the camp—a mix of old friends and new—complained that they couldn't understand why they were even in Argentina in the first place. Some wanted to go home; others wanted a clear timetable for the mission, and resented Taschner's refusals. His authority was waning, she could tell, compromised by his own anger and inflexibility.

Crumbling morale was the greatest threat to Bonehouse. Without greater care, one of the Reich's boldest achievements would end up abandoned, tumbledown buildings in a strange cluster on the *Pampas*.

No, this was a vital moment, a time for someone to intervene; someone with unique knowledge of the mission and its participants.

Someone whose appearance before the *Commandant* of *Der Knockenhaus* would be, to put it mildly, a considerable surprise.

***

She walked into the mess hall just after he'd finished eating. Any earlier, and Inge worried that Taschner might choke on his *empanadas*. He saw her, his eyes flickered for a quarter second, and then his hands were at his belt, finding his Luger.

It wasn't there. During breakfast, he was usually without his sidearm. And Inge must have known that, he decided quickly. Everything else laid itself out over the next few seconds while she enjoyed her little moment of theater.

"Oh, I'm so sorry to disturb your meal. Is there anyone who could take pity on a hungry girl and whip up some eggs? I'm just *famished!*" She was breezy and cordial, as though just back from a morning ride.

But Taschner was yelling, even as the local kitchen staff tried to take Inge's order, assuming her a visitor. "Explain yourself, now!" Taschner barked. A trio of U-boat crewmen had followed the shouts, grabbing MP-38 sub-machine guns on the way. "Or this 'surprise visit' won't last much longer."

The furious German dialogue meant nothing to the staff. They were only a dozen in number and planned to carry on as if Inge were welcome; visitors were so rare, and surely a good thing, that they couldn't guess how this woman had brought Taschner to such apoplexy. So, once Inge was surrounded by gun-toting crewmen and made to sit down at Taschner's table, two staff stepped through the stiff, Teutonic awkwardness, served her a plate of *migas,* and quickly withdrew.

The commandant himself was pacing around, ordering people to rouse the rest of the crew, to get Berlin on the phone, even to alert Vice-Commissioner Delgardo, their ever-obliging and oft-bribed contact within the local police. Taschner would have returned to his chalet and loaded his Luger, had it not seemed preposterous to leave a traitor unguarded among people prepared to help her.

It galled him, how easily she'd returned. The security at Bonehouse was as tight as he could possibly design it.

How the hell did she find us?

The crew gave him yet another puzzle; she had clearly enjoyed help from inside, no doubt from those pussy-struck crewmen who'd thought of nothing but Inge's unique charms since her 'eviction.' Now, he'd face the prospect of having to execute half his work force because of a stubborn and truculent blonde.

It was Neumann, predictably, who settled things down sufficiently for negotiations to begin. Until his arrival at the wooden mess hall, Inge's life had been in immediate peril.

"Sir, there's a good explanation. No need for any drastic measures," the acting captain said. "I'll tell you everything."

"And I'll gladly help," Inge offered, chewing her eggs and then flashing her eyebrows. "It's quite a story."

"I'll bet," Taschner said curtly. "All of you, stay here, on my order." He stalked back to his hut.

Immediately, a wave of murmuring began, but only Neumann had the confidence to approach Inge. She sat upright, but relaxed, as though beginning a job interview. "You're alive," he said. "I'm just saying that out loud, in front of people, to make sure I'm not crazy."

"Alive and *well*, by the looks of it!" a crewman joked, sending the others into raptures, but Neumann hissed at them to be quiet.

"He'll be back in a second. Now, Inge, you miracle, you dastardly bitch," he grinned as she blew him a kiss, "what do you need from us?"

"What does a girl always need?" she asked, and Neumann had to wave down more noise from the crew. "I need security," she spelled out. "I'm valuable to him, but he's too angry, and he'll try to forget that."

"Angry? He's fucking *furious* with you," Neumann warned, "so don't *you* forget *that*." Although Taschner had so far restrained himself from shooting anyone at Bonehouse, he'd come terrifyingly close, more than once. "I can see him losing his rag and reaching for the Luger. Only it'll be in its holster this time."

The crew's murmurs died the instant Taschner re-entered the mess hall, the overly-sprung door clanging behind him. *"Herr Neumann!"* Taschner called.

"Shit. Here we go," Neumann muttered, sensing that Inge's chances of survival dropped every time Taschner raised his voice. When the SS man was enraged, his noise and fury fed off each other. But it was only when they ignited the fuel of National Socialist ideology could Taschner's true genius for barbarism, his zeal for rooting out treachery, be unleashed. *"Ja, mein Herr Standartenfuhrer?"* Neumann reported crisply.

"We may need to perform an execution. If so, there will be no delay."

Neumann knew why: with the submariners' loyalties in question, Inge was more dangerous incarcerated than free or dead.

"Gather the necessary things, if you would."

"An execution?" Inge spluttered, but not out of fear; there were important practicalities he'd overlooked. "You're quite sure that you want to murder the only truly Aryan woman for hundreds of miles? Right here, on the grounds of a unique laboratory where Aryanism itself is being researched and perfected?"

Taschner's calculus was typically cold. "Treachery is a greater danger even than genetic corruption."

"And what will your submariner crew make of *that*?" she asked. "They are my friends, my informers, my enablers in this little scheme." When Taschner insisted on her unmasking those who'd assisted her, she said, "No, I won't give you names. That way, the entire crew is implicated."

"Then they'll all suffer the same fate," Taschner said.

It was mostly bluster, the theater to be expected from Taschner at a time like this. His position was weak, and Inge's return—sudden and genuinely surprising, at least to Taschner—was a direct challenge to him personally.

"Gunning down your own workforce," she imagined, nose wrinkled in distaste. "Your own researchers and experts. Yes, they helped me too, just as much as the lowly torpedo-men and chefs. And what about the *pilots* who connect this place to the rest of the world? Are you going to slaughter them, too?" Inge demanded.

"We are subjects of the Reich, servant-soldiers, beholden to the code of the *Schutzstaffel*."

"That's just rot. The old structures are collapsing, *Herr Taschner*," she said, giving the warning in a milder tone. "The world is being remade. Anything is possible—atomic power, flights into space, they're all within reach. And I'm here to help you achieve them *all*."

Word had now spread to every corner of the six-building camp. The residential huts emptied quickly, twenty or so crewmen woken from sleep to find not the start of their shift, but the prospect of a quite unique entertainment.

Their muster complete, the crew found they had the same questions: *Where has she been? How did she get here? And why is Taschner so freaked out about her arrival?* The local cooks and farm workers wondered something simpler still: *Who the hell is this?*

Inge exchanged surreptitious glances with several people, becoming almost shy at the sight of so many men who had shared her rough, functional 'quarters' in the torpedo room of U-99X. The rekindling of those alliances, not in the cramped confines of a submarine, but on the broad pampas at night, secret and alone, had made her plan possible.

But the risks were still enormous. Even as she felt the crew's many-hued warmth on one side, there was Taschner's incendiary fury on the other. She decided to give herself a fifty percent chance of surviving the next few minutes. Taschner's Luger was a hypothetical threat, but she already knew he'd choose strangulation, when the time came. It was too apt, too perfect a method to ignore.

Perhaps that was what Taschner and Neumann discussed while the crowd grew and buzzed with curiosity. More than one scuffle broke out, and Taschner remonstrated with crewmen who were barging each other for a better view of the proceedings. As he did so, Inge pushed away the sounds—so very masculine but not in a way she found interesting—and focused on her tactics for beating Taschner in the coming logic game.

He's an experienced interrogator, trained to find and exploit weaknesses. He'll look for tiny flutters in my body language, a change in the direction of my glance, a hesitation before speaking. He'll read me like I'm reciting a poem in semaphore.

Laborious note taking slowed the proceedings and gave Inge time to think. Ironically, she planned on being completely honest. A few weeks of reflection had showed Inge that her influence onboard U-99X could not have been allowed to continue. Factionalism, distraction, insubordination ... they followed her like a cloud of her own perfume.

But honesty, here in this perilous place, would strip away a protective layer of her psychological shell. She'd have to admit her crimes—a mere *bagatelle* compared to those of Taschner, and before him, Keck—but awful, nevertheless. She'd have to resist questioning from an expert, and when that didn't yield the desired answers, Taschner would have the entire range of torture methods available to him.

Violence for pleasure was sport; violence to extract information was cruelty. There would be cuts and bruises and burns and bites.

Surely, Taschner would loosen all restraints to reveal the truth, even recruiting electrocution or some backroom truth serum. There would be no stopping him, even once everything was out in the open. Cruelty would *become* his sport, all the more effective in front of a rapt, emotional audience who would never forget.

It would be purgatory. Her friends forced to witness her pained confessions. There would be nothing any of them could do.

Unless...

There was a place to which she could travel, *in extremis.* A time, back when she was a girl. In difficulty, she knew she could rely on a dynamo which spanned inside her, silent and prepared, a source of strength and anger, unknown to anyone else but indispensable to Inge. She forced herself to think back and recall that day. The afternoon snowstorm which blanketed their little town before her walk home from school. The crisp air, cold and memorably sharp in her throat. A scene of peace and serenity, until she heard other footsteps in the crunchy, crystalline snow. He caught up with Inge, distracted her and leeched her attention until they strayed onto an unfamiliar path. Then she was being dragged by her hair, kicking and biting and defying him with every breath, into the quiet of the woods where he struggled to complete a cold, awkward rut in the snow. Only weeks later, when she saw him in the street, did the real anger begin to flow, triggered by a devastating realization: he was headed to the synagogue. Inge had been subjected to the horror of defilement by a lecherous old Jew.

Not a word to anyone, even her best friend, Maria. She was gone now, taken by the fires of Munich, the only one she'd ever have told.

No. Instead, she would reinvent herself, create an identity rooted in defiant opposition. She took industrial jobs only recently made available to women, quickly gaining friends and admirers among the largely male cohort. When groups promising to rebuild the strength and honor of Germany met in her town, she would attend the beer-soaked events in cellars and church halls. Eventually, she found the courage to speak, at once impressing the ambitious, fat-bellied leadership with her clarity and drive.

They were both revolutionary and counter revolutionary. They would push back against the elites, the traitors of Versailles, the socialists and democrats who could plan only for a creaking, short-lived coalition government, who were simply stealing votes from her brothers and sisters in the National Socialists.

And she would push back—harder still—against the Jews.

Every one of them who fled, every Jewish businessman forced to close his doors, every rabbi beaten in the street, was *that* man, the filthy lech who'd forced himself on her in the snow. She found she could berate them with greater confidence, with the certainty that came from possessing the truth, but her friends in the brown-shirted mob soon graduated from hurling insults to cracking heads. Inspired and unshackled, Inge joined in, several evenings a week, meting out racial justice in the form of broken bones and smashed windows, always in carefully chosen districts. Again, there was no guilt; theirs was decent work, she and her comrades knew, and a benefit to society and the economy.

Many nights of this training meant that, when it came, Inge found she could kill. There was little emotional display, but in her private world, a place she showed to no one, each violent, final moment wreathed Inge in glorious pleasure. She had a reason to work—to rid Europe of pestilential vermin—and found her new position at the city jail most satisfying.

On its best days, when everything came together just so, it was exquisite.

Clear purpose and private enjoyment, harnessed in tandem, created an endless thrill, just under her skin, like the memory of a favorite lover. Later, attached to the concentration camp system, she was in her element, and her hand-picked crew served both the Reich and her own needs. But the draw of Reinhold—his access to the upper echelons, his obvious sophistication, his constant traveling—was intense from the outset.

And so, that initial surge of murderous, carnal desire had propelled her to this unlikely place, at a wooden mess table, opposite a furious SS 'superhero' whose expression demanded an explanation. He was so damned *certain* of everything, so convinced of his own rightness. But who could argue? He was educated, a veteran of four fronts, and if Reinhold's half-drunk confiding could be believed, a *time traveler*. Inge was but a lowly sergeant, specially skilled in some areas, but younger by ten years, and—no one would let her forget—a woman.

For some, that would connote weakness, but only those who had not yet met Inge Weber.

Taschner's discussion with Neumann was over, and he began gesturing for crewmen to get up and help him move furniture. "I will chair a plenary session of the *Knockenhaus* Operations Committee."

"Now?" Neumann asked. But then, it occurred to him. "A disciplinary meeting?"

He stopped bossing men around, turned and said, "Is that not appropriate, given the circumstances?"

"*Jawohl*," he said, and helped minimize the scraping and banging while twenty submariners hauled six tables into position. The plenary session included all the Germans—designers, geneticists, security team leaders, and submariners—though Taschner excluded any local staff and ordered the doors locked.

Just before they began, with the crowd leaning in close, Inge recalled Taschner's last order relating to her: *cast her adrift*. He'd left her to die alone on a crippled ship without radio or water, floating powerless on the wide ocean, a massacred crew her only company.

Four crewman escorted Inge to the improvised 'dock,' a quadrangle of tables with a chair at the center. As Taschner approached the table, she sat up extra straight and cleared her throat.

"Come to order," Taschner called out, then took his seat. He'd found a notepad and pen and seemed surprisingly in control. Where was the Teutonic fury of the vengeful Taschner, smarting and raw after being deceived by a conniving woman? Where were his shouts of treachery? Once the proceedings began, Inge found that her expectations of Taschner were quite wrong.

"This is not a disciplinary session, but a technical one," Taschner explained to a silent room. Every German at the redoubt was present, except Hader, who was still confined to his room in their simple wood hut of a medical building. "Ms. Weber was able to make her way from the coast to Bonehouse, carry out reconnaissance of the target, and make secret contact with loyal friends within." He lit a cigarette—another surprising down-shift in the level of tension—and asked, "Do I have it right so far?"

"Yes, sir," she said.

"On whose orders did you travel?" Taschner asked.

She stifled a laugh—such a preposterous question!

"I was abandoned by my commander," she reminded him pointedly, "on a damaged, foreign vessel which lacked a crew. By the time I was in contact with anyone, the war was over, and the *Schutzstaffel* was in turmoil." The coup against Hitler had brought predictable bloodletting and instability, including assassinations elsewhere in Europe. "The new United Nations has branded our SS an international terrorist organization."

"As if we'd sully ourselves with terrorism," Taschner couldn't resist saying.

"Those being the truths of the matter, I proceeded under my own command as an independent, irregular, forward-deployed unit of the German armed forces."

"The Inge Division," a wag called from the back.

"Wow! Where do I sign up to serve?" shouted another.

"Shut the fuck up!" roared Taschner. They obeyed instantly. "This looks like our mess hall, but today it's a court room. Discipline can only function well and benefit everyone," he said, part of a familiar lecture, "if people respect the traditions."

"*Jawohl*," muttered the crowd, unevenly.

The gulf between them was sometimes all too obvious; when they drank and sang their bawdy mariners' songs, Taschner would slink off to enjoy his schnapps and a precious LP of classical music. But they'd found ways to muddle along together, and it worked, as long as Taschner kept his temper.

"So, Inge, let us proceed," Taschner said, growling at the men to keep some kind of order. "You see, I find it very interesting that you were able to escape the freighter and find us."

She said nothing, but this was a tactic. She gradually allowed each part of her body to relax, beginning with the soles of her feet. By the time Taschner finished explaining the reasons for the hearing, her wrists and forearms were being sequentially drained of tension with each breath. Finally came her face; she let it fall, like a veil tumbling down, but then restored her features to project confidence and vigor.

I am to be trusted; I am your ally, even though I usurped your command authority, bribed, and bullied your men into lying for me, and spied on your secret base for three weeks. Put all that aside now. We can still do business together.

"Please don't be shy," Taschner said. "I'm sure we're all anxious to hear."

She was dressed not unlike a local woman, in a flowing, green skirt and a red-white blouse. Earlier, in her anxiety, the skirt was bunched at her lap, tightening the fabric around her ankles until they were locked in place. She was more relaxed, but still needed to feel the ground under her feet. "First, I'd like an assurance."

"I can imagine that you would."

"The regular chain of command was wrecked by the Armistice. Some SS people were arrested, others promoted."

"And some murdered," Taschner assumed, "to settle old scores?"

She nodded. "There were *a lot* of old scores. The organizational chart of the SS wouldn't have a single name you know, these days."

All the more reason that competence and discipline be quickly restored at the highest levels.

"So?" he asked.

"So, who's in charge?"

He rattled off a regulation about delegating command to lower-ranking officers in times of uncertain communications. "But we don't have a manual for Armistice. The only advice Berlin had for us was, 'Well done, please carry on.' So, with Captain Hader unwell, I've been in operational command, running the place day-to-day. With help," he added with more generosity than usual, "from Neumann and our enlightened team of specialists. Given how things were, my leadership seemed the right choice."

"Yes," she said at once. "You're the right person to lead. And you can offer me the assurance I need."

Taschner wasn't going to be played. "I can't promise not to execute a self-confessed traitor."

"Assure me this, then," Inge said. "You'll listen politely and make a reasoned judgment. In the end, if you conclude there has been treachery, I will carry out the execution myself." She gestured to his Luger, which sat on the table next to his uniform cap. "Will that be satisfactory?"

As the only judge, his opinion was final. "It will. Proceed."

***

"My coming along on the flight, that was Reinhold's idea," she was saying, five minutes into the fulsome account of her role in Bonehouse. "He saw I had skills that might be helpful at the redoubt, and I encouraged him to take a chance on me."

"Did you report directly to him while on the submarine?" If U-99X crewmen were prepared to help Inge's reconnaissance of the redoubt, perhaps they'd assisted in making a radio call to Berlin.

"No. I sent one cable to Reinhold's office, about ten days before we ran into the freighter. They replied after a week, saying that he was missing."

"Missing?" Taschner asked. "I'm not bloody *surprised* he was *missing!* Intelligence officers from Glasgow to Berlin to the Khyber Pass were searching for him."

"Searching ... for him? Why?"

She is well behind the curve.

Daily radio sessions with Berlin were Taschner's sole prerogative, transforming him into the redoubt's only source that was remotely up to date.

"My dear, I'm afraid *Herr Reinhold* was rather dishonest with you. And with his superiors, come to think of it."

Inge had quietly harbored her own suspicions and wouldn't let Taschner have this aggrandizing look-how-much-I-know moment. "He was a spy, wasn't he?"

Taken aback, Taschner said only, "Of a kind."

"He didn't trust Hitler. Reinhold used to say, 'The war was lost the minute we invaded Russia.' He thought empire-building was a waste, and always brought collapse. He told me once," she continued, humanizing a man known to Taschner only as a flawed but pivotal figure, "that he thinks Europe would be best as a federation. Germany, France, England, and everyone, together."

Aghast at the proposition, Taschner asked next, "Did that not seem to imply that Reinhold might be the agent of a foreign power?"

"I mean, not necessarily," Inge tried.

"He was a *double agent*. He left you on the submarine with us, flew back to France, and immediately alerted his contact to send the Royal Navy south, looking for us. He helped the British sortie a squadron of destroyers after us, Inge," Taschner explained because she really didn't seem to understand, "and that was *after* the Americans sent a whole carrier battle group to track us down."

The realization was like pins and needles, felt all over. "He knew I was onboard ..."

"Yes," Taschner said, waiting while the penny dropped.

"But he told the British—"

"*And* the Americans," Taschner pointed out, "just to be sure."

"How to *kill* us?"

"A despicable act. He helped design the redoubt and organize our manifest. He knew we had poured serious resources into this and sent key people on U-99X to help set things up."

"That bastard ..." she muttered, apparently more embarrassed at being outplayed than hurt by Reinhold's final personal slight.

"Don't feel singled out," said Taschner with a patronizing smile. "You were one of a dozen people he wanted out of his way. Officials who could complicate things for him, prevent him from getting what he wanted. Underlings, like you, who might know too much or cause trouble later. Then, there were experts and theorists like Zimmer and Baumann, who worked ceaselessly to perpetuate a war that Reinhold was desperate to stop."

She brought her emotions under control. "How did he die?" Inge asked. "Shame I didn't get the chance, myself."

"He was fleeing *Der Dom* after the earthquake bomb attack. Got caught by a marauding aircraft. That was all his staff could say. Except one more thing."

"That he's sorry for what he did?" she joked.

"SS men never say sorry," Taschner reminded her. "But I wanted you to know this: Reinhold envisaged taking control of *Der Dom* but only using it once."

The crowd knew this part of the tale. Taschner had initially learned it from Reinhold's demobilized staff, who became more talkative—and, more helpfully still, *speculative*—as Reinhold's victory over the Allied para-assault seemed close. The men mumbled together, "His wife."

"Killed during an RAF raid on Munich. Reinhold planned one trip back to bring his poor wife to safety before the raid, and then live with her in contented retirement. That's it. That's *all* he planned to do with that miraculous machine."

"Such limited vision," Inge said, expressing what she knew would be Taschner's own view.

"I heartily agree. And was it your 'vision' which spared you from death on the open sea?"

The meeting—or trial, as it certainly felt—was providing high-quality entertainment. The crew felt they understood part of the puzzle—Reinhold's espionage, and the equally treacherous capitulation by the 'provisional government' which led to the Armistice—but much still eluded them. Chief among the remaining questions was Inge's miraculous return.

She cleared her throat again, and the room fell into an agreeable silence. "I thought the U-boat was following you to Bonehouse with more supplies. I suppose now that the U-75Z was searching for the U-99X when they saw my freighter. I'd lit a fire, so I was visible for miles. Just needed a stroke of luck."

"How long had you been on board?" Taschner asked, taking notes. Any discrepancy would be scrupulously investigated.

"A few days. Maybe a week. It was a very strange time." This was as much as she'd say about her time spent becalmed on an already blood-soaked freighter, and many in the crew felt her reticence was all for the good.

Next came the most critical question. "What did you tell the captain of U-75Z?"

***

The day's work was forgotten. Researchers left their lab buildings empty; even Zimmer's noisily impressive engine experiments were put on hold. As information flowed, more of the local staff were brought up to speed. The challenge of communicating her story stretched the crewman's Spanish past breaking point, but they got the gist: *She's controversial and she loves causing trouble, but we need her.*

"Well?" Taschner asked. "What kind of yarn did you spin?"

"Yarn?" Inge said, offended.

"You were marked for death," Taschner explained. "The U-75Z was there to intercept and destroy our submarine, plain and simple. If he realized you were Inge Weber, or that you were connected to Bonehouse, or Reinhold—"

"A yarn, yes," Inge smiled. "They approached very slowly, warily, so I had time to be inventive. When they came close, I was at the rail, shouting for help in English. I must have looked an absolute fright." Neumann could only guess, but in his imagining, Inge had become a naked, feral creature on the freighter, prowling and snarling, content in her depraved solitude until a surfacing U-boat interjected, and forced a return to civilized ways. "I told them I was on a round-the-world sailing trip with my husband."

Warmly anticipating just such a tale of subterfuge, and devouring her testimony as though it were a vital newsreel from home, the crew and researchers found coffee and snacks and settled in for Story Time.

"Husband?" Taschner asked. He would transcribe her testimony and then check every single detail in the days to come. Even he found himself amazed at her audacity.

"Long gone," she explained. "I told them we'd had engine trouble and drifted for a couple of days before we encountered the freighter." Around her, the men had their own memories of that misbegotten ship, her slovenly crew, and their rank unprofessionalism.

"You told him you were rescued by the crew of the freighter?"

"Yes, but—"

"The crew you were largely responsible for murdering in cold blood?"

"Animals," someone cut in from the back of the crowd, bringing agreement from the others. No tears would be shed over Inge's victims who had done so much to ensure their own doom.

"Animals in fact and fiction, both," Inge said. "As far as the U-boat officers knew, they'd turned on us after the rescue, spying a quick buck and," she paused, bashful, "an unusually fetching companion."

"Hence the disappeared husband," Taschner knew.

"Over the side. Couldn't have him getting in the way."

"But then, we still have the three dozen corpses on the freighter. Unless you confessed to being violent, how did you persuade the captain …" He tried to get ahead of her. "Piracy?"

"Is it altogether *too* obvious?" asked Inge. "The U-boat crew swallowed it by the spoonful. I described a mysterious vessel, with no markings, and a strong, tall, African crew."

"You were a hell of a long way from Africa," Taschner pointed out.

"But it made enough sense at the time," said Inge. "The submariners believed I hid away during the pirate's ransacking of the ship, and that they never found me."

"What happened to these *pirates?*"

"Seems they couldn't get the boat running. Bad engine, flooding in an important system, I don't know. They took what they could carry and left. That's what I told the U-boat commander."

"And the submariners believed that?" asked Taschner. As tall tales went, it loomed impressively.

She made her first overtly provocative move—crossing her legs to reveal three inches of her ankles. "Have you never had the experience," she asked in a disarming, sultry tone, "of choosing to believe something because of *who* said it?"

"Out of the mouth of a buxom blonde," Taschner began. "U-boat types really are simpletons, aren't they?"

Before the submariners' complaints rose above a murmur, Taschner quickly turned to his crew and added, "Present company excepted, naturally."

"And SS men are all medal-obsessed aristocrats with friends in high places," Neumann fired back, good-naturedly. "Present company excepted, naturally."

He took it well, a thousand times better than Inge would ever have guessed.

"So, you were rescued by intrepid servants of the Reich, thousands of miles from home, and you thanked them for their service by lying to them comprehensively." Inge waited for a terrible, punitive finale to the rebuke, but instead, Taschner said, "That took big, shiny, brass balls, Inge."

She let herself laugh, a wonderful release of the tension in her gut. "I learn more about myself every day." The audience joined her, finding that the situation wasn't so unnerving or uncertain when they could laugh about it. Still, Inge had to tread carefully; she'd impressed Taschner, but her story had to be consistent, through to the end. "Once I'd explained everything—"

"Or just made it up," Taschner qualified.

"The captain agreed to take me to Montevideo. They were scheduled to do a port visit there anyway on their way home. I told them my husband's company had an office there, and that they'd be able to help me travel onward once I'd figured out what to do."

The sub struck Neumann as a lucky boat. "Better the South Atlantic than getting themselves sunk in the Bay of Biscay or the Baltic."

Taschner nodded. Submarine warfare was the only real way to carry on the struggle, and he privately wished the captain had decided to join Bonehouse, rather than give up the search and flee into the chaos of post-war Germany.

"Everything was fine until the submariners found out the news from home and wanted to leave," said Inge. "They prepared to sail, and rather than offering me a trip home, just handed me over to the Consul."

"And was the Consul helpful?" Taschner wanted to know. "Was he aware of our project?"

"Aware?" she laughed. "He was *expecting* me. Arrested me and threw me in jail only ninety minutes after I'd clambered up out of the sub. None of my tricks worked, and he saw through my false identities pretty quickly. Guess I wasn't prepared enough."

Concern filled the room. Inge's discomforts and dangers had become the crew's own, not least because among them were two dozen men with carnal knowledge of her. Watching her narrative unfold, quite unable to help but fearful of the outcome, they were caught in vortex of accused treachery, hopeful chivalry, and hidden lust.

"The paper pushers in Montevideo were informed of our mission by anti-Hitler forces in Berlin," Taschner surmised. "There are plenty in the capital who objected to anything that might rock the boat at the peace negotiations. Even something as important as keeping the

Aryan flame alive. One of them probably informed the Consul, hoping that he'd gain enough political traction to have us thrown out of South America. But agreements have been made with our Argentine friends," he reminded the men, pleased with his local diplomatic achievements, "and our future here is secure." He turned back to Inge, who squirmed slightly. "How was your treatment by the Consul's staff?"

How much to tell?

Inge's facial muscles bunched up tight.

Taschner asked, "Was he the one who helped you travel inland?"

"No."

He let groups of his men into my cell, an hour at a time.

"Then, how were you able to …"

Oh, hang it. This place is full of murderers, anyway.

"I killed three men. I don't regret it."

Taschner stopped writing, the pencil hovering. "Who?" He worried that there'd be a diplomatic mess to clean up.

"For some reason, the Chief of Police decided to escort me with his driver and a security guy. They got out to buy cigarettes at a gas station—"

"Literally?" Taschner asked, wincing at the amateurishness.

"Leaving the driver alone with me. Men are all too easy to distract," she said.

Arrayed behind her, seated on chairs and tables, the full German complement of Bonehouse seemed to endure a pang of jealousy. Most let it pass quickly; she'd used her charms to keep herself safe, and to reach the redoubt. The crew of U-99X were still her favorites, surely.

"I don't like guns, but I did what was necessary." This earned her some whoops of support. "Then I took one of the other cars and did my best to disappear into the continent."

Taschner could forgive a soldier a great deal, provided they showed the right zeal and determination when the time came. "A prudent reaction to a hopeless situation."

"I stole trucks and private cars, even some delivery vans. But my favorite was a motorbike. Easy and flexible. I traveled most of the way here on one."

Taschner asked, "How did you find the redoubt?"

"Some of it was memory, the rest intuition. Then, one evening just before sunset, I saw the biggest, most ridiculous aircraft come swooping down into one of the valleys. Six engines, enough noise to uproot the trees. And I thought, there are two possibilities. Either the Reich Air Ministry has lost its collective mind and licensed production of our experimental long-range aircraft to the Uruguayan air force. Or my old friends of the U-99X are alive and receiving visitors. I found Bonehouse the next day."

Frowning, Taschner admitted, "An arriving plane of its size was always a risk, but it brought in—"

"Fresh sausages!" she trilled, "refrigerated using a new technology. And oysters, and a side of venison!"

"How the hell did you know that kind of—" Taschner began.

"I bartered my motorbike for some supplies and blankets. Been camped out like a Girl Scout for three weeks, about three-quarters of a mile up the valley."

The thought of it made him immediately uncomfortable. "Spying on us? On the project?"

"Assessing your progress. I wouldn't give my loyalty to some half-baked lunacy, a misfire that's in danger of failure. My friends told me there was acrimony and frustration, and I needed to know how much. Otherwise, I'd be better off heading north, maybe to Brazil to join the other German communes. Or I could just ditch my travel documents and start over. Don't tell anyone," she confided, hands clasped hopefully, "but I had my heart set on a glamorous life in Hollywood."

Slightly less helpless in the face of Inge's charms than the other men, who gifted her a hearty laugh, Neumann muttered under his breath, "SS sergeant, spy, seductress, sadist. The book deal alone would set her up like a princess. If she manages to escape the hangman's noose."

Six years of war had made him cynical and brought out his most selfish impulses; like a quarry evading a hunter, his sense of things was stripped-down and sharp, obsessed with survival. But here, on a warm morning with rising humidity, with Inge still not safe, he smelled only fear—hers and theirs, both.

Reviewing his notes, and asking smaller, more specific questions about her journey, Taschner seemed almost finished. A hush descended, but it flickered with worry. Taking the temperature, Neumann didn't like what he found. The men were frustrated that Taschner was treating Inge like a prisoner, when she'd been a big part of their journey south. The interrogator caught this scent in the breeze and tried to address it.

"Comrades, friends, please don't think me unhelpfully direct," Taschner said, "but the last time Inge was with us, she caused absolute fucking *chaos*."

The crew weren't ready to blame her for anything, not when there might be available scapegoats. "The captain would have nipped that right in the bud, if he'd been well," Neumann argued.

"Well, he wasn't." Captain Hader, as everyone knew, remained very ill, effectively confined to quarters, suffering from an 'emotional malady,' whatever that meant. "And so," Taschner summed up, "Inge ran a U-boat like her personal brothel for a couple of weeks, as I remember."

"Aye, and remembering," someone behind Neumann commented, "is all we'll have, if you make her *shoot* herself."

"I won't have my orders questioned," roared Taschner. "*Herr Neumann*, regain control of your men."

"Come on, lads," he said quietly to them. "No good making things worse."

The crewman wouldn't let it go. "He's going to blow her brains out, right in front of us."

"Nah," Neumann said. "No chance. He's not an idiot."

"He's got the rule book tattooed on his balls," said the crewman. "You saw how he ran things when we first got here." Punishments had not fit crimes and, as the stark realities of life at Bonehouse sunk in, resentment gradually welled up. "If he thinks she's lied about even one thing—"

Taschner's fist, thumping the wooden table, called them back to order. For one thing, he was ready to get on with his workday. "Two hours have been quite sufficient," he said, "to gather the facts." With the crowd silent, many eyes fell on the loaded Luger pistol, still there on Taschner's wooden table. "It is self-evident that Inge risked the future of the Bonehouse operation by traveling here." He took the pistol but did not yet adopt a firing grip. "She could easily have been followed by MI6 or OSS agents based in Montevideo, or by local security."

The crowd thought this very unlikely, given the pains she'd taken. "Will anyone be permitted to speak in Miss Weber's defense?" Neumann asked Taschner, to general approval.

"No," he said at once. "Unless the traitor herself wishes to speak?"

Quiet for the last twenty minutes as she answered short, factual questions, Inge tried to rally, her voice a little unsteady. "I checked every day for three weeks, making sure no one was tracking me, and I found nothing."

Undermining her would take more, but he already had it. "Then, you should have let the U-75Z continue its mission unimpeded. They could easily have been spotted and sunk. You brought risk to a submarine crew in wartime because you thought only of yourself."

She threw back her head and laughed, perhaps the last sound the crew had expected. "Shall we review the submarine's mission, the one I *impeded?* It was to continue south and destroy *you!*"

He was still holding the Luger, and right then, she feared he might cut to the execution scene. "You ... cannot *be* here," Taschner growled. "You are a time bomb, with little to offer us, and these are delicate and vitally important experiments. Rockets, special materials, new electronic devices ... There's just no way you can—"

"*Herr Zimmer* needs a small amount of gold," she said suddenly. "For those new electronic devices in his rockets. The only jeweler up here is thirty miles away. If we send Zimmer, a flamboyant Italian and world-famous rocket scientist, he'll be arrested."

"And then there'll be an almighty confusion," the Austrian-Italian said from the back, "because one half of Europe thinks I'm dead, and one half of America thinks I'm already in outer space!"

"A severe, aristocratic German like Taschner wouldn't do, either," said Inge.

"I'll have you know," Taschner began, rising to the bait as always.

"But," Inge offered, "the affable, flirtatious blonde?" She flicked her hair appealingly. "Now, there's someone who could be a true asset. When a man sees a pretty girl, well ... let's just say that Nazis and spies and the SS are the last things on their mind. I can play on those assumptions."

"You haven't received proper field training," Taschner continued.

"You've seen that I'm gifted at obtaining things normally unavailable to others."

"Yes, but your effects on morale were *catastrophic*."

"And I'm known to be highly effective at persuading people to cooperate."

There was no denying her abilities to extract information. Usually in parallel with some teeth. "Go on."

"I'm someone who's capable of both devising," she said, finally rising from her chair, "and executing complex plans. Traveling hundreds of miles in a foreign continent, under six different aliases." She added defensively, "And they only identified me when I was betrayed by that bastard, Reinhold."

It was almost against his better judgment by this point—she would be a tremendous asset to any irregular warfare group— but Taschner leveled one more objection, as much to keep up appearances as anything else. "You've never seen combat. We may require you to fight ferociously for the cause. And, if necessary, to sacrifice yourself."

He had not yet instructed her to sit, and so she prowled for a moment. "Sir, may I make a request?"

"Of course."

"That you pause your note-taking for a moment. Some things don't belong in the record."

The pencil spun between his fingers as he decided. "Very well. We'll think of it as your having approached the bench," he said and dropped the pencil.

But she decided to tell not only Taschner but the whole room. They should know the person she had been, in her professional life, before being duped into undertaking this disjointed and ridiculous journey.

She took a breath and began. "I have killed seven hundred and twenty-nine people." Half a second's pause, a complete silence. "More than four hundred of them men, using auto-erotic asphyxiation during intercourse." A pin could have dropped and made a *clang*. "The others were mostly Jewish academics whose brains were to be studied. Librarians, teachers, and such. Those I stabbed with bayonets and kitchen knives. And also shot with a broad variety of calibers."

The first words the crowd managed were, predictably, *"How many?"*

"Only thirty-six women, all while under orders and against my own wishes." Her voice somehow held steady. "Seven children and two infants. All first- or second-degree Jews, and about eighty Russian prisoners of war." She grinned at Taschner, who was as pale as she'd ever seen him, even back in the sallow light of the submarine's interior. "The good-looking ones."

For Taschner, it was like watching a whirling dervish slow himself down and explain how the miraculous could be made possible. He'd never heard anyone simply state their record of contributions to the extermination program, and never dreamed Inge might do so publicly. Her ledger was open, and each page proved to be soaked through with red. All this she confessed without a flicker of guilt or disgust.

"And most recently?" Taschner couldn't help asking, as though he'd received telepathy from the crew.

Inge's face was flushed. "Someone Reinhold and I were working on, in Berlin."

"A prisoner?"

"A wing commander in the RAF, shot down over Holland. Seven months of torture, I assume by tepid, fourth-rate idiots, yielded nothing. I got plenty in my three hours, but then he closed the drawbridge. For good, I knew."

"How?" It was Neumann, representing the crew's fascination.

"Reinhold and I took him to a seventh-floor balcony. He still didn't talk. After, I delivered the *coup de grace* in the parking lot, below."

"Christ," said Neumann. "I'd scratch your worries about her being squeamish, sir."

He looked up and knew the situation would, for now, get beyond him. "I'd have to agree."

The lads went wild, and for a while, Taschner let them. Because although they were already knees-deep in conjugal fantasies, Taschner knew something they didn't. Although Inge would survive the day, perhaps even the week if she behaved herself, Taschner knew for certain that she could not possibly stay with them at Bonehouse.

He couldn't kill her; even to force her out, back to Uruguay, would be a deeply unpopular move. Sending her back to Germany would be to bet her life on a coin toss; since the Armistice, with radio contact fleeting and supply flights irregular, the Reich remained an Unknown Territory.

No, Taschner had a better plan for Inge than letting her swan around in the jungle, making everyone horny.

***

2 days later

Four-fifths of the U-99X complement volunteered to help build Inge's new hut, but Neumann chose only ten men and four local workers. Within a week, she'd have a home as comfortable as any in this remote region, and the privacy to which so many were looking forward.

Until he could hatch the rest of his plan, Taschner simply had to deal with her. "It's traditional for visitors to be given a guided tour of a new place, no?" he told her on her third day at Bonehouse once the crew's hormones had settled somewhat. "Or have you already learned amply from your spies within my ranks?"

"A tour," she said, "would be a pleasure."

The place was small enough to tour on foot, but the Commandant used a jeep, obtained from who-knew-where. "Construction went well," Taschner told her. "Everyone pitched in. Big expeditions into the forest to find trees of the right height; all-night sawing and hammering to seal the mess hall roof before the rains would come."

"I suppose," said Inge, "the prospect of having a roof over their own heads was excellent motivation."

After only seventy-two hours in the camp, Inge had found her feet. She could order men around—she was a sergeant, after all, and at Bonehouse, the incongruities of ranks, uniforms, and the chain-of-command mattered little. The hut they were building for her would be more than adequate, and she had already found time for quiet intimacy with several of the crew, not that Taschner would know for sure. Her lovers were unusually discreet for a group of young men; during this febrile time, when Inge's life hung in the balance, all recognized the value of silence.

Zimmer was banished to the far corners of the lot, where he could fire up rocket engines without endangering anyone. "I wish I could send him to a smaller camp," said Taschner, "way out there, but he needs his equipment, and it's unbelievably heavy." They spotted the Italian, fussing around the nozzle of an engine which sat, proud and potent, as if ready for blast-off. "He's in paradise, but we can't afford to give him angel's wings."

"You mean—"

"He's very unlikely ever to produce a functional rocket."

Inge immediately wondered why Taschner allowed the waste, but the inscrutable officer had his reasons. "And what about those buildings, with the black fences around them?"

"Biological science laboratories."

"What's in there?" Inge asked with an excited shiver. Hoping it would secure a visit, she peppered Taschner with questions as they slowed and parked outside the collection of basic huts.

"Inge, stay here." Taschner went inside through a noisy, temporary door on an overly strong spring. "Wonderful," he muttered.

Alone, Inge was a magnet for the men who worked in or near the Bio facilities, and all wanted to reacquaint themselves with her. "Not today, boys. The big, mean boss is coming out in a minute, and he'll think I've been wasting your time."

When they wouldn't move off, surrounding the jeep and asking Inge all kinds of things, she stood in the passenger's seat and screamed so that they ducked down in fear. "Get back to work immediately, morons!" They shrank from her like scolded puppies. "Move it, or I'll shoot every last one of you in the fucking face!"

They scattered as Taschner was returning. "Here," the Commandant said, either oblivious or indifferent to the confrontation. "Guard these two containers with your life."

"Me?" she asked as she was handed two strong, metal boxes, stacked atop each other. "What's in them?"

"You'll see," was all he'd say.

Completing the back half of the rough circuit formed by the camp's roads, they passed an old shepherd's hut, renovated with canvas added to make a rough homestead. "I think you can guess who lives there."

The most senior member of the crew was the only one she'd yet to see. "How is Captain Hader?"

He sighed, a welcome sign of compassion from someone barely capable of it. "In the twenty-first century, it was known as Post-Traumatic Stress Disorder. With therapy and medication, he might improve, but we haven't the means for either."

"He snapped? Permanently?"

"Nobody knows. He chased away the last people who came to visit. We don't even know what he's eating. *If* he's eating."

Taschner drove them back around the loop to his own quarters. "Come in for a schnapps," he said. "We still need to properly toast your return."

A schnapps, really? If he's thinking I'll just lift my skirt and let him ...

She stopped, uncertain what she'd do if he proposed it. Or if he insisted on it. She'd never considered him flirty, far from it. Like her, he was the type to take what he wanted, even if it were being given willingly.

Once they were settled and sipping, he decided to make short work of the discussion. There was risk of an explosion—he'd heard her, chewing out those men, of course—and if he waited any longer, the fallout would be worse still. "Inge," he said in as comradely a tone as she'd heard from him, "I'm very glad that you didn't die in the Atlantic."

"I can say the same of you," she said, raising the glass to him.

"And I know the men are overjoyed to have you back with us."

She sipped in silence, then waited for him to get to the point.

"Which is almost exactly why I can't let you stay here."

Her eyes closed. "*Herr Taschner,* if that's what I'm really supposed to call you, please consider the implications for morale of simply sending ..."

But he'd stood, Luger drawn and suddenly pointing right at her. "You question my name again, I'll shoot *you* in the fucking face," he hissed through gritted teeth. "Deal?"

She kept her composure through any lack of a reasonable alternative. "I apologize."

"Don't fucking apologize," he said. "You're too useful, too goddamned strong to be anyone's obsequious pet. For now, shut up and let me tell you the plan."

She looked up at him, finding the Luger was holstered. "I hadn't realized there *was* a plan."

"Oh, you'll love it, Inge, I promise. You're going," he beamed theatrically, "to Hollywood."

| 3 |

The Resistance

In the woods outside Carrickfergus, Northern Ireland, 1945

Osborne, Jenkins, and Keller were in charge of breakfast, and much else on what promised to be a busy day. Two fires were already going by the time Yanis woke up, each sending a thin, grey curl skyward. "Wonder if anyone else will see the smoke?" he asked himself. Through the slight haze of the ship's walls, he could see their little expedition coming to life.

"Hmm?" She was wrapped around him like he was a thermal blanket.

"Breakfast?"

"Yeah," she said, still four-fifths asleep. "Put the kettle on."

He subtly maneuvered her so that he could slide out from under the blanket and headed for the exit panel, now marked with stretches of rope on either side so that none would forget. "Another glorious day in Who-Knows-Where," he said and ducked into the forest.

"Here's what I want to know," Jenkins was saying to the others, pacing around the clearing in confusion. "How in the name of Eleanor Roosevelt's knitting do you have *bacon*?"

Too hungry to provide a full briefing, Keller said simply, "Cubed, freeze dried, rehydrated," and tipped a half-cup of boiling water into the metallic pouch, which seemed at first to contain only an uneven, green-yellow powder. Seconds later, chunks of meat and lengths of *fusili* could be discerned within the mix. Grinning, Keller lifted a forkful of restaurant-quality pasta to his mouth and chewed. "Better than your mother makes."

Jenkins bristled. "Don't let her hear you say that. She's fierce with a rolling pin when she's pissed." But he continued to stare into the pouch of pasta. "Ain't that the damnedest thing?"

"This is what we send into space to feed the German astronauts on the International Space Station," said Keller, genuinely. "Very efficient. Low mass."

"There he goes again," the Ranger sergeant exclaimed, theatrical and skeptical. "This *Buck Rogers* stuff don't convince me, you know."

Keller shrugged as he ate. "Be as unconvinced as you want, but it's all true."

"Well, I ain't gonna be caught out by no lies," said Jenkins.

"I'm serious," Keller persisted, "satellites and astronauts and trips to the moon. All true."

Terribly aware of both bursting a bubble, and potentially bringing on a psychological crisis, Yanis said, "*Still* true?"

"How do you mean, *still*," Keller began, but then he saw it. "Ah, you're supposing that we've permanently changed the timeline."

"Shit," observed Osborne glumly.

Jenkins was applying all the brain power he could muster after a disturbed, worried night. "So, even if we're in '43, like we should be—"

"Like *you* should be," Keller pointed out. Having departed from 2014, he was intent on returning there, and *only* there. With his commander dead and his team decimated, Keller was in no mood to continue fighting the battles of long-dead generations. Even if he'd developed a towering respect for these men during their courageous defense of the mine.

"Yeah, fair enough, so if we're in '43, but the timeline was changed in the past, and it's different now, compared to before, you know, then ..." Much faster than Jenkins had hoped, his brain reached its limits. "Crap," he uttered in the face of the complexity. "Say, professor, could you help a guy out?"

Yanis had hoped only to find Jillian some breakfast, or at least some coffee, but now he was doing his best to explain the intricacies of the space-time continuum. "The original timeline is the historical Second World War," he said, arranging some spindly branches in a rough line from his feet, across the little clearing, to where Keller was squatting while he clicked a tiny stove into life. "Overlord is a success, Hitler blows his brains out at the last minute, and Europe heads into a new era of ..." The image of Doc Brown from *Back to the Future* appeared to him, not for the first time, saying, "No one should know too much about their own destiny." Instead, he moved on. "Well, that's the original one. We'll call it R-Zero, the default reality."

Jenkins smirked. "I feel like I'm back in high school."

"Wow," Corporal Hyde observed from behind, always ready with his bone-dry wit. "You went to school in a spaceship?" the Royal Marine quipped. "Must have saved you a fortune on bus fare."

"No, I mean ..." But then he decided to let Hyde's joke fall harmlessly through the seventy-year gap in their senses of humor. "R-1," he said instead, laying a set of sticks which protruded from the same origin at his feet, but then skewed upward, forming an independent line, "is the reality Keck created when he made use of the time device. On returning to 1943, he instigated R-1. In this reality, Overlord didn't go so well, and somebody had to jump into Bavaria to straighten things out."

"Aren't you glad you volunteered?" Jenkins joked. It was dark humor; so many of his friends had died, he'd lost count.

"R-1 would have continued," Yanis explained, "except for the mountain collapsing on us."

"Continued?" Jillian asked. "Continued into *what?*"

"Well, for us, obviously," he coughed, "there wouldn't be a lot of continuing. We'd have been squashed by the mountain."

"Who would have been left in control of *Der Dom?*" Jillian asked. This seemed crucial to how the rest of the timeline would play out.

"Nobody. Unless the Germans managed to find a way in after the war. But that place was *wrecked*. I don't figure there's any way they could come after us. Not without the risk of creating more timeline junctions along the way."

More than one of the men puffed out his cheeks. This was becoming a mental stretch.

"It might help," Professor Miller advised them, "if you think of each timeline as continuing into a fully-fledged future. Imagine that they're all going on concurrently—R-1 and R-2 *and* R-3, where we are. Imagine we can kinda shift from one to the other, making new timelines as we go, depending on our decisions."

"Yeah," Jenkins was saying, pleased with some quiet mini-breakthroughs. "Yeah, I think I got it." He handed Yanis a battered, metal canteen of food which steamed slightly. He ate without paying much attention.

"Okay, now for the tricky part. We went and created R-3, our current timeline, when we bailed out of *Der Dom* and came here. As far as I can figure, the time device would still have been buried by the explosions, but we zipped out of there and arrived 'somewhen' else."

"You mean some*where?*" But Jenkins was catching on faster now. "Oh, I get it. Some*when*. Pretty freaky."

"If we're ahead of 1943, in the future relative to our original timeline, then we'll simply live through this reality, R-3, as though it were our original one."

"I really feel," Entwhistle warned, "like there's a 'but' coming."

"But ... if we traveled into the past, there may be several of us here."

Keller looked around and re-counted. "Sixteen," he confirmed.

"No, I mean ..." Yanis said, and then they dove into the world of doppelgangers, and their implied threats to the Conservation of Mass Law.

"You're telling me," Jenkins was fascinated to find, "I'll be able to *meet myself?*"

"I've already had the pleasure," Osborne quipped, "and I'd skip it if I were you."

Jenkins ignored him. "What about the NATO people, and Miss Qualmes?"

"If we jumped forward to a time beyond theirs, then the universe will have to resolve the equation. It saw nine people leave 2014 and arrive in 1943. If they're gone for longer than an instant, if there's any delay in them returning to the exact right time in 2014, the universe will have to catch up."

"And we trust it to do that?" Jillian asked.

A shrug. He could make no reasonable claim in this area. "I guess the universe could get tired of us jumping around in the continuum, and just scrap this timeline completely. Not sure where that would leave us, or even if we'd know it was happening." He'd already forgotten the breakfast that Jenkins' Airborne duo had provided, but his burps tasted of ketchup and animal grease. "Wish they'd brought a few months' of the German astronaut food," Yanis said. "They might know their constellations, but the Airborne guys are hopeless cooks."

"Next time make it yourself," Jenkins said with false haughtiness, then flounced away to find more coffee, grinning over his shoulder.

After breakfast, patrols were sent out, instructed to walk for about an hour, and then turn around. "Should give us a pretty good survey of the surrounding four miles," Osborne said, hoisting his LMG, the last part of a lighter, stripped-down equipment load-out. They would go west, planning to hook around to the north. Yanis and Jillian would follow them for a few minutes, and then head south to do the same left-hand hook. This way, the teams hoped to cover the whole area efficiently.

But moments before they started out, two or three voices called from the chamber. "You gotta see this!" someone was yelling. "Where's Miller? Tell him to get up here *now*!"

They were pointing to Jim Thompson. The orange of the medical bunk was intensifying, and although asleep, Jim seemed agitated, his feet occasionally jerking and curling up as though shocked by sudden cold. "He was talking," PFC Montoya told Yanis. "Numbers. Maybe directions, I don't know. Then he asked for you." The young Airborne trooper, his lungs only slowly recovering from the effects of tabun, looked equal parts confused and scared. "Is he gonna make it?"

Jim was shirtless, laying in the glowing bay; the fascinating historical artifact known as Jim Thompson's uniform was no more. His modesty was covered by a thin, plastic gauze similar to the cool, permeable layer which shielded the bay from the outside air. "Sergeant Thompson?" he said. "It's Yanis."

The sound came with effort, a long, whispered sigh. "*Where ...*"

"Ireland, Jim! The old country! We jumped out of Bavaria and landed straight—"

He was shaking his head, which took still greater effort. "*Where,*" he began again, "*the fuck have you been?*" he demanded, forcing his eyes open. "*Was asking for you.*" Then he coughed heavily a couple of times, bringing pain to the center of his congested chest.

"Sorry," said Yanis. "We've been trying to figure things out. Lots of questions to answer."

More shaking of the head; from the outset, Thompson seemed frustrated with Yanis, as though they'd been racing the clock this whole time, and only Jim had realized it. "*One answer,*" he rasped. "*Listen. No time. Write this down.*"

Just as Montoya had said, it was a set of highly specific directions from the chamber to somewhere else, using intercardinal directions and precise distances, though the unit of measure, to their surprise, was quite new.

"Jim," Yanis asked when the sergeant appeared to have finished, "you're not saying feet, or meters. You're saying lengths. How long's a length, Jim?"

"Long as I'm tall," he spluttered, coughing harder now. "*Six-one.*"

"Science welcomes a new unit," Jillian joked. "Ladies and gentlemen, after years of tyranny by feet and meters, I offer for your consideration ... the Thompson."

Somehow, amid his pain, Jim managed the faintest smile.

"Okay, Jim. We've got all that. Well done." Yanis paused, aware that he hadn't asked the key question. "Jim? Um, where actually will it take us?"

The effort was draining him, and Jillian frowned at Yanis not to ask anything else. But Thompson persevered, saying, "*Cave. You'll find him.*"

His eyes quickly making contact with each of the others, Yanis mouthed, "*Him?*"

"*At the entrance.*"

More glances and silent wishes left Jillian asking the question. "Who's *he,* Jim?" But the ailing sergeant was falling into slumber again, as though anesthetized. She checked his pulse, just to make sure. "He's completely out," she noted.

Yanis whispered, "Drugged?"

Jenkins had his own troubles in mind. "Wish I'd gone to sleep that fast last night."

"You want to try laying down in the other bay? See if it helps you sleep through the night?" Jillian joked. It did seem rather odd that the ship had provided *two* bays; unnervingly, it seemed the vessel knew more than they did, and was anticipating at least one more serious casualty.

"I'd rather follow Jim's directions," Jenkins said. "Did he say it would lead us to a cave?"

"Count me out," Entwhistle said. "I used to love being underground, but I reckon I've had enough of bloody caves and mines for one mission, thank you very much." Then, seeing as no one else had, he addressed the elephant in the room. "I take it Jim's not been in this particular wood before?"

"No reason to think so," Yanis said.

"No way he can know where we are, anyway," added Jillian. "He's been asleep, or unconscious, or whatever, the whole time."

"No, but," the Scot continued, "those directions, they were *very* specific. Like he was reading them out," said Entwhistle. "Wasn't that how it sounded to you?" Jillian looked thoughtful, so he continued. "I mean, like someone was giving him the instructions, and then he was passing—"

"Look at his left wrist," said Jillian. As the others turned, surprised, she added, "Tell me his skin hasn't always been that color."

***

The strange, grey-green patch on Thompson's wrist was completely new, they agreed. The skin around the joint had gained a dried, weathered texture, like stained parchment, but brightened by a slight, metallic glint. There was nothing obviously threatening about it, but in the hour after its appearance, Jim's movements stilled until he appeared lethargic, even beleaguered. Worried and uncertain, Yanis had Entwhistle bring over the others; until then, the Airborne and Royal Marine groups had been kept away, mostly through fear of the unknown.

"What," Osborne asked, like everyone else, "is *that*?"

"We need to talk about some kind of medical protocols," Jillian said. No one else had thought of it. "I know we've been surrounded by alien stuff for a while now, and they were good enough not to let a mountain drop on us, but we don't know *anything* about what's going on with Jim."

"You're saying it could be dangerous?" Keller asked, alert to unusual threats since their encounter with Keck's nerve agent.

"Don't know. Not going to know for a while," Yanis said, feeling that rising anger that comes from being expected always to have the answers. "It could be a feeding mechanism, something like the valve that helps him breathe. Or an antibiotic patch, to help cure an infection."

"Well, I don't like the looks of it," decided Keller.

"That makes all sixteen of us, then," Yanis told him, exasperated. "But like Jillian said, the aliens have gone out of their way to help us. Why would they poison Jim now?"

With a larger group of opinions, Yanis was right to anticipate a wave of ill-informed suggestions. "Could we not just cut his hand off? To stop, you know, *that* from spreading?"

"We don't know what *that* is," explained Yanis, "or if it's spreading."

"Still, though?" the Marine persisted. "As a precaution?"

"Isolation," was another idea. "Like quarantine. In case he's infectious."

"He's already isolated. And we've been here for thirty hours, without anyone becoming ill, so we're close to ruling out a contagion."

Without a decent option, they would leave Thompson in the care of the glowing, orange bay. He seemed relatively comfortable, even snoring at one point. Jillian stayed with him before Jenkins relieved her, and between them, all they heard from Jim was some mumbling in his sleep.

But in the morning, as Keller got their fires going again, Jenkins quietly stopped Yanis at the chamber exit. "It's worse."

"How much worse?"

"His whole hand, except his thumb and two fingertips," explained Jenkins, almost too quiet for Yanis to hear. "Looks a little bit," he said, trying to find the right analogy, "like snakeskin, only the snake's made of rock, or something." Yanis would have to see for himself; the phenomenon was peculiar enough to defy easy description. "Real spooky, professor, ya know? Even for a FUBAR mission like this one."

"Yeah," said Yanis. "Shit." With a To Do list already crammed with the unknowable and the impossible, the last thing he needed was aliens doing some kind of half-assed experiments on their best sergeant, the man who was their natural leader.

"What you want me to tell the others?" asked Jenkins. He looked exhausted from worry, and from his all-night vigil by the medical bay. "They were asking."

"Jim's going to be fine," Yanis announced. "Whoever is caring for him, they know what they're doing. They took good care of me. Well, actually, the ship took care of me. But it's like they're trying to build trust."

"We can *trust* them?" Jenkins didn't care for investing heavily in the Little Green Men. "These aliens went and let a fuckin' *Nazi* use their machine, Miller. Completely screwed up human history. You think they care about the results that had?"

Neither Yanis nor anyone else knew the first thing about the aliens' intentions. "I can't say, but what about the directions Jim gave us? Worth a look, don't you think?"

They made an agreement. Jenkins would do nothing to sow fear among the men, and Yanis promised never to deliberately mislead anyone about Jim's condition. If the sergeant appeared to be in danger, they would pull him out of the bay. Until then, they'd leave him to rest, which meant putting their faith in the machine. And in whatever great mind would make its decisions.

***

Gratified to be doing something concrete, Keller quickly finished his German astronaut's breakfast and began planning for a reconnaissance of what Jim had called "the cave."

"At least we know to bring flashlights," the lieutenant said.

"But that's all we know," Yanis needed to mention. "How many of us should go with you?"

Keller revealed an intricate plan which would minimize legwork and maximize safety, about which he was completely obsessed. Three small teams would set out, one following Jim's instructions and the others in parallel, staying within sight of each other as they approached the objective.

"There's no point asking, is there," Osborne said to Yanis, "how come your sergeant knew all of that?" He was trying to wash his hair using only a canteen of cold water and an empty travel-sized shampoo bottle. "Bloody Nora, that woke me up."

Jenkins passed them both and tossed out the cooled dregs of his coffee against a tree trunk. "Let's see if any of it is actually true," he advised, "before we start another round of guessing games." For the most part, Jenkins was informing the others that Thompson was resting quietly, and that they had good reasons for optimism. Privately, though, the unexplained discoloration gave him a hot curl of worry in his gut.

Without Jim, maybe me and Yanis and the German can keep things together, but if one of us is lost or captured...

"Saddle up, Airborne," Keller called. Then quietly, to Miller, "Was that right?"

"Huh?"

"I saw it in a movie, *Aliens*. You know? That lieutenant, the ... how do you say, the *pen pusher*? He's trying to act tough, and when he sends out his sergeant, he says, 'Saddle up, Apone.' It is right?" he asked, showing a more vulnerable side. "I know it's ridiculous," he said, managing to laugh at himself, "but they are all such strong characters, such amazing individuals, and I guess I just—"

"Want to sound like you're one of them?" It was a tall order, given the seventy-year gap. Not to mention Keller's German heritage.

"Like I said, ridiculous."

"You're doing great." In truth, Keller and the other German NATO troops—like Schachter, his C.O., now long since departed—had gone the extra mile to make friends with the Allied forces. With their numbers now so few, these connections, and the mutual respect they fostered, were beyond priceless. "Ready?"

Osborne was wasting no time in taking his two Marines, Hyde and Brooks, straight down the line of Jim's directions, led by his compass. Yanis received a quick salute from Keller and watched the officer pace away to join his own team. Then he turned to see Jillian emerging from the spacecraft while helping a pale, bandaged Airborne trooper hobble down the ramp alongside her.

"Dennis?" He approached to help them reach the ground, but Jillian had things covered. "Sorry to say it, Private Dodson, but you can't possibly hope to go on the recon …"

But the young man's aspirations were smaller. "Just wanted a bit of fresh air, sir."

"How's *this* for fresh air?" Professor Miller offered. "You get to call me Yanis."

For a nineteen-year-old, it was like being told he could call the school principal by their childhood nickname. He smiled, "Roger that, sir."

The three trios set out, with Yanis joining Jillian and a blond Airborne PFC named Hart. He was exhausted, like the others, but still had a hundred questions. Yanis kept him busy, asking about Hart's hometown, and his plans for after the war, while Jillian's eyes swept their route through the forest. Every few seconds, she'd see one of Osborne's Marines through the trees to the left, beyond which would be Keller. He'd taken along PFC Irwin, who spoke some German and liked Keller personally, as well as the unflagging Sergeant Jenkins.

Hart left the others to relieve himself in the woods. "Feels completely ordinary, doesn't it?" Jillian mused.

"I'll take ordinary over *Der Dom* any day of the week," Yanis quipped.

"Gets me thinking that Keller might have been right," she said, "like this is all some high-tech con job, and a camera crew is going to pop out and tell us, 'You've Been Framed!'"

"They'll get themselves shot doing something like that," said Yanis. "No, it really seems, by some stroke of luck, that we've earned ourselves another bite of the cherry. People don't normally get third chances."

There were shouts from his left, but they didn't sound urgent. "Reckon they've found the cave?" asked Jillian. She spotted Hyde jogging over to fill them in, and as he arrived, told him, "I'm not exactly thrilled to be going underground again. Not after last time."

"This is different," Hyde said. "There ain't no geometric archway, and there ain't no elevator." The cave was tucked away, hidden by the lip of an overhang, with moss and forest plants crowding the rock all around. "Gonna need some equipment."

Before they'd even started figuring that out, Entwhistle interrupted in his bright, Scottish brogue. "Oh, aye, it's nice doon here!" He'd scaled down the damp, mossy walls, free climbing the unfamiliar terrain, entirely indisposed toward any form of unnecessary hesitation. "Picture postcard stuff," he said, looking down to find good hand- and footholds on the uneven surface. From above, where the search teams stood and watched, the crevasse looked to have been made by a giant with a paring knife; the rocks were separated by a deep, geological incision through which water had labored through the years to create a sequence of chambers. "Alright, then. Chamber ahead, going to see what we've got."

Reaching the lower depths, some ten meters below, Entwhistle found himself alone and cut off from the densely wooded little valley above. After weeks in *Der Dom*, the cool, green quiet of these rocky walls felt like a balm for his soul.

"Wait for us, Harry!" called Osborne. He and his men had reduced and simplified their gear but would go into the cave fully armed. Until they knew more, this could be no ordinary expedition.

"No, no, hold it," Entwhistle shouted back. He sounded suddenly concerned. "I found something." After a moment, a spine-chilling addendum. *"Someone."*

***

It was a body, and whoever it had belonged to had died long, long before. Six of the explorers huddled around the find, a forlorn bundle of disarticulated bones partly covered by lengths of browned, rotted fabric. The body lay on its front, with both hands seemingly outstretched in different directions. Picked clean but then largely undisturbed, the bones were mostly intact, but darkened and brittle.

"Well, I'm afraid we're not going to be able to do anything for him," Entwhistle said, regarding the pile of remains. "Got to be a hundred years he's been here, no? Maybe more."

The discovery might have seemed innocuous to soldiers who sometimes found bodies in strange places. But the ancient, desiccated corpse removed Yanis' last excuse for keeping his cool. He pulled Jillian aside, out of the tight squeezes which formed the entrance.

"What?" she asked. "You sick of confined places, too?"

"Of all the things we could have found," Yanis was saying, "we find a *dead body*. Precisely where Jim Thompson told us to look around. Don't you find that ..." He searched for the word.

"Creepy as fuck?" Jillian tried. "It's almost worse than if we'd found someone alive in here."

"Yeah." The others were heading past the body, into the cave itself. "No wonder this place remained hidden. Look at the *shape*." It seemed the cave had been deliberately designed to occlude its secrets using a kind of visual labyrinth, complex and twisting enough to keep prying eyes away from the inner sanctum. "How does it look further in?" Yanis shouted through.

Entwhistle was taking the lead, despite earlier reluctance. The appeal of pure exploration was strong, as was the chance to show off his free-climbing skills, and his capacity for steady leadership in a dangerous spot. "Four squeezes in a row," he said. The labyrinth was apt to prevent entry, as well as obscure sight lines. "Tighter than a duck's arsehole. We can go one at a time, but it'll be a hell of a—"

Keller's CB radio, one of only two remaining, crackled loudly in the echoing chamber. The voice on the other end kept mentioning Jim Thompson.

"What's he saying?" Between the echo and fizzing static, the message was almost lost.

"It's Jim," Montoya was saying. "He's awake, and he's angry."

"Angry?" Yanis asked, very worried.

"I can't explain it," Montoya said, "but Thompson *desperately* wanted to come to the cave."

***

"It's all he'll say," PFC Montoya reported from within the spacecraft chamber. "'Get me to the cave,' or 'Need to go to the cave.' Things like that." Yanis had encouraged them all to reach within the orange bay and make contact with Jim, but after finding the patch of discolored skin, he'd forbidden any physical contact. Now, though, Jim grabbed for anyone he could see; he was animated and energized by the cave, and any thought of visiting. "What you want me to do, sir? Can we do as he asks?"

"No," Yanis said. "Jim was poisoned with nerve gas, or whatever horrible shit they threw at us, down there. No way he can walk a couple of miles, and back, and hardly any way of transporting him there."

As if he could hear, Jim began poking at the outer membrane of the bay with his foot, trying to swing one leg out. "No, you don't,"

Montoya warned. "Stay still, okay? They'll be back soon, and they'll explain everything."

But there was no appeasing him. Every sentence, every utterance, contained the word 'cave,' as though Jim was crossing the desert, and the cave would be his oasis. He pushed at the membrane, and at the soft ceiling of the bay, but they would not yield, as though the alien technicians operating behind the scenes had seen the danger. Still, it was unnerving to have Jim thrashing at the membrane, so single-mindedly desirous to visit a place of which he could not possibly ever have heard.

Within an hour of sunset, the three trios of explorers returned to the ship, better informed than before, but in ways which only generated more confusion. Yanis and Jillian came straight to Jim, worried that he'd still be struggling against the bay's in-built security. But he was still, and extremely pale, as though worn out by his exertions. Jillian knelt by the bay and reached into the membrane to find his hand; it was icy cold. "Shit, Yanis, is he dying?" she asked, panicked. "Feel this."

To Yanis' touch, Jim had already gone. "No, no, no, don't you dare!" he bellowed. "Not after all this!"

But there was movement, a flutter in his eyelids, a tiny, trembling crook to his finger. And he spoke, a single, predictable word, a desperate plea: *Cave.*

***

It took hours. The orange bay released Jim reluctantly, apparently concerned that the patient wished to leave before his treatment was complete. Jim couldn't stand, and his eyes remained closed most of the time. A litter was constructed from the simple resources available—thick branches from the forest, and a doubled-up poncho. It wasn't perfect, but they managed to hoist Jim onto four shoulders and convey him through the forest. Osborne mocked up a US Marine Corps cadence, and the carrying quartet kept up a good pace:

"I don't know, but I've been told,
Alien pussy is mighty cold..."

Arriving at the cool, wooded spot where the hill gave way to broadening cracks in the limestone, they began to think about how Jim could be lowered into the cave itself. "Reckon if we had about thirty yards more rope," Entwhistle estimated, but Jim Thompson stopped them all with a single gesture: a spread palm, held skyward. It was an appeal, a request for intercession, beheld in sudden silence by a group equally fascinated and concerned. The grey, faux-lithic coloring now covered Jim's entire hand, and almost to his elbow.

"Three diurnal cycles since arrival," spoke Jim Thompson. It was his voice, his accent, but most decidedly *not* his words. "Eight diurnal cycles until local aphelion. Four diurnal cycles since local estival solstice, axial inclination twenty-three point four-four." Yanis found he was writing, subconsciously taking down every word. "Local latitude, equatorial plus fifty-four, local longitude, meridian minus six." Then the hand fell back, and Jim was still and quiet, breathing deeply on his stretcher.

No one knew what to make of it. Jim's pronouncements had come like those of a prophet, a man who offered a conduit to a much greater mind. At least his condition had not obviously worsened, despite the stresses of being carried out to the cave. Jillian held his hand once more while Yanis paced around the edge of the limestone fissure, looking down into the soft-greened, subterranean haven, and then up at a cobalt blue sky.

It's summer. Notions began to coalesce, if only slowly. *He mentioned the equinox, didn't he? What did he say?* "Jillian, check me here, would you?" They read his notes together, but she couldn't add any meanings. "Diurnal," Yanis knew, however, "means 'day.' So, Jim knows we've been here for three days."

"*Jim* knows?" asked Jillian. "Or *Jim's handlers* know?"

He shrugged this away; they were working a list of three basic problems—*where, when,* and if possible, *why*—and concerns about the extent of alien involvement were currently down at number six. "And he said it's been four days since a solstice."

"Yeah, what word did he use? It wasn't winter or summer." A flash of worry; if the local seasons could not easily be defined, perhaps they were not, after all, on a familiar Earth.

"*Aestivus,*" Yanis said, puzzling it through out loud. "Latin for heat. Gives us estival, meaning summer."

She stared at him, scarcely ever more impressed.

"The benefits of a classical education. Blame my folks." He worked the rest of the numbers. "Twenty-three degrees, he said. That's the Earth's axial inclination ..."

"Huh?" Jillian asked. She wasn't alone; the others were dividing their attention between the stilled Thompson and the newly animated Miller.

"Don't worry, it's good news. Not every Earth is inclined like ours." It was more proof that they had not left the planet. "Now, if we're at fifty-four degrees north, and six degrees west—"

Osborne was with him, until this point. "Wait, how did you—"

"Equator and meridian," Yanis spelled out. "Latitude and longitude."

"Holy shit," breathed Jillian. "And Jim somehow *knew* all of that?"

"Not *all* of it. Did you bring your iPhone, like I asked?" The battery showed only nine percent, but the machine powered up, and Jillian was able to launch the default astronomy application. "No service," she warned, "but the onboard data should be helpful." There were star charts, and tide tables, and all manner of data on conjunctions and eclipses. Yanis read, made notes, and performed some notebook calculations involving the area of the surface of a sphere. Then, he shut down the phone and handed it back to Jillian.

"So, do we have the first idea what Sergeant Thompson was talking about?" she asked, without much hope.

For the first time in ages, he gave her a full and sunny smile.

"Yanis?"

He was standing, waving for the others' attention. "Want to know where we are?"

Osborne played it cool. "Kinda curious, is all."

Yanis checked his math once more, then announced, "We're in the northern half of Ireland."

Eight different versions of, "Huh, really?" were his reply.

"And it's about eleven o'clock in the morning," he continued, thrilled now by his own acumen, "on Wednesday, 27th of June, 1945." He grinned at them, then knelt by Jim again. "That sound about right, big man?"

"Bingo," croaked Thompson. "Yeah. Real good." He was regaining some color, but remained very sickly, so Yanis was staggered to hear him say, "Now, where to, Miller?"

He stared around the group, but no one knew what Jim might mean. "*Where to?*" he parroted.

Jim reached for Yanis' hand, took it with a surprisingly firm grip, and whispered, "Picture it, and we'll go there. All of us."

"But Jim, where can we go?" Out of their own timeline, and beyond even the new event strands they'd created, Yanis had to think quickly to find a place that might be safe. "Where's the safest place for us?"

"Not Korea," she said. "And behind the Iron Curtain sounds pretty awful."

"Behind the what?" Jenkins asked. Yanis explained for a few moments, and the young sergeant shrugged. "Good name for it. Especially with that big wall about to go up, like you say."

"Maybe steer clear of revolutionary China, too," Jillian advised, picturing them arriving into a unified, fiercely independent Communist China using a time machine found by the Nazis. "And anywhere else we might be executed as spies."

"Alright," Yanis had his eyes closed. "I think I know." He held the image of the room in his mind. There was that red phone on the central table, European maps on the walls. The cloying odor of wartime cigarettes and, worse still, wartime coffee. He could see the ever-helpful, supportive man whom Yanis fervently hoped would still be manning his desk. With the image as complete as he could manage, Yanis took Thompson's hand and gripped it as though preparing to haul the sergeant to his feet. "I've got it, Jim."

"Yeah," said Thompson quietly, "yeah, alright." The world around them began to turn in two directions at once, like an astronaut's training chair tumbling end-over-end while yawing hard to the side. There was noise, and nausea, and sudden cold. Someone shouted— a man, a question. Beside him, Jillian was there but not there, flashing in and out of reality. It lasted seconds but seemed to stretch to fill all the time they'd stolen from the universe, and all that they ever might.

***

The shouting collided with the spinning, each slowing the other until words formed in the air like ice crystals. Yanis could almost reach for one, but the nausea and dizziness were absolute in those first few seconds, and the words sparkled, out of reach. He was being asked a question, over and over, but couldn't yet make it out. A presence to his left could have been Jillian. Or she could have been a billion miles away. Perspective failed until there was a click within his head, like a synapse snapping back into place, and the scene cleared.

They were being yelled at by about a dozen armed, angry men.

"On the ground!"

"Don't move!"

"Drop your weapons!"

It wasn't the most auspicious start, but at least he was being screamed at in *English*.

"My name is Professor Yanis Miller," he called out, trying to get the soldiers' attention. "Miller, M-I-L-L-E-R, here to see Mr. David Walcott." Someone recognized the name, and the shouting eased off while a confused corporal asked a confused sergeant what their confused captain might want to do. "We are members of Operation Asphodel," he said, making sure the whole team had their hands aloft.

It was working; Walcott and Asphodel both meant something to the guards. Things moved quickly, and instead of being shouted at, they were kept at arms' length and herded into a conference room. It looked familiar, but only in layout, and in the less hectic moments after Yanis and the others were led inside and told to sit down, an old, old joke occurred to him.

Up on charges for the third time this year, Paddy O'Hearn strolls into a Dublin court room, walks up to the judge and informs him, "I do not recognize this court!" The judge is furious, insisting that the defendant submit himself to the court's authority. When Paddy refuses, the judge demands an explanation. "Why on Earth would you not recognize this court?" he asked.

"Well, here's the thing," Paddy finally explained. "It's been painted since last time I was here!"

Then, the room identified itself in his memory. This was where it had happened, where he'd been hauled up from his cell to face questions fashioned from skepticism and asked with unconcealed derision. It was in this room that he'd been freed from the barbarism of the asylum and set on the course which would lead to the freezing-cold doorway of a C-47 at midnight over Bavaria. For all that had happened in the interim, being here again was as strange as returning to the womb, and to Yanis, it felt like a giant step backward.

Why did I choose Walcott's offices at MI6? Why not ask Jim to take us to a nice beach in the tropics? What's wrong with palm trees and freshly-squeezed, dusky maidens?

From just outside the door, they could hear only part of a heated discussion. Yanis picked up, "The Prime Minister is aware," and then, "enormous security implications," and some mention of "distortion spheres."

After several minutes of arguing, the older voice gave way to the younger, and the room's door opened. "Yanis?"

"David!" Yanis exploded.

From the look on Walcott's face, Miller and his comrades might have been ghosts from another dimension, strange apparitions appearing unannounced out of nowhere.

"Yes, David, it's me! Yanis Miller!" Three awful, silent seconds passed during which Yanis' darkened mind composed a timeline in which Walcott had never met Yanis, was unaware of *Der Dom*, and would shortly be arranging for their arrest.

"It *can't* be."

"David, do you remember when Winston Churchill fired the head of MI6, right in front of us?" He pointed to the central chair in the horseshoe of desks, where the indefatigable war leader had brutally curtailed the man's career. "The *look* on his face ..."

"Yanis Miller," Walcott said, separating the words, finding them hard to believe. "Professor Miller from Asphodel. I can't ..." He needed a moment. "I literally can't believe you're all here, but I'm going to have to, aren't I?" He looked around the ragtag group; he'd interviewed agents returning from months in the field, even some who had escaped Gestapo torture. But to him, no battle survivors had ever looked so exhausted in victory.

He had so many questions, but the very first of them was impossible now: *Where is everyone else?*

Walcott knew, and the immensity of the loss was only beginning to dawn on him, like a looming, slow-motion avalanche.

"There will be," Walcott warned them, "a *great deal* of catching up to do."

4

Sam's Story

Manhattan, New York, August 1944

Williams had told him it was a job interview. "Easy as pie," he'd even called it, a desk job likely to position Sam Clark within sight of the typing pool. Just a quick chat about his background, and then he'd be on a straightforward promotion track. "Don't worry about which aerospace company it is," Williams had said. "They're pretty much the same, and they're all hiring like crazy right now."

It was a lie, but such things were Williams' profession, so he made Sam believe him when he said he was an 'aerospace industry representative,' and a 'contracts broker,' and later several other things. Sam was happy to keep on believing, as long as Williams took him to lunch twice a month and buttered him up until he felt like one of American engineering's hottest young tickets.

All Williams ever asked in exchange was for Sam's blameless help in keeping his ear to the ground. You never knew, the 'representative' often told him, when opportunities would arise. It was all about scanning the horizon and building the US capacity for 'deep-future thinking.' For a boy who'd read little but science fiction for nearly twenty years, it was nirvana.

That Sam had not even *qualified* yet, let alone risen to a rank where he might juggle opportunities, seemed not to matter to Williams. Besides, they got along, even if Williams drank a bit too early in the day. Nerves from the war, Sam came to assume. Everyone was coming back different, in one way or another. But in the rumors of an upcoming invasion of France, like a lot of people, Sam had seen the seeds of final victory.

By the end of the first week of June 1944, though, the world learned the truth: this was not the beginning of the end, but the inception of a terrifying new era. It was the very week Sam Clark graduated from Croftman College, placing tolerably well in his class. But he was not an instant, no-brainer choice for a big aerospace firm like Grumman or Lockheed, as he'd so fondly hoped these last four years.

And so, he fully expected to land among the thousands of newly qualified engineers looking for work, among them men who could boast war experience to burnish their academic credentials, or years in management with other businesses. Men who would see him off in these initial employment skirmishes, sending him scurrying away as surely as a subway rat.

Climbing up from the steaming, crowded subway into a breezy Manhattan mid-morning strewn with sunshine and newspapers, he imagined the line of hopefuls stretching down the block. They'd be nearly identical, most of them in their first ever suits, clutching an old Army duffel, or a brown suitcase, or, if they had enough money to look classy, a proper, leather briefcase. The haircuts would be 'regulation,' even in a business without such rules, but American men of the 1940s conformed to preconceptions out of duty, and a desire never to be seen as *different*. He imagined them waiting, two or three deep, an endless line of men better than him.

Either he was in the wrong place, or it was the wrong day. He checked the address again, and then a third and fourth time, and then asked two passers-by to confirm. Nobody was waiting outside, except for a cab.

"You've got a tongue in your head," his mother used to advise him, "so make use of it!"

The receptionist was doing eight things at once, but still found time for him. Yes, he was expected, and no, there hadn't been any mistake—this was the right place. She could shed no light on where the others might be. "Why not take a seat? Someone will be with you shortly."

Sheepishly, like a trespasser already discovered, Sam found a chair near the lobby piano and tried to sit still. Everything around him was an arrival from another world—the suited bellhops and elevator attendants—an *elevator*, for heaven's sake—and the smart lobby bar with its gleaming taps and rows of mysterious spirits. He couldn't read any of the labels, but they looked expensive. *In this day and age, how anyone could afford to ...*

It was Williams, in characteristic pose, one foot on the floor, the other on the rung of his bar stool. He was partway through a beer, though a smaller glass stood next to it. It was just after nine thirty in the morning.

"Jack?" Sam asked tentatively. The 'representative' turned and gave Sam a big grin. "Wow, Jack, did I screw this up? I mean, they said I'm in the right place but there's nobody—"

"Relax. Have a drink." He waved for the barman.

"No, thanks," Sam said. "Not twenty-one, anyway."

"I won't tell, and neither will he. Come on, I insist."

Insist? What the hell was Jack Williams even doing here?

"Sure," Sam relented. "But just one. I got this interview to do, still."

"What time?" Jack asked as the barman pulled Sam a crisp, cold pint.

"Ten," he said. "Thought I'd get in early, you know, see the lay of the land."

"Yeah," Jack said. "Got some news about your interview, Sam."

"Huh?" Was this opportunity about to fall apart after all? Had he wasted the cost of an overnight train from Illinois? Sam felt his stomach start to drop; as usual, it would all be too good to be true.

"It's not at ten o'clock." He raised his glass, unconcerned that Sam was staring at him, perplexed.

"Huh?"

He set down the glass and smiled, kindly and affable. "Sam, your interview started a few minutes ago. And so far, you're doing fine."

***

Up in one of the rooms on the twenty-first floor, from where Manhattan rolled itself out to the horizon like an urban fog bank, they made a deal. "Gonna ask you a whole mess o' questions," Williams promised from his armchair by the window. "A *whole* mess. More questions than you ever got asked in all your life before."

"Like a quiz? Or a test?" Sam asked, spotting a chair by the small, pine bureau.

Cryptically, Williams nodded while also saying, "No, quite unlike either of those things."

"Huh?"

"Sit down, Sam. If you answer everything as honestly as you can, once I'm done with the questions, it'll be your turn to do the asking. Anything you want. Sound alright?"

He guessed that it did, but there were worrying unknowns. "Could I ask one now?"

"Sure."

"Is this still an interview for an aerospace company?"

Again with the nodding. "Does Lockheed normally interview people in nice hotels? Does this *look* like an engineers' job fair?"

"Nope."

"Then, you know more than you think." He waved to the chair again. "Sit, seriously. This ain't an interrogation. I'm just here to get to know you better." In places, this would be the truth. "Tell me about home," said Williams. "Doesn't have to be specific, just things you remember from growing up."

Sam found this an odd, unsettling way to start. It was too open; didn't there have to be a right answer? "Like, things I achieved, tests I passed?"

"Didn't you submit all of that with your application?" Jack checked.

"I sure hope I did. That was all they asked about."

"Then assume we know all of that. Tell me about *home*. Growing up. The farm, your family."

Like most people, he felt he should begin with, "There isn't much to tell, really." When he was a child, theirs had been a perfectly normal, traditional farming family from Wisconsin. Quite unexceptional, really, even a little dull. "We had the cycle of the school year, and the cycle of the farm," he said. "Things ticked along pretty regular. Not a lot out of the ordinary."

"Little League and church, and the county fair," Williams predicted. "A big effort for Veterans Day, or the Fourth of July, everyone mucking in."

"You got it," said Sam. It sounded as though Williams had grown up in a similar way, but his mannerisms, his practiced sloppiness and devil-may-care bonhomie, carried more of the city than the farm.

"But then, things changed for your family, didn't they?" asked Williams. He was speaking without recourse to notes and took none of his own. "After your dad graduated with his master's. When you were nine."

The Big Move was most definitely young Sam's greatest challenge. "Dad didn't think he would get the job. Didn't even tell Mom. So, it was a helluva surprise when the letter came." Dorney Aviation, a fast-growing Chicago manufacturer of big maritime patrol planes, offered the newly qualified Ray Clark an engineering position, starting immediately. It was his dream ticket, and it would change everything.

"Sixteen days," Sam remembered wistfully. "We sold about half our belongings, then gave things away until we could fit everything in. They gave Dad an Army truck for the move, and it was like we were driving into combat, or something. He was fired up, ready for a change."

"How was it, settling in and making friends?" Williams asked. He'd brought a second beer up to the room, and the glass now stood empty, but for suds.

"It was okay at first. There were kids from Wisconsin, downstate Illinois, rural Indiana, other places like that, so we stuck together." He stopped, eyeing Williams' empty glass.

"You want one? I can call down, no problem."

"It's no big deal," he said. "Guess all this talking made me kinda thirsty." Williams reached for the phone, but Sam stopped him. "I should probably keep a clear head. How about coffee?"

"On the way," he said shortly after. "They're good here. Very quick."

"You come to this hotel a lot?" asked Sam. "Seems like you know the place."

"Do something for me, Sam," he said, folding his arms and looking differently at the young engineer; with all that was going on, and after the briefings he'd been given, Sam's status had changed. He'd been a lump of clay, albeit an interesting one, but now he was a potential asset. "Drop me into your final year of high school like we're both on parachutes, okay?"

Immediately wary, but helplessly intrigued by all of this, Sam said, "Parachutes?"

"Pull back and give me the big picture, then focus more and more on the most important thing."

Sam identified the strange sensation that was making his stomach itch: *Williams knows a hell of a lot more about me than he should.*

"You're going to have to help me there, Jack. I can tell you've done your homework, so why don't you just come out and—"

"Your stammer."

Three knocks at the door, just as he was on the cusp of answering. Once the coffee was set up, Sam's willpower broke, and he asked the waiter for a beer. Williams interjected to make it two *each*, just so they'd have a backup. The man returned with the tray in double-quick time, serving with neat flourishes of his white-gloved hands. "Anything else I can get for you gentlemen?" he asked, and then as he withdrew, glanced at the wall clock, and then at the four cold beers, and grinned, "Nice work if you can get it." The door closed with a firm click.

"So. My stammer," Sam said.

"Yeah."

"Not my work on the 'flying wing' concept, or the new type of tricycle landing gear I proposed, or the—"

"I know it's strange, but I need you to go with it."

The unfairness was mounting. *Go with it?* The only thing likely to 'go' anywhere was his anger, which rose faster than he'd have believed. It might have been the first beer talking, or just the frustration of being lied to, but he heard himself demand. *"Go* with it?" His temper rose until he decided, yes, he *was* going to swear at Jack Williams; the moment demanded it. "What the *fuck* is this, Jack?"

Williams froze for a moment but didn't seem unduly alarmed. "Come again?"

"You lied to me about this interview, and now you're doing some … I don't even know, some goddamned cartoon psychoanalysis. So, I repeat, and forgive my French, what the *fuck*, Jack?"

The inscrutable agent was cornered, but he'd rehearsed this part of the playbook, too. "I'm gonna put my hand on the Bible, and I'm gonna swear to tell you everything. I mean," he added quickly, "everything that's in my power to tell, just as soon as you finish telling me about your stammer." As he made the promise, he found the room's Bible in the bedside table drawer. "I'm completely serious, Sam. I ain't no saint, but swear I'll tell you what you want to know."

"Once I tell you about my stammer?"

"Damn right. But it'd better be the whole tall tale." He waited for Sam to drink half his second beer in a single pull. "Parachute me in, son."

He sat back, wiped his mouth. Absent the beers, Sam couldn't honestly say whether he'd still have been sitting there; he was fond of Williams, but this was a hell of a sleigh ride. "Well," he began, "shit. Alright. So, I never shook the farm boy thing, right?"

"Hayseed, bumpkin, yokel … Recognize all those?"

"Yeah," he groaned. "That was my lot for the duration, and, hell, I looked the part. Still do, some say. So, I went along with it. And you know what that meant?"

"That an expensive high school, fit for the wealthy son of a Chicago-based Dorney Aviation engineer, generally provides a first-rate education?"

"Well, I mean, yes, and—"

"And that such schools have social cliques which are crucibles of terrible social savagery?"

Eyes down, but prepared to go along with it for now, Sam said, "No lie."

"I'm gonna guess there were a couple of friendships that got needlessly smashed up by stupid 'Spoiled Rich Boy' bullshit?"

"It's like they'd carefully planned a social operation," Sam explained, "to shut me out of their circle. Only they'd do it gradually."

"You didn't fit in, and that was all that mattered, right? You didn't play the right sports."

"Fucking *hated* sports."

"Or go to the right, um, house of worship," he felt confident enough to add.

"Didn't go to *any*. Wasn't time on the weekends. Dad was never interested, and Mom just about put aside her rosary after she got married."

"And then, even when it seemed you'd built a kind of bridge, and that maybe she liked you back ..."

"Jesus, Jack," Sam groaned. "Were you watching from the fuckin' bushes, or something?"

"All I have is the sundry findings of my long and bitter experience," he said. "And it tells me your heart was broken, not by the girl, but *The Parents?*"

"Nixed it. Kibosh. Never had a *prayer*."

"And it was all you could think about for weeks and weeks."

Another nod. The man was damned near telepathic. "It wrecked my last summer in Wisconsin. Can't even remember half of my first-semester college classes, because I was still hurting so damned much. I never wanted to think back to those days, ever." Sam polished off his second beer. "And then," he said theatrically, as if the break-up wasn't enough, "I flunked one of my freshman-year classes because of a stupid mix-up."

"Your fault or theirs?"

"Mail problem. Ran out of time. Gonna blame *The Parents* for that, too," he replied. "I was still a mess."

"Their fault, for sure, but it doesn't say *that* on your transcript, does it? What happened next?"

This time Sam fixed the agent (investigator?) with a firmer look. "Why don't you tell me, Nostradamus?"

"Lot of money to pay out for a class, only to watch your son flunk it. After working those long hours at Dorney, the weekend shifts doing essential war work ..." He saw Sam flinch, and for a quarter-second, was certain a beer glass was heading, hard and fast, in his direction.

"You gonna talk about my dad?" Sam shouted, standing. "You think that's what you're gonna do? Huh?"

"Calm down, for Christ's sake. He did his duty, he smoked too many cigarettes, and he's gone. I'm sorry." Very matter-of-fact, the tone Williams found best when cooling off a hothead.

"Yeah, he is." The glass clunked back down on the table. "I miss the old bastard. Don't mind telling you that," he said, sitting once more, and feeling foolish for standing in the first place. What was he going to do, square up to Williams? His first job interview, and his first arrest for drunken brawling, both on the same day; what would the late, great Ray Clark have made of *that*?

"I know you do, Sam. I also know he just about caught *fire* when you told him about that class."

"It was like," Sam recalled painfully, "his hero had been found out to be a crook. He took it *so* hard. Couldn't believe I'd done it, told me the school had to be responsible, that I couldn't be responsible for something so *stupid.* But there was a special meeting, and they stood by their decision, and my dad was left with this impression of me that was just ..." It would be a shitty word, whichever of them said it. "Imperfect."

He stood again, but not with anger. He just didn't want to be looking at Williams while talking about this stuff and turned to the window. "Yeah. For the first time. He couldn't get over it."

"Got to be hard."

"It nearly killed me, Jack, I'm not kidding. He was *certain* that I'd permanently screwed up my chances of working at somewhere like Dorney."

"Never going to follow in Papa's footsteps ..."

"And that I might as well quit college now, before I waste any more of his money." It was the heady, lunchtime beers, he told himself, as he had to flick a tear away.

Williams was there, standing with him, overlooking Seventh Avenue through frilly, white drapes. "There wasn't time, was there?" he asked quietly. "To make it right?"

Eyes closed, he confessed it. "They said he had twelve weeks, and I couldn't afford to get back there from the east coast more than once or twice. So," he sighed, the pain still so close to the surface, "I saved up for five weeks, hoping he would wait for me. But he couldn't."

Jack took the shaken young man by the shoulders. "It's only been a few months. Give yourself time. And," he added, in case it hadn't come across, "I'm sorry, son, really." He let Sam have some space, visited the bathroom and then the lobby to check for messages. When he came back, pleased to find Sam hadn't chosen to skip the remainder of this unorthodox, cloak-and-dagger psychology, he found the engineer in a better frame of mind.

"I shouldn't drink in the mornings," he said, by way of an apology for some over-reacting, earlier.

"Each to their own," Williams shrugged.

"Can you I ask something?"

"Anything, like I said."

"Why me?" asked Sam. "I mean, we've gone over the problems I had with classmates, tests, and such. Why would I be a good candidate for whatever this is about?"

Williams sighed. "Fishing for compliments?"

"Not at all, I ..."

"Relax." He brought Sam's file out from his satchel, turned to a page he'd marked with a blue cross, and read aloud. "Mr. Clark's performance on the aptitude tests was satisfactory, though special mention must be made," he paused, making sure Sam was with him, "of his capacity for memorization. During testing, Mr. Clark achieved 100 percent recall, when the group's average was 42 percent. In a follow-up test, Mr. Clark was observed memorizing an entire deck of cards, then recalling all 52 in the correct order."

He felt pretty good, despite himself. "Alright. So, I'm good at remembering things."

"That's called *savantism*," Williams explained. "They used to call people like you an *idiot savant*, but I've just taken to thinking of you as a unique boy who has a computer for a brain."

"Really?" It wasn't the kind of thing adults normally said to him; most were either too intimidated by his brain or hadn't got to know him well enough.

"You're one of a kind, kid. That's why you're here."

He glowed for a quiet moment. "So," Sam proposed next, "shall we proceed, as requested, to the command performance of *My Stammer in a Nutshell* by Sam Clark?"

"Sounds like a powerful thing, Sam."

"*Powerful.* That's one way of saying it. The stammer bled my confidence like a leech. Starting college, I was a bag of nerves, but after a few months, I couldn't talk to *anyone*, even to thank the girl in the grocery store for bagging."

"So, what happened to it?" he asked. "You sound fine. No needless repetitions or hesitations."

"Beat it. Overwhelmed it." He found it hard to describe. "I'm not exactly sure, but it took eighteen weeks of intensive speech therapy with the kindest grandmother in Illinois."

"Ah, yes, Mrs. Kassianedes."

His eyes were screwed shut. "This is like a goddamned sci-fi novel, Jack. Are you reading my mind or something?"

"I sent her to you."

"Huh?" he exclaimed.

"Mrs. Kassianedes. She handed you her card at the freshman's fair. Do you remember?"

Staggered, Sam located the memory after a moment. "I think so."

"She was there specifically to meet you, on my orders."

The remainder of the puzzle began to slide together. "The Illinois Young Adult Communications Fellowship?" he said, immediately sure his silent but generous funding source was not what it had seemed.

"You like the name? It was the dullest I could think of."

"The stipend for my room at Croftman College, the money for Mrs. Kassianedes ... that was all you?"

"Not from my own pocket, you understand, but yeah."

Before anything else happened, Sam's upbringing kicked in. "Thanks, Jack."

"You're welcome."

"I mean, it was thousands and thousands."

"Yeah, it was. And do you wanna know why the U.S. government spent thousands, just so that some young buck engineer could speak straight?" He reached back into his jacket, hanging on the chair, found an envelope and handed it over. "Because fancy high schools turn out future academics, and good colleges turn out fine engineers, but I want to know if you can be both. Or if—"

"Or if the whole thing just crushed me like a bug," Sam summed up.

"Can you take stress, and remain functional?" Williams asked rhetorically.

"I've been functioning fairly well, I'd say, despite the beers. And this was pretty goddamned stressful."

"Well, good," Williams said. "Because if I'm right about Sam Clark, then he's gonna have a great long string of fuckin' *incredible* things to say in the next fifty years. I figured it best if they came out right."

***

It was an invitation of a kind Sam knew he couldn't possibly refuse. He would be commissioned into the Army Air Force as a Lieutenant, "with the rights and responsibilities of that rank," and stationed somewhere called Fort Duke. But these details mattered less than the brief description of Project Prophet: *To acquire, study, replicate and improve captured enemy technology, specifically the 'X-weapons' used in Normandy.*

He folded the letter back into the envelope and waited for Williams to return once more. Though Sam believed only that Jack was giving him time to compose himself, the agent had three of these interviews at the hotel today, each at different stages and with varied chances of success.

Williams came back in looking purposeful and stood by the doorway. "Well?"

All Sam could do was shrug, really. Without knowing more, he couldn't be sure whether this was an opportunity to advance in the sciences or to spend a year getting coffee for more important people. But to Jack, the young engineer's reaction was troubling. "Why am I getting the sense," Williams asked, "that you're just a little bit disappointed?"

Embarrassed, Sam tried to cover. "No, no, it's not that, please don't think I'm—"

"Top secret high-technology not interesting enough for you?"

"It is, honestly, it's like a dream come—"

"The chance to *change the world*?"

"Alright, dammit," he cursed, feeling obliged to spill the beans. "I thought ... I thought you were recruiting me to become a spaceman," he blurted.

"A ... spaceman?"

"You know, to go up there, like the Germans are trying to do." If he'd ever doubted it was a forlorn hope, Jack's reaction confirmed it. "Okay, laugh it up if you must," Sam said, "but you're the one who invited me here without giving me a clue about what's going on."

Still laughing, he beckoned Sam into the hallway and put a companionable arm around his shoulder as they walked to the elevator. "I don't doubt we'll do it. One day, I mean. Go into space," he said. "And if we do, there's no point someone like *you* being at the top of the rocket."

"Hey!" Sam objected. "I'm a *lieutenant* now and everything!"

"I meant," said Jack, stopping short of the elevator, "that you're the guy who should be designing and building the thing. Ain't no one else gonna help us, and we know for sure the Germans are racing ahead. So, what do you say?"

"To what?"

"To coming on board and making sure that technology ends up powering *our* military, and economy, and space program, and never *theirs*. Because wherever they came from, its inventors sure as shit didn't intend for the worst imaginable humans to get hold of it. And," he added, "because you're ready for this."

Skeptical to the point of pessimism, Sam asked, "You think?"

"Well," Williams admitted as he ushered Sam into the elevator, "almost. You will be, by the end of next weekend."

"What happens then?" he asked, but all Williams did was smile.

***

8 days later, near Clayton, upstate New York

It had taken three days, but he was sure this was the right place. A final 'orienteering' exercise, rather different from the traditional jaunt across the countryside, had sent Sam three hundred miles from Fort Duke, north to Ithaca, and then into the quiet, Amish backwaters of upstate New York. He'd been given nothing but an address and some money—not enough to hire a vehicle or a driver, but buses and trains were cheaper. In the end, the train to Albany had been a nice ride, and some amiable hitchhiking gave him a chance to decompress after a few ludicrously packed days.

Sergeant Cole had called it training. Sam's lower back, knees, feet, and powder-burned fingertips all called it abuse. Much had been learned in ten days—combat driving, shooting at all kinds of targets, and then screaming through the first six seconds of a parachute jump but loving the rest of it. Sam Clark might have been of little practical use at The Front, but his confidence was achieving take-off.

The address he'd written down was a timber yard, and it was closed and completely deserted, which left Sam nonplussed. On the positive side, he was by the water now, after days of rattling buses and drafty train carriages, and it was blessedly quiet except for the low monotones of warning horns sounded by ships out in the channel. Connecting the Great Lakes and Canada to the Atlantic, the St. Lawrence had never been more strategically vital, and more than one Nazi submarine had braved its waters, hunting for prey.

Sam walked down to the water, just beyond the timber yard, and sat on the riverbank for a while, watching a pair of warships escorting several merchant vessels steadily down the channel. Behind him, there was the crunching of footsteps on gravel, and he turned.

"Ah, good, you're here. Come on." The briefest handshake, and they were pacing down the little street which flanked the river. Sam trotted quickly to catch up, but before he could ask much of anything, they reached a boat slip where a 21-foot motorsailer was waiting. "Do you sail?" the man asked. He was tall, with a distinctly military bearing.

"A little bit. Tried it last week."

"Ah, yes, I heard about that," he said. It was a numbing impact, as it meant this man was part of the assessment, and Sam was still being examined, or graded, or whatever the *hell* this all was supposed to be. "Didn't they have to call out the Coast Guard?" the man asked.

"Yes, but that wasn't me," Sam affirmed quickly. "One of the others, how do you say, *got into difficulties.*"

"He flooded his engine, got his sails all cock-eyed, and then expected someone else to help him. You shan't be seeing him again," the man said. "Anyway, jump onboard and see if you can make yourself useful."

Sam recognized enough of the boat's functions to know how to stay out of the way. "Sir, if you don't mind me asking—"

"Hold your fire, *Lef*tenant," he said. "There are certain things best discussed over a glass of scotch in front of the fire. And some things," he added, tapping his nose, "can *only* be discussed that way."

Instead, they sailed for twenty minutes or so with the boat's thrumming engine as the only sound. The man was obviously an experienced mariner and rather familiar with the area. A couple of times, he'd shout over the noise of the engine, identifying a landmark or naming one of the islands and Sam would nod, none the wiser. But in pastel-golden afternoon sun, with the waters clear around them and the ship's prow smoothly parting the water, Sam felt terrific.

After all, the whole week had been like this, a sequence of stumbling guesses and bits of luck, apparently sufficient to see him through myriad tests and trials, almost all of them entirely new to him. Well, he *assumed* he'd passed them all; otherwise, why would he be here, taking up this man's time? With his gruff, experienced demeanor and sleek, classy sailboat, he was clearly someone of significance. If Sam's ears weren't playing tricks, he also had a British accent.

Some twenty-five minutes from the docks, out of nowhere, Sam's pilot throttled down, leaving the engine at idle. "A quick pit-stop, before we continue to my island. Would you step forward and take a seat? Yes, opposite me, here," he gestured, and Sam stepped very deliberately and slowly toward the round perch before sitting down. "Good. I need to ask you something. It's important."

"Of course," said Sam.

"Before I tell you who I am, I want you to tell me something."

"Alright."

The man reached under the boat's console and brought something out. Sam's guts leapt like a startled rabbit—it was a revolver, which he placed on the console between them. "Would you ever sell out an operation, if offered all the money you could ever spend?"

"No!" Sam answered sharply.

"Did your parents own their farm?"

"Yes," he said, before he could even wonder how that was important, and why there was a gun.

"Any debts, I.O.U.s, that kind of thing? A girl to whom you owe money? You know, perhaps for ..."

"No, none at all. Dad paid my way through college, and I had a stipend." Would this mysterious Brit also know that the Illinois Young Adult Communications Fellowship was an agency front? Probably, but no matter; Sam knew it was important only to be honest. "I've got enough saved up to pay my first month's rent, whenever I figure out *where* I'm going, but that depends on finding a job."

"I'd say you've already got one of those," the man said. "One last question. Why was it important that we defeated Nazism?"

The standard answer came to mind, but Sam took another way, rooted again in honesty. "I don't know if they're completely defeated, sir. Their government is still kinda shaky on ideology. And on morals," he added. "We don't know much about what's going on inside the Reich."

"Righto," the man nodded and turned back to the ship's wheel, his hand on the throttle control.

"Wait, why did we stop?" Sam asked.

"Hm?"

"You could have asked me those things at the docks, or wherever we're going."

"Hartsmoor Island," the man said. Could Sam detect a hint of pride?

"Alright, but you could have asked me there."

"Yes, but then, what would I have done with the body?" he said without turning. Off to their starboard, a freighter loomed large in the middle-distance; the deep, rhythmic thrum of its engines would have been audible from here, were it quiet.

"Body?" It came out as a strange croak.

"I asked if you'd ever sell out an operation. You didn't evade, blink, procrastinate, or ask for more details, you just said 'no.'"

"Of course I did."

"And that was excellent. Because if you'd done any of the other things, I'd have shot you in the head, tied those two breeze blocks to your feet," he said, waving to the incriminating pile of murder accoutrements by the boat's stern rail, "with that chain, there, and dumped you over the side." He spied something ahead which confirmed his navigation, and nodded, gratified. "So, like I say, excellent choice, Sam."

"Jesus Christ, sir," said Sam.

"Like they told me in training, back in the day," he quoted, "If you can't take a joke, you shouldn't have joined a comedy troupe."

An island, one of dozens which sprouted up within the channel, grew larger in front of them until Sam could see his pilot was planning to dock there. "You know what to do, lad?"

"Yes," Sam exaggerated.

"Splendid. I'll just light my cigar a little early, then." With that, his hands left the controls. The engine remained at two-thirds throttle, but the wheel began to spin to port almost at once.

Sam grabbed it, but realized he'd been given only a sliver of time. "Sir? Um, we're getting very close to the shore, sir."

Quick puffs of tobacco smoke were followed by, "Well, you'd better do something about it, hadn't you?"

Uttering something equal to the disgust he felt at being deceived again, Sam slapped down the throttle and grabbed the wheel. "Co-pilot has the *conn*," he said, forcing an official handover of responsibility. "And if you're just going to sit and smoke, do it in my seat," he said. "This is difficult enough without having to stand up."

Roaring with laughter, the man relinquished the seat and watched Sam bring this disorderly approach under control. It was a cruel challenge to toss straight into a tired man's lap, but he didn't rate it as demanding exceptional skill. Well, ordinarily, anyway. He'd quite deliberately set Sam up very badly for an approach to the little docks, angling the bow to spill the wind from his sails, and then leaving the rudder nudged just one-eighth over to starboard. It was unlikely Sam would even notice, he judged, even as he inadvertently rammed the docks with his sheering bow.

But Sam was equal to it. He spotted the rudder bias and brought the controls back to midships, then used the engine, revving hard in reverse, to back up and buy some time. Once he'd oriented the boat again, coming in so that the wind would help to slow him, not accelerate him to disaster, some more judicious use of the engine brought the motorsailer neatly alongside the little wooden docks.

"Champion," the man said, bounding out to grab lines and tie the vessel up. "Couldn't have done it better myself."

"Then why didn't you?" Sam said, tossing a rope back at him angrily. He was piqued at the insult; apart from anything else, it had been a terribly dangerous, un-seamanlike act, especially with a passenger. "Huh? What is this? Another goddamned test? You've threatened to shoot me, then nearly got us both drowned—"

"Scotch," he said. "Once there is scotch, and a fireplace, all shall be made clear." Barely mollified, Sam glared at him. "Not trying to be unhelpful, not trying to hurt your feelings," he explained, without fuss. "It's just the way we do things."

A rough path led away from the docks, through an overgrown copse to a better-tended lawn area where a white-painted, wrought iron table and chairs were set out. The house, much larger than Sam would have guessed given the island's dimensions, was a sturdy, wood-beamed farmhouse. A single story, but broad and spacious, fit for a weekend fishing party of six or eight. A fire was already going, he could see from the chimney smoke, and a black-and-white sheepdog was excitedly prowling the lawn, awaiting someone's return.

"Boots off, mind your head, no swearing in the parlor, lavatory's on the left." The man slung his jacket on a hook and kicked off his boots as though he'd done so, in just this way, ten thousand times. Then he headed for the fireplace and the oft-promised scotch which sat out on a two-shelved glass side table; the lower level held a pair of thick tumblers. As he came back from washing up, Sam found the man contentedly stretched out in front of the fire, smoking while warming tired feet, scotch finally in hand.

"Please, sit, make yourself comfortable," he said as Sam approached the fire. "My name's Stuart Menzies. In this capacity, I answer directly to Downing Street, often handling very sensitive matters which arise at the intersection of government and the military. Do you understand?" he asked smoothly.

"I think so, sir."

"Good. And please don't worry if that's your most common answer from now on. I'm going to be dishing up some pretty heavy fare. I trust," he smiled, "you've brought an appetite."

***

"I hate to put it as simply as this, but 'All the rumors are true,' as they say." While he talked, Sam listened, unable to shake the sense that someone was rearranging the inner workings of his brain. "The Germans acquired a considerable amount of very advanced technology, we think, during the autumn of 1943. By the time Overlord was launched, Hitler's *Westwall* was enhanced with rifles, mortars, artillery, even *tanks* which had originated in the future."

"The mortars, I didn't know about, but ..." He stopped as though he'd walked into a pillar. "The *future?*"

"Does it not make sense, when you think about it? The level of foreknowledge they had? The weapons, too, from a decade far beyond our own."

"Stone the crows," breathed Sam. "So, when you said, 'All the rumors are true,' you—"

"Meant it absolutely seriously? Yes," Menzies replied. "Try a few, and I'll tell you."

Off the top of his head, Sam could think of three. "Okay. The newspaper carried a report from Navy servicemen onboard battleships which were sailing in to support D-Day. They said it wasn't bombs that came at them, but *missiles*, powered by a motor all the way to impact."

"True."

"Shit."

"No swearing in the parlor," Menzies repeated. "Boots off, and no swearing. Only two rules, Sam, not difficult to remember, eh?"

"Sorry." He fumbled for the next example. "On the beaches, the Marines said they were pinned down at night by snipers, as though they could see in the dark. But," his eyes pleaded with Menzies, "that can't *possibly* be true, can it?"

"It's called a starlight scope," Menzies explained. "We'll show you one soon."

Shaken as though by an earthquake and staggered at how Menzies had already metabolized these calamitous findings, Sam reached for the ludicrous. "Aliens from outer space," he said. "A newspaper, one of the 'comics,' my Dad used to call them, printed a story that the time machine wasn't an amazing, new German invention, but part of a crashed alien spaceship."

Menzies sighed heavily and set down his scotch. "I've done this ... what would it be, four times, now?"

"Done what?"

"Spilled the beans. Initiated someone, as it were. And, you know, they've all been completely different. I wonder how this one's going to go?"

It went relatively well. The stricken engineer barely moved a muscle until he asked just two questions: "How long ago," and, "Are they going to come back," neither of which Menzies could answer. Somehow, even once Menzies had spilled all the beans he had, Sam remembered the rule about swearing in the parlor.

"These people are *real?*" he asked. "I mean, people from the future have come back to 1943?"

"Professor Yanis Miller, who is a mathematician, a talented police investigator named Jillian Qualmes, and six officers from a Pan-European counter-terrorist force, sent to protect them. They're in England, based at the biggest little airstrip no one's ever heard of. It's from there that we'll plan Operation Asphodel to take the mountain. But your concern is Operation Prophet, the mission to retrieve and decode these weapons."

It took a few moments, during which Menzies did nothing to rush him. "Okay, sir," he said. "I don't even ..." It took a little more time, and to cushion the blow, Menzies topped up his scotch. "Well, sir, I don't know how I'd have explained this to anyone else, but I've got to hand it to you. No one ever blew my mind with a gentle breeze before."

Menzies loved this. "Well, let's just say the practice is making it easier."

"What happened with the other guys?"

Wincing as though having to describe how his granddaughter flubbed her role in the school nativity play, he said, "One chap just sat there for a second, then bolted for the door and jumped headfirst into the river."

"Wowsers."

"Had to get the skiff out, pick him up. Nearly caught his death, the silly bugger."

"Glad I didn't try something like that." A question occurred to him that he'd not yet thought to ask. "Um, sir? Did anyone ever get picked up from Clayton but never make it to this island?"

He was offended, to Sam's surprise. "What on earth makes you say that?"

Sam stared, then said, "Sir, you threatened me with your revolver, said you'd dump me over the—"

"Oh, for heaven's sake, man. There's no way I could shoot someone like that," he said with a fond uncle's smile.

"That's a relief."

Menzies knocked back the rest of his scotch. "Of course." He coughed. "I had the safety on the entire time."

***

Early the next morning

Out on the water, amid dawn silence, each deep breath ushered in a wave of fresh, cool oxygen, apparently enriched by the wooded hills. And each one helped Sam to feel perhaps half-a-percent less hungover.

"You realize something, Sam?" Menzies said. He was smoking, cigarettes this time, and enjoying a hot toddy from his thermos. "There could be a Nazi U-boat, right underneath us, and we'd never know."

Sam couldn't help peering down into the still deep. "Comforting."

"Professor Miller told me," Menzies said, continuing the weekend's thread, "that in the late twentieth century, there are comprehensive sonar arrays, all the way from Norway to Scotland to Greenland, so nothing can get by undetected."

He pondered it. "An undersea radar system which can see *everything*?" How would naval warfare even be fought with stealth and surprise nullified?

"And he told me there are submarines, I mean non-military types, which can carry cameras and equipment to the very bottom of the ocean. Seven miles down. He said," Menzies leaned in, "they can pilot *themselves!* Can you *imagine* the applications?"

They tried, together, and found the limit only to be their capacity to imagine new uses. As they brainstormed, the sound of an aircraft asserted itself above the watery soundscape.

"Speaking of piloting," Menzies said, "Alistair is smack on time, as usual."

The sound grew louder until it turned into a lumpen, flying shape, skimming low over the water, off to their left. "It's come in from Canada?"

"That's right. Al is my regular *confrere* on these trips, you see. RAF liaison with the Americans. When he's not busy helping obliterate Germany from a great height. Makes sense to travel around together, just the two of us. Easier to visit certain people, you know, and do quieter things like this."

They watched Alistair land the seaplane, an unlikely performance that was as graceful as physics would permit, given it was the barely controlled coming together of a metal fuselage and a terribly unyielding body of water. "First rate. Row us over there would you, there's a good chap."

Grunting at Menzies' capricious delegating, Sam grabbed the oars and got them moving. Naturally, it couldn't just have been a peaceful early morning fishing trip. Of course not. There had to be a goddamned *seaplane* show up in the middle of it. Sure, a seaplane! Why not?

"Will you be traveling, too, sir?"

"I'm going to stick around for a few more days. There are a couple of American politicians who need classified briefings on all this stuff. New people who've come in since poor old Roosevelt had to give it up. Honestly, there's nothing half as much fun as inducting incredulous Yanks into our little club. The looks on their faces ... Well, I don't need to tell *you* that."

Wheeler was standing on one of the plane's floats, shirtless, bellowing like a tyrannical slave master. "Heave!" he cried. "Heave! Put your back into it, man!" Then he laughed, slapping his belly. "I hope you've brought breakfast, or we'll have to land in bloody Halifax again."

"Coming!"

"Morning, Sir Stuart!" he called.

"Squadron Leader!" Menzies saluted. "Take good care of this chap, would you? He's not as abject as he looks."

"Don't know about abject, but I've seen better rowing from a bloody statue!"

"This thing's damned heavy, you know!" complained Sam.

"Ah, yes, sorry about that. Not really intended for a single oarsman, especially over," Menzies guessed, "a quarter mile. It's a spy boat, you see."

"A what?" Sam puffed.

"Hollowed compartments in the bow. Supposed to be filled with explosives. Simple French fisherman, half a mile from a docked Nazi warship, not bothering anyone. He sets the rudder, quickly disembarks onto a friend's vessel, and quietly sails off, leaving the spy boat on its final course. And then, *boom*."

Wheeler was a long-time convert to the plan. "I'd have given anything to watch one of those bob into the U-boat pens at Saint-Nazaire, and tear the arse end off a brand-new Type Nine."

"*Before*," Menzies emphasized, "it has the chance to sail quietly up the St. Lawrence, here, and cause bloody havoc."

"Amen, brother."

Rowing heartily as this exchange wafted over his head, Sam was nearing the plane. It was far grander than he'd expected, the kind of thing the royal family might use. "Good morning, Squadron Commander! Permission to come aboard, sir?"

After a heavy night, an early start and a rough landing, Wheeler had elected to swim, naked and shouting with cringing complaint, in a St. Lawrence river, as yet barely warmed by the sun. "Jesus, Mary, and Joseph, that cleared my sinuses!" he said, pulling on clothes. "Right, then. Al Wheeler."

They shook hands. "Lieutenant Sam Clark. They gave me a rank, so I guess I should use it?"

"Definitely," he said. "Women find the high-class allure just irresistible."

"Really?"

"Once you see where *Lieutenant* gets you, imagine what happens once you become, *Squadron Leader.*"

"I can barely imagine," he said.

Wheeler flicked a sequence of switches, then changed his mind about one and switched it back. "Not," he said, flicking more, "even barely."

The engines re-started, as graceful as a pair of bull elephants coughing on the silent river, and Wheeler soon had them underway. "You've done jump training, right?"

"I wouldn't necessarily call it that," Sam said. The exigencies of time had meant compressing Sam's education as a parachutist into just four terrifying afternoons—one of them involving *three* descents under a canopy—and then a night-time jump, with combat equipment, followed by a short navigation exercise. Sam passed by a whisker; for long moments after the jump, he could barely find his own feet, let alone the objective, seven hundred yards across a dark field.

"Well, let's see," Wheeler said. "Did you jump, fall, get pushed, or otherwise depart an aircraft in mid-air?"

"I did. Six times altogether."

"Did you die, on any of those occasions?"

Sam's fingertips tapped his feet, knees, chest, and head. "Nope, still here."

"Then you successfully passed parachute training. There's one behind your seat. Any nausea, lean over and open a window. Pee bottle in the canvas bag to your left."

Sam did have one pressing question. "Squadron leader, um, where are we going?"

Wheeler checked once again for boat traffic, finished his hard-left turn, and judged the implied line of wave crests to be reasonably well aligned. "First rule of flying in The Circus," he said, moving the throttle forward. Within moments, they were moving with startling speed, unnervingly now in neither a boat nor a plane, but a boat-plane which might still decide the split for itself. "Don't ask fuckin' stupid questions." The plane lifted off and half the roaring and chaos fell away.

At school, Sam hated being sworn at; he took each jibe personally and replayed the moment to himself that night when he couldn't sleep. But in the last few days, he'd regarded it as a badge of honor. "That's a problem."

"It is?" They were ascending through two hundred feet without unduly taxing the engines.

"It is, because I've got dozens of questions, and they're probably *all* fuckin' stupid."

He grinned but waved a finger. "Now, don't get the wrong impression. I'm just the guy who drives Menzies around. Sometimes, yes, I venture over certain parts of Europe and drop certain things from my plane, but I'm a cog in a bigger machine, Sam. I probably don't have any better intelligence on this stuff than you do."

Intelligence.

"Shit, that reminds me," Sam said. He momentarily feared Menzies' rebuke, then found it funny; he was not in the elderly man's parlor now, but at three thousand feet, just south of Montreal, heading northeast to follow the river. "Menzies gave me something. Told me to read it on the flight."

"That'll keep you quiet," Wheeler said as Sam brought a generously thick envelope from his duffel. He hadn't even seen Menzies toss his bag into the spy ship; probably too bleary-eyed at 0445.

By the end of the first page, there was no chance Sam could possibly be quiet. Everything was far too fascinating and impossible and unbelievable to keep to himself, and Wheeler was on the security list for the folder anyway. By the time they were on approach to St. John's, the pilot was being invited to review the exploits of one Yanis Miller, professor of mathematics.

"Miller? Oh, yeah. I met him once, after a briefing at Tempsford."

Bug-eyed, Sam asked, "You *met* someone who came from the *future?*"

"You'll meet him too."

"I *will?*"

"That's how come we're not stopping off in Iceland for some salmon fishing. Too pressed for time because of Asphodel. It'll be a merry bloody circus at Tempsford, I can tell you. 'Mouse' Fielden is a good man in a flap, but he'll have his plate full."

Whoever Fielden might be, Sam didn't care. "I can't wait to meet Miller. Was it strange to meet someone from the future? He wouldn't have been born until ... until I'm an *old man*! Forty *years* from now!"

"Actually, yes. He did the queerest bloody thing, I remember it vividly. I was, you know, introducing myself, so all I said was, "Squadron Leader Alistair Wheeler, but you can call me Al," and he just started, I don't know, laughing all by himself, and then he was dancing around and making like he was playing the guitar in mid-air."

"What a strange man."

"They give them funny drugs before those parachute drops, you know, so they don't throw up in the airplane."

"Might explain it."

"Might do."

5

Somewhen Else

MI6 Briefing, Putney Green, London, 2 days after Yanis' arrival, July 1951

He usually read his paper at breakfast, sitting at their little table with the red-and-white cloth. Anne liked it when he'd read an article aloud, something about books or all the new sciences the experts were studying, while she finished preparing breakfast. Anything other than politics, or the Cold War; she'd had enough before 1939, and a dozen years later, she'd far rather listen to a theater review, or hear about the amazing, new labor-saving devices the factories were churning out. The rest was just a dark well of fear.

But today, Anne Walcott found that her husband, David, was completely lost in thought. He'd barely touched his oatmeal and wasn't interested in the usual silly breakfast time back-and-forth with little Fay. She sat watching him, quiet but not unduly concerned.

"Daddy has a funny look on his face," the six-year-old told her mother as she sat down, bringing coffee which David ignored. "Is he happy or sad?"

"I don't know today, dear," she said. "Daddy's working on something in his head, I think."

It was almost a trope of their time. How many breakfast tables around the country, she wondered as she watched David in silent thought, were silenced by awkwardly unspoken worries about the future? About the world's five massive—and fast-growing—nuclear arsenals? About those stockpiles of horrible military chemicals?

It was a child's guess, nothing more.

"Working on a secret?" she whispered to her father. To Fay, he was the most incredible person imaginable, a scientist-soldier-historian who knew everything about everything.

"Just trying to do something for some people," David to his daughter. "People who need my help."

He knew everything, *and* he was a selfless superhero, rushing to shelter others from harm. Other girls had a 'dad,' but she'd overheard her mum call him *SuperDave*. They would make a comic book or a movie about her dad one day. He was always racing around Europe in a special plane—she'd *seen* it, one day at the big airport, bringing him back from somewhere—and giving advice to all the most important people.

But Anne knew that David was speaking in code. He'd suffered terribly, these last six years and more, pained by just how many families' breakfasts, and dinners, were subsumed within the grief and sadness of an empty chair.

"An *invention*, Daddy?" One of Fay's favorite new words.

Her father's mouth opened to answer, but the white lie didn't form quickly enough. Anne stepped in. "Daddy can't tell us, darling, but maybe you're right! It could be a new invention to help keep us safe from the Germans and the Russians."

He reached for his spoon, then let it go with a soft clink. "Keep us safe, yes." Brow furrowing, he was soon away again into the world of worry. "And to bring everyone home, no matter how far."

"David?" she asked under her breath. "No need to worry Fay, love."

"Sorry?" he said, snapping back to it. He seemed surprised to find a bowl of oatmeal in front of him, and an effervescent six-year-old chuckling at his expense. "Oh, right. Yes, an invention at work." He turned to Fay, "Something very tricky, very important."

"Ooh," she thrilled. "Tricky." It was another favorite word at the moment and had come to describe anything that was both fun and difficult to accomplish. "Are you using *all* of your brain, Daddy?"

"Every smidge," David Walcott assured his daughter, tousling her dark ringlets.

"Lots of people are helping Daddy with their brains, too," added Fay's mother. Anne had her own high-level security clearance through her work at the Ministry of Defense, and though she wasn't strictly cleared for David's projects, he kept her loosely informed.

This latest news, though, had arrived yesterday afternoon, like the proverbial thunderbolt. Only hours later, he'd felt the need to whisper it to Anne in the dead of night. "It's about Asphodel. But I don't know much yet. They say some of them have come back."

"Come *back?*" It sounded like an answer to so many prayers. "But how?"

"The cable from MI6 didn't give details," David told her. He was aching to know more.

"How many?" she asked hopefully.

"There's sixteen of them, flying in today. I can't believe it yet," David whispered. "They said I shouldn't break their quarantine until the group reaches Tempsford, but I'm desperate to see what's what."

"Of course you are, darling. I mean, the time you've spent, and, well …" No time to dwell on the nightmares; if the reports were true, some kind of redemption might finally be at hand. "Is Menzies with them?"

"He's finishing one of his trips. Flying straight into Tempsford once we've given him the all-clear."

"About what?"

"It probably doesn't matter. One of the guys fell ill. Thompson, the American sergeant from the Rangers. Likely it's just a skin rash, or a chemical effect, something like that."

Anne understood just enough of Asphodel to be worried about dangerous alien beings, or capricious and incomprehensible time-travel devices, or terrible, asphyxiating chemicals. She knew that his nightmare was of the walls closing in, the roof tumbling down onto them. But *hers* was the tabun, a chemical killer which only struck because you *breathed.*

"Promise me you'll be careful, please," she said. "I know how much they all mean to you, Yanis and Thompson and the others. Just remember," she said, finding his eyes with hers, "they've probably been through a lot, just like you have. Their returning like this was always a possibility."

"'A strong and compelling probability,'" Walcott quoted from his own thesis on the subject, *Present Imperfect: Strategies for Adjusting to an Unexpected Timeline.* The 700-page tome had been roundly ignored by its intended audience until, Walcott assumed, sometime last night, when it suddenly became required reading for a couple hundred ministry officials and the eighty permanent Asphodel staff at Tempsford. In it, Walcott theorized a margin of error in Yanis' 'chrono-coordinates,' caused by damage to the time systems. Millions of calculations, done using one of the new, single-room 'SuperComputers,' showed it was likely either that they'd arrive within a few years of their intended date, or not at all.

"You wrote that more in hope than expectation, David. And it was good for you to write it," she emphasized, taking his hands in hers. "You learned a lot, worked through *so much*." She was proud of him, even if his research consigned her to spending most evenings alone for three whole years, just when their marriage should have been at its most passionate and spontaneous. "What I'm saying is, you're ready, and you're the best choice in all the world to help them land safely."

"Thanks, love."

"It'll take time, and I don't want you to rush." She kissed his forehead. "Did you sleep much?"

He'd given up trying around three, kept awake by the whirl of emotions and speculations, letting his worries take him over. So many questions and unknowns.

As soon as his alarm went off at five, he was out of bed, eager to get the early train. But in his lengthy reverie he'd left his oatmeal to cool into an unappetizing, grey lump.

"Didn't they specifically tell you," his wife reminded him as he packed the things he'd need on the flight to Tempsford, "not to show up early? Something about a quarantine?"

"Yeah, and they can shout at me all they like. I've waited seven years to lay eyes on these people."

The phone rang, and David caught it quickly. "Yes, this is Walcott." It was a ministry functionary, someone he'd probably forget as soon as the call was over. "Yes, I'm hoping to ..." he said, but seemed to hit a wall. "Look, it's been seven years, and nobody's said anything about the conditions they're traveling in, or anything about this—how did they call it—this 'rash' Thompson has. What kind of a ..."

His face told the story of an incoming fusillade, and within moments, he was promising to 'be good.'

"Alright, it's fine, really, I'll just go to Tempsford and meet them there."

Anne hugged him and walked him to the car, making reassuring but instructive, 'slow-down' gestures as he anxiously tapped the gas by accident. "I'll call you."

"Remember not to say anything controversial on the phone."

"How about something world-changing?" he asked.

"Sure," Anne decided, waving him off. "Provided it's good news." That way, she hoped his nightmares might begin to lose their grip, and the terrible drama of Asphodel could finally end.

***

16 Miles NW of RAF Tempsford, later the same day

"All I'm saying is," Jenkins leaned across the cabin to yell, above rotor noise, into Keller's face, "it's got *no bloody wings on it.*"

"Will you *relax*, please?" the exhausted German advised. "I flew in these things a hundred times, back home." A place which was, dizzyingly, sixty-plus years in the future. "It's just a car with the engine on the roof," he said, grinning.

Osborne had more easily made the transition to rotary-wing travel. "We all whizzed over to Ireland in something much bloody weirder than this, mate. Just relax, okay?"

In formation, the six helicopters approached RAF Tempsford and flared to land on a broad stretch of concrete, newly cleared of the base's own aircraft. Watching them arrive, around the perimeter of the landing area, were perhaps two hundred senior officers and representatives from ministries and universities. None knew what to expect, but the atmosphere was almost giddy, as though Yanis and the others were emissaries from the stars, rather than the past.

Walcott saw that they'd found civilian clothes for everyone; their original gear was useful now only to forensic scientists, and then a museum. Jenkins, Osborne, Entwhistle and Keller stood and saluted the reception party, a knot of generals flanking the Prime Minister and his wife.

Yanis looked thin, but he was alive and somehow unhurt. He was glancing around as though lost, only gradually realizing that Tempsford had grown significantly since 1944. A dozen new buildings had sprouted, some still under construction, but the administrative hub for Asphodel, a broad, two-story office building overlooking the hangars and flight line, stood ready to receive them. Walcott couldn't bear to wait alone in his cubicle, so he mingled with the others in the anteroom of Menzies' office, like curious schoolboys awaiting the results of a friend's disciplinary committee.

At length, Menzies bustled out, a wash of conversation following him. "Walcott, I need you, and your best time-science chap."

"Ah, that would also be me, sir," he said truthfully.

"Alright, then, *both* of you come in and meet one of the Yanis Millers." He chuckled to himself. "Now, David, no reason this can't be a little celebration, eh? Other things notwithstanding?"

One of the 'other things' was the likely death of nearly the whole force. David always knew that, when they gave him the final number, when they told him how many of those brave men were left, he'd ...

"David?"

Sixteen ... Was it a triumph, when set alongside the alternative?

"God almighty, David Walcott!"

Perhaps it was, yes. But to see so dreadfully few was heartbreaking.

He stared, numbed by the tininess of the group, until Yanis Miller actually grasped his hand.

"I wondered when they'd let you in!" A gaunt, pale Miller took David in a surprisingly strong hug. "We're home, man!" said Yanis. "Well, kind of. We're alive, anyway."

"I can't ..." he stammered, his brain unable to work with the facts he was seeing. "I mean ... *How?*"

"I know, it's *bonkers*," agreed Jillian Qualmes.

"Jillian, you're ..." As he embraced her, the relief solidified in a brief gust of tears and elation. "It's a miracle, a bloody *miracle*. How did you—"

"All in good time," Yanis said, "if you'll pardon the pun. There's a lot of catching up to do."

"For both of us," David agreed.

"Sir Stuart said there'll be a briefing, but even covering the basics will demand a really top-flight intelligence officer, he reckons. Told me he'd hired the smartest guy at Tempsford to give the briefing." Someone handed him coffee which smelled marvelously sweet.

"I don't doubt that's true," Walcott said, polishing his glasses.

"So, who's giving it?" Yanis asked, but Walcott just grinned back at him.

***

RAF Tempsford's new briefing hall was six months old, and still smelled of fresh paint and wood dust. Arriving from all over the UK, some flying down at a moment's notice, were a hundred eighty officials, experts and researchers. Not since the build-up to Operational Asphodel itself had Tempsford's runways been so busy.

Amid a dizzying whirl of questions, in both directions, Walcott and two MI6 staffers walked Yanis, Jillian, and the team's ambulatory soldiers from Menzies' office in the austere administrative building across to the Lecture Hall. The coming meeting, Walcott explained, would be a kind of rolling, continuous professional conference. "We don't even know what we don't know," he said, "if you see what I mean."

"*Known unknowns*," Yanis recited from somewhere, and "*unknown unknowns.*"

Making a note on his pad, Walcott said, "Interesting, yes, very good. Can I borrow that?"

"Go crazy."

Inside the hall, chairs were set out in precise, military rows, but Walcott hoped for different ways of organizing the delegates. "I'd like people to feel able to think freely. You know, outside of their usual constraints. Physicians thinking like airmen; navigators thinking like nuclear scientists."

"You'd fit right into the twenty-first century academic conference scene," Yanis observed. "It's all about cross-disciplinary stuff." He'd have said more, but Walcott was noting this expression, too, fascinated.

Maybe I should just speak plainly for a while, so people aren't so distracted?

Knots of people arrived, and all eyes were either watching Miller, or trying to figure out which one of the plain-clothed men was him. The classified briefing document had given scant clues, leaving the delegates intensely curious. Walcott deliberately kept Yanis and Jillian off to the side, pointing out important figures but insulating them from undue scrutiny.

"Sir Stuart is in overall command, still," said Walcott. "He insisted on staying until either Asphodel was resolved, or he was forced to retire. I think," the analyst added, "he's taken the burden personally. A lot of us have."

As Menzies greeted some of the delegates and ushered people to their seats, Yanis saw the years fall away. Who could have withstood the stress of such an operation, the years of uncertainty, without a terrible emotional cost? He seemed to take a moment, between comments or greetings, just to look around at the Asphodel team and give his own quiet thanks.

"One other person you're going to hear from is Alice Chernowitz. She's our operational security chief." He pointed out a woman of perhaps forty in a severe grey suit. "Anyone puts a foot wrong, forgets to sign in somewhere, loses their key-pass, she descends on them like the proverbial ton of bricks."

Three other men, as yet unidentified, sat together at the very back of the hall, almost conspicuously distant from the others. Yanis didn't recognize the blue shade of their uniforms, but all three had very short hair, part of their austere, military bearing. "Miss Chernowitz, you said?" he said, committing the name to a memory already crammed with details. "Okay, so who are those three dudes, way back there by themselves?" Yanis wondered aloud.

Crestfallen as if handed a sudden and odious responsibility—one of Walcott's most common facial expressions since Asphodel—he chose to be vague but concise. "Three guests from an Allied agency." Not every aspect of *this* 1951 would meet with Yanis' approval, Walcott knew; in fact, it was distinctly possible that, upon learning just *how different* things were, the whole team would lose their minds.

"Which agency?" Yanis asked.

Walcott just glanced nervously at the three men.

"I mean," Yanis said, concerned and curious enough to eschew Walcott's subtlety, "they don't look like Brits."

"It's all okay, really," Walcott was saying, "they're kosher. No need to ..."

But Yanis was already striding toward them with his hand extended and suspicion in his mind. "Professor Miller of Jerusalem Polytechnic," he said very deliberately. "Who may I have the pleasure of addressing?"

Shrinking back in unison, the three men were perplexed and confused by this display. None spoke. In fact, Yanis felt at once, it appeared they didn't speak English.

"David Walcott!" Yanis brayed, turning and using the man's full name like an irate mother. "You're gonna tell me who these characters are. Because things have gotten weirdly cozy lately, and if it turns out they're fuckin' SS, or German intelligence, and that we've been—"

"Yanis, for heaven's sake," Walcott said, keeping his voice down. "They're not SS, nor are they German." He came closer and hissed, "This is an important time, Yanis. Calm down, would you, please?"

"But ..."

"Remember, crawl comes before walk. Trust me, alright?" He turned to the trio. "I'd like to introduce Colonel Yevchenko, and Major-General Artyukin." The two men stood with the precision of automatons. Precisely synchronized, they clicked heels and saluted, their chins elevated high and proud. "With them is Captain Bykovsky, their translator. We speak only with him."

"The other two guys never say anything?" asked Yanis, yet more curious.

Bykovsky now stood and performed the same neat salute. "*Akademik* Miller, I bring the comradely greetings of all the workers, soldiers, and peasantry of the Union of Soviet Socialist Republics."

Surprised, both at the stentorian volume of the announcement and that, against the odds, these men were *Russians*, Yanis opened his mouth to reply.

"Our common struggle," Bykovsky boomed as Menzies quickly sidled over in case anything went pear-shaped, "to achieve peace against the evils of tyranny, has required the greatest sacrifice. And for you, the most dangerous experiments. For this, we intend to honor *Akademik* Miller, and each of the brave survivors, with The Order of Lenin."

Yanis thanked the man formally, but Menzies made much more of this, approaching to thank Bykovsky personally for the offer. His relative obsequiousness before a Soviet official spoke volumes; these relationships were fragile, and Menzies clearly valued a mutual trust which was all too easily undermined.

"Comrade Bykovsky has been an important figure," Menzies said, though his eyes ably communicated the rest to Miller: *This is just another portly, unimaginative* apparatchik, *but needs must when the Devil drives.*

"A man called Sam Clark will fill you in, later. He's anxious to meet you."

"Him, and a whole airbase full of people," said Yanis.

"Come on." Menzies saw that the bustle was settling as the hundred eighty or so attendees found their seats. "I think David's ready to start."

***

Walcott took a few minutes to get his notes ready, standing away from the lectern. There was no use rushing time travelers, he'd already decided, no matter that his own nerves were jangling. Menzies had a thousand questions for them, as did Wheeler, Fielden, Bykovsky, and a host of others. With invitees from a dozen departments, it was set to be a lively meeting. No, Walcott thought, 'meeting' can't describe a gathering like this. A conference? A debriefing? Then he made a note as he thought of it; an 'informational-temporal synchronization.' Fay would love that one, next time they played Silly Scrabble.

The group kept things deliberately light, emphasizing their unlikely return, rather than the absence of so many. There would be another time for those sad, inevitable duties.

For now, though, Miller had a beer in hand and was being ushered to a seat. Walcott's voice just barely carried over the throng, "I don't want to break up the party, but we need to get some information into these people's heads, pronto," he explained. NCOs are natural-born organizers, and they were soon seated, hushed, and reasonably attentive. Yanis sat beside Jillian in a row which included Keller and Osborne. His Marines were behind them, with the Airborne guys on the other side. Entwhistle brought up the rear, observing events from behind a cloud of smoke. He looked relieved to be here, but wary of what might come; in his experience, being gathered in a lecture room by an officer was the usual prelude to something unspeakably dangerous.

"Alright. Quick introductions. With Professor Miller is Miss Qualmes," Walcott said, eliciting some craned necks and intent peering over the heads of others, "and the remaining members of her security team, Mr. Keller and Mr. Clavel." He thought it best to dispense with ranks and nationalities; this was not the 1951 anyone leaving *Der Dom* would expect. "82nd, would you care to introduce yourselves?"

With enthusiasm, Jenkins stood, snapped out a salute, and said, "Sergeant Jenkins, presenting Corporal Dodson, whose leg isn't as bad as it looks, and Privates Irwin and Hart. Montoya is in the infirmary."

"How's he doing?" Jillian asked over her shoulder.

"Gonna be alright, if he gets first-rate care. His lungs were wrecked by the tabun."

Walcott checked his notes. "Also in the infirmary, in a quarantine ward, is Sergeant Jim Thompson. He's alive and has been conscious. His condition is stable," he said, skipping all of the complicated unknowns before turning to Osborne. "And then, we have our friends from the Royal Marines, 1944 vintage."

"Best until last, and all that." He stood to acknowledge the room. "Corpr'l Osborne, here with Corpr'l Hyde, Lance Corpr'l Stewart, and Marine Brooks."

Entwhistle exhaled a grey cloud into the ceiling before introducing himself. "Apparently, the Americans can't manage to say 'Company Quartermaster Sergeant Entwhistle,' so I'm 'Sergeant Harry,'" he joked. "I like to go underground, and to blow things up, so I was a shoo-in for this one."

Introductions over, Menzies gave Walcott the nod to formally begin.

**

His first duty was a painful one: to explain to the Asphodel group that theirs had been the only miraculous arrival from Bavaria. "We waited for any sign, thinking some of you might have been rescued somehow by the ship. Or that you'd come in separate groups, or to different locations. There was so little information, and we had no way of knowing which control settings you—"

"The whole thing was on fire," Yanis recalled with a shudder. "Control wasn't really available." *Jesus,* he thought to himself. *That was only a few days ago.*

"Ah." Walcott shuffled his papers. "Well, in that case, I'd say we've been *damned* lucky," a sentiment with which the group heartily agreed. Their applause sounded more to Yanis like relief than celebration. The fighting might have stopped, but the last seven years of peace had brought precious little respite. Menzies and his confreres looked drawn, older than their years, pressurized by unrelenting fear and uncertainty.

Walcott had the ambitious aim of bringing the confused time travelers up to date, something Menzies expected would take two weeks or more. Other figures would help, thankfully, including a bevy of scientists from Boscombe Down, the UK's much-expanded weapons research center, a large team of behavioral scientists, and also experts in something called 'quantum physics,' sent by both Oxford and Cambridge Universities.

"Someone's told you by now that *Der Dom* was attacked by a squadron of Lancasters?" Walcott checked. Most decidedly, they all knew this much. "Right, well. All that comes next is our best estimate of what happened. At about the same time the Germans lost control of the mine, there was some kind of a coup attempt at Hitler's residence at Berchtesgarten. It seems he was placed under house arrest there by a cabal of generals, and that several of his staff and security detail were shot."

"A *coup?*" Yanis was on edge at once. "What kind of coup?"

"It was chaos," reported Walcott. "British intelligence was contacted by three different senior Nazis, all desperately trying to establish a channel before any news of the tabun gas attack could reach Downing Street. The Foreign Office received two different peace proposals *on the same day*, each sent without knowledge of the other. For a good seventy-two hours, we really didn't know who spoke for Germany."

Menzies took over. "Keitel made a play for the top job, but someone blew up his car, just as he was arriving at a rally of his supporters in Hamburg. Former SS people carried out mini-coups across Germany, seeing their chance to usurp the civilian government. We've got estimates that upwards of nine hundred serving military officers and ministry personnel were shot, and some three thousand arrested and removed from their posts. Ironically, many were sent to Treblinka, including one of the men who'd originally approved the camp's design, back in 1942."

"Couldn't happen to a nicer bloke," Entwhistle opined.

"We finally received formal word that, from now on, we'd be dealing with the Reich Government of National Unity."

"Wait," Jenkins interjected. "Wait ... where's Hitler in all this?"

"Oh, they shot him on the third day," Walcott said. "On the terrace at Berchtesgarten. Along with Bormann, Speer, Goebbels, and six others." The photos were simply unforgettable: ten bound, uniformed Nazis, defiantly facing a firing squad under gleaming, Alpine peaks. "The provisional government had no choice. They needed major concessions from the Allies, and removing Hitler was their way to start those discussions. It also changed Stalin's calculus in the east, and he was more amenable to a ceasefire than we'd expected."

At the mention of his name, the three Soviet officers at the back straightened noticeably, as though the General Secretary might suddenly arrive in person, to inspect Asphodel.

"The war was crushing Soviet society," Menzies said. "We had it tough during the Blitz, but this was on a different scale entirely. The Germans initiated so-called 'scorched earth' tactics as they retreated west. Twenty million Russian casualties. With Normandy a stalemate, the SS Panzer Divisions could be sent east, and unless Zhukov was incredibly lucky, his advance into Poland would stall."

Yanis was made to consider a victorious Nazi Germany completing her drive to the east amid ceaseless, helpless slaughter. But before that, and after, a much larger thought assailed him. He missed what Walcott said, only slowly able to pick the lock of his creeping unease.

"If the news from the front turned bad, Stalin feared a general uprising in the countryside," Walcott was explaining.

His temper rising fast, Yanis soon found a name for the unbearable stench which hung around Tempsford, around Menzies and Walcott and these gathered dignitaries. The stench of *capitulation*.

"We feared food riots, mass defections, perhaps a rebellion by the new, reconstituted officer class—"

"We *gave in to the Nazis?*" Yanis screamed. In the silence after, the insanity of the notion rang out like a bell. "They killed Hitler, and we responded by *surrendering?*"

"An Armistice," Walcott clarified. "Not a surrender."

Menzies put it most clearly. "The war was concluded as a stalemate, a high-scoring tie. Since then, we've adopted a posture of continuous surveillance and battle preparedness. There have been incidents, but none were allowed to flare out of control.

"A Cold War, people are calling it," said Walcott.

"You don't say," Yanis muttered.

"The western powers agreed to reduce tensions, returned units to their bases. The U-boats were a problem ..." A hundred groans told their own story. "We spent two months tracking them all down, and some refused to believe Hitler was dead, carried on to the end." And so, months after hostilities had ended, young men were still dying in the cold Atlantic as their metal hull cracked open and admitted the sea. "If it gives you an idea, the *Kriegsmarine* all but *told* us where they were. Helped to build trust."

Unable to keep it in, Yanis' last act under any kind of control was to stand and take a deep breath. "*Trust*, you said? Did I hear that right? We're gonna *trust* the Nazis now?" He looked around pleadingly, sure others would see this as lunacy also. Only Jillian was moving, and it was to calm him, to no avail. "Because I'd say that 'trusting' the Nazis, and working tirelessly toward their unconditional surrender, well, they're kinda the *opposite* of each other, aren't they? I *really* thought we were all doing the *other* thing," he said, his voice continuing to rise.

"Yanis, I know this is all very new and sudden—" Walcott began, but he knew he wouldn't get to the end.

"Twenty million Russian lives! Sir Stuart is right," Yanis affirmed. "Numbers like those make us weep, make us stop and sit down in fucking despair." He turned to the Troika. "Right, comrades? Numbers like that, they make us want to put history through the editing suite, cut out the worst parts, ensure we save as many lives as we can. And their troops, too," he said, gesturing to the Troika again, though without any kind of response. "God knows how many million ruined bodies and minds. If the Armistice closed out that bloody chapter even a day early, then I guess, I do have to applaud it." His tone was far from conciliatory, and everyone was waiting for the *but*.

It came from Jillian, who was standing with Yanis, providing both wisdom and reinforcement. "But you've abandoned *millions* of people in occupied Europe. You know full well the extent of the camps, David, and Sir Stuart, both of you," she said, turning to the distinctly uncomfortable intelligence director.

"How *could* you?" was all that came out when it was Yanis' turn. Around them, feet shuffled in discomfort as delegates recalled those anxious, unprecedented days. Only the most delicate diplomacy had created a safe path through the minefield of the Armistice.

"Please. We're not monsters, Mr. Miller," said David defensively.

"No, maybe just careless," he shot back.

The delegates uttered a dull rumble of concern, faced with a discomfort unknown to those from other timelines. Theirs was a terribly fragile Armistice, a mere document which offered scant protection for so many millions of lives and was threatened by the Damocles sword of German aggression.

"We would never have agreed to a status quo in Europe," Menzies explained. "Agreements were put in place for elections in Germany and in about half the *Reichscommissariats*—"

"The what?" a dozen Asphodel people asked.

"Belgium, Holland, Norway, bits of the Balkans, they all became states in their own right, administered from Berlin." The hum of lingering approval in the room showed Yanis that these elections had gone well, though the different regions remained effectively occupied and subjugated.

"And then there was the Air Agreement," Walcott added proudly.

"That was the key," said Wing Commander Alistair Wheeler, the obvious choice to explain. "It meant both sides were allowed to fly unarmed reconnaissance, pretty much wherever they liked, to observe activities on the other side. Helped to build," he added tentatively, wary of another explosion from Yanis, "um, helped us to build trust."

"Wow," Yanis said. "Eisenhower proposed an agreement like that, for us," Yanis told Jillian, "to avoid our first satellites 'overflying' other countries."

"Pretty neat way to do it," Jillian admitted.

"But a reconnaissance plane can't see inside a death camp," Yanis pointed out to the group.

A portly, dark-suited figure rose to speak. "Mr. Miller, as director of the department dealing with interned and displaced peoples …" His welcome was not universal; there was a history of difficulty and disagreement here, Yanis could tell. "I'm glad to say," the man soldiered on, his fondness for many of the officials around him clearly very limited, "that the Nazi euthanasia and concentration camp programs are officially over. Inspections took two years, but we've verified that the Germans closed down those facilities, and now, almost without exception—"

Sudden controversy sparked shouts of disapproval from every section of the crowd. Some stood to voice their views. "*Exceptions?* There were twenty-seven *thousand* exceptions!" someone yelled.

"How can you say that?" demanded another of the beleaguered functionary.

"Christ," Jillian whispered. "What's happened here?"

"The system is now dismantled," the administrator concluded, reddened by the reaction.

When Walcott invited him to explain to the Asphodel team the reasons for this sudden ruckus, the bureaucrat withdrew and sat down, apparently unwilling to help. Or perhaps just too embarrassed.

"Alright, I'll tell them," Walcott said to general approval. "Not our finest chapter, and heads have already rolled. And with good reason." It turned out that the Germans had constructed two more large underground weapons facilities, down in the Alps. "Much deeper, and better hidden, than the others. Really learned their lessons from Nordhausen and *Der Dom*, got much better at hiding their activities from local people, and recon planes, both."

"They were building a whole *mountain*," Menzies emphasized, "full of distillation chambers where the outside air would be chilled down and liquefied. This gave them oxygen for rocket fuel, and other uses."

"How deep?" asked Entwhistle, just as Hyde said, "What kind of weapons?" A second later, Jenkins wanted to know, "Who the hell was *working* down there?"

"Making all kinds of things. U-boat batteries, jet engines, rocket planes, guided missiles—"

"They'd completed hundreds of aircraft," Menzies said, underlining the failure. The Germans had successfully built up their high-tech military arsenal, even under the strictest constraints.

"They were getting ready," Walcott gulped, "to make enormous amounts of tabun. We think maybe sarin gas, too, and an illegal chemical agent called C-Stoff, a kind of rocket-plane fuel. They somehow hung onto twenty-seven thousand slave laborers, had them living in the tunnels for years. They falsified paperwork and kept the Repatriation Commission in the dark. A week before we found the place, laborers were digging out a massive, new section. At their deepest," he said, finding the Scottish speleologist, "they were digging four miles from the surface."

"Jesus," half the team uttered, but Entwhistle was already wondering how he might gain permission to explore such a singular place.

"We know only that they planned a huge underground centrifuge facility, to refine uranium."

"A what?" Dodson asked.

"A big factory that makes little factories that make fuel for atomic bombs," Osborne spelled out. He nudged Yanis. "Oi, not too bad for a simple corpr'l, that, was it?"

"It was *quite* the scandal," Walcott said, glaring at the dismal ministry man. "Could have completely fucked up the … sorry, Jillian, screwed up the Armistice." It wasn't simply for show; since 1944, the most common policy reminder to every Western civil servant and military figure was, "Don't Fuck Up the Armistice."

She stood. "I'm not sure that *I* wouldn't like to screw up the fucking Armistice," she said, loud and clear. "This is *absolutely unacceptable!* The 'Greatest Generation' can't possibly have yielded so meekly."

"Read the whole agreement, first," Menzies told her, as always aware how this would look, "and you'll find your elders are still actually in possession of a backbone." As one of its architects, Menzies was ready to defend the achievement; Germany faced terrible punishment for any threat against her neighbors, could not deploy forces overseas, and was forbidden from operating or building warships or long-range military aircraft.

"The public hated it, at first," Walcott said to the Asphodel group. "About two-thirds of them had the same reaction you did."

Wheeler chimed in. "Down the pub, people were complaining that Old Winston and FDR had lost their nerve and given up, just like the German generals in 1918. Couldn't stick with it to the end. A lot of people felt betrayed, or like the Germans had somehow broken our spirit without us realizing it."

"People," Menzies fired in, "who had never been heartbroken by a casualty list and could be certain of never appearing on one."

"Here, here!" came the endorsement, giving the room a momentary flavor of the British Parliament.

"Our newspapers savaged them for weeks and weeks," Walcott remembered. "Men were resigning, left and right."

"The government damned near came apart," Menzies confirmed.

"And one American general based in Britain, a man who shall remain nameless, proposed a 'caretaker' arrangement which sounded awfully like a bloody military takeover."

"There have been other setbacks," Menzies explained, "but the ceasefire held, day by day, and now the casualty rate is down by nearly a hundred percent. We all cling tight to that basic fact, especially on the darkest days."

"And what about Alien Peak?" asked Hyde, one of Osborne's Marines. "Did they ever find anything?"

Recently promoted Wing Commander Alistair Wheeler described the scene on the night itself. "I was there, *right* there, when it happened." In his modified de Haviland Mosquito, Wheeler played a pivotal role, relaying communications and attacking SS forces in the valley. "It was like looking down into a burning dragon's nest or something. Warwick reckoned he saw some kind of *glow,*" Wheeler recalled of his co-pilot, "but the flak was so fuckin' thick, who even knows what he saw."

Menzies carried on. "The Germans have given us an account of their assault on the mountain. The record is thin, owing to the large number of casualties."

"How many?" said all the 82nd Airborne boys at once.

"You want the official numbers?"

"Yes!" they replied enthusiastically, as a unit.

"The *Liebstandarte* Adolf Hitler SS Division deployed eighteen thousand men to the operation. Their missing or KIA outside the mine was just over three thousand."

"You're welcome," Wheeler grinned.

"An estimated seventy-eight hundred stormtroopers went into the mine. None came out alive."

The air was momentarily thick with emotion as the Asphodel warriors punched the air, the chairs in front of them, and each other. Some reacted differently, marking in silence this extraordinary total. They had destroyed an elite SS motorized division, in part using bombs fashioned from water pipes, fuel cans, and a tar-coated sock.

They'd survived chemical warfare, flamethrowers, and an impromptu, unplanned journey through time.

But the elation was soon muted by the numbing weight of reality; losses on their own side had been above ninety-nine percent. Their casualties came from two different *centuries*, and one of their number was ill in a way no one had ever seen before.

Walcott finished this section. "According to official channels, including your president, and the Prime Minister, the Zitternberg mountain is being protected as a shrine to our war dead. We've admitted that an audacious airborne raid went in, trying to capture a unique Nazi weapons facility."

"That's one way of putting it," Yanis scowled.

"There is no general public knowledge that Captain Keck, nor anyone else, traveled through time."

"It's a secret?" Jillian asked. "Still?"

One of the Cambridge academics was invited to add something. "It's also a belief commonly held that time travel is, as such, impossible. Though, of course, we know different." He sat again.

Yanis was catching up, and something about all of this bothered him badly. "So, the sixteen of us, we didn't travel through time either, then? Officially, I mean?"

For the first time, Walcott looked around for some help. "I'm not trying to be evasive, Dr. Miller. I just didn't write that part of the planning document."

"Professor?" a woman said, inviting the scientist to continue, but he'd reached the limit of what he knew for certain. "Well, that sounds like my cue," she said. "We don't plan to make a public announcement of your arrival, but we do have a number of options for getting you home. Each will need careful consideration. Until then, we keep tight security. No information leaves this base." If anyone were asserting themselves as the operation's disciplinarian, it was she, Alice Chernowitz. She was no stranger to Tempsford and its operations, having run Maquis agents for the Resistance. "If the Germans realize you've returned, they might try again to reach the spacecraft."

"Again?" six people said.

"There was a tunnel," Chernowitz explained. "The Germans swore they were amateur collectors, threw them in jail for a dozen years, but the whole thing looked state-sponsored. So, we keep all details of Asphodel buttoned up. The penalties for treason," she warned them, "have not lessened in the last seven years."

"Alright," Yanis said, trying to sum things up. "So, there's absolutely no way to access *Der Dom?*"

"No. A small, multi-national force keeps an eye on things," said Walcott, "but the place is just an ugly, jagged hill now. No one's allowed in. About once a year, some loony gets shot trying to breach the security fence, claiming there are 'aliens' in there."

Given the enormity of the Asphodel mission, it seemed inconceivable that word had not leaked out. "There *must be* survivors from the project, the engineers or SS men who spent time at *Der Dom*," said Yanis. "Keck wasn't exactly bashful about his leaps through time. Maybe someone knows, but isn't saying?"

A brand-new term encapsulated their policy. "Information management," Walcott said. "Remember, the morning tabloids are just collections of ink and paper, but people *believe* what they say."

"And these days, it's pretty important that they say what we *need* them to say," Menzies added. "It's never been difficult to make outlandish claims look ridiculous."

Jillian sighed at how familiar it all sounded. "Fake news," she said with a slump. "Nothing changes, does it? Even when the clock goes backward."

"The loony conspiracy types believe *we* invented the aliens story, as a cynical explanation for the wasteful deaths of thousands of paratroopers," the grey-suited Chernowitz told them. "Otherwise, why risk assaulting the mine, when the Lancasters alone could have denied it to the Germans?"

"So, half the world thinks we're lying, and the other half thinks we're over-ambitious and incompetent?" Yanis asked rhetorically. "Half thinks we've made alien contact, which is profound, by the way, and the other half think we've conjured the alien bodies and the ship as ... as what? A ruse to cover our own military blunders?"

"Something like that. Nobody said it was going to be perfect," said Menzies.

"Awesome," Yanis grimaced. "So, where does all of this put us?"

In a new era. There was no quick way to bring them up to speed. "We finally learned through experience," Menzies said weightily, "that we have a collective responsibility to restrain military technologies and ensure we don't destroy mankind."

"Your actions at *Der Dom* were crucial in forcing the peace settlement," Chernowitz told him. "You see, we didn't know the tabun was coming, but we always had 'sniffer' aircraft over the battlefield, testing for chemical traces. Their data confirmed that the Nazis had used the weapon on the battlefield."

"Pandora's Box," Menzies said, "was not yet open, but the Germans had definitely found the key." He depicted a period of spiraling atrocities, one more brutal than the next, as the *Luftwaffe* and Allied air forces doused each other's territory with an airborne pharmacopoeia of death. Plans were being drawn up, in that fateful week, to decimate Germany's working-age population. Without industry, they would sue for peace; but without restraint, there'd be no survivors to sign it.

"The epic fighting at *Der Dom,* and the famous attack by 617 Squadron's Lancasters, really grabbed public attention. People were asking, 'What else are the Germans making down there? A biological toxin? A nuclear weapon?'"

"'Where might they hit us?'" Menzies paraphrased. "Mothers began sending their kids out of London again." It was a huge step backward, a punishing moment for allied morale.

"But once the provisional government came in, and showed it could make the ceasefire actually stick," Chernowitz continued, "the Chartwell Debate was held, and broadcast on the radio a few weeks before Armistice, during ceasefire." In a deeply consequential debate, former ministers, retired generals and academics discussed a new and terrifying notion, only recently brought into existence by the Germans. "The panel asked us to imagine that the Asphodel mission ended in a different scenario," he said of a program which had been discussed on buses and in pubs for weeks after. "In their version, the SS drop tabun into the mine, but then they posited an RAF response against Duisburg with mustard gas, causing sixty thousand casualties. That was the beginning of the debate."

"What did they decide?" Jillian asked.

"They coined an expression: Mutually Certain Destruction, or MCD."

It was Keller who spotted it. "Could I make a suggestion? Perhaps *assured* destruction?" Struck by the resulting acronym, the room praised Keller's sharp sense of humor. "Sometimes these things just come to me," he joked as Jillian rolled her eyes theatrically.

"Well, MCD or MAD, whatever we'll be calling it," Chernowitz concluded, "was something the British public could understand. It was a civilian version of trench warfare. Still based on attrition, not of soldiers, but of the workforce and its morale."

"Once the Germans opened that gate with the tabun attack, the whole perception of the war changed. It became something we had to end before technology inevitably overtook our capacity to control it. And then, well, there were just so many setbacks in 1944."

"In the Atlantic, with those sodding U-boats," Wheeler growled, "and then the seven-day long fuck-up that was Overlord."

Walcott said, "About the same time, two or three of our big bomber raids got chopped up. Found ourselves intercepted by dozens of fast, new aircraft—"

"Fuckin' 'orrendous," Wheeler confirmed.

"And then Gerry deployed a new radar, streets ahead of ours."

"Once your feet got dry over Holland or France, things were just impossible," Wheeler remembered, leaning forward in his seat, his hands steepled. "Warwick bought it during that week, right before the bloody Armistice," he added, still angry at his friend's loss. "It was those nippy, little rocket planes, you remember, boys, how they used to race up toward us?"

"You could just about follow their exhaust smoke, but no bugger could ever hope to actually *hit* one," another experienced pilot confessed.

"They'd stand on their tails, heading straight up, accelerating all the time. Fired a whole cloud of missiles at once. Bloody mayhem, it was."

Faced with these reversals, Arthur Harris resigned, and RAF Bomber Command suspended operations over Europe. Broken and haunted, 'Bomber' Harris died a year later.

"But once we called a halt," said Menzies, "it made the Germans think about following suit. Opened some doors. Not everyone liked how it happened, but we started a dialogue."

"A dialogue which is still ongoing, thank Christ," Walcott added. "It could have broken down a hundred times, but we've each kept the other from pushing the button." He tried quickly to flesh out the new relationship between the Allies and the Reich. "They decided not to return to autocracy. The Reich is run by a cabinet of about twenty people, and it's been a stable group. There have been elections, of a kind, as I said. Reconstruction has been swift."

"I thought the economy would be ruined," Jillian said. "Years of war, all the bombing."

"Never underestimate the power of holding key patents in every critical area of late twentieth-century technology," Menzies spelled out. "Germany is now a massive exporter of consumer electronics, cars and, of course—"

The entire 1951 team said it together. "Weapons!"

Miller screamed in his frustration. "You *let* the *Nazis* export *weapons?*"

Menzies sighed the deep sigh of those who had already tried their hardest, many times over, and failed. "There is some version of the Armistice where we strangled Germany's economy, but it's not this one. And this is the one we've got."

"But!"

"Nobody wanted a repeat of Versailles," Walcott said.

"Huh?" said Jenkins.

"Nineteen-nineteen, the Treaty of Versailles," Jillian began. "Germany got itself humiliated, stripped of territory, bankrupted by reparations payments. Ruined the economy and paved the way for Hitler." Her colleagues were staring. "What? I liked history at school. Coming in handy now, isn't it?" she joked. "I'd have paid even more attention if they'd told me I might try sodding *time travel*." She turned back to the dais, where Walcott hovered. "So, all is sweetness and light with the Germans now? Best of friends that ever there were?"

"Far from it," Walcott warned. "Our inspections stopped a while ago, and though the overflight program is still basically in effect ..."

"Sort of, maybe," Wheeler cautioned. "The Germans want to scale back to 'occasional' recon flights with 'specific' objectives."

"Don't trust them," Yanis said. "*Ever.*"

Jillian knew it wasn't the right time to remind Yanis not to tar everyone unfairly with the same brush. Negotiations took time, and they took *two*. Peace was better than war, whatever form it took. There would be a lot to discuss later.

Enough to last the rest of our lives, I'd say.

Walcott was filling in other details. "The refugee situation is still pretty awful, and the system we're trying to build with the Germans ... well, it's been slow going." The much-troubled Repatriation Commissions had almost no means of pressurizing uncooperative governments, and the negotiations became rancorous, marked by naked racism. "Even getting accurate lists of names has been a *huge* task."

Mind and body divorced by stress and confusion, Yanis found himself standing and pacing around between the two aisles of seats. "You gotta wait," he said, "you gotta give me time to think." Menzies announced a twenty-minute break, and two hundred people lit cigarettes at the same time. Jillian headed outside, bringing Yanis with her, as much for privacy as for fresh air.

"Fuck," he breathed. "I'm beginning to understand why they all smoke so goddamned much."

She'd found a flask of coffee and poured them each a mug. It was two hours before lunch, but Yanis had suffered such disruption to his body clock that it could have been midnight in Siberia.

"Well, look at it like this. We've got peace," Jillian said. "Not a bad achievement, given how things were."

"Peace at any price?" Yanis countered. "Sounds like a re-run of Munich, only this time it's Churchill, not Chamberlain, bowing and scraping in front of the fuckin' *Nazis* until they tell us just the right kind of lie."

"They've closed the concentration camps," she added. To her, though highly imperfect, this was a timeline worth investigating; much of what they wanted was already in place. "No one can access the mountain. The map they showed me," she said, "has Poland as a separate state, recognized by everyone."

He'd seen the same map, and found it revolting. "Recognized, but divided in two, and occupied by Germany and Russia, just like under the Molotov-Ribbentrop Pact."

"But it *exists*, Yanis. That means there's a chance for—"

"You know what *else* exists?" he demanded. "A German nuclear arsenal."

"And an American one," she pointed out, "and a British one, and the Russians are building ..."

"You really think Messerschmidt and Heinkel have stopped designing military aircraft?" Yanis said, almost panicking at the obvious danger. "You think they couldn't convert a passenger plane into a nuclear-armed bomber, in half an afternoon?"

Back in her training days, a no-nonsense French Army nurse had shown her how to deal with a hyperventilating patient. Her first recourse wasn't available to everyone; she put her arms around him and kissed him, bringing his panicked rebuttal to a halt. Then, she held the mug for him, deliberately giving him slow sips of coffee laced with brandy. "It's not Prozac, but it's the fifties, and we do what we can."

With her arms around him once more, Jillian coaxed Yanis to synchronize his body with her own, taking slow, deep breaths. It was a more powerful tonic than coffee or Prozac could ever hope to be. "You're not wrong about this version of events" Jillian said. "This rerun of 1951 is really imperfect, definitely not the one we'd have chosen, but all I'm saying is, let's look on the bright side. No German family is gonna die tonight because Wheeler and his friends were ordered to drop high explosives on them."

But to Yanis, this artificial timeline was a great deal worse than imperfect; it was an impostor. The anger he'd restrained in the briefing now smashed its bonds; he broke Jillian's embrace and let it out, as he had to.

"If you could *promise* me that not a single Jew will be beaten up today," he ranted, "or have their business confiscated, or be shipped off somewhere, then I'll see that 'bright side' with you. Until then, those motherfuckers are still *Nazis*," he said, his eyes in a hard, stern meeting with hers, "and I still fuckin' *hate* them."

***

When they returned to the hall, after Yanis' necessary five minutes of cooling off while pacing around outside, Jillian saw that he wasn't alone in having serious reservations. The Marine-Airborne-NATO coalition was of a shared viewpoint, expressed very bluntly by Osborne: "Total war doesn't tolerate peace deals." Attractive though the Armistice might have been, none of them found it commendable, or even acceptable. "You put the Nazis in the ground. That's what you do," he said, speaking for everyone. "No ifs, ands or buts. Total surrender."

With five years' pedigree, the agreement had general public support, and the objections of these returning heroes bothered Menzies and Walcott. The briefing was suspended while they sat with the Asphodel team in a rough semi-circle; most of the other officials stayed, fascinated with men's reactions. The Russian Troika stayed too, fascinated with seemingly everything. The room was tense; all the explosions so far had been emotional, not physical, but the Asphodel team couldn't but feel betrayed by the events which ended the war.

"You're looking at it through the lens of your own timeline," Walcott said, "and that's absolutely natural. But, let me ask you this: Would the men who trained you, led you into action, ran your units and advised your governments, would *those* men throw in the towel without some *serious* guarantees?"

Walcott explained the Armistice as an exercise in 'containment,' but each and every concession they had made to the Germans—on rockets, industry, refugees, a hundred issues—was met with appalled shock. The worst was surely an agreement that the Reich would continue refining nuclear fuel, 'for peaceful purposes only,' which struck Yanis as tantamount to handing over the blueprints for the Manhattan Project. In fact, hadn't Walcott already told them that Germany had its own nuclear *arsenal?*

"*Containment*, is that what you're calling it?" He was losing his temper again, but what could he do, when those around him had been played for such fools? "Well, *containment* isn't working," Yanis said bluntly. "You said no nukes, and they got them."

He felt foolish, but this was Walcott's job, today. "Yes, in very small numbers."

"You said, no foreign interventions, but I'm reading here," he said, lifting a thick dossier, "that German volunteer forces have popped up all over the British Empire, from Cape Town to Simla, helping foment rebellion."

"It's true, that's unfortunate, but those deployments are very small ..."

"And what am I reading here about rockets?" Yanis demanded. "About a goddamned *successor* to the V-2!"

"It's part," Walcott said, reddening, "of their civilian rocketry program. Later today, we'll have a separate intelligence briefing on the technologies. Clark will cover all the ..."

But a dozen voices were throwing around the word "*civilian?*" as if it really didn't belong, amid growing pandemonium. The agreement was far, far too lax; the Allies had been made to swallow a poison pill, someone argued. Appeasement would only bring World War III, said another. "The *wasted lives*," said another disbelieving trooper, again and again.

It took fifteen minutes. A couple of times, sleeves were rolled up, and offers made to settle the question outside. In the end, Entwhistle roared above them like a Highland bull moose. "Has anyone got," he demanded, "a time machine in their pockets, right now?"

They did not, it seemed. Heads turned toward Entwhistle and conversations, sometimes rudely, wrapped themselves up.

"Look, lads," he began, "and lassies, too, forgive me. Seems to me, we're here in 1951. We don't belong here, but I don't see any signposts marked '1944,' and even the great Professor Miller doesn't know how to get the machine re-started."

"Or even where the goddamned controls have gone to," he muttered darkly.

"Aye, that'd be right. So, if I were a man of learning, I would compare our arrival here in the fifties," he wondered, "to the arrival of Cortez in the Americas."

"Ah, interesting!" Walcott piped up. "I see the analogy. Yes, very clever."

"Enlighten us?" Jenkins asked through a yawn. It had already been a long morning.

"Cortez encouraged his men to make homes in the New World and consider their lot there permanent. As an inducement, he burned their ships. So they couldn't get home."

"I'd say we *buried* the *enemy's* ship," Wheeler commented, "rather than burned our own, but I take your point."

"And now there might be another time chamber," said Walcott, "the one which brought you to Ireland, but we know nothing about it, and can't operate it yet." He stopped, checked his notes. "In theory," he said, smiling helplessly at the raw ambition of it, "that should bring you basically up to date."

***

2 hours later

He could have been a movie star, fresh from playing the dashing cowboy's precocious sidekick. And so, Yanis spotted Sam Clark quickly in the small crowd outside the mess hall.

"Last time I saw you," Sam enthused, "you were as green as grass."

"In both experience level and skin tone," Yanis remembered. His nerves before the take-off for Asphodel were of a kind to make a mere mathematician vomit. "And you were the new boy, trying to catch up, whereas now it looks as though you're in charge of things."

"And I was the new boy, running to catch up. And now look at you! Legends, both!" Sam said. "At least, in our research community, you are. None of us ever expected to actually meet a *time traveler*."

"*Legends*, he called you!" said Wheeler, joining them for the trip to the hangars. "How do I qualify, eh? Do I have to travel through time, and what not?"

Yanis expected to walk across the airfield, but Sam had a jeep and driver ready. "Can you tell us anything about your research?" asked Jillian as they set off, passing the row of six helicopters and heading to one of the new hangars. Change had overwhelmed Tempsford in the years they'd been gone, with new accommodation blocks, offices, and a new parade ground. Most noticeable, though were the five enormous hangars, each with space for a dozen aircraft. Literally everywhere, Jillian noted, were anti-aircraft positions; further away, radar masts scanned the horizon.

"We're doing all kinds of things," Sam told her. It was invitingly cryptic, rather than dismissive. "If I showed you all at once, you'd go cuckoo on me, so let's just start with the *Rafwaffe*," he said.

"The what?" asked Jillian. It sounded familiar, but somehow wrong.

"Wait, aren't our Russian friends going to follow us?" Jillian asked, unable to spot them.

"They know as much about all these planes as we do," said Sam. "Their pilots rotate through, learning the new types, but they keep to themselves."

"Yeah, at the briefing, the Troika just sat there, mute."

"That's because no one is allowed to talk to them, except about a specific plane, for a specific reason."

"Sounds tense."

"You get used to it," Wheeler said from the passenger seat.

"It's functional. That's what everyone says, about a bunch of things these days: It ain't great, but it *functions*."

Sam cruised at the 15mph maximum, heading past more parked aircraft—a sleek, high-speed demonstrator, a weird fighter which stood upright with three jet engines in a circle around its belly, and then another behemoth, a converted He-177 bomber, her skin blistered by electronics domes and spiked with antennae.

"The *Rafwaffe*," Sam said, keen to resume. There was *a lot* to get through. "Let's say," he explained as they followed the interior roads, "a German recon pilot gets himself a bit lost, and winds up flying over neutral Sweden, or Iran, or somewhere, and they force him to land. The British government contacts the Swedes, or whoever, and we buy the plane."

"*Buy* it?" said Jillian.

"Or maybe the pilot of a fighter plane decides that life in Scotland or Malta sounds better than what he's got, and of course, they know we'll be grateful for the charitable donation of their aircraft—"

"Just *ever so grateful*," Wheeler grinned lasciviously. Outside of combat, getting one over on *Luftwaffe* counterintelligence was his greatest thrill.

"In one case, a mint condition version of their latest long-range bird. Some of the others, we bought on the black export market, through mediators."

"Combat aircraft," Yanis wondered, "bought 'under the table' like Kalashnikovs."

Sam had no idea what a 'Kalashnikov' might be. "Well, as a motivator, hard currency is phenomenally effective. Helped make a few interesting things just walk off their airfields, across Germany." They parked outside a hangar, and Sam encouraged them toward the massive building's door with enthusiasm.

"But then, what do you do with them?" Jillian asked.

Sam recited the *Rafwaffe's* mission. "We receive, analyze, repair, and fly captured enemy aircraft. And by the way, buying these things is a fantastic investment. I mean, take a look at this big ol' sucker," he said, leading them to an incongruously small doorway. Looking up, they saw the hangar's shell, a yawning mass of metal and brick. "To prevent fragments in an attack, and as a firebreak," Sam said when Jillian asked why the hangars were surrounded by sloping piles of earth. "The stuff in here, we don't wanna lose."

The door opened to reveal a monument to gigantism, a hangar completely filled by the looming, slate-grey bulk of a single, huge aircraft. Wing tips nearly touching the walls, its span created a vast acreage of metal, supported in places on scaffolds. The cockpit area was like a military greenhouse, composed of a dozen glass panes, the better to view the enemy. Eventually, one's attention had to shift to the six massive engines; each looked plentifully able to lift a cathedral.

"Holy fuck," said Yanis. "It's bigger than a jumbo jet."

To their surprise, Sam burst out laughing. "That's just a *great* name for a big plane! Might have to borrow myself that one. The *Jumbo Jet*," he chuckled, making a note.

They walked around the giant patrol plane, a long-range Me-264 with additional fuel in big, bulbous tanks under the wings. "These engines are first-rate," he said, "as good as anything we've got. They're becoming real masters with refueling mid-air, too." In this and other areas, as Sam explained, the *Luftwaffe* now led the world, often by some margin. "I could show you the list of records, but the Germans attacked technical problems like they were competing in the Aviation Olympics or something. They went faster than us, then higher than us, then *much* higher than us, and *then* some lunatic rode a rocket plane so high, all of the atmosphere was below him, and he broke the sound barrier. That was in early '47."

Pinching his nose, Yanis asked hopelessly, "So, you've never heard of Chuck Yeager?"

"Who?"

"Shit. What else?"

"They set distance records that blew our minds. One of these," he said, thumb pointing up at the marquee-like wing of the converted bomber, "took off from Hamburg, headed north and just kept on going. Over the North Pole, down the other side into the Pacific, over the South Pole, until they *circumnavigated*. I'm serious! It was around Christmas '48, and they did a whole propaganda thing about visiting Santa Claus." Supported by gigantic tanker planes, the Me-264-ER was refueled in mid-air dozens of times, an unprecedented technical challenge.

"Every few weeks, we see something new," said Sam, showing him grainy pictures of strange, airborne shapes, taken at odd angles from a distance. "We've seen these five times now," he said, pointing out a bright, shiny, snub-nosed fighter plane, compact and aggressive, with a twin-boom tail. "They're not allowed to paint the Swastika or obscure the natural metal finish. Makes them easier for us to see, in case they stray where they shouldn't."

"And do they?" asked Jillian. "Stray, I mean."

A resigned slump of his shoulders. "All the time. They're forever testing our boundaries. Figuratively and literally." The mutual reconnaissance agreement didn't permit aircraft to loiter over a foreign nation or probe its airwaves with sophisticated intelligence-gathering equipment. "They love seeing what they can get away with. The Russians too, sometimes."

"Surely, they could hide some kind of weapon on one of those enormous patrol planes?" Jillian assumed. "We wouldn't know until it was too late."

"We thought of that. Every time the Allies intercept a surveillance bird, their pilot has to follow instructions, or risk being shot down.

Includes opening his bomb bay so our interceptors can take a look. So far, they haven't tried anything. That we know of."

"But there have been other incidents?" asked Jillian. She'd read an article on Cold War 'shoot-downs' of unarmed imposters; this incredibly tense stand-off with Germany, the fractured Italian states, and Japan was sure to have produced similar clashes.

"Yeah. Three of them, and I hope that's all we get. I reckon everybody could tell you where they were during those moments."

"I certainly can," Wheeler said. "I was in a cockpit, on fifteen-minute alert for nuclear war."

"One was just a collision—basically pilot error," reported Walcott. "A German fighter jet clipped a Superfortress doing electronics work, carved off a wing. Sixteen killed, huge diplomatic row."

"About a year later," Wheeler continued, "a young pilot, flying in the dark, reported he'd found an 'enemy reconnaissance plane,' illegally off course, and engaged it. Problem is, the flight was a civilian passenger jet, peacefully heading back to Norway." He winced, remembering the ten days of terrible diplomatic fallout. "Seventy-six casualties. The pilots did all they could, but it crashed into a row of houses in Berwick. Nearly wrecked the whole agreement."

"There have been others, and, well," Sam sighed again, "I'm sure in your timeline, you had some real dicey, real delicate moments in history, right? Real finger-on-the-button stuff?"

"Cuban Missile Crisis," said Jillian.

Wheeler mouthed, "*Cuba?*" incredulously.

She thought back to the article she'd read. "Couple of real-world nuclear alerts because of faulty equipment."

"And even if some hot-head jet pilot makes a dumb decision, or some equipment goes faulty, governments try to work it out, right? To pull things back from the brink, I mean."

Yanis said, "Jillian and I probably wouldn't be here, if they hadn't."

"Well, it's like that, for us," said Sam, finding the simple explanation. "We forgive and move on, because we have to."

It was deeply unsatisfying to Yanis, a cobbled-together treaty which left Germany virtually unrestrained. "They're probably breaking this deal, under the table, on a daily basis. Hitler did the same in the '30s, sent his air force overseas for their training, out of sight, disguised one type of plane as another."

"Not going to argue with that. We've seen plenty of evidence," Sam confirmed. The walls were covered with photographs of airbases, planes in flight, and underground assembly lines. "They try something, we discover it, they pull back. But we've never been in a place where we'd have risked the general annihilation of mankind."

Thoughtful, they followed Sam up the giant aircraft's metal steps and through a small door which, in flight, sealed the crew compartment from the outside air. They clambered through and found themselves in a bright, surprisingly spacious flight deck. "When you've got six engines and all the fuel in the world, you can afford to build big, eh, Sam?" said Wheeler, bringing up the rear. Then, more seriously, "Look, you two. I'm cottoning on to just how bloody *weird* this whole business must seem, so I've got to clue you in about something. Sam, you can hear this, too. It'll be a good thought experiment."

They took seats at the fold-away dining table, where the bomber's crew would play cards and pass time. It was as good a place as any for a quiet conversation. Sam Clark hovered in the mid-section, near the navigator's position, within earshot.

"Let's say we'd done it differently, and kept on fighting rather than signing the accord," posited Wheeler.

"Now you're talking." Yanis couldn't understand why this hadn't been the immediate choice.

"Who would control—what did your mate call it—Alien Peak?"

"*Der Dom*, or what's left of it. The Germans, I suppose. But you saw what the Lancasters did to the place."

"I did, but then I might just," he said slyly, "have a better imagination than you. Present yourself with the problem," he said like a school physics professor, "of moving *one billion tons* of rock, earth, and debris."

"Okay."

"Then give yourself a labor force of ten million conscripts, immediately available, and cheap to employ."

She tried to picture it, and saw a fearful mass of humanity, impressed into a labor which was dangerously inhumane. "*Digging* the spacecraft out?" Jillian said. "Seriously?"

"The Egyptians built the pyramids, the ancient Britons erected Stonehenge, and given the chance, if what you've said about him is true," Wheeler said with his own brand of certainty, "Keck, or someone like him, would *definitely* get the mountain back, and *definitely* dig out that spacecraft."

"As long as the Armistice holds," Jillian deduced, "the Germans can't do any digging."

"What happens if it *doesn't* hold?" asked Yanis.

Sam had his own answer. "Then the owner of a time machine could charge just about any price they liked for tickets out of here."

"Very funny," said Yanis, leaning left to spy the young engineer loitering by the navigator's table.

"No joke," Sam said. "The US Institute of Atomic Energy, the scientists who built the Doomsday Clock—"

"Yeah, we've got that, too," Yanis said.

"They predicted that a total nuclear exchange would kill *everything* except the toughest microbes. Those are the stakes. That's why we pull back when some *Luftwaffe* jock decides to pop off one of their new missiles and kills somebody. Because not doing so kills *everybody*."

"I get it, Al."

"I'm talking about preserving life on Earth, itself, Yanis."

"I said I get it."

"That's great, but a few hours ago, Miss Qualmes suggested tearing everything up, because the Germans are still, well, *German*," Wheeler reminded them.

"That was before I understood a lot of things." It wasn't necessary to be defensive; the military men knew this was a brand-new experience, packed with difficulties.

"Glad to hear. No one likes to contemplate ending the Armistice. I suppose there are parallels for you."

"The thirty-eighth parallel, in fact," Yanis said, his pun serendipitous. It was true—the tense, stalemated conflict was the best example. "But I guess there's no Korean War, now?"

"Korea? You mean the Japanese-Held Korean Mandate?"

"Ah." Yanis and Jillian exchanged a glance. "Well. Just be glad that you skipped that one."

"We caught a break?" asked Sam. "Wow, there's a first."

"But there's absolutely no reason to be glad," Yanis added bitterly, "that the Japanese Empire, just a bunch of thugs with a flag, really, still govern one-third of Asia."

Like a lot of people, Sam had learned since 1944 not to concern himself with larger themes over which he had no authority. "It's not quite like that. You'll see," was his gentle delaying tactic. Sam's job was to prepare Yanis and the Asphodel team to use and understand the technology of the 1950s, not to help partition the Dutch East Indies, renegotiate the PALS submarine agreement, or translate for the famed Truman-Stalin-Atlee summit in Iceland. No, Sam would adhere to the most suitable, most common, and very much the prevailing attitude: No one eradicated humanity during my shift, so it's been a good day.

He escorted the dazzled pair of time travelers to the neighboring hangar, equally huge but home to some twenty aircraft, some under repair and others apparently ready to fly. Yanis didn't recognize a single one.

"I'll write the book on all this, one day," Sam said, leading them under the wing of a sleek, delta-winged *Luftwaffe* attack plane, "if we ever declassify Asphodel and Prophet." He steered them to the far wall, where Prophet intelligence staff had created another display of photos and memorabilia.

"What's this?" asked Jillian of a long, paper read-out. "Looks like a lie detector test, or something."

"Oh, that's Herr Major Saalwächter. His first radio transmission, as heard from Jodrell Bank."

"Huh?"

"His voice broadcast, captured by the new radio-telescope array in Manchester." Sam paused, worried that there was not only an information gap, but a crevasse. "Surely someone's told you ..."

"I think that's your job, Sam," said Jillian. "Who's Major Saliva, or whatever?"

"Hans-Peter Saalwächter was the first man in space."

They both screwed up their eyes, then opened them again in hopes of being greeted by a less objectionable reality. "We urgently need to invent a word for this feeling," said Yanis.

"Yeah," agreed Jillian. "Ironically enough, it'll probably be one of those long, German words."

"The sensation of realizing—in our case, *yet again*—that one's own timeline is just one of many possibilities. I mean, look at what the Germans managed to do, for heaven's sake." He examined the printout, which was flanked by photographs of the launcher, and of Saalwächter's cramped, single-porthole spacecraft. Pictured before being perched atop the rocket and encased by a metal launch shroud, the capsule was a sleek, black teardrop-shape. In every picture, and from every angle, it looked hysterically unsafe.

"With rockets, they notify us in advance, for safety and for political reasons, so we keep an eye on them. That said, they didn't officially announce the flight had a pilot until Saalwächter was already back on Terra Firma, in good shape."

"How the *hell* did they manage it," Yanis wanted to know, "so soon after the war?"

Jillian tried to compute the size of the achievement. "I mean, 'our' World War Two ended nearly a year later, and ... what year was Gagarin?"

"Sixty ... two?" Yanis tried to remember.

"Seventeen years. And the Germans did it in, what, *five*?"

"Who's Gagarin?" asked Walcott.

Yanis groaned in exasperation. "That's like someone coming to your timeline and asking, 'Hey, this Queen Elizabeth character, what's she all about?'"

He examined a map of Saalwächter's route, a cannonball arc heading east from the Baltic coast, then high over Russia. The major splashed down safely, under revolutionary high-speed parachutes, in the South China Sea, to be met by the *Kriegsmarine*. "Okay, okay, so he didn't actually go into *orbit*, then," concluded Yanis.

"Not yet." An oft-updated list on the wall, however, detailed all of Germany's orbital satellite launches. There had been sixty attempts, of which a third were failures. "Jeez, they don't mess around, do they?"

"Swords into plowshares," Sam said. "Old V-2 rockets, re-purposed and given a big, big upgrade. "Plenty of 'em around, at the end of the war," added Wheeler.

Yanis broke off from the others, just to make space for himself to freak out. "Wait, wait, wait." He pushed away invisible attackers, armed proxies for the awfulness of these agreements with the Nazis. "They were allowed to keep the V-2?"

A suite of photographs told the story, part of a display intended to bring the Asphodel troops up to speed. "We absolutely bust our gut," Walcott recalled, "working with the Germans to end their rocket program but got nowhere. They claimed only peaceful intentions. Even had the bloody cheek to question the military usefulness of a one-ton warhead, given the rocket's unit cost," he recalled, looking revolted.

"Made plenty of one-ton holes in British cities, as I remember," was Wheeler's comment.

"In the end, we shook hands on a deal, and Fritz was as good as his word. Decommissioned every warhead, and all their mobile launchers, the ones we were really worried about."

"Blessed with a solid understanding of camouflage techniques," Wheeler said, "good missile crews can make their launchers an absolute *bugger* to find in the woods."

"We usually had no idea where they were," Walcott despaired, "until they were already flying."

Yanis still couldn't fathom how the Allies had ever agreed to a deal which merely scratched the Wehrmacht's paintwork. "All I can say is, wow."

"I mean, they changed the world, professor," Sam said. "I've loved science fiction since I was a boy, so ..."

"So, what, everything's forgiven now, and the Germans are your new heroes?" Yanis snapped. Then, quickly, "Shit, man. I'm sorry."

"Forget about it," Sam shrugged, good-naturedly.

"That was lame. And it wasn't what I meant."

"I get it," said Sam smiled. Yanis was a man twice displaced from his own time, dropped anew into a well of confusion.

"It's just, *the things those bastards did ...*"

"Professor Miller," Sam said, never bolder than this, "I was with Prophet from the beginning. I went into Germany with the first research teams, when the Nazi leadership was kinda still there, and keeping real tight-lipped about a lot of funny stuff. They gave us the run-around, told us the wrong directions, you can imagine. But *still*," he said, "nobody missed the big picture. I saw things just by the side of the road which turned my goddamned stomach. Things that came along and asked me some big questions, you know? My deputy, Terry Foster, he ... well, he handed in his notice because of all this."

"Moved to a Scottish loch, doesn't talk to anyone," said Wheeler.

"They sent him to visit Nordhausen, the forced-labor camp for the Nazis' underground rocket plant. He came back permanently changed. I'm not talking about how things were for your G.I.s in your '45, Yanis. These places, the camps, they weren't liberated, God no, they were still *functioning* concentration camps. Couldn't shut everything down immediately."

"Why?" asked Jillian, already sensing it was naive to ask.

Wheeler sighed, almost a growl. "Because the local Nazi *Gauleiter* would have let loose his Brownshirts on the inmates, and then blamed drunken Russians, or a 'false flag' operation by Czech nationalists. How does 'Herr Happy Hour' say it on the propaganda radio?"

"Oh, man! That newsreader guy? He's *amazing*," opined Clark. "I never heard basic truths so completely twisted using only very short words."

Walcott performed a bit of a send-up, adopting the propagandist's stereotyped demeanor: the angry, resentful, minimally-reformed Nazi stooge. "Zese cowardly and despicable acts," he raved, "are now proven to be ze work of *rogue, demobilized Polish inzurgents.*"

"*Vengeful, anti-German partisans,*" Sam tossed in.

"*Agents of illegal sedition,*" added Wheeler.

"*Counter-revolutionary splittists.*"

"*Armed, rebellious dissidents.*"

"*Mobsters, racketeers, and criminal elements.*"

"*Thieves, turncoats, and parasites.*"

"Oh, man," Sam laughed, "*turncoats* was always *my* favorite! I really can't *wait* to meet one!"

"Alright." With his temper coming to the boil again, Yanis was finding this rather less funny. "So, you saw how awful things were in Germany, and thought to yourself, 'I know what this ruined, racist slave-state really needs ... to restart its hyper-expensive rocket program!' Yeah, that's a great idea! Let's shove a few thousand Jews into a cave and beat them until rockets come out the other end."

With a lot more firmness than the usual gentle tug to get his attention, he was being dragged off to another part of the hangar, heels skidding on the concrete. "Hey!"

"Shut the hell up," Jillian said, putting her back into it.

"Huh?"

"See those three men in this hangar?" she said, halting his baffled retreat just outside of their earshot and turning Yanis to face Walcott, Clark, and Wheeler. "Yes, those three. Please indicate which one of them single-handedly wrote the Armistice."

"Oh, come on, I know they're not *directly* responsible, but—"

"Complex negotiations always produce shitty, residual elements. Nothing is perfect. There's always a remainder to the sum. One side gives slightly more concessions than the other, and some of them might prove very unpopular afterward. Sometimes," she said, still holding his arm, but pleading now, not punishing, "even completely inexplicable."

"Like letting Germany keep its fucking rockets?"

"Yep. Now, go and apologize to Clark."

Damn it, she's right again. "Okay."

The affable farm boy breezed through it. "Sir, with the war you all have had, I'm amazed your head's still screwed on straight."

To the relief of everyone, Sam steered them away from politics and the Armistice, and toward his favorite species of minutiae: rocketry.

"Instead of firing off a warhead to London, the up-rated V-2 could propel a tiny, five-kilogram package all the way to orbit. The Germans sent up radiation sensors, cameras, all kinds of stuff, way ahead of what we can do, even today. Their civilian science program was exempted from the agreement," he said with another apologetic grimace to Yanis, "so we haven't been able to see most of that technology."

With its growing list of launches and tiny but ambitious science satellites, the Reich had evinced its technical superiority with an enviable Buck Rogers panache. On the wall next to the list, confirming the impression, was a photo frame almost completely filled with the bright, hazy, green-blue-brown disc of the earth, as seen from space.

"Oh, yeah, this was pretty neat," Sam told them. "Once the Germans developed their three-stage rocket, they sent up a sophisticated satellite with a color camera. It took a dozen pictures from record altitude, thirty thousand miles, then separated and re-entered using a heat shield. Germans picked it up in the Baltic."

"Don't tell me," Yanis said, remembering the famed 'whole Earth' image from Apollo 17, "it blew people's minds, didn't it?" In the 1970s, a single photo had effectively spawned the environmental movement; what could the same experience bring to people in the war-weary 1950s? Might a machine of war, ironically, have lofted the instruments to provide photographic proof that we are tiny, and lonely, and helplessly dependent on each other? "Things were never quite the same, right?"

"Right. It's taken time, and there are enormous challenges, but yes, those photographs definitely changed things. Communications satellites became more common, too. So cheap, they replace them every few weeks. They link German diplomatic and research people in Japan, the Reich, and South America, and handle secure phone calls for foreign governments. Best security and encryption in the world."

"Well, of course," he sneered. He thought back to the Enigma, the discovery which had pushed him over the edge and onto this insane roller-coaster ride.

If you're breaking laws, best do it in code.

There was a research hangar specifically dedicated to devices. "Planes are pretty hard to steal, but a periscope lens, or a time-delay fuse, or a fancy, new circuit board, they're easier." He gave them a brief tour, aware of the sheer volume of information. "You know," he said, hoping to reverse the flow for a moment, "we've been hoping, all of us, that you'll be able to help us understand the time machine. Just as a research project, for completeness' sake," he added hurriedly, "not planning to go over there and dig the thing out." Culturally and professionally, in 1951, any notion which risked the Armistice was akin to proposing genocide.

When Yanis simply puffed out his cheeks, his brain fried, Jillian said, "Time travel? Oh, there's nothing to it, as far as I can tell."

"Really?" asked Sam excitedly.

"All you do is curl up on the floor in a strange, blue room and hope you don't die. Then, *poof*, you're in Ireland." She laughed when Sam actually grabbed his pen and started to make a note.

"For my report," he tried to explain, a refrain which would come to explain almost every line of inquiry, but Jillian was helpless with laughter.

"How about a break, Sam?" It was three o'clock; hours had spun by, and Yanis was sure his brain was actually full.

"Sure, yeah. We can pick up tomorrow. You guys look kinda ..."

"Completely worked over by events?" Yanis asked, bringing Jillian to him for a tired hug.

"Completely," Sam agreed. "Quite a ride, huh? I can show you to your ..."

Jillian was already leading Yanis back to the car, arm in arm. "Yeah," she said, anticipating some sleep, and some long-awaited privacy, "that'd be *great*."

***

Early the next morning

He did his absolute best not to wake her, the springs groaning slightly as he levered himself up. Tip-toeing between the two twin beds, he grabbed the civilian clothes he'd been given, and went looking for a shower.

"Anything you need, sir?" a young corporal asked, startling Yanis.

"Oh, g'morning," he said groggily.

"Coffee?"

Ten minutes later, Yanis decided that British Army coffee had improved immeasurably in the last six years. He also recognized that his new favorite pastime, when not worrying about the utter chaos of the world, would be quietly watching Jillian sleep.

The corporal agreed to escort him back to Hanger Two, where they'd repeatedly had their minds blown by Sam Clark. "Can't let you go in alone, sir," he said, so Yanis suggested he come along.

"Oh, no, sir," he said severely. "I mustn't be going in there. Strictly off limits."

The impasse was resolved when Al Wheeler came striding by the hangar on his way to breakfast. "Officers' digs are on the other side," he explained to Yanis. "Fastest way is right through the middle, even if I have to show my pass about ten times."

They walked steadily by some of the displays, a creative effort by the Prophet intelligence team. They hadn't shied away from the unprecedented task of telling these travelers how their actions irrevocably changed the world, and not decisively for the better. A simple narrative had to be found from a situation wreathed in complexity: *We made a deal with the enemy, and so far, they haven't broken it. Happy days.*

"Al?" said Sam. "I was going to say something yesterday, but there wasn't time, with everything ..."

"What's up?"

"South America. I think Walcott mentioned it, something to do with their radio communications." He found and studied a panel which showed the orbits of Germany's growing satellite fleet. "See?" he said, pointing to a pair of thin lines. "These two lifted off from Peenemünde, on the Baltic coast, and got boosted into an orbit which passes over Montevideo and Berlin, both."

"Passes over plenty of other places, too," Wheeler noted, though his own reaction was somewhat troubled.

"Sure," Yanis admitted. "Just seems, I don't know ..."

"What?"

"Odd."

Wheeler let out a quick, skeptical laugh. "If it wasn't odd, it wouldn't be happening at Tempsford."

"And whatever happens at Tempsford," Yanis joked, "stays at Tempsford."

Entirely unaware of the expression, Wheeler laughed again. "I'd say Alice Chernowitz would *insist* on that!"

Someone had woken Jillian and led her through the shower-and-coffee routine, then driven her to the hangars. "I almost," she reported, "feel human again. Did I miss anything?"

He pointed out the resources Germany had invested in ensuring satellite communications with a broad swath of South America. "I'm probably just being paranoid," Yanis said. "They've got embassies down there. Got to stay in touch."

"Yeah," she said sleepily. "Normal, right?"

But at breakfast, a sequence of thoughts piled up, leaving him quiet and worried. "Can I get some time with Sam Clark this morning?" he asked Walcott when the analyst popped in to make sure the Asphodel team had slept well and were being taken care of.

"Don't think you'll have any choice," Walcott laughed. "He's been standing around waiting since before you got here." At 4:45 a.m., Yanis remembered. *Someone's dedicated to his duty. Or just obsessed, maybe.*

Yanis hurried his breakfast, distracted by his suspicions, and quickly found Sam afterward, hovering outside the mess hall. "I need you to fill me on South America," he said without any pleasantries. "Are the Nazis doing something down there?"

Sam had hoped to spend the morning talking rockets, missiles, and radars. "Ah." He frowned.

"Ah?"

"The best answer I can give you is *probably*."

Yanis fixed him with a deliberate and penetrating look. If the Armistice had been close to his worst-case scenario, this promised utter disaster. "Tell me everything."

***

"I've got to be clear," said Sam. Schedules were adjusted, leaving him with Walcott, Menzies, Yanis, Jillian, and Corporal Jenkins in a smaller briefing room. "Our local assets aren't as dependable as I'd like. Reports have been intermittent, and sometimes incomplete."

"Great," Yanis murmured.

"Most of our intelligence resources are focused on Germany, and those that aren't," Menzies explained, "are oriented toward Russia and Japan. I'm afraid South America has been something of a backwater for MI6."

Still, Walcott and Sam presented what they thought they knew. "We had some reports from local sources. And some unusual, but otherwise trustworthy, intelligence from a long-standing source in the *Kriegsmarine*."

"At least," said Menzies, "we *think* that's where he was from. Hard man to pin down. Something of a legend."

"He was a solid source, until he got himself mixed up in Asphodel. Tried to escape the valley, but Al Wheeler was trailing him and blew up his car. Until then, he'd been giving us near-daily updates on a submarine that was heading south."

Bright lights, flashing and scary, went off in Yanis' brain. "Wait ... *what submarine?*"

***

"Three different times, we thought we'd sunk her," Walcott remembered. "Sent two carrier groups to the Bay of Biscay, hammered her for days."

"Destroyers, aircraft, the whole nine yards," Sam assured him. "But no luck. We assume U-99X made it to South America, but there's no way of knowing if her crew, passengers, and cargo are still there now."

"*Assume?*"

Yanis was astounded by the badly skewed intelligence priorities.

"Some might have made it home, who knows?" said Menzies. "The submarine was probably part of a rat line, some SS officer's last-ditch escape plan."

Notions both absurd and terrifying formed themselves up for inspection. "Hear me out," Yanis said. "Because I can think of at least one SS officer who might conceive of an audacious submarine escape."

"We did have some intelligence that an SS sergeant named Taschner was on board, and a female sergeant called Weber arrived later. We never made much sense of it, but our source—an intercept from the German consul in Montevideo—intimated that Taschner wasn't actually who he said he was."

"No? Why? Who did he say it might really be?" Yanis asked, but he knew exactly what was coming.

***

Walcott felt the worst. He recalled the difficult hours of interrogation, Yanis' lengthy spell in a mental hospital; his appalling treatment came from the decisions of lazy, stupid people who had since lost their jobs, but it had been an unforgivable way to treat a priceless, unique intelligence asset.

"He was a target, you have to believe that," Menzies explained by way of an apology. "We tried everything we knew. Even sent three hundred aircraft to hit a railway station we thought he might use."

They'd been chasing smoke. As usual, Yanis saw, *Sturmbannführer* Kristock Keck was several steps ahead.

"OKW reported him missing in action at *Der Dom,* and he was later declared dead. That's all we have on him, but Keck's adjutant was named 'Taschner,' and he was reported KIA near the valley. We assumed it was a duplication, or a radio operator mixing up the names."

"It wasn't," Yanis had already decided.

Was he leaping to conclusions? Did this evidence really support a supposition that Keck had somehow fled to South America, to continue the war?

Even as he spoke, his own level of certainty gradually increased. "I want you all to work on the theory that there is now an active, organized, well-funded Nazi SS cell in South America."

He was adding to a lengthy list of problems, and it was difficult to get the others to see the potential in this historically unfruitful area of intelligence work. "Verifying any of that is going to take a great deal of effort," said Menzies." We never ignore useful avenues, but we're stretched pretty thin."

"Can't you ... I don't know," Yanis guessed aloud, "intercept their communications?"

To the extent it was possible in 1951, this was already being done. "We can't yet pull signals off their satellites. Maybe in 2014, there are machines which can link into enemy broadcasts, or orbital battle-robots which can shoot down satellites with lasers ..."

"David, old chap, what *have* you been reading?" Menzies muttered.

Yanis wasn't going to disabuse him. Besides, the future was as yet untold, and *this* 1951 was a different kettle of fish, quite entirely, from

Yanis' own; a manned suborbital flight in 1948, a little constellation of satellites by 1950, and they were advertising the first overnight trans-Pacific passenger flights.

"Recon!" Yanis exclaimed. "Just fly up and down taking pictures of everything, until we find it."

"It's someone else's airspace, Yanis, but, apart from that ... David, what's the staff of the photo-recon analysis suite looking like, these days? Two thousand? Three?"

"Nearly four, since we started daily flights at the Soviet submarine bases." An entire cadre of young men and women were learning how to take flat, two-dimensional images taken from great height, and use them to interpret the enemy's shifting, elusive three-dimensional world. "But to cover Argentina at the right level ... maybe double it?" He turned to Yanis apologetically. "Do you remember telling me about that remarkable World Wide Web service?" he said, awkwardly mouthing the unfamiliar syllables. 'Doodle Earth,' or what was it called?" He explained to Menzies, humming with the possibilities. "The Doodle company bought millions of images taken by commercial photographic satellites and *stitched them together*." As he carried on, Jillian watched a man in his early sixties, who as a young lieutenant had bled with his friends at Passchendale, try to metabolize the idea of orbiting robots, and high-resolution photography, and gargantuan data files sent through the ether in an instant.

"Can we," he requested mildly, "return to our own time?" Speculation and creativity were wonders to behold, especially when wielded by Clark and the Prophet team, but if they were going to neutralize these rogue Nazi threats, he'd need to go backward, not forward. "In the absence of flying cameras and eavesdropping robots, we'll have to do this the old-fashioned way."

"How do you mean, sir?" Wheeler asked.

"Well, back in my day, if you wanted to know what someone was up to, you went and visited them."

***

The submarine's course would have taken it to Uruguay, a common method of Nazi access to Argentina. Nothing would have been known about any of the civilian passengers, except for an extraordinary stroke of luck. "The last page was transmitted electronically, so that both sides in the divorce could sign. One reason listed: *my husband absconded to Argentina without me.*"

"Our eavesdropping won't reach late twentieth-century levels for a while, but we're not doing too bad, eh?"

"Who was it?"

"A guy called Carl Friedrich Baumann. We pulled his file, but if you're looking for Nazis down there, I don't think he's your guy."

"Why not?"

Sam tried to remember. "He works with cattle, or something. Breeding."

It came together with horrifying certainty. "Breeding?"

"Yeah, you know, making stronger horses, or meatier pigs, or—"

"Stop." There was no way he was wrong about this. "Nothing is known about DNA in 1951. Right?"

"DNA? What's that, now?"

"Alright. So, if you're going to produce the perfect Aryan, you couldn't ask a geneticist. Instead, you'd need an expert in breeding."

He asked dozens of questions while Sam and others tried to find the relevant materials. "Have there been any unusual financial transactions? Big sums moving around for no good reason?" But they lacked the resources for a comprehensive search. "Have there been rumors? About experiments or strange animals, down there?" As the threat of Keck and his submariner friends crystallized in Sam's mind, he became more frustrated at the lack of intel.

Within an hour, fired up and worried, Yanis' only suggestion was that he and Jillian personally lead an expedition to Argentina, to track down Keck.

"Believe it or not," Menzies told him, "we've already thought about this. If a base exists down there, it'll be near-impossible to find. Figure the local cops are on Keck's payroll, and the rest will be either too uninformed, or too well bribed, to tell you anything useful."

"So, what else am I going to do in 1951?" Yanis complained. "Get a job?"

"Actually," Menzies said, "we've got an idea we'd like to run past you. It's based on some solid intelligence from California."

"California?" asked Jillian, perplexed. "What on earth are *Nazis* doing over there?"

| 6 |
Roots

Berlin, after Inge is dispatched to US, 1951

It was slow going, but he was finally developing the Zen-like patience of a veteran traveler. Keck knew the engine noise would—eventually—come to an end, and the seaplane's floats would—maybe even one day soon—touch down. Perhaps even on a calm ocean. Until then, he would simply breathe, and await the bump of the seaplane's meeting with the water. Between meals, drinks, and moments of grandeur from the window tempered by impatience, he practiced mindful control to moderate his feelings; Keck would need a steady hand on his emotional tiller in these coming weeks.

It took six days of this patient, observant calm—of flying, waiting, eating, sleeping, and flying again—for Keck to derive any true gratification from his trek north. He was in another thrumming seaplane, ninety minutes from landing in Cape Verde, the Portuguese mid-Atlantic archipelago. Halfway from Bonehouse to Berlin, it was a significant milestone, and Keck was already feeling his spirits lift. Charming, well-to-do Portuguese newlyweds asked to borrow Keck's copy of *Der Zeitung*. They talked briefly about world events, and only then introduced themselves, but the new bride interrupted Keck, confused. "Argentina? But ... I was *certain* you were Portuguese! You speak it like a native! Doesn't he, dear?"

Six years of language study, mostly alone and using his own methods, had paid off. Keck quietly exulted for the rest of the trip, his reserves of confidence replenished by the smoothness of these encounters. At airports and cafes, he found his Zen calm becoming elevated and honed into a guardian's watchfulness, his senses sharper as the journey advanced—flight after flight after droning, lengthy flight.

The rest of the time, he read books, wrote in his journal, stared out the window, and engaged the other passengers in conversation. "My ranches are in Chaco, in the north. Have you been up there?" Keck asked. His English was very competent, but it was tough to keep a Spanish accent behind everything in his second, third, and fourth languages. He was speaking with his next seatmate, a British trade official also returning from South America on the Lufthansa International Seaplane Service. "The finest lamb in the world comes from Chaco, I promise it by all the saints!" Before they parted company at the seaplane docks in the Azores, Keck made sure to give the ministry bowler-hat the card for his burgeoning ranch business: Cabrera & Son. Underneath the name it read: *Finest Meats for Export.*

Business could come from anywhere, and Keck was traveling to Europe precisely to do as much new business as possible, so he wheeled out the same patter to each new neighbor, to other passengers waiting in line, people standing in the hotel lobby, and the businessmen with whom he shared a cab.

"And is it lamb that brings you to Germany for the first time?" he was asked on the Lufthansa Euro-Jet service to Lisbon, on the seventh day of his trip.

"Lamb, yes! For export. And beef also!" he said. The Cabrera family were always loudly proud of their family ranch. "Also, I administer our financial portfolio. If I am lucky, we will invest in one of Germany's wonderful, new technologies. So impressive!" he exclaimed, then chose to slip briefly into the 'International German' which had become so popular in the last year or two. "*Nicht war?*"

"They've been very impressive, yes," his British fellow traveler admitted, betraying a strong and lingering distaste for German success. *We didn't fight them almost to the death, just to watch them turn around and get rich by selling us luxury cars.*

Lamb, beef, and electronics appeared in every conversation during his journey. The world loved Germany's new devices and personal radios, and exports were driving reconstruction. IG Farben was to the world in 1951 what Apple and Samsung would be during Keck's 2014 visit, he remembered.

"*Recognize* it? What, Berlin? After all that's changed? Hardly." Sharing a table at a hotel bar in Lisbon, Keck asked the impressions of another onetime emigre who had left Germany to design trains for the Americans. "I should have stayed at home. Every designer and architect and painter in the Reich was *making* something. Whole streets were cleared and transformed in a few weeks."

"How was that possible? The bombing was so very—"

"Modular construction. A method," he touted, "invented by our technologists. The houses will last fifteen, twenty years, and by then we'll have the resources to build better. More permanent."

Modular construction, you say? Keck felt another surge of pride on a trip which was to be full of them. *You're welcome.*

"If you've got the capital, they say Germany is making the best of everything, these days," said another coffee drinker with time on his hands, an exhausted, chain-smoking Frenchman coming home from Vichy-administered Cayenne. "Little beeping, spinning things, up there in space!" he wondered, circling his fingers in unlikely orbits. "Controlling our minds, no? Influencing behavior with," he stammered, "with *microwaves*. It's true!"

"Speculation," Keck decided.

"Read it for yourself in the newspapers!"

Keck knew most of the dailies were little better than comics, feeble entertainment for the feeble-minded. The flow of *real* information was guarded much more carefully. "I don't have time for such things," he said, ever the single-minded businessman without a second to waste.

"We must not ignore the world," the Frenchman warned, stabbing the air with his cigarette to emphasize the point. "Evil may return."

Keck could have allowed his anger to rise, fueled by the Frenchman's blinkered idiocy, but the maritime vibrancy of Lisbon harbor helped buoy his mood. As did knowing that he'd once again passed for a native, this time in French.

The Frenchman had been right to warn against evil, but Keck knew enough to recognize *true* evil when he saw it—right there on the front page of today's *Der Zeitung*. Keck bought a copy at a kiosk outside his Lisbon hotel, then read the article in the cab to the airport. 'No More Guessing for Guest Workers' ran the headline. The government was issuing new rules, relaxing the restrictions on foreign-born workers staying in Germany after their contract. From fifteen days, the limit had already been raised to thirty. But now it was six months.

And in those six months, how many young, white German girls will get knocked up by horny Turks or Moors or Slavs? The threat to racial purity bothered him as he boarded the jetliner and turned his stomach enough that he had to refuse the in-flight lunch service. 'Guests' were not 'residents,' Keck thought scornfully as he bitterly re-read the article, and 'workers' were most certainly not 'citizens-in-the-making.' Least of all were any of them even remotely 'German.' Words still had to have meaning, and for Keck, *that* one would never change.

But ... today's flights were both remarkable, so amid his concerns as he read, Keck made sure to enjoy himself. *A paying passenger, a mere civilian, breaking the sound barrier?* It sounded utterly fantastical, a soldier's daydream, until his Lufthansa flight, itself a curious piston-jet hybrid carrying over a hundred, made its arrival in Barcelona. There, from his transfer gate, Keck saw the ultra-sleek eight-passenger business jet with its distinctive, stainless-steel gleam, waiting to fly. *My God. A mini-Concorde, decades early ...*

Onboard, with his notebook put aside, Keck sat through something the attendant called a safety demonstration; he was polite, grinning only privately at the suggestion that a seatbelt might keep any of them alive in a depressurized, spinning, supersonic jet. His buzz of anticipation easily counteracted the frustration of a short runway delay. Then, as the engines of the aircraft—or was it not officially a *spacecraft*—gave forth their famed whining sound and the plane headed into its take-off roll, Keck found himself thinking, *In my original 1951, only a handful of people had ever been to Mach 1. Now there are six supersonic flights a day, on this route alone.*

Something which felt like a herd of giants came rushing up behind them, pushing the jet off the mark and then accelerating it down the runway before flinging it skyward. Then, they did nothing but climb ever higher, leaving the weighty, resistant atmosphere behind.

Forty miles out into the Mediterranean, the pilot announced they would begin, 'the quietest and fastest stage of our cruise.' With that, he pushed the engines forward and the dart-like jet climbed out of the atmosphere and into the supersonic realm.

Keck relaxed into his leather seat, cruising at Mach 1.1, almost overwhelmed with pride. He would always be cautious of such a wily emotion, but there were genuine reasons to reward himself, and he ordered a drink. "*Dein bester Champagner, bitte.*" Quietly and miraculously skimming the highest clouds, was this jet not a summation of all he had achieved with *Der Dom?*

The sensation re-doubled as the jet passed over southern Germany at 58,000 feet. He saw networks of broad, new highways under construction. The outskirts of Berlin, as they descended, looked orderly and neat, with groups of smart residential towers built in the efficient *Neueur Konkreter Stil.* Tempelhof was an airport re-born, tripled in size to accommodate Germany's sustained, parallel booms in business and tourism. The sensation had taken hold and now stayed with him:

I helped make all of this.

A silver-grey Mercedes pulled up, bristling with German confidence. The cadet-aged driver even addressed him in commendable Spanish before whisking him downtown on a road built for the traffic of the 1980s, not 1951. A sweeping overpass showed the extent of the new layout, generously broad to insure against a much busier future.

All derived from *his* designs, the descriptions in *his* reports, *his* photos from the future. *I am Father of all I see.*

Keck let the driver practice for a few minutes before revealing Cabrera's functional but accented German. "Everyone's learning *Deutsch* these days," the driver said. "This is how Germany can be friends with the world again." This time, Keck's satisfaction came in reverse, as he played a German-speaking Argentine who convinced the driver he *wasn't* a native speaker.

Outside his window, Berlin was rising, triumphant. The giant six-phase rebuilding project was well underway, as Keck had expected, but the really striking change was among the people. On some street corners, there were more non-white faces than German. "Oh, well over a million now," the driver told Keck when he asked about the influx, "and another million coming, they say."

"From where?"

"All over. Every country you could name." Large communities of workers from Belgian Congo and French Cameroon, as well as Ethiopians from Italy's protectorate in east Africa, were putting down roots. Families were applying for residency, and with the Nuremberg Laws now entirely struck down ... the very thought made Keck nauseous.

He distracted himself by quizzing the driver about these new roads and suburbs and learned about the government's ambitious plans to pedestrianize much of Berlin's shopping district. "They're going to do it like Paris," he said, "you know, a boulevard with street musicians and decorative lights."

"How charming." *Importing culture from the French? What the fuck has Germany come to?*

His hotel was in the center, one of a new chain catering to business travelers; there were a handful of tourists, but the only non-Aryans there were employees. Quiet and comfortable, it was the nicest room he'd stayed in since his days of being feted like royalty by the SS.

Two stretches of six hours' sleep, a bath, and a couple of solidly German meals were enhanced by some good-quality tobacco. The package boasted: *Chinese Grower, German Roaster, European Perfection, World Renown.* After enjoying such civilities during his first day in Berlin, Keck was ready to begin his mission.

But first, he had to be Jose-Luis Cabrera for a full day, in Germany, for the first time. He gave himself an encouraging wink in the mirror, as Cabrera might when meeting an interesting woman. *"Tranquilo, amigo,"* he said. *"Eres un profesional."*

***

Later morning, third day in Berlin

They were all ex-military, of course, the men with whom he'd meet today. Representatives from Thyssen, Siemens, Junkers, BMW, and many thousands of smaller companies, all here to showcase their products, tout future plans, or just take the temperature and seed some useful IPO rumors. One could tell the former officers from the others; they were confident and knowledgeable, but not used to being interrupted, overly flashy and impatient. They would rely on old networks of favors and connections. The former sergeants, on the other hand, brought in some camaraderie, a little showmanship, and the gift of the gab.

Most of the stalls clustered with people who in turn attracted others, so that a snake of people made its way steadily around the gathered groups, trying to peer over the others. Both the former officers and the former NCOs, it seemed to Keck, were doing just fine.

Keck's driver made sure he was hand-delivered to Herr Scholz, a Berliner and industrial insider and provider of 'innovative solutions.' Keck presented his card, and explained his twin objectives, but Scholz misunderstood and told him about an upcoming agricultural show.

"My ranch operates very efficiently already. I wouldn't propose to build anything myself," Cabrera told him, "but I'm interested in finding organizations and ideas which have yet to be properly supported."

"Ah! A Valkyrie Investor!" he exclaimed. "Swooping down to save brilliance from doom!" He pumped Keck's hand. "So few people have any actual *money* to invest. A few thousand here, a quarter million there." Capital was tied up in building both a symbol and an engine of Germany's rebirth: the remarkable infrastructure which had speeded Keck's journey.

Scholz continued, "But some of these fledglings, are proposing extraordinary things. I'm serious, they leave you just staring at them, wishing you had enough money to give them all a proper start."

"What kind of technologies do you mean?" Keck asked.

Straightening his back and preening, Scholz reached his favorite part of being an 'industrial solvent.' It could easily have been his catchphrase: "May I introduce you to some interesting people?"

Keck smiled. "By all means," he gestured.

***

It became an exercise in controlled impatience. Keck learned a great deal about advances in shearing and slaughterhouse technologies, none useful to him; Cabrera's setup was already optimized, and expensive changes only brought attention. He took some business cards, asked a few questions, but then steered Scholz toward the stalls displaying the blinking lights, flashing screens, and whirring mechanisms for which Germany was becoming globally renowned.

"You'll never *lose* or accidentally *burn* another piece of paper, because you won't be *using* any!"

"It can do the work of a whole *room* of calculator girls, in a fraction of the time!"

"Why sit in traffic when you can fly over it? Introducing the HoverKraft 55."

Still not satisfied, Keck asked where he might find companies developing computers and personal devices. "Communications, data storage, wireless technology, that kind of thing."

"I mean, nobody knows if that stuff is really going to fly," Scholz warned Keck. "A telephone, that doesn't even need a line? No wires? I mean ..."

"I want introductions to those people," Keck said at once, then added bluntly, his impatience finally showing, "Some of these others are interesting, but you should ask the 'flying car' people to leave."

"Why? They've had good crowds all morning."

"Because investors shouldn't be distracted by pointless lunacy."

"Now, wait a minute, what makes you so certain ..."

Keck strode off toward the crowd which surrounded the mocked-up, wood-and-canvas 'flying car' model. The technical guy was thrilling the audience with the 'vectored thrust' idea. "To shift from forward to vertical flight, the exhaust nozzles can swivel down like this ..."

No, no, you idiot! I included these in the engine's dossier in 2014, but for Luftwaffe *attack aircraft, not Disney-fied cars, for God's sake ...*

"Lift off from wherever you want," the rep claimed, "land wherever you want, either on a road or straight down onto your own driveway."

Keck had to do it, or the parts of his brain dedicated to running Bonehouse would nag him all day. "Sir, I wonder if helicopters might be preferable as personal transports. Seems to me that cars are too heavy."

The suave, tanned sales guy swung in to assist his technical rep. "With an engine this powerful, there's really no problem with—"

"In which case, aren't you concerned about noise?" Keck asked next.

Sales Guy was ready. "The cities of the future will be more crowded and noisier, that's a natural part of—"

"All of your artwork," Keck pointed, "depicts the cars in urban environments. What if someone loses control and crashes into an apartment building?"

Again, the preparation was solid. "Our patented Fly-By-Clockwork design ensures constant ..."

Sweet Jesus.

"Alright, listen, please, for your own good," he said, the crowd puzzled but fascinated. "Firstly, no one's going to buy one. The prototypes will be museum pieces, at best. Secondly," he said, "it's regressive. Cars made for rich individuals will be a bust, a waste of design effort. Focus on public transport and domestic air travel instead."

"Our market research shows that—"

"And thirdly, if you'd ever heard one of these turbofans, up close, you'd know the noise is a deal-breaker."

"But," Technical Guy objected, "that's not possible! You can't have heard one of these yet, we've only just ..."

But the bearded stranger was already gone, disappearing into the crowd. There, he searched out Scholz and found him looking for Keck with a worried expression.

"Ah, good! Did you do any business?" Scholz asked, glancing around to check that Keck wasn't being pursued by angry graduates whose bright idea he'd just squashed.

"No, but neither will those idiots. For that, I feel a lot better."

Unwilling to argue with an Argentine whose net worth was rumored to be among the highest on his continent, Scholz led 'Cabrera' to, "the computer people," as requested. "The person I'm looking for," Keck told him, "is probably a man, between twenty and thirty. He's single, and may be alone at his booth, or with his only close friend. He's got an idea which will transform humanity, but, these days, and in here," Keck waved to the gargantuan expo hall, "it's only one among thousands."

Scholz trailed Keck as he paced down the three long aisles which were packed with stalls and booths for sellers, makers, and inventors. Another sales rep was boggling at the giant pile of paper on his table, comparing it to a single reel of magnetic tape, held aloft like The Good Book. "Every word Goethe ever wrote, or all of Schopenhauer, or of Shakespeare ... each on a single tape!"

It's a start, but come back to me, Keck grumbled impatiently, *once you can fit all three authors on the same reel.*

Most invited potential investors to consider a physical product, but a highbrow few, almost secreted away toward the back of the hall, were a much-misunderstood group, the world's first software engineers. He listened for a few moments, filled in the rest while the team stood, gawking, and then answered questions until they had it.

"So," the young, bearded man said to Cabrera, "every time you press a key, the backup copies it, too?"

"Not every keystroke," Keck said. "That would be inefficient." The software was to be called Control-Z, and Keck expected it to make millions. "Once per minute for coders, or per five minutes for everyone else. Every mistake you made would be un-doable." Keck laid out his larger strategy, a Reich computer network to rival that of the 1990s. "What kind of hardware would that need?" he asked them.

The youngsters had to think exponentially. "You're saying, if every office desk in Germany had a computer, and all of them were connected to the telephone system at the same time?"

Then, he invited the dazzled engineers to consider moving *terabytes* of data down those same lines. "Best think big," he advised, leaving them slack-jawed but enormously fired up.

He patrolled the stalls, advising some quietly, others noisily, and actually deciding to drop some hard cash on several of the teams. "I'm not going to be breathing down your neck. I live in Argentina, after all," he said to the group of 'transponder freaks' who he was guiding to build a location service based on radio beacons, a nascent German GPS system. "But from you, above all, I expect regular *communication*. Yes?"

He turned, full of swagger and old-money pomp, only to run headfirst into Ludwig Graf von Brennau, resplendent in his bristling uniform.

Thank God! Brennau, finally!

He was red-cheeked, overweight, hyper-conservative, and in other ways perfect for Keck's purposes. *Now, is he too soused and addled, or might the curmudgeonly old fart recognize me?*

Brennau gave a pen-pusher's harrumph and complained for a moment about being walked into, before regarding Keck with optimism. "Ah …" he began, his eyes suddenly glinting with recognition and excitement. "You're here. I can barely believe you're actually *here*."

"A long journey, but quite fascinating." Ultimately, Keck had decided for himself, the Zen philosophy was mostly just repetitive crap; hour after hour on a rattling seaplane numbed your ass just as certainly, whether you were communing with cosmic eternity or not.

"Fascinating, yes. Ours has become a *most* fascinating world, wouldn't you say?" He led 'Cabrera' to the far edge of the hall, past seats set out for the press pool, and around the back of the most remote stalls and toward a swish, officers' mess-type setup with tablecloths and quality silverware. They were virtually alone in this hidden

VIP area, which was so much the better, for their talk would be of treason.

"You don't report to me, my friend," Brennau assured him when Keck tried to launch into a formalized update. "This isn't an annual review. Bonehouse has been off the Reich government's books for over five years. It's your project, and you're running it like clockwork, as far as I can tell."

He almost let out a laugh but decided instead to bring out documents from his briefcase, almost covering the table. "We're discussing lambs and steers, remember. I'm just a *ranchero, nicht war?*"

"Lambs that can hit a bullseye in the dark," Brennau joked, "and nuclear-armed steers."

"These days, it's not only steers," Keck explained. His geneticist, Baumann, had only agreed to participate in the more controversial of Keck's experiments if granted time and resources to resurrect an ancient beast. "He's bringing back the old European aurochs."

Brennau saw this for the unnecessary distraction it was. "Big kind of bison, something like that? Didn't know we'd lost it."

"Six wealthy families who own hunting lands funded research to create a genetic facsimile of the great aurochs."

"Giving renaissance to an extinct species," Brennau asked, "all so they could hunt them down and kill them again?"

Keck shrugged, his own arguments already exhausted. "Baumann insisted, and in return ..."

"Yes?"

"Well, I shouldn't say too much." The experiments were at an especially delicate stage, he explained, with still many variables, many 'unknown unknowns' to be discovered. "Viability has been more difficult to achieve than we'd hoped."

Brennau sagged; their great plan had to be preserved, but the tininess and fragility of Keck's outpost worried him, not least for his own reasons; supporters of Bonehouse were all promised full access to the Elixir research. Brennau had lived sixty years with a bulbous gut and was anxious to have news. "When do you think you'll have an example of ..."

"We will not rush," Keck said, "to fulfill arbitrary deadlines, whether fixed by us or by others. Nature is being harnessed, and like a green-broke horse, she will take stern mastering."

The metaphor lifted him. "Masters of nature!" he exclaimed, almost too loud. Keck needed Brennau's enthusiasm but could not respect over-excitement; giddiness about these things was the opposite of what Bonehouse needed: scientific, rational, secretive men. And, he reminded himself, the occasional, remarkable woman. Their genetic experiments were far from some brute combat between man and nature. Instead, one would gradually seduce the other.

He ran Brennau through their other work, on rockets and materials and radios, while the elderly former general drank it all in. "Everyone's fully committed," said Keck. "One large camp and two smaller ones." He omitted to mention a fourth unit, but their work was none of Brennau's concern; some of those acquainted with Keck's Bonehouse plan lacked the foresight needed to see the larger picture, and how Bonehouse might fit into a larger strategy to defeat the Armistice. Brennau was useful but had the imagination of a kitten.

"Where will you go next?" he asked Keck as the documents were being folded away. In all, their meeting had looked convincing—a German dignitary in a routine meeting with a foreign investor.

"That depends. Could I possibly ask a couple of favors?" Anything he needed, of course, twenty-four hours a day. "Is the General Census fully completed?"

"Oh, yes," Brennau boasted. "My old department brought it in, on time and under ..."

"Excellent. I'll give you some names, if I may."

"Of course!" Finding the address, service record and even medical history of every German was now as simple as typing into a search box, provided one had proper clearance. Keck had even taught Brennau to pass on a mantra to his engineers: Search, Don't Sort. And it had worked like a dream. "Anything else?"

He smiled. "Don't suppose you could spare me a car for a couple of weeks?"

"It would be my pleasure!" he said, patting his pocket for a notebook to find the right phone number. "I'll call Karl, and he'll get a BMW ready for you, one of the new roadsters. There's no speed limit on the new *Autobahn*, so you can ..."

"Something more," Keck forced himself to say, even against his ego's raging instincts, "inconspicuous?"

***

2 days later

Germany still had an internal security service, even if was a shadow of its former self, and Keck knew each one of his journeys had to be justifiable. 'Cabrera' had a legitimate interest in farming, and so here he was, driving across Germany on a fact-finding mission. He stopped at a tannery, which stank even worse than the cattle enclosures at Bonehouse, and then visited a burgeoning manufacturer of beef jerky. By then, his interest was waning and patience thinning, so he skipped one of the 'cover' stops on the route east. He wanted to reach his destination by dark, but the one farm in the Reich he actually *wanted* to visit was still four hours away.

Progressing down the *Autobahn* was closer to flying than driving. The mid-range BMW ticked over effortlessly at 110 mph, and Keck could sit in the middle lane, sliding past slower vehicles with graceful ease. He turned on the radio but found most of the news so disgusting that it angered him, and he accelerated past 120 mph without realizing it. Slowing again, he found a classical music station—Bach, Beethoven, and Schubert these days, not Wagner, *never* Wagner—and was happy to let the *Brandenburg Concertos* accompany the rest of his luxuriant journey.

He stopped for dinner at a large restaurant by the highway, another business built with the future in mind; the giant parking lot was nearly empty, but the service was impeccably attentive. He ate pork schnitzel and wrote some more in his journal before re-reading Brennau's secure telegram from the previous day.

"Gerhard Adolphus Keck," it read, "age forty. Caretaker and manager of the Keck Estate since 1942." *Only because I was deploying east again,* Keck thought, *and couldn't do it myself anymore.* "Married, 1937, to Esther Margareta Knabel, who died without issue, 1939, complications following surgery. Married again, 1940, to Brenda Dietrich, a war widow and former governess."

So many mundane young men snagging these strong, sharp, no-nonsense war-wives. Once the honeymoon was over, the marital dynamic must have reminded them of Basic Training.

"Estate was divided, December 1944, between Gerhard and his only surviving relative, Hans Paplisch."

Cousin Hans? God's truth, I thought he'd died in uniform, out east. Was he captured and repatriated, or ... ah, I see, yes. Early '45. According to Brennau's census, a quarter million Germans had gone into Soviet captivity during the reversals of early 1944, with half never to return. *Lucky bastard, our Hans.*

"Paplisch subdivision was sold. Plans for migrant housing. Gerhard subdivision partly leased to the state as a convalescent ward."

Finally, some good sense! Even if a greedy housing developer were to raze their elegant forests and plop down rows of identical little boxes on Paplisch's land, at least Gerhard's portion was dedicated to helping Germany's wounded veterans.

The gesture made him marginally less likely to kill them both.

***

Keck Estate area, eastern Germany, same day, late evening

After exiting the highway, Keck soon found he was completely lost. Nothing was familiar here, only three miles from the edge of the estate, where new roads carved routes which redefined the neighboring farmland. The old Henschel farmhouse was nowhere to be seen, until he found it rebuilt, a mile away. "Roads everywhere," he muttered. "Even through an old man's farmhouse, for God's sake."

Sometime past ten o'clock, he found it. The track was paved now, which made everything else seem different, like driving into a parallel universe. A light was on downstairs, and they'd surely hear his approach. As he turned the BMW to park by the farmhouse, his headlights swept their two barns, and a madly barking dog, chained-up. "You, dog, whatever your name is," Keck said as he got out of the car with a lot more reluctance than he'd expected, "you are *not* Misty." She'd be eighteen now; a forlorn hope.

"Are you the inspectors?" came an angry voice from the doorway of the farmhouse. "I told you people, I *told* you, the law doesn't allow unscheduled visits. Why didn't you pick up the phone like a normal person ..."

Then he saw the face, noted the thin, slightly hopeful smile, and found he was extending a hand. "My God ... Kris?"

"Cousin Hans," Keck said, the noun becoming a sunny adjective. "It is so late, and I am uninvited, and I must apologize a thousand times."

"You'll do no such thing!" Hans insisted. "Come in, come in. Jesus have mercy, where have you *been*?" He took the tired officer's coat and bid him loose his boots after such a long drive. "My Marie, she's up at her mother's in town. The old bird hasn't been looking too good, you see."

Depending on your behavior, we'll soon see whether Marie will be organizing one funeral, or two.

"I'm sorry for her troubles," said Keck. "I really don't want to be a nuisance, it's just I was given leave, and my next flight was out of Dresden, so I thought ..."

"Of course, of course!" Hans said. "A drink? Old Mr. Henschel's Riesling vines are three years old now, and he let me have a case after Lent. Not half bad, for the price." While he busied himself with a corkscrew, Keck headed to freshen up. Once the bathroom door closed, Hans almost dropped the bottle, setting it instead on the stone countertop.

He comes at night, when I'm here alone. No invitation. The Keck family's illustrious black sheep, the mysterious, much-promoted hero, returning like this? Something's up.

His father, Ernst Keck, thought his brother, Klaus, to be a good family man, a hard-working provider, but a terribly inflexible parent. Young Kris knew the sting of a belt across the rump, early and often, and to look at him now, with his glitzy BMW and neat, slicked-back hair, his manners so very polished, Hans had to admit the punishments had worked. None of the other Kecks had ever amounted to much, but this one, Kristock, had risen to become some kind of—what was it—an official? A *spy*, perhaps? Onkel Klaus knew only what he learned from Kris' sporadic, often bitter correspondence, and those read more like bulletins from his post than heartfelt letters home.

"The place looks good," Keck told his cousin as he returned and accepted a glass. "I didn't know what would happen, you know, with the war and everything."

"One hundred and eighty miles," Hans said, clinking glasses.

"The Soviets? In '44?" Keck asked, aghast. "*That* close?"

"It was the Armistice, or ..." Hans drew a finger across his throat. "We were done for, all of us. The Russians would have slaughtered us, then raised generations of godless communists on these farms."

"Then we were spared hell," said Keck, "by God's providence." *And by the judicious use of alien time travel technology, naturally.* Would the two be identical, to someone like Hans?

God had provided much else during the years of peace. "Marie's sister, Magda, has *seven* now. Six girls and a boy, the youngest."

"Poor little bastard," Keck chuckled. "Every felicitation to her, that's wonderful."

"And do you remember Horst the bakery boy, with the bicycle?"

"The way things are going, I wouldn't be surprised if they'd made him mayor."

"Close. He caught the eye of Lillian Richter, you know, the—"

"The girl whose father owns Richter Pharmaceuticals?" He whistled. "Nice catch, Horst."

"Biggest goddamned wedding I was ever at. Three days, it went on!"

Keck let Hans prattle like this, recounting the tiny ups-and-downs of a dozen meaningless existences. He was trying to care, he told himself, but the distraction of the land sale was overwhelming. Finally, Hans circuitously brought it up. "You see, the southern plot was going to be taxed like a dairy pasture, but we plowed that under and re-sowed with grain, you know, for the ethanol. We'd not have broken even, especially with prices going loopy every couple of years."

Keck listened with the impatience of someone with much to say. *And probably at least one thing to do.* First, he nodded. "You did the mathematics, Hans. You sat down and worked it out. You know better than I do."

Forced to depart from the script, Hans just blinked.

"I was away, doing *my* job, and *your* job here was to make good decisions for the Keck Estate."

Hans always called it simply The Farms, which spoke eloquently of the gap between the two men. "That's ... kind of you to say, uh, Kris. It wasn't an easy decision, you have to know. Weeks and weeks, we puzzled over it."

Keck set down his wine glass. "You should have puzzled a little longer."

Hans clutched his, nervous now.

"You know who's coming to live on that land, don't you?"

"The district council told us it was for social housing."

"For *refugees!*" Keck bellowed. "Detritus from the world's many other calamities."

"People whom a Christian would help, if they could," Hans retorted, getting to his feet.

"People," Keck screamed back, "we fought a fucking *war* to keep out! But *you invited* them here!" All pretense was lost now, the true meaning of the visit finally clear. "Pregnant Indian girls, and toothless crones, and radicalized zealots from tribal militias. You welcomed the contagious, and the feeble-minded, onto *my* family's land."

"Our family is the same one, Kris," he said, arms outstretched. "We were raised playing in the same meadows. You'll always be family, however long it is between visits."

"Oh, you misunderstand," Keck said, drawing his pistol from his waistband. "This visit is most certainly my *last*."

***

He carried on east once it was done. The estate nauseated him now, a shrunken embarrassment of a place. Hans' young son would run the place now, someone who could more easily be made to delay the land sale. And eventually scrap the idea altogether, he hoped.

And to think he'd dreamed of his own coat of arms, and the dignifying elevation to Von Keck. Then, a comfortably rebuilt homestead, a family of his own.

He slept at a motel near the highway, but had disturbed dreams of being pushed and pulled, competed over. He woke finally at four and took time only to shower before continuing east. The empty lanes on either side of the BMW gave the journey a luxuriant feel, as though he'd been given free rein at the company's test track. At such speeds, it took only two hours, and then, tired and hungry but undeterred, he found himself actually staring up at the sign, even as groups of visitors walked past him, into the complex.

Arbeits Machts Frei.

He knew by now that the camp system was essentially gone. A handful of the old facilities were in use as mental institutions but faced closure and demolition. For Keck, it was a capitulation to the raw stupidity of racial equality, a tragicomedic about-face, performed naked, in front of the world, as if to say, "Look, everyone! Come and see! In our *Neues Deutschland,* our pests are our friends, and our friends are insane dictators who deserve to be toppled!"

It was enough to give him whiplash. Or a bilious eruption onto the gravel, something he averted only narrowly. *Courage, Keck. We must see what lies they're telling themselves.* Then, he might know how to throw the process into reverse, by using those same pressure-points which made the people *demand* action: jobs and crime. They'd vote for someone who made those two issues the very center of their promise to the people, all while new agents of the Fourth Reich re-kindled enthusiasm for 'final' solutions. Past experience would help guide secrecy and efficiency. At last, there would be a national celebration, a Germany unimpeded by squalid invaders, newly scrubbed clean.

The docent began with statistics. "Only one other leader has ordered so many put to death in such a short span, and that was Ghenghis Khan. The world will judge the two alongside each other, perhaps."

But Keck was overwhelmed with pride. Each great civilization yearned to create something everlasting, and in the machinery of death surrounding them, Germany had shown a great power to cleanse herself. Like London's giant Victorian sewer system, perhaps, carrying away the city's filth. At each staggering figure, each indictment of the Nazis' unique barbarism, he thrilled inwardly.

Finally, he chose to step away from the tour and enjoy some of the areas alone. Much was preserved exactly as it had been when the last canister of Zyklon-B was emptied. The loss of such efficient functionality bothered Keck, but then, new methods would surely emerge.

There, inspired amid the crumbling concrete of the gas chambers, he saw a brilliant future. The world would see Germany not humiliated and infested by her pests but roused to new greatness by *cleansing every last one.*

***

'Domstadt,' Bavaria, the following day

"This is complete fucking chaos," he said to the otherwise empty interior of the BMW. The tailback stretched for nearly two miles, and both vehicles and drivers were starting to overheat. Behind him, a VW van full of students were passing the delay with *We Shall Overcome*, to Keck's cringing distaste. There were hippy types everywhere, and he could have sworn he smelled marijuana. "People have died for less," he seethed, watching their naive singalong in the car's mirrors.

He shook off the distraction. Ahead of him, beyond the snarl of traffic, was The Mountain. Only, that was no longer strictly true. *Der Dom* had become a jagged, alien boulder-field, only now beginning to re-green itself with intrepid seeds blown in from more peaceful valleys. Its once-sharp flanks were overwhelmed with rocky debris from the collapsing peak. To the traveler, walking in from the forest, what could be called the core of the mountain would be almost completely hidden by the remains of its former self.

"Officer, what's the hold-up?" he demanded of a policeman who was facing many such questions.

Mercifully, the man took pity on what appeared to be a confused Spanish tourist in a well-chosen hire car. "Protest at The Hill again."

"Who's protesting?" 'Cabrera' asked, disappointed to hear the once-proud *Zitternberg* so demoted.

"Who? Everybody!" The officer finished answering another irate motorist, and then stepped to Keck's window. "You're a visitor?"

"Yes, from Argentina. On business," he said by way of an opening. "Why are they there?"

"Well, these days, people can think whatever they like," the officer said. "Some say there are ghosts there, or alien beings, or magical dwarves. Every bullshit theory you could make up, someone's already written a goddamned book about it. Once the student types get their hands on this stuff ..." He tailed off, waved to the fuming line of traffic. "We'll all have to be patient today, sir."

It took another hour; Keck's use of the steering wheel as a stress toy was starting to leave marks. "Follow the car in front of you," the gate official said. "Do not leave your vehicle."

Dismayed, Keck nevertheless complied. He'd hoped for some kind of access to the tunnels where the fighting had taken place. "Why haven't they dug out some of this rock by now?" he asked the BMW.

Visitors' facilities were minimal. "By order of the Bavarian state government, access to the viewing point for *Der Dom* is strictly limited to seventy-five persons per day," he read in the introductory brochure handed to him by another stern-faced official. The atmosphere of the place was severe, almost reverent, as though they feared the mountain and what it might do.

"The viewing platform?" Keck complained to the car. "One can only *see* the ruins?"

But what ruins they were. Directed to a parking space in the shadow of the looming wreck, and then literally tethered to his assigned tour group, Keck shuffled together with them along a wooden walkway, following a guide.

"The research center was in the galleries of the old salt mine," the group were told. "A small team was developing synthetic fuels to help bring light and warmth to German homes during wartime winters. And for this, the British punished them with the heaviest special-weapons raid of the whole war." The anticipated mutters of objection emanated from the group. "To destroy a fuel research station, Lancasters demolished an entire mountain."

"War is insanity!" called out one of the group.

"If it really helped to stop the war, they could've brought down *two* mountains, for all I care!" said an elderly woman.

"The very same week, it was!" another tourist wanted them all to know. "Out of nowhere, we had a revolution against Hitler, and then an agreement to end the war! A second armistice, but with honor!"

This was approved by the group, with only a couple of detractors; still, some had not come to terms with Germany's great, global rapprochement. "All within *days* of what happened here," the man said in conclusion.

"It's not a coincidence. It can't be."

"You mean, if it was so important, it couldn't have been a simple fuel lab, like he said?"

The tour guide was as familiar with crowd control as he was with the 'received' history of the mountain. "Ladies and gentlemen, unfortunately, there isn't time to stop our tour and debate. If you recall, up until only a year ago, visitors still wore gas masks because of the lingering tabun gas, and we don't want anyone becoming ill up here."

This shut down most of the discussion, except two students, who continued animatedly agreeing with each other in whispers.

"We think as many as thirteen of the British 'special weapons' hit the mountain. The material you're standing on," the guide said, "was excavated from a depth of twenty meters by the explosion. Some of it was thrown three hundred meters out to the side."

"Could the old mine be explored again, one day?" asked Cabrera. Others were keen to hear the guide on this, too.

"No," he said. "There'd be no point. Nothing could be recovered after an event of this magnitude. The enemy paratroopers were all crushed to smithereens, alive or dead, so we'll never know why they were so determined to destroy the lab."

"That's a little pessimistic," countered Cabrera.

"Well, the research station is gone, and all the galleries, so that's that. It'd take a hundred years to excavate down. Digging here is banned *completely* by the state government, by the way."

The group sagged, having quietly hoped for some sliver of an answer.

"Alright, our next stop is just around those green boulders there. We'll be able to see the rough location of Tabun Point. This is where the local commander decided to use chemical weapons on the enemy paratroopers, one of the most important decisions of the war, and maybe one reason why the Allies came to the negotiating table so quickly. Nobody wanted that stuff being dumped in the sky over their capitals, I guess."

Cabrera held the guide as unnecessarily pessimistic, but only for a few more minutes, until the monumental scale of the challenge became clear. A regiment of Titans had apparently assailed the mountain with pickaxes, chopping great pieces out of its slopes to form a slowly heaving river of flinty debris which threatened the valley beyond. By the time these twentieth-century Titans were done, *Der Dom* was smashed to a stunted cone shape, its entire peak artlessly hacked off. "By all the saints, I can't imagine how you'd do it," he said quietly to himself.

"The Chinese say you can move a mountain by first carrying away small stones," the elderly tourist reminded them all.

The guide knew the quote perfectly well already. "That might be true, but we're talking about a *billion tons* of small stones."

Even the most ardent optimist would have yielded, Keck saw. One could more easily have adjusted the orbit of a planet.

No, it was as obvious as it was gut-wrenching: recovery of the time device was simply impossible.

***

Hamburg, the next day

Short on fuel, he left the highway an hour short of Hamburg and found an agreeable meal in a restaurant run by a group of grizzled artillery veterans who'd converted a huge barn. Piles of sausage, roast vegetables, and even half-decent beer restored Keck, though he deliberately ate in the quieter corner of the barn.

The journey had begun to bother him. A sensation only a few hours old, it was hard to pin down, but as he ate and drank and ignored the carousing and inebriation and pork fat splattering around him, a voice cut through with crystal clarity:

You're afraid to meet your own child.

Could Brennau have been wrong? Could the census-taker have made a mistake?

The record was routine—a child of five, born to one Anna Magdalena Schmid. The memory of her was like a sunlit park, ever welcoming and congenial. In his mind, and in his loins—*that's for goddamned certain*—the encounter meant far more than just a few hours in a comfortable bed. It was his Statement to the Universe, his act of defiance against fate, right before it would drag him down to the docks and force him into the all-male confines of U-99X.

The memory of her youthful innocence, her supple smoothness, distracted him almost completely from the Autobahn, and he reduced his cruise speed to 95 mph until the feelings left him.

And you're afraid to meet the child's mother.

A 'comfort girl,' she'd been, in essence. Someone to temper the cauldron of fear which roiled in every deploying soldier's gut. But she hadn't been offering herself at the docks; his partner in the genetic lottery was not, at the very least, a 'lady of the evening,' but a well brought-up Christian girl who'd simply found a dashing SS captain overwhelmingly attractive. She was only human, after all.

And you're definitely afraid there might be a man, 'parenting' your child in your stead.

He'd killed Hans Paplisch for selling family land to accommodate human refuse—*Untermenschen* from the sodden jungles of the world, unfit and unworthy. What in God's name would he do upon finding that his *child* was cast adrift, parted by events from the good ship of moral conduct? If the 'father' was a drunk ... No, the greater problem in Hamburg was the new range of opiate drugs. "You're welcome," Keck muttered, yet again, and if he was using, perhaps to obliterate memories of the war.

Will the child look like me?

The thought surprised him. He'd contemplated other genetic traits, but never appearance. Would he see himself in the boy's eyes? In the line of his jaw, his bearing, his laugh? Would he see something of the playful child Keck had been before the demands of family and war stripped him of so much?

The house was in a smart row which had been spared the firestorms of '44. The coal-blackened brick was at least solid; it was a good home, he saw, neat and orderly with a small vegetable patch out front. He drove by slowly, and then again, seeing no movement but finding the street pleasingly tranquil on this quiet afternoon.

She might be at home, making plum jam in the parlor, or reading by the fire. Would she beam with delight and throw herself into his arms? Or berate him for a reprobate, a fool? Another selfish wartime shirker? A witless would-be Casanova with offspring scattered carelessly all over Europe?

You can't go in there.

No one would know.

She knows your real first name, whispered in the dark. She knows you were deploying from Hamburg, just when U-99X left for Argentina. And she doesn't know Cabrera.

Could he pass off the mustache, the carefully revised haircut, as those of a demobilized veteran searching for a more modern look?

No, a woman remembers. And then, she'll wonder what the fuck you're doing in Hamburg, five years later, wearing a disguise.

After so much anticipation and so many nights in his bunk at Bonehouse, spent wondering, it was awful to be so close without meeting them.

And so, he spoke with a local attorney the following morning, and drew up a financial instrument which would mature on the child's twelfth birthday, and another which would provide a lump sum for college tuition, on his eighteenth. There would be a letter, too, on the day of his majority, encouraging him to see the world and learn everything he could. Leaving it with the attorneys, to be handed to the boy on his birthday, he felt the smallest glimmer of hope; in a chaotic world, his offspring would have a modest but important head-start.

A small secular charity appeared to be responsible, and there was an address in East Prussia, but the boy's letters of thanks, sent over years, would all go unanswered.

7

Hollywoodland

2 to 3 weeks after Inge's arrival at Bonehouse, spring 1945

In the end, they'd decided the flight would be worth the risk.

Two former *Luftwaffe* pilots brought their giant seaplane skimming in to land just off the Argentine coast, and then dockyard laborers ferried crates of supplies to a smaller aircraft, a modified Ju-52, which could 'land on a Pfennig,' according to the intrepid pilot, Helmut Wolf. They made a dozen journeys to Bonehouse, and to its two satellite camps, each mercifully without incident. The fresh fruit, LPs, and tobacco were cheered the loudest, except for the bag of mail from the Reich, of course.

On their final flight with the Ju-52, back to the coast to reclaim their waiting seaplane, Wolf and his co-pilot were accompanied by a single passenger, seated quietly in the drop seat behind them. It took her a while to become chatty, but after she warmed up, the two pilots found her to be solid entertainment. The long flight passed while she tried out a few different 'characters'—the haughty socialite, the imperious school ma'am, the alluring and waifish vicar's daughter. Each reacted hilariously to the view from the window, or to things the pilots said. "God, it's a long way down, *innit?*" she asked the spluttering pair, in character as her 'Hamburg Hooker.' "I could drop my knickers here and they wouldn't hit the ground for hours!"

They showered her with applause. "Just practicing my routine," she seemed to joke, though it was perfectly true. She napped for part of the journey, awaking an hour after dawn as the big plane swooped low over a startlingly blue Caribbean.

"A very warm welcome," Wolf said, "to Curacao. The only *other* German colony in the Americas," and the only friendly harbor in the Caribbean. At the moment of touchdown, everything was azure ocean and dancing spray, and then the rumbling calmed and they briefly became mariners once more. Slightly numb and assaulted by the equatorial heat, Inge stepped down into a small local boat which took them through a maze of fishing vessels, nets and—strangely—tourist boats crammed with Europeans. Their white skin was already melting to a rare, roast-beef pink under the ceaseless flame-thrower of the sun. This, and their pronounced corpulence, marked them out as Germans. No one else behaved with such entitlement these days when abroad.

Wolf insisted on two rest days, and gave Inge the run of Curacao, a pleasant colonial outpost ceded to Germany by the Dutch during the Armistice. She found a good restaurant and made it her home for an afternoon, writing letters and sampling most of the menu. The red snapper, a fish she'd never heard of, was *very* good when blackened, with lime and salsa. It made her ravenous for the limitless food choices of California, just another reason she was anxious to get going. In the evening, and later, she found that the pilots, though exceptional in the air, were each only passable in bed.

The following day was spent preparing for the second leg of the journey, and an hour before sunset, fueling could begin while Inge's various things were loaded and prepared. With just enough light left to see the horizon, the monster's six engines churned, and the seaplane plowed its own watery runway, lifting off and turning north once more.

But not back to Germany. Wolf would not make his usual clandestine refueling sojourn in the Atlantic. Instead, in dark, foggy, intemperate conditions, but with just enough moonlight, they slid into the gap between British Honduras and Cuba and headed out over the Gulf of Mexico.

Sunset approached, and their mission became a military one. The plane's massive fuel tanks easily drained a conventional fuel truck parked right by the jetty. Helmut filed a legitimate flight plan but would follow it for illegitimate purposes. He'd considered flying an 'intruder' profile, mingling with the sparse commercial and military traffic to avoid detection, but it was safer just to file the paperwork. The aircraft would land where it was supposed to, at a pier in southern California, but it would also be dropping off a passenger on the way.

Inge was alive with excitement about her upcoming mission, hardly able to think of anything else, but she kept up her theatrical practice with the boys; they loved her 'spoiled princess' bit, though her English was already streets ahead of theirs.

"This all seems a little much," Inge said, hands on hips as she looked at the mass of equipment to be delivered. "I mean, couldn't someone just row a gal ashore, like before?"

"Not this time, I'm afraid," Wolf told her, giving her shapely ass a slap.

"I could get used to that kind of treatment."

He simply arched an eyebrow, unsure which treatment she meant—being elegantly rowed, or less than elegantly slapped.

"We have to do it this way. The plane, you understand," said Helmut, and of course, she did. Their modifications dictated her insertion method—the plane offered a quiet night-time ride cross the United States, but nowhere to land besides lakes or the coast, clandestine or otherwise. "Even without landing gear, as we are, *Big Boy* is way too heavy to land on concrete."

But Inge continued to argue her case during the long hours of the flight. Even a few minutes before their approach to her drop zone. "But, couldn't I just land with you, on the coast?"

"We've been over this," said Wolf. "It would put you on their immigration books."

Inge tried, "Not if we landed without them knowing."

"M'lady," Helmut cautioned, "have you ever attempted a night-time seaplane landing in enemy surf?"

"And what about all these crates?" the co-pilot wanted to know. "How are you going to transfer them?"

"Hire someone to drive them to the ..."

"Customs Inspection would come first."

"Out of the question," she objected.

"Then we have to do it this way." Two different modern devices confirmed his geographical position, as well as speed and altitude, though both still used dials. "And we're almost there."

"I'm the one who has to do it this way," Inge pouted. "You get to land, all comfortable and warm."

"Warm? We're dropping you into California. You'll do just fine. And as for comfort," Wolf grinned, "I'm told there are plenty of strong, tanned surfers who'd just love to ..."

"Jealous?" she whispered.

"Get out of here already, you crazy bitch," Helmut told her fondly, "before the Americans realize this big old thing isn't what I said it was."

She pecked his cheek like a daughter thanking her father for the ride to the party. "I'll call in as soon as I can."

"Be safe!"

The co-pilot helped her through the final checks, but she knew she was ready to go. *Be safe*, is that what he'd said? Helmut knew little of her mission; they could only be told so much, for security's sake. *Besides, where's the fun in being 'safe' all the time?*

She tried not to hold her breath as she jumped, but it was instinctive, as though she would shortly splash into water. Instead, the upward snap of the parachute's opening expelled all of Inge's air in a giggle of unconfined excitement. "I'm flying!" she laughed, kicking her feet. The engine noise and the cold faded to memory, and her descent became a slow-motion tour of the orchards and farms laid out beneath her in moonlit serenity. Three parcels of supplies preceded her from the seaplane, and she turned and spotted all three, happily under full canopies. First one, then a second, touched down near where a road bisected a plowed field.

Her own landing was even worse than the training, a heavy, graceless flop into the dirt. Bruised and winded, she struggled to control an unruly parachute in the middle of an otherwise silent, broad field. The scents were of agriculture, of the baked-hard dryness of the daytime and the freshness of night air. She found her bearings and began gathering her equipment at the fence line near the road—both for inventory, and in case she was discovered and needed to destroy it. Everything looked intact, including the precious glass vials in their protective rubber containers.

Then she was just waiting, taking a few minutes to sit and enjoy the moment. She was in *America!* The air felt alive with promise, and a late thunderstorm over to the west, felt like a fanfare of welcome.

Right on midnight, triple-flashed headlights gave her the signal, and she emerged from her crouch behind the fence line to see a pickup truck, waiting in darkness, flanked by two men. They beckoned to her, and a third headed off across the field to the crates, shrouded under their collapsed, white parachutes.

The entire Nazi network in North America just expanded by twenty-five percent, and yet we'll all fit comfortably in a pickup truck. There was a great deal to be done.

But first came the warm smiles and embraces. Everyone had taken enormous risks to be here, they agreed.

"This is a new platform," one of her new mini-cohort announced. "The launch pad for great things!"

Oh, God, she smirked to herself, *another of Zimmer's cosmic dreamers.*

"I prefer not to make promises I can't keep," Inge told the three men as they prepared to drive back toward town, and the railway station. "So, for now, let's just say that the Americans are in for something special."

She let herself relax once they reached the main road, trusting these three at least to keep an eye out. She began to doze, her head already dancing with her dream-of-choice.

Some of them, I will make heroes. She carried it now, there inside her jacket, a cluster of vials, warmed by her heart: the secrets of rejuvenation. Six identical doses of Keck's first 'working prototype' for the Elixir of Life itself. *Yes, some of them, I will make immortals.*

And others, she smiled sleepily, *I will purposefully destroy.*

***

Aboard the passenger airship *Centurion*, 1 month after Asphodel arrival

A waiter whisked across the red carpet of the busy little lounge and set down two cocktails just as the young couple were recounting the funniest part of the story.

"And you said, something like, 'But, sergeant, they've *urgently* requested our presence,'" Jillian remembered, impersonating a stern-faced Yanis.

"Wartime travel restrictions still in effect, ain't they?" Yanis recounted in a lazy, civil servant accent, his take on the most unimaginative, least helpful British pen-pusher. The man had been wittering on about 'tightened regulations on non-essential travel' when Yanis chose to suddenly and decisively pull rank. Not since the mine had he given into his urge to just *lose his temper*.

"The look on that guy's face," she said after her first sip. Their paperwork was fast-tracked—*work of national importance in Washington, D.C.*—and permitted them a two-week journey on 'any reasonable route.' "The thing is," she told Yanis, "encounters like that make me rather determined to spend an entirely *unreasonable* amount of Uncle Sam's money." Not least on a new wardrobe for them both; a green evening dress and a very smart tux gave them exactly the look they'd hoped for.

Luxury ocean liners, although enjoying a renaissance, were generally crammed with boisterous, *nouveau riche* Germans. So, when Jillian noticed another, quite different option, gratifyingly more costly still, she was insistent. There was a double cabin available. The brochure promised a pianist, and they were already getting to know the highly creative barman. With no hydrogen, the cooks could *flambé* and sizzle; on the first night, with everything fresh, the chef often liked to show off. Yanis was easily persuaded that five uneventful days in one of the new, heated, pressurized gondolas, slipping west over the Atlantic, sounded like the perfect break.

Even if it would lead them straight into a massively important secret mission.

"Here's to, um, the next step," she said to Yanis, raising her Manhattan to meet his.

"Gonna be something else," Yanis promised, clinking glasses and taking a sip. "Wow, this is pretty good."

"Should be. It cost the Pentagon a fortune."

"Just by telling them not to bother with 'Star Wars,' we've saved them a hundred billion." His eyes were drawn to the broad windows opposite them; their view from 25,000 feet was of the Bristol Channel, a spacious dark-brown swath, busy with vessels of all kinds. "Anyway, 'Miss Davidoff,' are you ready to make some movies?" Yanis asked, sipping again. It really was delicious, and doubly so on Uncle Sam's dime.

She sighed. "Kinda." Around them, people sat in modernist armchairs of leather and chrome, reading newspapers, often while smoking, or stood at the bar with cocktail, trying to look fashionable and generally succeeding magnificently. There would be interesting opportunities to people-watch during this five-day journey. "The problem is ... well, our plan, really," she said, troubled. "It just doesn't feel right to me."

"What do you mean, it doesn't *feel* right?" Yanis saw no complications, either moral or otherwise. It was also, by some way, their best shot at infiltrating Fountain.

"You're not feeling even a little bit guilty about, I don't know, say, imaginary future copyright infringement?" asked Jillian pointedly.

"In our case, that would be a victimless crime," argued Yanis.

"Doesn't feel that way to me."

"Well, you keep reminding me you're an investigator. What's a 'feeling' got to do with it? The fact is," he reminded her, still buzzing with the brilliance of the plan, "we've got sixty years of red-hot movie ideas in our heads. Ideas no one has ever had."

"Yes," she agreed cautiously, "and that's all well and good ..."

"But ..." Yanis said for her. He knew their plan bothered Jillian, but Yanis was convinced by its expediency. Successfully spying on a whole raft of aging Hollywood elites would be far easier as a script-guru than as a jobbing actor or a lowly technician.

"But they're someone *else's* ideas," objected Jillian. "The victim in your 'victimless' crime."

"Let's say," Yanis proposed, "that we invent a device just like one that's patented in our time. What then?"

"That's different. We need special skills to mock-up an iPhone, but we only need to have seen the movie to steal its script."

He puffed out his cheeks. "Well, if it makes you feel better, we could send half of our royalties to the Spielberg estate, and ... oh, no, wait, we *can't* because he's, like, five years old, and his parents wouldn't know what the hell we were talking about."

"But it's *stealing* characters and plot lines."

"Besides, he couldn't have made those movies if the Nazis hadn't lost the war, and in this timeline, there was an Armistice."

"*Stealing* other people's jokes."

"What, you're going to arrest me for taking a movie plot without permission?"

"*Stealing*," she repeated.

"*Adapting* a plot for a film," he insisted, "one which otherwise won't be made for decades! We'll be bringing in great ideas, and that'll open the right doors."

"Open them by just ripping people off left, right, and center."

"It's making use of our resources, Jill. I mean, if you think we should get jobs sweeping the studio floors, if you think we'll meet some really major, serious, *key* people, just by rubbing shoulders with lighting directors and prop handlers, then fine. But the *interesting* types," he leaned in closer, "the ones who might have heard from you-know-who in regard to you-know-what, going on down south in you-know-where," he leaned back, "*they* spend all day reading scripts and deciding where to invest their cash. To meet *them*, we need a movie idea that's coming in nice and slow, right over the plate, ready to be smacked out of the stadium."

Beyond the moral problems were some practical ones. "But, I've never written a movie script before," Jillian objected.

"Judging from the kind of dialogue some screenwriters include in films, neither have they! Besides, it's not like we're building a rocket. If it doesn't work, there's no harm done. We just go elsewhere or try a different script."

"We don't *have* a script."

"Well," he said, bringing out his black-bound notebook, "let's see about changing that, maybe?"

There was plenty of time for brainstorming, and for other things; the Zeppelin, despite its upgrades, needed eighty hours to cross the Atlantic. "It makes up for its steady pace," Jillian read to Yanis during a break from people-watching and stealing James Bond plots, "by connecting to a global airship network.' You can be anywhere in a week, I think this says." She held up a schedule which spanned the world. "No wonder Berliners call Lufthansa The Flying Railroad."

Not everyone was convinced, even those who'd parted with money for a ticket. Across the lounge, a white-haired old Briton, one of those bullish, parliamentary types, was complaining loudly to his wife. "It's unsafe! Wholly and unacceptably unsafe! Why, it's like the demented, bastard child of the *Titanic* and the *Hindenburg*." Most of the lounge heard this oration from the man's lounge chair near the piano. The player, to his credit, kept on tinkling; on his ninth voyage, he'd seen his share of eccentric passengers. The elderly complainer wasn't done. "And now the waiter," the man pointed accusingly, "tells me we're going to see *German military aircraft*, 'escorting' us partway to Canada!"

While the man's wife tried alternately to settle her husband, and to smile in placation at the surprised passengers seated around them, Yanis regained Jillian's attention. "Hey, it's okay. Ignore that old idiot. The Germans are just showing off their new long-range jets. Airships and their rich passengers always generate positive press."

"Provided everything goes to plan." As an airship neophyte, and a member of a secret intelligence organization, she had no wish to end up in the newspapers for the wrong reasons.

The old man was still haranguing his wife, who kept patiently sighing and hoping the old codger might one day learn some god-damned manners. "And look at us! *Hanging* here, like a huge kite without its string! It's intolerable!"

"Dude, come on," Yanis pleaded, *sotto voce*, "I thought everyone knew these things are filled with—"

"Non-flammable helium," said Jillian, cutting him off like a scalpel. "I *was* ignoring him. But who's the guy in the grey suit, three tables closer toward the windows from the hysterical old geezer?"

Yanis honed in and found the suited figure. He was pale, in his forties perhaps but with thinning hair. He sat legs crossed, smoking a cigarette, but his eyes were attentive. Yanis didn't recognize him. "No idea, sorry."

"Maybe a security guy? For one of the passengers?"

"Or the airline?" Nothing identified him as such explicitly, but it was the way the man's eyes swept the passenger lounge, not so much admiring the gathered cognoscenti, but assessing them.

"Look away," warned Jillian. "He'll make you."

"Make me do what?" he said, glancing at her, then back at the enigmatic, smoking figure.

"*Make* you, I mean. Identify you."

"As whom? Neither of us are born yet, and there's no record of us even—"

"I said look *away*," she growled.

"Okay, but a minute ago, you said to look at him."

"Not so bloody obviously. You must've made eye contact." She sounded appalled.

"Shit. I'm sorry." His eyes gripped the carpet now instead, which made him feel more ridiculous still. "Who do you think he is?"

"I just asked *you* that." She was checking furtively on the man, but then also in every other direction, as though anticipating a flanking threat. "Not the moment for some high-stakes James Bond fight scene," Jillian muttered.

"We could re-enact the one from *Indiana Jones* where he throws the Nazi out of the window for having no ticket," Yanis recommended, not yet sure how worried to be by this calm, observing stranger.

"Shut the hell up." Suddenly, it was time to be worried. "He's coming toward us." Certain their bags would be searched by German, British, Canadian, or American immigration officials, Jillian hadn't packed a handgun, but she reached for her purse anyway. "Fuck." She thought quickly. "Yanis, If I say, 'Glad to meet you,' hit him in the face with the ashtray."

The broad, thick glass looked fatally solid. "Roger that."

She rose with a charm which seemed effortless, making herself tall and instantly feminine. But to gather herself, so quickly in those scant seconds before she extended her hand to the oncoming gentleman, took more composure than she knew she had. "Jean Davidoff," she said, "always nice to make the acquaintance of fellow passenger." Her British accent had become a lot closer to *Are You Being Served* than to *Eastenders*. Very deliberately, Yanis knew.

The man stopped in partly disinterested surprise. "Uh, yeah. Hi, I guess. I'm Eli Caan."

"Nice to meet you. And this is Mister George Tower," she said, introducing Yanis, whose eyes had just left the hefty ashtray.

Caan shook his hand, but as he did so, the newcomer was awkward, all angles and elbows. Either he was unsure physically how to smile, Yanis figured, or was faking it. "Uh, hey, how ya doing?" asked Caan.

"Just fine, just fine," he said, losing his twenty-first century mannerisms and trying his best to sound '50s. "Isn't the view simply splendid?" Though a little more clouded than before, it was still worth a look. "Ireland will be coming up soon," guessed Yanis.

"Sure, yeah, splendid." The man kept his focus on Jillian and Yanis, however. "Gets a little old over the water, they tell me. But," he added with an awkward weight, "making friends is the way to go."

"Sure," Yanis said amiably, thinking the guy a weirdo.

"Are you traveling all the way to New York?" Jillian asked.

"Uh, well," he said, uncomfortable without any apparent reason, "that kinda depends on the two of you, really, doesn't it?"

Yanis' threat sensors, already warmed up, now became overloaded. "The hell you talking about, buddy?" he hissed. When Caan had no immediate reply, Yanis said, "Or should I ask a little louder, maybe get security?"

"Relax, for Christ's sake. Didn't you hear the pass phrase? *Making friends is the way to go?*"

"Huh?" He hated moments like this, when he felt left behind by events he'd himself initiated.

"Fella, I'm Eli Caan. I'm your confidential intelligence contact for Prophet."

"Our ... you're our ... what's that now?" Jillian said, amazed she'd just heard all those words spoken out loud.

But Yanis was already smiling, both at his own macho overreaction, and at Caan's good-natured bumbling. "I don't think you're really supposed to tell anyone that."

"Yeah, I know," he said, appealing to the heavens, "but I've never done one of these before, and I didn't really know how to come clean with you. Didn't anyone tell you to expect a friend on the airship? And the pass phrase?" he asked again.

"They might have," said Yanis, a little embarrassed, "but there were so many instructions."

Jillian had a little dig, but it was really a criticism of them both. "Spies are supposed to be able to remember instructions, *George.*"

"I've been ... kind of winging it. Haven't you, *Jean?*"

Jillian tried to fill the gap but couldn't. "I thought we were meeting someone at the airport in Newhaven, or wherever it is. There really was a lot to absorb." She scowled defensively at them both. "It's not like I could write it down for easy reference."

Feeling as storm-tossed by events as ever, and already two Manhattans deep, Yanis confessed. "I thought they meant, you know, it's a long trip, so maybe meet some new people, make conversation, help pass the time."

"Wow, Mr. Superspy," laughed Jillian.

"Sorry. Guess it worked out, all the same."

Eli was signaling for one of the bar staff. "Well, I do try to pass time in good company, as they say. What do you say to a pitcher of those Manhattans, and then maybe we'll figure out what the fuck we're all doing up here."

More affable and less nervous by the moment, Caan made sure he had their names and basic biographies straight by the time the pitcher arrived. "So, what did they tell *you*, if it's alright for me to ask first?"

"That you're completely plugged in to Hollywood and can put us in the same room as lots of influential people."

"I don't know about that," Caan said, reaching inside his jacket for cigarettes. "I'm no Hollywood hotshot. I just made some movies, stateside, for Stuart Menzies and his people."

"Propaganda movies?" Yanis guessed.

"War bonds, enlistment," he explained, "the morale-booster before the main picture. He helped adjust …" The waiter arrived and was efficient, but Caan wouldn't even look at Yanis and Jillian until he was gone. He lit a cigarette in a smooth, practiced motion involving only a flicker of his jacket, and then the click of the lighter. Even the smoke seemed to disappear behind and below him. If he wasn't a spy, Yanis reasoned, he'd certainly have played a convincing one on TV.

"Menzies wanted us to achieve certain psychological effects. Gave us important words to include, that kind of thing."

"Not exactly Oscar-winning stuff," said Jillian.

"Maybe not," he chuckled, "but MI6 paid better than the bloody studios. Worth every penny, too, we were. Craftsmanship." He puffed on his cigarette. "You don't see much of that these days."

The couple conferred discreetly for a few moments, then Jillian spoke for them both. "Okay, Mister Craftsman," she said with a smile. Caan was an odd fish, but the pair were glad to have made contact with their OSS liaison, in any event. "How do you propose we get done what needs to be done?"

"It's a matter of using people I know. They might know others who can be helpful."

"Networking," Yanis said.

"Yeah." He brightened a little, as though habitually engaged by novelty of any kind. "Networking, nice. I'm going to *network* the hell out of my buddies in Tinseltown, and they're gonna put you in the same place as a particular category of people," he said, puffing on his cigarette. "I guess all I need is to know who."

"Nazis."

"No fucking shit!" he exclaimed in a splutter of hot smoke, then apologized through some lengthy, distracting coughing. "Gotta switch to filters," he finally admitted.

Once he was done, Yanis made to confront him; given the importance of tracking down Keck and the Fountain members, he'd expected Caan would have been thoroughly briefed. "They didn't tell you about the mission?"

"They said," Eli managed, handkerchief to this face, "you two needed to meet the best in the business, especially the older crowd who had a—*how the heck did he say it, that old fucker, Menzies*—a full Rolodex."

Caan was the first American to swear in front of Jillian without apologizing, and she liked it immediately. "Correct."

"But he didn't say *anything* about cock-sucking Nazis," said Caan, visibly uncomfortable.

"That's not us, you realize," Yanis clarified. "I'm Jewish. Here to eradicate a terrible, lingering Nazi threat, probably based in South America."

"And I'm not Jewish," Jillian said, "as far as I know, but I'm buggered if Kristock Keck is going to personally shape the human gene pool."

"I'm buggered, also," Yanis said, still not completely sure what it meant.

"Okay, you can tell me in a minute all about Kristy and Gene and their pool. I'm sure it's a great story, but first, tell me one thing, and tell me straight, alright?"

Yanis wiped his lips with his embossed napkin. "After two of these things, I'm not completely sure, but go ahead and ask."

"Are you two actually from the future?"

"I was born in 1981," Yanis said, "in Belgrade, Montana."

"And I will have been born ... No, wait..."

Yanis tried, "You were to have will been birthed..."

"*Are* to have going to been birthed?"

Caan wasn't in the mood. "Prove it to me, Buck Rogers, or we don't got a deal here."

Jillian frowned apologetically. The man had obviously upturned his career to accompany them across the Atlantic on this lunacy of a flying invention which unnerved Caan as surely as it scared the curmudgeon in the smoking jacket. As a World War II veteran, Caan just dealt with it better. "We knew you'd ask about that," said Jillian.

"We don't have a huge number of physical objects from our own time," Yanis explained briefly, "but here's just two things. Take a look. It's alright, you can pick them up." He placed on the tablecloth a single, small piece of plastic with the word *Visa* and some numbers.

"This is ... what, like a passport, in the future?" asked Caan. "For ports of entry?"

"Um, not exactly. It's a kind of money."

But Caan was already gingerly lifting the solid, glass-metal-plastic rectangle and admiring the smoothness of its edges. "Wow, that's something. What's this, a flashlight, or something?"

"Well, yes, that's one thing it can do," Yanis said, turning the iPhone on, "but watch this."

Yanis found Caan to be an interesting figure. He seemed to stand with feet in several camps—law enforcement, intelligence, the Pentagon, and, somehow, Hollywood. If there was someone better suited to help Yanis and Jillian succeed in Prophet, he knew that Menzies and the others would have gotten them, instead. Caan was unruffled when confronted with the future, certainly compared to some others.

"It's quite a thing, I'll admit it. Like something out of a movie, or some futuristic expo," said Caan.

"Sam Clark wouldn't let it go without a fight," said Yanis. "We had to promise him permanent access to all kinds of things from the NATO guys, just so he'd let us have it back."

"We'll need it for recordings, data storage, images, and so forth. Also, we've been building our Compendium," Jillian said. "It's like a working document."

"Compendium?" Caan asked, reluctantly passing back the extraordinary iPhone.

"*Compendium of Historical, Estimated, and Actual Time.* Or CHEAT, for short. It's absolutely everything we can remember about everything we ever learned that pertains to anything."

"The proposed subtitles are, 'The Great Anglo-American Brain Dump,' and 'How to Survive in the Twentieth Century.' We're still debating," Jillian told him.

"This is Print Version 9.18.6. We do a new one every week when we're not traveling." It was the size of a desk dictionary, bound in a kind of interlocking metal case. "Eli, go ahead and give me a year between 1975 and 2014," Yanis said.

They tried to be casual about all this, as though they were clairvoyants at the fair, but Caan felt the creep of an unusual sensation, as though he were abutting the perimeter of a complex, forbidden territory. "Erm, you mean, you're gonna tell me my future?"

"Not yours, specifically. The world's, as best we can recall it."

"This isn't the word of God, either. Just the pair of us, don't forget."

"And the NATO guys contributed some, before heading home," Yanis added. "But I'll swear on any book you give me that it's all one hundred percent true, according to our timeline."

"Alright," Caan decided, "I'll bite. Give me 2010." He laughed at the very idea. "I'll be a hundred fuckin' years old. What can I expect?"

They told him, and he found that he reeled, time after time. All of it seemed perfectly reasonable and explicable—familiar themes in politics and society and war, really—but also quite utterly alien, as though reported by those not from another timeline, but from a different *dimension*. A future where all the variables had been violently shaken, then left to float down to their new positions; a geopolitical snow globe, made anew each time.

"That's really somethin', I gotta tell ya," Caan said, his nerves betraying his New Jersey police sergeant background, "*really* somethin'. I mean, I keep telling my kids, they don't know they're born, but with you two ... I mean, you ain't even *been* born yet! It's crazy!"

The passenger lounge was spacious but animated by foxtrot numbers from the piano, and each table at least partly shrouded by tobacco smoke, so the three spies could converse with a certain degree of freedom. "Mr. Caan," said Jillian with the same engaging warmth, "it's quite alright to take some time with a notion as nutty as this one. Isn't that so, Yanis?" The professor nodded. "We've had our own struggles with time," Jillian continued, "and how it can be twisted in the service of evil. I hope you understand that we're here to stop someone."

"Yes," he said, completely serious now after the real-life parlor tricks. "Captain Keck."

"He's a singular officer," Jillian conceded, "one who has acquired, or seeks to acquire, genocidal capabilities."

His face stony sober, Caan nevertheless leaned forward and said, "I really want to know how freaked out I should be, but I didn't understand half of that."

Yanis took his turn. "It's okay, Eli, a lot of people reacted this way when we came here to 1951 from 1944. And when I showed up from 2014 in 1943, there was, let's say, an *enormous* amount of skepticism. How about you refill our drinks, and I'll tell you the *Reader's Digest* version of The Story So Far."

It took twenty-five minutes, but only because he skipped most of the really appalling stuff. Like the tabun. And before that, the mental hospital, back in England in '43. And more recently, the pants-shitting terror of a combat parachute jump in the dark.

"Most of the team has dispersed. We've been back over a month, after all, and the mission's over. It's not like they could place nineteen combat veterans under indefinite arrest because the government couldn't figure out what the hell to do with us. So, after assisting Mr. Clark in his endeavor, we've been killing time in a little burgeoning resort in the Mojave Desert. Supposed to be the next big thing, I hear."

"You didn't feel like going home, too?" Caan asked, gobsmacked time and again.

"We're not even sure we can," he said, skipping a semester's worth of doctoral seminar work in quantum physics. "It's complicated. But, once they'd showed us a dozen fuckin' enormous hangars full of stolen Nazi gadgets, we knew for sure their technical advantages flowed straight from Keck's acquisitions."

"That one Nazi grabbed all that stuff from the future?" he asked. It sounded utterly absurd.

"Hardware, designs, ideas, you name it. He 'twinned' himself when he came back, like I said, but only *one* of him was definitively accounted for."

"The one those Lancasters went and buried under a whole fuckin' mountain," Caan recalled.

"I think I remember that, too," Jillian shivered.

"So now," Yanis said, "we're chasing the *other* one."

His neural circuits were very nearly blown out by all this, so Eli was glad of a question from Jillian, a chance to move on. "What brings you into our little conspiracy, Eli?" she asked. "Who came to you for help? And," she smiled, "thanks for doing this, by the way," she added, reaching to take his hand appreciatively. "It's complete madness, all of it, and we owe you a lot just for stepping forward."

He patted Jillian's hand companionably, then lit another cigarette. "What can I say? I'm a sucker for service."

"That's it?" Yanis asked. "They asked, so you answered? Simple as that?"

"I wish for even *one* simple thing in this whole deal, Mr. Tower. Although, I don't mind tellin' ya," he smiled, "they went and doubled my pension when I balked. Kicks in at fifty, too, so that's pretty sweet."

They toasted their coming success. There would be time for more, even before they reached Washington, but the three had collectively reached their limit; talking about this ridiculous business was always emotional, and exhausting.

***

1855 Redwood Rise, Hollywood Hills, Fountain Meeting #1 of 2, late 1950

David and Lydia Feldhemler arrived in America with nothing but their own ragged clothes, three weeks after Passover in 1938. Settling where they could, in New York, they worked hard and raised twin boys. After the war, their once-tiny divorce law office went gangbusters, and the family could afford to swap the growing smog for a suburban home in California, where friends were setting up a movie production company.

The architect for their wooded lot (another refugee from Europe, as were so many) conceived of a beautifully precise glass-metal-wood curve, quietly set back under a steep ridge line overlooking Los Angeles. There was also money to give to charity, and to invest, though how one invested was invariably linked to who one knew. Feldhemler's friends ran clubs, and allegedly, one or two rackets. Still, the lure of becoming an 'artistic entrepreneur' in Hollywood was considerable, and with plenty of room for entertaining, the Feldhemler house at 1855 Redwood Rise became a vibrant gathering place for Hollywood writers, actors, and investors. The hosts liked it best when established names gave some space to the hopeful dreamers; real *gems* could be found that way.

After some modest success with light comedies, the Feldhemlers really made it big with their own take on the lavish, Biblical classics of the age: the acclaimed, controversial *Skin and Sandals* genre. Three Egyptian-themed movies stormed onto the screen, appealingly splashy and risqué. The third was subject to cuts by the censors, generating usefully garish headlines. No purveyors of prurience, the Feldhemlers defended their work. "It's not about whether the nipple is *necessary* ..." David often had to begin. In a world of shifting, uncertain morals, the MPAA was tasked with protecting the impressionable, and the film faced a ban if its director wouldn't yield.

It was a PR brush fire, nothing more. And without more movies in the same vein, the Feldhemlers could have expected things to blow over.

The opposite happened, breathtakingly quickly. Allegations surfaced connecting David with a pornography ring. There were soon rumors of photos, supporting the claim. The couple fought back, condemning 'a malicious, baseless, and ultimately anti-Semitic conspiracy,' but then came the *coup de grace:* photos of David in the most compromising possible position with a startled, anonymous young Asian man. The charging documents, most damningly, later called him a 'boy.'

The FBI had no choice but to make the arrest. Friends wouldn't answer the phone; even one of the Feldhemlers' bank accounts was seized. Then, a few days before David finalized his plea deal, the family's lawyer received a letter with an extraordinary, unsolicited offer, only two percent under the asking price. Such a beleaguered couple had no choice in this matter, or any other, and telexed the reply: *Your bid for 1855 Redwood Rise in the value of $92,250 is agreed.*

A conventional auction would have been slow and costly, the lawyer warned, and the buyer—a single woman, apparently—was offering a large chunk of the sale price in cash, just when the couple were hemorrhaging legal fees. To complete the deal, a safe deposit box was established, housing several ounces of diamonds; they would not regret access to discreet, portable wealth, David told his wife at the time, once these injustices were straightened out. It was their last phone call before his sentencing: eight years, hard labor.

Once the cash was transferred and the deposit box key handed over by a functionary, Inge Weber took possession of 1855 Redwood Rise. Much more, though, she felt the need to take *ownership*. "The grounds of the house," said 'Sabine Ehrlinger' to the realtor, whose head still spun from the pace of events, "are the worst kind of derivative, bourgeois shit."

Commands were given and calls made; men and machines moved. A long-tended garden and rockery were bulldozed away, giving space for a terrace with wineglass-dropping views. "It actually *celebrates* the location," Sabine trilled to the builder, who was proud of this nicely detailed, honestly almost-vertiginous perch on the green hillside. 1855 Redwood Rise would be no museum, Inge decided—*no, it's Sabine, everything's Sabine from now on*—but a place of ... what was the word? Yes, *dynamism*, that was it. A place of change and science. Of unique meetings of bodies and minds.

Her contractors were confused only by an order to clear some remote, coastal woodland to the north, without building there. "A festive clearing, for parties," she told them. "Pig roasts, big haunches of venison ..."

From day one, 'Sabine' was a massive hit with the workforce. "Any chance of a pig roast invitation?" tried one optimistic wag.

There was not, of course, but let she each of them down gently. The site foreman, six inches taller and built like a Swedish miner, however, received a different kind of invitation, three times before the terrace was finished, and twice after. But then his Nordic stoutness made her homesick, and she sent him away. Then a ginger-haired bricklayer, but it was the same. Then a quiet, pleasingly inexperienced air conditioning guy. None provided what she needed, and all reminded her of what she missed.

The last of his work was to complete a sprawling, new wine cellar. But now, months later, only a few cases had arrived, and tradesmen still toiled somewhere down there during the day, a mystery to the staff.

None had time to stop and wonder. Cocktail parties always started at five o'clock sharp, and dinner parties—which, naturally, began with cocktails—just after six. Industrial quantities of vermouth, Pernod, and scotch were always close by, with everything prepared in advance as the housekeeper, Karin, insisted. Efficiency was their watchword.

1949 had fifty-three Fridays, and Sabine threw a party on exactly forty of them. Also on twenty-three Sundays, and a dozen of their Wednesday poker nights. When Senator Forbes died, the local chapter of the Party held its forty-person 'after-wake' at her house. There'd even been a fun 'Splash and Splurge' for the families last August.

The staff were becoming *exceptionally* efficient.

Composing the guest list for each *soiree* was a fascinating intellectual puzzle for Sabine. Her clientele, as she saw them, were people of means (which often meant some amount of fame and, Sabine hoped, taste) who might one day join Fountain as Participants. Alongside this, their core enterprise, ran several other strands of ongoing and delicate negotiations, for there were always things the Project needed. Or, more accurately, things that the research going on in Keck's remote little outpost could not do without; chemical and biological 'samples' of one kind or another, cases of laboratory cultures in petri dishes, *und so weiter*. She sourced rare metals from industrial chemists—Vanadium, Palladium and even a few grams of non-fissile Uranium which arrived mercifully intact, in contrast to their first attempt to ship optical-grade glass. Everything was horrifically expensive, but her connections helped create leverage, which could be much more cost-effective.

And when neither money nor fear seemed the suited method of motivation, midnight assignations were promised, and sometimes even delivered. Loyalty could be purchased and bought discreetly by careful spending of Sabine's ample currency.

This string of useful men, as well as some truly enfeebled sycophants, came to form a many-colored fabric: the garish, often experimental tapestry that was Sabine's sexual life. Well-practiced by now, she excelled with her sultry, Lauren Bacall demeanor. *Desinvolture*, the French called it; she'd learned a lot recently, in several languages. It all took time, and work. She'd fumbled her earliest social engagements, an awkward investor luncheon and a confusing cocktail bash at Rupert St. Martin's place. It was the *accents,* and how quickly language changed. She worked to overcome shyness, simply because she had to. Looking as she did, men usually couldn't help approaching *her*. Slowly, she found a more casual, approachable touch, and they found her irresistible.

With the women, it was different. "I feel like I can talk to you, because you've been through so much," she heard more than once. "You've managed to assert yourself in a male business," said another, convinced like everyone that 'Sabine' had fled Austria as a recently graduated film student. It just so happened, a student with family wealth and some very special connections in the pharmaceutical industry. "You didn't let them keep you down. And your looks are just so *real*, and *authentic,* when everything these days feels 'high-techno' and fake."

As her confidence truly blossomed in the California spring of 1950, Sabine began to bring an unmistakable sensuality to her meetings. The financiers and film distributors found her quickly disarming and engagingly sassy, but when needed, straight-backed and knowledgeable. After a year spent meeting literally everyone, and with each investing success fueling the next, she was nothing short of transformed. "Sabine? Oh, she's a walking *Who's Who,*" said a starstruck Loretta Lehrer to a reporter, one day in 1950. "She gets invited to everything but only seems available to … well, a select few."

It was only natural for Sabine's female friends, a bevy of producers' wives, older actresses, and semi-retirees, to wonder aloud: *What kind of special food is she eating? What pills is she on? Something from one of these 'bio-techno' labs?* But Sabine was tight-lipped, admitting only to 'a strict diet' and something called 'mindfulness meditation.'

But she harvested from this vine-like network by making sure *she* heard *everything*. Any rumors about events at 1855 Redwood Rise, or the enigmatic Sabine Ehrlinger, were trimmed like one of the estate's decorative hedges: neat and definitively short.

During the building phase, she was the mean, intemperate 'boss lady,' the slavedriver. It was a role that came naturally for her when among burly men, and they were jaw-dropped at her whole act, the ball-breaking 'hurry ups' to shorten a respite, and what the foreman called 'slave driving with a smile.' If nothing else worked, she became diminutive, almost submissive, wearing an expression that said, "You wouldn't stand up a pretty girl on a rainy night, would you?" None could resist.

But Sabine's new role, that of the charming and affable hostess, was a dazzling leap for an SS sergeant. Back in Germany, she liked to think of herself as perhaps half a notch above working class, in manner and appearance. She was strong and firm-boned without being fat—she'd never had enough money to overeat. For years, in Poland and Germany, she'd worn a uniform cap or a wool hat, incarcerating her shortened curls.

But now, 'Sabine' sought a new allure, something even beyond sultry—a half-teaspoon of Marlene Dietrich, if one cared for that kind of thing, and a lot of men did. She revitalized—*rediscovered*—her hair, and experimented with fashions, leaving behind the waning, European styles. 'Sabine' needed to embody something altogether different.

For weeks, she window-shopped and experimented. Then she saw the chic, unflappable, ultra-modern Loretta Lehrer as the suspected murderer in *The Danbury Trial,* early in 1950 and Inge knew for sure: her fashion sense, her whole look, was frankly drab. Sensible navy blues and greys were too pre-war, too militaristic, even. In the mirror, 'Inge' looked dowdy and dispirited, destined to marry a middle manager and raise two very ordinary kids in Poughkeepsie. Keck's orders involved attracting the attentions and affections of a large group of modern, affluent men, the kind who could have anything they wanted. 'Dowdy' wouldn't do at all, not for the chic, updated 'Sabine.'

She hired a student doctor as a kind of intern, and they patiently analyzed Sabine's gait using one of the new, hand-held movie cameras. Specialists visited Redwood Rise to help improve her posture, and she created an ambitious physiotherapy routine, based on documents from Keck's 'Future Library.' It took months of tennis lessons, again held discreetly at the house, before she was confident enough to drop the right hints around the right friends and received the invitations she most wanted. The drip of information revealed who might most urgently need Sabine's services, and whether they had the means to engage her. After two lazy sets—and an even lazier mid-afternoon glass of wine—three affluent socialites were priceless sources of information. And after three glasses, they became a veritable torrent. She made tennis a regular part of her networking schedule.

Just after her parachute arrival, back in 1945, she'd stood in front of a mirror, reminding herself of nothing so much as a sack of potatoes who'd ill-advisedly tried on a slinky, red dress. After a year in California, she looked tall, toned, and confident. Friends gravitated to her naturally, after that. And the *men.* Sabine had her pick of the bunch and could be highly selective.

They'd arrive for dinner, looking a little sheepish, saying something like, "I hope you don't mind, but I've brought along my old college roommate, from a thousand years ago ..." Sabine loved these surprises, for the unannounced 'plus one' was invariably from a similar demographic, which was—let's just face it—affluent, older, and vulnerable to illness and injury. Everyone was dealing with something, be it back pain or gut trouble, or the uncertainty of a fluttering heart. And so, just quietly, almost as though doing so *without* trying to get noticed by a giant potential client base, Sabine began providing 'personal health advice.'

She would take people to her private rooms; the women, she brought into her own bedroom. She would sit with them, dispense hard truth in plain words: *time is becoming unkind.*

Sometimes, she'd help dry some tears. Only twice, finding that broaching the subject had been a misjudgment, Sabine slid into a harmless, alternate script about face cream. But only twice. The others listened, read, saw for themselves, and all signed up, right there on the spot.

Loretta Lehrer was Number Seven, and she helped to recruit Number Nineteen, Number Thirty-One and, as of tonight, nearly twenty others. Among them were two of tonight's guests, Nathan and Amelie Dearborn, and they in turn had received permission to induct their lifelong friend, Tim Courtley, into Fountain as a Participant.

For inductions, Sabine always liked to prepare carefully, taking time over her appearance while she toured the house, checking on things. She included Karin on everything except the inner workings and her growing corpus of spoken rituals. "Nothing too special tonight," Sabine explained to the housekeeper; this was Fountain's forty-third meeting. "Catching up with our members' networking efforts and discussing their health reports." She sipped tea, shimmering slightly in her silvery dressing gown.

"Sounds thrilling," Karin said.

"From the looks of it," Sabine quipped, "you haven't been 'thrilled' since the Weimar Republic." She checked her notebook for tonight's date. "Ah, yes, I mustn't forget *that*." It seemed there would be an additional frisson of excitement: a disciplinary matter. One of their newer members, Number Hundred-Twenty-One (none other than Rupert St. Martin), in a moment of inattention, perhaps, had been overheard discussing his diet regimen. It wasn't strictly an 'indiscretion,' in the parlance of their order, but it was foolish, and contrary to their code.

A brief discussion would be enough, Sabine generally found, in one of the upstairs rooms. There was no need for the party to be disturbed by any screams.

"Tell me, Karin," said Sabine, "my old battleship, my fortress against the idiots, how does the place look tonight?" She asked a version of the same question, an hour before each day's Main Event.

"Very good," the efficient, Hungarian former housekeeper replied.

"Any failures to reply to invitations this time?" Sabine knew Karin's temper flared like a Roman candle when people showed they lacked the *common decency* to put pen to paper.

"Only Rupert St. Martin," she said, pronouncing the name with distaste, as though a comedian had made it up.

Ah, the transgressor. "He's coming later. I'll be seeing him alone, upstairs."

"Very good, Miss." Not once in five years had Karin let slip the least disfavor, or even an opinion, about events 'upstairs.' Or indeed, for any of the various goings on 'downstairs.' Surely, on the most vigorous occasions, it was not only Karin but the whole house that was shaken awake, and so she felt her own commentary was hardly needed.

Sixty and indestructible, Karin Horváth ran the catering staff, and two gardeners, with a massive distaste for inefficiency and a drill sergeant's abruptness. One night, even Inge snapped to attention at the sound of Karin's shouted kitchen command, purely on instinct.

Fleeing Hungary when the Serbian army shelled her village and finding her new home in Graz absorbed into Germany by Hitler's *Anschluss*, Karin had registered as a Hungarian refugee in 1945 and been granted asylum in America. Never married, she was now quietly and permanently braided into the fabric of Redwood Rise, with a small, tight-knit social group. It was good to speak her childhood Hungarian, once in a while.

The two women inspected the dining room together, finding two of the all-female staff carefully preparing the platter for a seafood buffet; shrimp and abalone would sit in a chilled basket atop graceful swan's neck towers of ice. Champagne sat bubbling on a side table, twenty-four glasses fully charged. Canapes would come through as the second group of guests arrived. The barman was in position, freshly showered after obliging Sabine with a session of afternoon stress relief. Adequate or better, he would remain on the mansion's permanent event staff. His predecessor ... well, all a girl could do was 'tut' and shake her head in disappointment.

"Ice sculptures and special foreign cocktails," Karin noted disapprovingly. "A lot of fuss over some rich lunatics. Doubt they'll even notice."

"They'd notice," Sabine explained yet again, "if those things *weren't* visible. Some of these people live in a different world from you and I."

"I live in the servant's quarters, where I belong," Karin said, proudly a martyr to her own social immobility. "And if *your* world needs hundred-dollar chunks of ice to look beautiful—"

"Don't be ridiculous."

"Then I *really* don't know ..."

"The sculptress was very reasonable, actually, we've used her before—"

"Can't even imagine—"

"Imagine?" Sabine said sharply in surprise, halting the banter. "You've all the imagination of that frozen swan."

"I can imagine thrashing you with a garden rake, that's what I can *imagine*."

"That's enough out of you."

Karin was quiet for all of eight seconds. "Will there be another of those horrid rituals, downstairs?"

A sigh and a grumble. "They are an important part of the ..."

"Voodoo and hoodoo," she said, her face puckered as though ready to spit on the carpet.

"No one invited you," Sabine reminded her. "Besides, you're not a Participant."

"Hah! If I had money to piss away like that, I'd sooner spend it on fancy cakes, and a ride in an airplane."

"I'll get Wolf to take you on a joyride across the Caribbean in *Big Boy*, then throw you out, somewhere between Mobile and Cuba."

"Ah, peace at last," she hummed. "From air to water to nothing. There are worse ways to go." With that, she headed off, straight as a dart and twice as sharp.

Tonight's group was deliberately small; inductions were best done in an intimate setting. Sabine had time to greet each new arrival as their cars swung round the circle to the steps. "What an *outrageous* place!" Tim Courtley said, arriving with his friends, arms spread in wonder.

Sabine smiled and extended her hand, and as she did so, her affable, charming Hollywood persona slid firmly into place.

"The only outrage," she said as a maid deftly caught Nathan Dearborn's tossed jacket, "is that it's taken so long to get you here!" Heels echoed in the double-height reception area; the installation of a quarter-ton, sparkling crystal chandelier made sense of the cavernous space. "Why don't you head on through to the bar?" she said. Weeks of practice were finally polishing her American idioms. "I told Jeremy to pour us a special *aperitif*."

"Something refreshing, I hope! We're—*how do you say*—parched!" Amelie Dearborn said, finding the word with an agreeable little laugh. She was a constellation, a smile of diamonds and sequins wreathed in an elegant, black gown and a chiffon scarf. "This way, dear," she said, "mind your step on the—"

"I can manage, stop fussing." Nathan Dearborn tottered after his wife across the broad, sunken living room, finding the kitchen to his left busy with three chefs, and then passed what looked to be a study or library before hitting the stairs. Beyond them was the house's old drawing room, expanded to form a more modern living room with long, sleek white leather couches. Full-length windows gave a view over the wooded estate, the Pacific, and the sinking sun beyond. "You could charge a million bucks for that view," said Dearborn, admiring the play of light on the sparkling ocean. "Maybe two million."

"Why, are you interested in buying?" Sabine asked as she helped the trio get comfortable in the living room.

"I really doubt I could afford this place. I mean, how on Earth did you …" Courtley received, just in time, a very dissuasive look from Dearborn. "That's to say," he said, trying to cover.

"Would it be too embarrassing to admit that my family invested in Škoda, back before the last war?"

No one voiced an objection. "Business is business. Doesn't matter what they make, provided they made you money," said Nathan Dearborn, sounding more sober than he was.

"Kind of you to say," Sabine smiled. "Although, one million dollars or two, I'm afraid we'll have to do without the vista for the first part of the evening," Sabine told him. "Prying eyes."

"Shame," he said, a little surprised as a team of maids shuttered the windows with neat, coordinated twists of the rod. Darker and somehow smaller, the room became more intimate, and the quartet—Sabine, Nathan, Amelie, and Courtley—sat close and talked earnestly about Fountain.

"I can only offer guidance and some practical help," Sabine said, keen to set out her *caveat emptor*. "The exercises, the diet, all that's up to you. But I promise you'll feel better, lighter, younger ... more ready for fun and games, if you know what I mean."

"He does," Dearborn said, "oh, Lord, he really does."

She explained Participation, what it meant and what it cost. Courtley had decided before arriving and signed a check before going alone with Sabine to another part of the house, leaving Amelie and Nathan to explore the early 20th century art on the walls. "God, is that a Klimt?" Amelie gasped.

"That *can't* be real ..."

"*Got* to be a copy."

"Yeah, *got* to be," Nathan said, uncertain and peering closer.

Upstairs, the lights were almost as low as in the living room, and in her slinky red once more, Sabine seemed to lead Courtley like a paramour, out of reach but utterly desirable. At the door to her room, she paused and turned to him. "You won't tell anyone, will you? I don't normally ..." she smiled, her eyes now light-blue pools of lust, "do things like this."

Tim Courtley had paid for services everywhere from Hong Kong to Casablanca, but was left staggered, indulged, more convinced than ever that Sabine and Fountain would be an excellent investment.

He did not see, neither did any of the others, the hand-held movie camera placed discreetly on Sabine's dresser, hidden under last night's lingerie.

***

Venice Beach, California, 1952

The Great Director was sitting contentedly, legs crossed, luxuriating with a cigarette and an enviable view of the beach, when Yanis, Jillian, and Eli Caan arrived. He stood in a single, swift motion and became surprisingly tall, like a white-haired mystic.

"Can you believe," he said first, "that they're still thinking of building a *highway,* right through the middle of here?" His yellow suit jacket blossomed open, revealing a purple shirt, as he exclaimed with arms outstretched, "I mean, who'd put a highway through *paradise?*" Huge sunglasses completed the look; Willy Leitz made movies, but was also himself a continuous motion picture experience, a rolling homage to freedom. This was how Leitz had chosen to celebrate life, creativity, and his own unlikely survival. An orphan, family friends spirited him from the Reich in 1937.

"Willy, Willy, always so effervescent! And at your advanced age!" Caan joked, leaning in for a cordial embrace. "Did someone feed you?" He shot the kitchen a glance, or at least its red door. "The staff can be slow."

Raymond's was entering its mid-morning lull, a quieter meeting time which reflected Willy's preferences; his evenings were replete with artsy madness and cocktail-fueled vulgarity, but *mornings* were for work. Occasionally, even Willy would admit, cocktail-fueled work.

"The staff are delightful," he said, stubbing out his cigarette. It had one of the new filters, the slender, white ones with the smart-assed jingle:

The Filter Man keeps your lungs in shape

By removing that par-ti-cu-late

"And I ordered my cocktail not thirty seconds ago, so be still."

"Well," Eli said, "at least they gave you a table outdoors."

"With an ocean breeze like this," Leitz rhapsodized, "who would drink cocktails inside? Besides, it's so stifling in there, and I wouldn't want our new friends to die of heat stroke before we've gotten to know each other, now would I?"

Eli handled the introductions. "Mr. George Tower, and Miss Jean Davidoff."

"Charmed," Leitz said, shaking hands with the pair and motioning for the staff to set up his new friends with whatever they wanted. "Eli's been in my ear about you two young bloods, *literally* every day, for the last two weeks."

"That's the thing, Willy. You're seeing two people," Eli said, putting some energy into a sales pitch he hoped would yield splendid dividends, "but what they *actually* are, is a motion picture toolbox." If Willy's eyebrows were any guide, Eli was bang on course. "They're magicians, Willy. Script doctors, set designers, lighting conjurers ... and wait until I tell you about the camera techniques," he said sumptuously, as though anticipating a legendary dessert.

"All-rounders, eh? A Jack," he grinned, "and Jill of all trades."

The slightest tremor, near undetectable, betrayed only to Yanis his partner's discomfort. *At least he didn't call me Jillian Qualmes of All Trades, Oh, and Interpol.*

"And you're, what ... thirty each?" Leitz asked, generously shaving off eight years between them. "Such range, such *vision*, and so young!" The precocious pair could only have been in the business, what, eight or ten years? "Where did you learn? Around here?"

"I started in local rep theater and amateur dramatics, but after we started working together, we got our break and shadowed Pat Cartwright at Elstree," Jillian said, wheeling out part of their established backstory, an artful mix of half-truth and invention.

"Cartwright!" Willy exclaimed of the much-touted Oscar hopeful.

"He made us run errands for a year."

"Making the tea, sweeping the editing room floor ..." Willy imagined out loud.

"Before we started working on set design, lighting and, well, a bit of everything."

"He gave us some time and studio space to work on a few things." Barring an expensive international phone call, Cartwright would remain unaware that he was Yanis and Jillian's unwitting guarantor; they needed to give Leitz a major name in the business, and his fit nicely.

"Most of the big studios weren't prepared to take risks on brand-new technology," she said, struck as ever by the anachronisms. Their 'brand-new' ideas would have been novel only to her grandfather, cribbed as they were from every Hollywood movie the pair had ever seen. "So, we experimented with smaller, local outfits in Scotland, and then around London. Bits and pieces, really, until a friend invited us to work on a project in New York."

Yanis—or 'George' for professional and espionage purposes—picked up the thread where 'Jean' left off. "Eli was doing some legal work for the cast, and we got chatting. I showed him some of our designs, asked if he knew anyone who might want to invest in something absolutely new, something audiences haven't even *dreamed* of."

"Audiences can *dream* quite a good deal these days, Mr. Tower. You've seen Cecil B. De Mille, and his casts of thousands? Gives new meaning to the word *epic*."

"Within a few years," Yanis tried boastfully, "imagery generated partly using computers will largely replace expensive crowds of extras. Anyone will be able to recreate those effects."

"Alright, okay," said Leitz, feeling a little challenged now by Yanis, "what about Chuck Schneer and his guy, ummm ..."

"Ray Harryhausen," Jillian said, glad not to have forgotten the genius animator.

"Yes! That new stop-motion photography? I mean, if he can make skeletons come to life, surely we're approaching some kind of outer limit," claimed Leitz. "The furthest reaches of movie-making technology."

In piercing his balloon, Jillian surprised herself, but it felt great. "Forgive me, Mr. Leitz, but that sounds just a little ridiculous."

Yanis squealed silently, then prayed her intervention was a prearranged meeting tactic he'd forgotten about.

"The transistor is only a few years old," Jillian said. "Soon, we'll have much more powerful computers, able to compose and manipulate entirely new imagery. We owe it to the public," she said. feeling rather grand, "to embrace these opportunities quickly."

"Because if we do," Yanis added, "the new technological surge we're experiencing might be only the tip of a tidal wave. Once everyone sees what's possible, what computers can do, they'll invest in personal versions, miniaturized to fit on your desk, or even in your pocket."

"We want to help you become ready for a time in the near future," Jillian offered invitingly, "when everyone has their own devices."

"When Oma used to leave me to my own devices in her attic," Willy leered, "I'd get up to all kinds of mischief."

"Behave yourself, now, Willy," Caan requested. "She's getting to the good part."

"I'm sorry. Devices," he prompted.

"A time," Jillian now had space to continue, "when people watch theater-quality presentations on big screens in their own living rooms."

"A *home theater?*" Willy wondered aloud. "A picture house of your own design, right there in the home. Wow."

"And upstairs, their two kids watch two entirely different movies, all connected by a computer network."

"A *network*," Willy struggled, "of computers? Talking to each other?" He looked at Caan as if for help. "Individual movie theaters, in the palms of our hands?" Willy's hands met at his forehead, and then exploded outward. "It's cosmic! I mean, I mean ..." he enthused, "it's like meeting an emissary from another planet! Where did you *get* these ideas?"

Continuing their mash-up of quasi-truth and outright fiction, Yanis spun a yarn involving graduate-level research work in the sciences, while Jillian looked Leitz in the eye and told him she'd been, "lucky enough to see the world," as an embassy staffer at the State Department. The lies came remarkably easy, when so much was at stake.

Willy had a ravenous side to him, for food, drink, opinions, and information. He'd already polished off his first cocktail, and his last forkful of salad, while listening. He re-ordered, then resumed fluently extemporizing his way through life. "We'll have to write a movie about *you two*!" Leitz proposed. "There's so much drama, and hard work, and ... dare I say, romance?"

Jillian replied less stiffly than she might have. "For professional reasons, we prefer neither to confirm nor deny."

Willy clasped his cheeks and shook himself to make sure Jillian truly belonged to reality. "Oh, this is to *die* for!" His eyes flashed with curiosity, and his smile seemed, at turns, to promise the salacious and the rejuvenative. "A glamorous, trendy couple, set to transform the movie business," he said like an impresario, with spread hands and a saccharine smile. "Very forward-looking, yes, very progressive. They tell me I should be on the lookout," he reported, "for the rise of something called *feminism*. Personally, I think it sounds *wonderful*."

Rising quickly and steeply in Jillian's estimation, Leitz told them he was warm to experimental techniques, but had to be wary. "There's a small part of me," he confessed, "that worries I'm going to be wasting my time with weird bullshit." Another apologetic look toward Jillian. "Sorry again."

"Not at all."

"You know what I mean, right? Naked actors covered in candle wax, then imprinted with jackboots. Scenery getting set on fire. That kind of caper."

Eli nearly spat out his sip of water. "You really do take in a broad variety of performance art, don't you, Willy?"

"I do my duty," he said, "to the gods of art."

"Amen, brother," said Jillian, extracting a snorted laugh from Leitz.

"So," Leitz asked once his plate was cleared away, "here's what I want to know." He scratched a bald tonsure ringed by curled, unruly grey, "are you an industrial salesman with an interesting catalog, or another 'plonker' with a guitar to smash and a score of Beethoven's Fifth to set on fire," he asked, pausing for laughter from Eli, "or are you actually a borderline creative genius, as I've been told?"

Jillian gave Yanis' hand a firm squeeze, which was either a stern reminder of their mission, or an expression of love and encouragement. He needed both.

"We've got some ideas for using cameras and lights to really transform the look of movies. They're entirely new concepts, some of them, and we need the chance to experiment, and figure out what works."

Leitz had been briefed by Eli, and anyway could see Mr. Tower's intended direction. "So, I'm to employ you as, what, research contractors?"

"Research engineers," was the title Yanis had already decided he liked best.

"We're making movies, you know," Leitz said, a little too mind-blown by Yanis' aggressive modernism, "not trying to race the Germans into space." He was courteous enough to let Eli try to mollify him—*it's smart and incremental, it'll hardly cost a bean, and everyone else will be doing something like this soon, anyway*—until the likely benefits seemed heartily to outweigh the risks. Caan had been working on Leitz, passing on and fostering Yanis' idea: a dedicated special effects subsidiary called Merlin Inc. which would blow the doors off the competition.

"So, it'll be just you and your assistant?" Willy asked, quite innocently. "I can offer you a room each at a hotel, or maybe an apartment in Burbank to share?"

To Jillian, this sounded like another subtle probing of their relationship status. "A two-bedroom apartment would be ideal."

"I respect your privacy, naturally," said Leitz, clearly about to risk invading it, "but there's no need to be shy. All kinds of new pairings and couplings are going on in Hollywood these days," he said. "Refugees from Europe, rehabilitated Japanese." He wiggled his eyebrows, adding, "Even the occasional defecting Soviet," and leaned in closer to advise, "so, watch how much you say at the caviar bars."

Caan harrumphed. "The Soviets are fine by me, so long as they don't let the Germans get going again. Nazis keep me up at night."

"Really?" Leitz joked. "You should move to a better neighborhood." He shushed Caan's objections to his sense of humor. "You're right, anyway, Eli. It's not like they all disappeared underground as soon as the Armistice was signed. I don't care if it's called the Government of National Unicorns and Cotton Candy, it's still run by people who were Party members. Don't quote me, but I'd say there are probably more active Nazis in the world today than in 1939. But with the nuclear whoop-de-doop, the 'post-Nazi' government talking annihilation, I guess the offer of peace was just too tempting."

"Did you feel the Armistice was the right thing to do?" asked 'Jean.' It was a question she posed to almost every new person she met, but Leitz's dispute with the Nazis went deeper than questions of history or sovereignty. "I'm sorry if that's indelicate, given everything, Mr. Leitz," she added after he'd been silent for longer than was comfortable.

"I'll say this," he said, dispelling an urge to say much more. "No one covered themselves in glory, not least these hardliners, these *idiots* braying for war with the Soviets. 'The *next* great threat to democracy,' they call them." With Japan's aggression neutralized by a generous peace deal, Stalin loomed large over eastern Europe and Persia. "The death camps are closing down. First glimmer of hope Europe has seen in years. And call me Willy, please," he requested. "Mr. Leitz, and his father, and all the other Leitzes, were herded into a dark room and then went up in smoke. I'm just poor Willy, another war orphan." It was the kernel of his oft-told origin story, performed while admiring the evenness of the salt around the rim of his margarita glass.

Caan swiftly distracted Willy, catching him up on the latest goings and comings in Hollywood—mutual friends who had been married, divorced, caught cheating, arrested and, in one instance, found dead—giving Yanis and Jillian time to decode the menu.

"Atomic oysters," she read, "harvested from the playfully radioactive band of ocean south-east of Japan, these little guys come by the mega-ton. Six bucks for all you can eat."

"Huh?" He'd found another head-scratcher. "Not sure that's a great idea, given that my stomach was doing some nuclear launch sequence the past few days."

"Yeah, what was with that?" Jillian whispered.

"Just didn't feel like myself," Yanis explained. "Not sure why. But I'm better now. What in the world is Kyoto Bass?" Then he found the description. "Inspired into new and surprising forms by prevailing conditions, Kyoto Bass are fascinating artifacts of evolution, and they're absolutely delicious!"

Though Caan was in mid-story, Willy halted him to let the couple in on a secret. "Ten bucks says the radioactive stuff is just baloney. Oh, but speaking of atomic, did you see that piece in the *Los Angeles City News?* About the ..." He paused, looking over his shoulder momentarily, then resumed in a whisper, "that Clark guy out in the Nevada desert, you know, in Groom Lake, that area where they do all that atomic testing?"

Yanis sat up straight, recognizing Sam Clark's name and mission.

Jillian caught her breath and blinked, "What's that?"

Leitz leaned over, nearly spilling his drink, "They say he's moved some sort of *intergalactic spacecraft.* If you believe in that sort of thing."

The remaining trio were stunned into silence, until Caan masterfully erupted in a hearty laugh, slapping Leitz on the back. "Intergalactic spacecraft stored at an atomic testing range," he snorted. "Now *that* sounds like a million-dollar plot if I ever heard one. Gonna be a blockbuster. You two should get on that."

George and Jean chuckle-sighed as Leitz nodded and quaffed his drink. As he set it down, he continued, "Back to the oysters, a huge swath of the sea between Okinawa and Taiwan was permanently off-limits, but I'm not convinced. It was only *one* submarine, after all, that was carrying German uranium and got itself sunk. Seriously, ten bucks says it's whitefish from around Catalina, with food coloring added."

Without breaking stride, Caan seamlessly continued his story, funny and convoluted, involving the crews of two movies—one planning to make a sex-ed video—being inadvertently sent to the same studio. "And by the end of it all, the director finally turns to the cameraman and says ... he says ... 'Did you get all of that?'" Relieved to have reached his punchline, Caan cracked himself up.

Willy chuckled politely, but he was moving on; time was money. "Speak to me some more, Mr. Tower," he said as the waiter brought more slender plates of chips and salads, "of your consulting business."

"We've got a suite of ideas," Yanis boasted, "for presenting dialogue in much more interesting ways."

Leitz seemed nonplussed; he'd expected some new camera filter, or a post-production technique involving miles of tape. "Dialogue? What's wrong with the way we do it now?"

"It's too much like the theater," Yanis argued.

"Too stylized," agreed Jillian. "Not enough motion. We're always on our feet, these days. People want a bit more 'crackle and pop' to their motion picture experiences," she said, snapping her fingers energetically.

Leitz chuckled to himself. "Is a motion picture experience the same as going to see a movie?" He lit a cigarette—only when drinking—and tried not to blow smoke at the others. "You know, ever since this goddamned *avalanche* of technology started, this *surge*, they're calling it, everyone wants everything *instantly*. We've lost the will to delay gratification." He gave Caan a cheeky, lascivious wink. "Except in some things, obviously. When you're in capable hands, a little delay can be a fine thing." But then he remembered that they had a lady at the table, and half-stood in his anxious hurry to apologize. "Miss. Davidoff, I have the grace of a baboon," he said, genuinely embarrassed and gesturing to the half-empty glass by way of explanation. "Forgive me?"

"Oh, relax, Mr. Leitz," she said, unsure for a moment how to follow it. Her guess that technological breakthroughs might have accelerated social change, perhaps allowing women and others a freer voice, was quite a risk, but it was also hopeful, and that felt right. "Besides, I've always said," Jillian decided to try, "why struggle to make one course last all night, when you can have a banquet?"

Hysterical joy overcame Leitz, who stubbed out his cigarette so he could laugh without trying to smoke at the same time. "Oh, that's priceless! Somebody," he laughed, "somebody write that down! Absolutely *priceless*!"

They decided against the oysters. One of the dishes sounded convincingly like fish 'n'chips, so Jillian went for it. Yanis ordered eggs, 'slathered with our homemade Nuclear Sauce,' which he hoped might be *huevos rancheros*.

Laughing to himself in cyclical mini-bursts of glee, Leitz munched through his second brunch—or was it lunch, by now—a ceviche of unusual shellfish, while Jillian and Yanis laid down a dozen different techniques they were anxious to try in the studio. "Some will change cinematography forever or revolutionize sound editing. Some, we admit now, won't work well in practice, but we've really tried to cast ourselves forward, into the future," Yanis explained. "We asked ourselves, 'What will a night at the cinema be like in 2015?'"

Excitable as a puppy, Leitz spilled out his own *ad hoc* vision. "We'll all be watching movies in outer space, won't we? Floating around and enjoying ourselves. I read *Colliers*, with all those ambitious plans. Ooh," he thrilled, "that *artwork* of space stations in orbit. Just *glorious*! I can't wait to make a movie," he said, already framing the scene with his hands, "about landing on the moon, or on Mars."

"That's going to be available to us," Yanis said rather enigmatically, channeling his inner prognosticator. "So are the most enormous screens, more than eight floors high. So big, it makes you feel like you're right there, in the lead car at Le Mans, or going into space, or riding a roller coaster," he said, gesturing the basic idea. "Even down to the vertigo you'd experience."

"Sounds awful!" Leitz scoffed. "Everyone in the first three rows is gonna yak all over each other! Now, Smell-O-Vision?" he said, moving to a happier prospect. "*That's* got a future!" While Yanis waited, his patience not infinite, Leitz wasted their meeting time with an extemporization about the mingling of scents in a movie theater.

"It's a fun idea. Maybe as a novelty?" recommended Jillian. Both of them knew that audiences would no more smell their movies than they would commute into the city by helicopter, or eat beef intensively farmed in vast, skyscraper-like *farms*.

"Most successful changes come through evolution," Yanis charged, "and Smell-O-Vision just doesn't have anywhere to go. It's confusing, a gimmick, really. And expensive to install."

"You got to love a man," Leitz said, laughing again, "who just spits it out like it's hot."

Yanis explained as succinctly as he could: their movie technology projects connected to larger themes in the business, and most would result in gradual changes. "We've got to persuade other trendsetters to buy into the ideas and show the world they're possible. But your support will guarantee we do more for the movie industry than Smell-O-Vision ever will."

Leitz was draining his third cocktail, leaving only an icy brine at the bottom of the glass. *How in the name of Jack Daniels does anyone get any work done around here?* "We'd need about a month," said Yanis, "ideally, that is, but—"

"But we'd take a week," said Jillian.

"We need only a small crew, maybe six, and some studio space for filming. After a week, we'll know if some of them work. After a month, the best ones will be ready to show you. You keep everything we build, all the rights to the technology we create, less a fair percentage."

"Which we think is fifty percent," Jillian said. Yanis' foot, only an inch from hers, quickly shifted into contact.

"Do you, now?" Leitz cracked up again. He was enjoying Jillian's fiery, feminist shtick like she was auditioning for a part. "My mother could drive a bargain, so they tell me, but *this* lady ..." He stood, slightly wobbly but not the least self-conscious about it. "Every sports car," he announced, slapping his ample stomach, "needs the occasional pit stop. I will consider your offer, in the place where my best thinking happens." He tottered off, watched by an admiring Caan, sitting with his arms folded.

"I can't tell," the fixer confided, "whether he's enamored, or just hammered, but he's very fond of you two."

"Awesome," breathed Yanis.

"He *loves* it when things just come along and blow his mind. And people, young people, he adores them. The kind who say things like 'progressive' and 'radical,' who want peace with the world, and maybe a bit of premarital you-know-what." These two were young, sure, but definitely bright, and worldly, somehow, as though more had been crammed into their years than was usual. They were *driven*, something Caan knew Leitz always prized. And they were committed to making better movies, the one thing that got people like Caan and Leitz out of bed in the morning.

"Sure, but will he actually introduce us to people?" Jillian asked, then leaned in to emphasize, "The *right* people?"

Returning to the bright sunlight, Willy shielded his eyes and mopped his brow. "You know what we got here?" he asked them rhetorically. "A very characterful couple ..." He stopped himself. "A pair of characterful *equal partners*, I mean, and I just love what you've got going on, alright? So," he said, wiping his mouth and apparently checking in with his extremities to make sure they were still answering bells. "I'm going to give Rosa the details, and she'll make the calls and pass everything along to you," he said, looking up and down the street for a cab.

"That's fantastic, Willy," Eli said, rising. "They won't let you down, I promise."

He tossed cash onto the table as though it didn't matter—even in 1952 dollars, Leitz was a multi-millionaire—and said, "People don't walk around with the belief that I invest in idiot schemes, so be careful with my reputation, alright?" He spotted a cab and began gesticulating; it veered over and headed for the curb. "I want results, but I don't need them tomorrow. Take a month. Actually? Fuck it, take *two*, really try some things out. You can be my Research and Development division. Just make sure you 'develop' something fantastic!"

"You can depend on us," said 'George.'

By the curb, 'Jean' leaned in to kiss the director's cheek. "Thanks for taking a chance on us. You won't regret it."

The yellow cab pulled up. "Bye, now!" he called over his shoulder, tottering slightly until the cab's door handle steadied him.

Caan watched Leitz leave and then asked, "So, hey, I guess that went pretty well, huh?" He raised a glass and they all clinked.

"To a great start," Jillian said. Then, much lower, "If he loves our stuff, it'll be the *perfect* way to get on some movie sets and meet the kind of weirdos we're looking for."

"Don't forget, Jillian, here," Yanis emphasized, "*we're* the weirdos. And did you hear what he said about Sam Clark and the intergalactic craft? No wonder I've felt so ... *off* the past few days."

Jillian smiled, understanding that Yanis felt a connection to the ship, though she didn't understand the connection in and of itself.

"Anyone else up for more margaritas?" asked Caan, who felt like celebrating. If their joint venture worked out, the finder's fee would buy him a new Volkswagen. And more importantly, Willy was the perfect conduit through which to meet all the major Hollywood figures—producers, actors and their agents, technology people and publicists. "I hear everyone does margaritas after brunch. Or is it before? I can't get used to this new European crap."

"Sure, but let's mix them at our place," Yanis suggested. "Jillian and I have plenty to think about."

***

San Francisco, Fall 1950

'The Nazi Stink' they were calling it. Any association with Hitler's regime, and a person could be blacklisted. It almost didn't matter who they were; an accomplished, fifty-ish director of *noir* thrillers was briefly barred—from his own club, mark you—following revelations that his accountant had once worked for a former Nazi. The Stink could cling on like that for years, destroying careers in a way that was piecemeal and incremental, but inevitable. It was Death by a Thousand Cuts, in public.

Two very different men had faced this paralyzing revelation in the last month: Keith McLandis and Everett Lord—one a board-treading comic, the other a well-reviewed thespian. Neither would ever work again, and Lord was lucky to escape his Kirkwall estate with his life, smuggled out by a loyal butler.

When history came for the acting career of Loretta Lehrer, however, the first cut was bloodless. It was just a warning, delivered in private, though the encounter began very publicly. Inge appeared on Union Square at her most luxuriantly fashionable—even by the furs of today—in hopes of snagging Loretta's attention, even just a jealous glance.

The ruse had not failed. "You've *got* to tell me where you found those shoes!" Loretta trilled, pulling Inge aside by the Beaux-Arts facade of the swanky City of Paris department store where Geary dovetailed into Stockton Street.

But their discussion quickly moved on from shoes and autographs and the usual, "I just *loved* you in such-and-such ..." Before Loretta's signature was completed, Inge said, not unlike a concerned family physician, "I've actually been keeping an eye on you for a few weeks."

"An eye?" Loretta asked, finishing the autograph with care.

"And I've decided to come out of the shadows and speak with you."

"Hm?" Every day in the City promised several random encounters like this, and Loretta was due to meet Marcelo at the Top of the Mark in less than twenty.

It was the tone which made Loretta look up. This woman was suddenly talking about Loretta's father, making some kind of accusation.

"I'm sure you're already aware that his born name was Albert Leitner, not Lehrer. Made the change at Ellis Island in 1929."

"So. you went digging in the records and found my dad?" Were there no lengths these creeps wouldn't go? "Well, what about it?" she asked angrily. "What's wrong with changing his name? Plenty of people did it."

"Of course, and you're both entitled to whichever name you want," Inge said, taking the pen from her hand, "but your father's *brother* is Julius Leitner." She screwed the cap back on. "To give him his full title: Herr *Lagerführer* Leitner. From 1942, he was Deputy Commandant at Ravensbrück."

"Julius? Who is Julius?" Loretta demanded, looking confused. "And lager-what? I don't speak any German, so …"

Could the family have hidden such an awful secret? "Your father never mentioned a younger brother?" asked Inge, almost amiably, as though her discovery of this dreadful man might somehow bring familial happiness. "Julius stayed in Germany with his pregnant wife, you see. Only your father, Albert, made the journey in the end. Julius advanced quickly in the Party, while your father began his new life in America."

"I've never even heard of a 'Julius' in the family," Loretta said, more than ready to end the conversation. "And 'the Party?' You mean, *the Nazi Party*? That's horrible, impossible. Who are you?"

"We should talk somewhere more private."

Inge's targets usually chose a nearby cafe or restaurant, often a place they knew, where two 'Ladies who Lunch' could be seen uneventfully doing just that. And more than most, Inge expected Loretta Lehrer to be able to act a part. "I'm telling you, this 'Julius' guy is news to me," she said as they found a booth in a quiet corner.

"As you said," Inge dispensed quickly with the waiter but ordered Loretta something strong. She'd need it shortly, to take the edge off.

"And this is creepy, by the way."

"Creepy?"

"You usually come up to complete strangers in the street and start talking like this?"

Inge did her best to *avoid* being intimidating. Instead, she played the amiable interlocutor—not an accuser, but the solemn, duty-bound conveyor of awkward tidings. "You're saying you've never had contact with Julius Leitner?"

"Of course I haven't," she snapped, "because he doesn't exist. That's why it's creepy, you see?"

"That's a surprise," said Inge, "because he knows quite a lot about you." From what seemed to be a large dossier of information, Inge placed two recent photographs of Leitner on the table. "I spoke to him about you by telephone, just a few days ago. He asked me to pass on his best wishes for your engagement."

Loretta was ashen now, her defiance visibly crumbling. She stared downcast at her diamond ring while the waiter brought their cocktails; she ignored hers, but Inge set about her own Manhattan with zeal.

"He's sent you letters in the past, and gifts at Christmas time. You wrote him a card to say thank you," Inge recalled, "which opened, 'Dear Onkel Julius.'"

"Alright! *Jesus*," Loretta hissed. "Alright. Just ... lower your voice. I think ... I'm maybe starting to see what's going on." She took a few seconds to collect herself; this was supposed to be a relaxed morning of shopping, not digging into the murky and terrible past. "I don't know where you got this from, but Dad never mentioned Ravensbrück, or anything like that. He said his brother was in the Army Reserve. Did his duty, survived the war, got discharged. Nothing to write home about."

"I'm sorry," Inge said plainly, "but that's not true." She opened the half-inch thick dossier, but gave Loretta just the basics, out loud and without any dimming of the facts, of her uncle's tenure at Ravensbrück. Built solely to house a female labor force, the camp boasted a large medical section, led by Dr. Baumann, whose assignment to U-99X on 'special duties' rather curtailed the lab's macabre medical experiments.

"Your uncle believed in gaining maximum efficiency by working people to death and replacing them, rather than feeding them adequately," Inge explained, using just two of the images to reinforce the point: huddles of emaciated, wafer-thin women, close to death. "He isn't facing any criminal charges as yet, probably well-connected or wealthy enough to avoid them so far, but who knows? The new government could decide to go looking for him. Maybe ask some questions about responsibility for certain things."

Once Loretta was really sobbing, Inge softened her body language and moved a little closer. "It's not your fault. It won't help to hear that, but I mean it. This is nothing to do with you at all."

"Then, why do I feel like …" Loretta cried, "like I protected him, even though I didn't know?"

"It's bad luck, I guess," Inge said. "Another evil man, doing more of their evil things, only this one happened to be a relation."

It was too raw. "It's unfair, though! If you're right about him, then I'll have to live with the stain of something really terrible."

"These days, that's true of almost everyone I know." She excepted herself, naturally; Inge's conscience was as clean as the cafe's pristine floor.

"So, how does this work? Who are you going to tell?" Loretta asked, then the rest of the awfulness started to hit. "My father will be absolutely *devastated*. Mother, too."

"I won't be telling anybody about this," Inge told her. "It's going to stay between you and me."

Loretta gave a tired sigh of realization. "So, it's about money. People *always* want money. Why didn't I guess?"

"Miss Lehrer, let me stop you," Inge said, "Blackmail doesn't interest me. My reasons for contacting you like this weren't quite so trivial as that," she added, hiding the truth behind something more enticing.

"So, what, I'm supposed to do you some favors?" She quickly evaluated the woman opposite her in the light of Hollywood's contemporary appetites. "You wanna be a star, is that it?" Sure, she was carrying off the 'blonde bombshell' caricature well enough, with her stern little pout and obviously expensive attire. "Newcomers like you will always need a hand getting auditions and screen tests."

"I was interested in some introductions, yes," Inge said, not interrupting.

"So you can snag some decent parts before you're too—"

"Old?" Inge said.

She sighed. "Experienced, I was going to say." It was the latest, and least offensive euphemism, and better than most. After all, once you'd banked enough years away, Loretta had begun to think, the compound interest made each of them really *worth* something.

"But there are hidden costs to those experiences, wouldn't you say, Miss Lehrer?" Then, more wistfully but nonetheless penetrating, "The passing of time condemns us all, in the end."

She made to stand but changed her mind. From her seat, she glanced around, perhaps for a waiter or to find a phone. Inevitably, she lit a cigarette and found she'd taken a pull on her drink. "Are you gonna carry on sounding like a goddamned Gypsy fortune teller, or are you gonna spit it out? *Why* it is you're here? Just to ruin my morning?"

"I'm here to offer you something," Inge said.

"What, some unconfirmed Nazi crap which will just slowly poison my career?"

She signaled for the waiter and smiled. "Actually, I want you to think of it as more of an endorsement opportunity."

***

2 weeks later

[Cable from US to Bonehouse, Fall 1950]
<u>Report on Subject 7/LL</u>
Following induction to Investor Level, a single dose of Preparation Nord-G was administered. Four post-injection monitoring visits (days 2, 5, 10, 14), no signs of organ poisoning or depression in this patient.

7/LL reports she feels 'younger,' and that her skin is, 'refreshed and tight.' Cardiovascular health was above normal during tennis. Libido has increased markedly. Subject reports having, 'plenty of energy all day.'

Recommend: continue Nord-G doses, twice weekly. Diet and lifestyle to remain unchanged—Vegan, hydration-intensive, low carbohydrate—with periods of intermittent fasting, days 20-22, to address subject's weight loss goals.

Subjectively, 7/LL's progress has been rapid and impressive. Her outer appearance is brighter, and she is clear-eyed; morning doses of monoamine oxidase inhibitors discontinued. Importantly, her friends have noticed the change and begun asking about it.

Actions / Conclusion: Subject 7/LL is an excellent candidate for an Advocate role. To be proposed during next home visit.

***

Parliament Studios, Burbank, CA, 6 weeks later

Leitz visited Merlin Inc. once, about a month after the experiment had begun. He left enraptured with their ideas and enchanted once again by 'Jean' and her spunky wit. Within a day, he'd thrown a second, much larger chunk of money at the project. "We'll wring the best out of these things," Caan promised 'George' and 'Jean'—*he never, ever used their real names*—"and if they work, Leitz will make you both incredibly rich." He hired a bevy of people on month-long contracts; there were experienced electricians to handle the high-voltage stuff, and to Caan's relief, some young engineers who spoke the right language. Work began quickly, and just kept on accelerating.

"What did they make of the 'walk and talk' idea?" Yanis asked, toward the end of a day. He and 'Jean' were being chauffeured by Caan, all the way out to their secondary backlot property. Given the distances, it was easier to drive between them. "That new thing with the reticulated arm?"

"At first," Caan laughed, "half of them couldn't even *say* 'reticulated,' but Jeff Westerman showed up like a champ, just 'cause I asked nicely, and he went and slapped everybody into shape." If it had a lens, Westerman could improve it; so went his well-earned industry reputation. "He's kinda made himself the site foreman, nowadays. Won't take shit from *anybody*. But he cranks out results you wouldn't believe. He's been working on this walking thing for three days already."

These updates were important; neither of them had been to the backlot in nearly a week. Jillian paused taking notes for a script. "Westerman is that chap with the ..." she gestured, "you know, the beard, right?"

"Capital T, Capital B," Yanis confirmed.

"And, Jeff liked some things that came out of the walking thing," Caan reported, "especially with a slow, consistent speed of motion." Their earlier attempts had been dizzying, with dialogue-heavy scenes being filmed like games of tennis, zooming back and forth.

"Well, if they think it'll be worth showing to Willy in the end, tell them to try it," Jean advised.

"I tell them to try everything," Caan said, flicking his half-spent cigarette out the car's window. "The money's already spent, and we got a dozen other irons in the fire. Most of our failures still cough up something useful. Like, for example, radio control of a speeding car does *actually* have range limitations."

"Yeah," Yanis slumped. "Sorry about that."

"It wasn't your fault," Caan said charitably.

"Yes, it was." He hadn't tested the mechanism properly and ended up driving a perfectly good Buick Roadmaster into a backlot wall at seventy, filming an ambitious chase sequence with a biplane. The Buick had fared better than the wall, which was demolished, but the car was still a write-off.

"Alright, it was your fault," allowed Caan, "but it looked *unbelievable* on film, and we *learned* from it. Plus, you're dealing with more important things than antennas and remote-control mechanisms," he said, taking the final turn along the slightly improved dirt road which connected the two properties. "You two are doing six days a week at the office, right? We hardly ever see you out here, but by the sounds of it, you're there together cooking up scripts that are gonna knock 'em out!"

"Let's see," Yanis said, tempering Caan's enthusiasm. "We've had some nice phone calls from interested parties."

"Interested doesn't come close, my friend."

"But I want the money in the bank before I pop the champagne."

"Are you *kidding* me?" Caan brought the Plymouth to a less-than-graceful stop in the uneven patch of land behind the backlot, next to a pair of trailers. "That idea you had, the one about the kid who travels through time?"

"*Past Forward*," he said. A cough. "Working title."

"Makes it sound like a football movie," Jillian said. "I still think '*Back to the Future*' is better." Yanis grimaced at her, then silently pleaded, but she was unmovable. "And did you like one where all the toys come alive to help the little boy?" she asked next.

"*Game Tale*," Caan remembered. He climbed out of the driver's seat and fumbled for his sunglasses in his top pocket; it was about a hundred and four outside, he guessed. Like walking around in a pizza oven. Even Tunisia, serving in 1943, hadn't helped inure him to the heat. "Absolutely loved it. What was the hero guy's name? Oh yeah, Larry Lightyear! 'To the Cosmos, and Beyond!'"

"We didn't sell that one yet," Jillian reported glumly. "But..." it was her cue to Yanis.

"Oh, yeah, we called that guy back, the producer guy in Santa Clara."

"What producer guy?" Then it clicked, and the meaning of it was huge enough that Caan almost drove off the 'road'. "Bix Nielsen?"

"Yeah, he left us a message to—"

"You just called Bix Nielsen, the guy who brought the world *Ivan Krieg*?"

"Alright, so he's kind of a big deal."

"And *Cape Retribution*. You called that genius, 'the producer guy,'" Caan said sternly. "Never do that again."

"Roger Wilco," Yanis said, admonished.

"What did he have to say?"

Yanis passed it back to Jillian, who explained, "I basically sold him that underwater movie I told you about," she said. "Remember, the one with the renegade nuclear submarine?"

"That one was too complicated," he said. "All kinds of technology."

"He loved it, and he says if his people can make a camera-toting *bathyscaphe* that doesn't leak and destroy its own film stock," Jillian said, "he'll buy the script."

"Also, he has influential friends in the US Navy," Yanis said of Nielsen, "and plans to borrow a couple submarines."

"You see the crazy shit you two are kicking off?" Caan said with a conspiratorial smile. "I love it!"

Backlot existence was dominated by the rolling cycle of construction and its opposite, but Leitz's workshop buildings felt more permanent. "I didn't know Willy already had a building here," Yanis recalled. "Kinda perfect."

"It was a town hall in some big crowd scene. Proved too useful to part with." Originally a kind of elaborate lean-to, the four-sided structure now had a simple roof with built-in slats to control the natural lighting, and to some extent, the flamethrower daytime heat.

On the short walk to the workshop building, Yanis dropped back with Jillian to plead his case again. "Do we *have* to steal the original movie titles?" *Past Forward* wasn't unforgettable, but it was serviceable, he thought.

"In for a penny, in for a pound," she said.

"I have no idea what that means."

"We stole the plot, that gives us the title, too. Besides, the originals are *good* titles. Ours are terrible."

"Ours are fine," countered Yanis.

"*Broken Cop?*" she scoffed

"Another working title," he said defensively.

"You think '*Lethal Weapon*' was no good, but you think *Broken Cop* will cram the theaters?"

"It's not that, I mean ... wouldn't it feel better to put our own stamp on these movies?"

"We're making them thirty years early," she hissed at him. "I'd say that's a pretty indelible stamp."

Caan walked some way ahead of them; these kooky 'creative couples' and their endless discussions. It sounded more like an argument, this time; couples needed to do that, too, creatively or not. Despite the heat, he lit another cigarette. "Ah, good, someone's hammering," he observed as they arrived. "It's not really a movie set unless there's hammering." The trio were ushered into the building by one of the crew, all instantly glad to be sheltered from the sun.

The space was quite large, a surprise which reminded Yanis slightly of walking into the storage chambers at *Der Dom*. They were filming an office scene, trying to get the Aaron Sorkin 'Walk and Talk' right. Veterans of the stage and screen Tim Courtley and Nathan Dearborn were mulling over a sheet of script together, both brandishing pencils. Neither looked impressed with anything going on around them.

"Why would Caan hire those crusty old so-and-sos?" Jillian asked, surprised. "This project is about novelty and fresh thinking. Those one-track old fools have been playing the same dapper, entitled, debonair role since ... God, the early *thirties*."

Caan explained while shuttling between arbitrating with one group and scheduling something on the phone. When among movie people, he was never still, a one-man cottage industry of filmmaking. "Willy told Tim and Nathan to come over and have a look at what we're doing. I can't even begin to guess *why*," Caan said, exasperated at this new awkwardness, "except that The Great Director had three cocktails before lunch again."

"*They're* doing the 'Walk and Talk?'" Yanis asked. "Those two?" Ideal for the roles, they were not, but they were *truly* ideal as potential friends with connections *everywhere* in the industry.

"It's just an experiment," said Caan. "We can try capturing some gestures and interaction, maybe swing the boom out and change angle as they go."

"I like it," Yanis nodded. "Phasing one in, and the other out."

"That'll help show more of the interior, too," Jillian said. "Like the opening chapter of a book, setting the scene."

"Gotcha." Caan approached the actors, his enthusiasm entirely feigned. "Gentlemen of the stage!" he bowed. "You are welcome to our meager home."

"Say, Eli," Dearborn said, extending a hand. "What's Willy got you doin' out here in the desert?" He sounded, and formerly had looked, like an Atlantic City lounge lizard, straight from central casting. Now, at fifty-six, his hair thinning, and rumors of recent surgery, Dearborn wasn't going to get any more tough-guy or buddy-cop roles. Or much of anything else, if the rest of the rumors were true.

"Trying things out, is all," Caan said, almost dismissing the project. *Nothing to see here.*

"Pretty expensive stuff," Courtley said, looking around at the array of equipment. "What the hell are those?"

"Gauze screens for the camera lenses," Courtley explained. "We're trying different thicknesses, materials."

"What's wrong with what we have now?" Dearborn asked.

"And there," Eli muttered, "is our problem."

"Hm?"

"Ah, nothing." Eli motioned to their copy of the script, now quite heavily edited. "You guys felt like stepping in, then? Helping out?"

"Figured we'd make ourselves useful."

"Unless you want us to make ourselves scarce, instead?" Dearborn asked.

"Oh, yes, we wouldn't want to muscle in on any secrets, would we?" said Courtley.

"I could tell you …" Dearborn began.

"But then I'd have to kill you!" the pair said together.

"I *adored* that line!" Dearborn gushed. "Pure genius! *Operation Hope*, wasn't it?"

"You're too kind," said Yanis.

They got to the task at hand but found that Courtley was troubled. "You want us to read our lines while charging around the place, line abreast, tracked by a zooming camera?"

"We're pretty sure it's going to look silly, Tim, but we're making a point of giving *everything* a shot."

Dearborn chimed in, "What do you mean by this, rapid and intense?"

"You're two very busy, very competent people," explained Jillian, "catching each other up on a case."

"While on our way from A to B," Dearborn confirmed.

"Wouldn't it just be better to catch me up in my office?" asked Courtley.

"Probably," Eli shrugged. "Alright! Places, people!"

***

Jillian looked as closely as she could, through different lenses, and simply couldn't shake the certainty that something was *odd* about Tim Courtley. As an actor, he'd been capable of only a limited range, but now he was giddy, almost childish, full of an energy which eluded most people his age.

"Yanis?" she said quietly as he zipped past on another errand. "Can I talk to you?"

It was hard to put into words. "I'm a professional investigator, so I'm not really supposed to use words like 'hunch,' but boy, oh boy, I've got myself one."

"About what?"

"Courtley, of course!" she said, motioning discreetly toward the actor, who was plowing through another questionably successful take with Dearborn. "You don't notice something strange about him? Like he—*I don't know*—snorted coke before showing up here today? Something like that?"

Yanis tried not to stare, but her accusation made him fascinated. "I mean, he's got a spring in his step, no mistake. Did he find a new girlfriend, maybe?"

Jillian gave a brief but expressive cough.

"Oh, alright. A boyfriend, then?"

But not even a new romance could explain the transformation. "We could ask him his secret," Jillian suggested.

"Whether we do or not," Yanis said, "we should get to know him."

"My thoughts exactly." She already had a plan. "We'll tail him after this test session."

"Not quite what I meant by getting to know him," Yanis laughed, "but, sure, Miss Investigator."

***

Courtley veritably tap-danced out of the experimental shack, just as his driver brought the car round. After hearing his stereotypically British, "A very good day to you, my man!" Yanis and Jillian watched him leave the backlot.

"*The Devil and the Bishop*," Jillian said as the car pulled away.

Yanis adjusted his tie once again; it was part of his *cultured idiosyncrasy*, but the damn thing had a mind of its own. "Is this the start of a joke?"

"1947. That one, and *The Adventures of Don Palazzo*."

"Huh?"

"Timothy Courtley," explained Jillian. "*Sir* Timothy, eventually, just before his death. Aged only forty-one, as I remember."

"How do you know all that?" Yanis asked.

"Grandma Qualmes, Oma, watched old movies on TV, one after another, after Granddad died. I used to sit with her then and at the nursing home, later. I must have watched a hundred films with her. She was like an encyclopedia. Come to think of it," she said wistfully, "by the end, movies were all she could remember."

"That's sad," he said, "I'm sorry."

"Tim Courtley played a bunch of dashing hero characters, then some arrogant bullies and a corrupt mayor, and then played nobody at all, because he was drinking himself to death."

"When was this?"

"Relative to now," she calculated, "he died about eight weeks ago."

"Wow. Looking good, isn't he?"

They caught up with Caan as the session was ending. The camera teams broke for lunch, leaving their experiments for the moment. There were filters and booms, reels of tape and lenses, from one end of the shack to the other.

"What about him?" Caan asked as he drove them back to their apartment.

"He's made this amazing turnaround," Jillian said. "In our timeline, by '48, when he did *Caramel Moon*—don't bother, it's dreadful—he was wearing makeup to hide the bags under his eyes. Grandma Qualmes pointed it out one day, said it was a symptom of The Demon Drink."

"So, did he kick the booze in this timeline, somehow? Got help and straightened out?"

"That's one thing, kicking the booze. Quite another is to begin exuding *veritas* and energy and—"

"Wait, exuding what?" asked Caan from the driver's seat.

"*Veritas*. Life force."

"You're saying," Yanis said, going slow in case his brain might give way, "Tim Courtley is a Jedi?"

"A what?" Caan asked, feeling that he'd quickly fallen behind, as usual.

"No, I'm saying he's using advanced Nazi chemistry to reverse his aging process."

"Shit, Jilly. This is like a thriller, or something. We've got Nazis, *and* strangely rejuvenated actors, *and* some secret elixir, and now we're looking for clues?"

They mulled over the evidence, wishing it was more abundant, until arriving at the apartment. Caan bid them a good day; he had to report to HQ, then do some travel of his own.

As theories go, it was pretty good, but Yanis sat there, chewing his lip. In some ways, it was like Jillian had claimed a jackpot before the bells went off. "If Courtley is really taking something, how can we prove it?"

"Hang onto your hat," she warned, bringing out her Dictaphone, "and keep your ears open. You'll hear background conversation and noise but listen for Courtley's voice." It was reedy but projected, like a Heldentenor, carrying easily over the hubbub.

"Oh, they're getting better, I'd say, learning to be more civilized. Step by step, month by month. And along the way, well what would you know? They're knee-deep in new ideas which might actually help the world, not poison it, or blow it up. Amazing what a bit of peace can do, isn't it, for human ingenuity and trade?"

"And ..." she said, drawing out the syllable until the tape wound forward to the correct spot, "there's this."

"I mean, it sounds awful to say, and I know you'll understand ... they were just so very orderly about everything, weren't they?"

Agreement, quick but quiet, surrounded him.

You knew exactly where you stood. It was black and white: raze it all to the foundations, absolutely all of them, gone. It was brutal but it was simple. And now they're sending them to us, or to England, and people just don't want them."

Someone argued that upcoming elections might hinge on the issue.

"The British government can barely look after its own, can't afford the big welfare projects they promised. Military spending at some crazy percentage of their overall budget. All over fear that Germany will do something stupid. I tell you, they're not *stupid. They've got some clever ideas about society, just like they've got clever ideas about new mechanisms, and little artificial moons."*

A question began about Courtley's possibly attending a rocket launch at Peenemünde, but Jillian stopped the tape.

"Whoa." To hear such vile drivel from a noted Hollywood star was unsettling, and terribly incongruous, like hearing Daffy Duck recite the SS oath of allegiance. "How did you manage to make the tape?"

"I'm a detective, Yanis."

"I know, but ..."

"Years of training."

"Sure, and that's all great, but ..."

She sighed. "Is it because I'm a woman? And, 'women can't do high-level police work,' hmm? Is that what your tiny brain is telling you?"

"Now, wait a second—"

"It's the *1950s*, Yanis, not the Victorian era. Girls can *do* things now!" she said, her deadpan exterior finally breaking as she laughed. "Even sometimes arrange for conversations to be recorded."

"But how?" he needed to know.

"Sabine pays her staff well," Jillian summed up very concisely. "I just paid one of them better."

| 8 |

Festivities

1855 Redwood Rise, 2 weeks before Finale Day, 1952

First, 'Sabine' decided, she'd have breakfast. Coffee and a croissant, at the very least; it was only civil, after such a late night. A glance at *Der Zeitung* and the day's mail and check the new answering machine. Only then would she deal with the American radar problem.

"Hey, there's no need to call me things like that!" Helmut Wolf objected. "It's getting harder, like I always said it would. I can't just blend in. Their radar is improving, and last time I was spotted on my way out over the Gulf of Mexico by a fighter plane, Christ knows where it came from."

"I thought the skies over the Caribbean were getting 'busier every month?'"

"They are."

"Well, it sounds to me like that would make things easier, not harder."

"It's not just volume of traffic. I can't blend in like before," her pilot told her. "Their radar—"

"Yes, you told me," Sabine said, her temper rising.

"We knew this would happen, eventually. I'll was able to reach Curacao this time, but from here on, we're going to have to think of another way."

"Am I still talking to Major Helmut Wolf?"

"*Former* major." As commander of a disbanded squadron, Wolf was demobilized and, at forty-one, would have been living off his *Luftwaffe* pension. Bonehouse, Keck, and Sabine paid a hell of a lot better.

"Helmut Wolf," she said, waxing rhapsodic, "A man whose fearless penetrations ..."

"Steady."

"Of American airspace in the service of the Reich—let me finish, you rotten little shit—are certain to inspire many legends."

"Are you *mad*? No one can ever hear a *word* of this."

"That same hero, that same God-like airman has been demoted to 'Curacao Courier?'" Sabine scoffed. "A tragedy, for one to have sunk so low."

"California is exceptionally dangerous," the former *Luftwaffe* pilot reminded her. "The new American radar system is for air traffic control. It's sensitive, even by German standards. *Big Boy* has *six* engines, remember; we'll be as clandestine as a horny baboon. If someone comes up to take a look, decides we're hostile and shoots us down, I've got fuck-all for deniability, and the Americans don't have *any* sense of humor about this kind of—"

"OKAY!" she bellowed down the phone. "I hate hearing *can't*, Helmut, even if it's completely fucking reasonable."

These restrictions would hurt; the old ways gave them an ingress route that was solid gold: fly from The Ranch direct to Curacao, spend a day on a world class beach, then parachute at night into the California farm belt, usually smack on target, with their small group of friendlies converging quickly. Wolf had a dozen successes, no failures, and an ardent desire to keep things that way.

"So, we find another route," suggested Sabine. "Let's get ourselves into the Curacao to Fort Lauderdale air freight business, or something like that."

"Is there much, um, trade between the two places?"

"You know what I'm looking at?" she said, still marveling that the phone's wireless reception was so clear, even forty yards from the east veranda.

"I'm picturing you ... outside a crowded bar," he guessed, "in Harlem, and you're about to go in and settle a debt. There's gonna be broken glass, cracked jaws, and all manner of fisticuffs ..."

"I've got two banana plants here in my backyard, you thundering dick."

He said nothing for a while, then, "So, you, um, like bananas?"

"I like the idea of bringing them, hot and fresh, from Curacao to Florida."

"Hot and ...? I'm not sure you grasp how bananas work, Sabine."

"Get back to fucking work, Helmut. I'm expecting another call."

"Boyfriend?"

"Yeah, yours."

"Funny."

"A work friend. From Kalamata Metallurgy."

"Sure you'd like to roll off his tongue."

"What?"

"I said, 'I'm sure that rolls off the tongue.'"

"Funny."

It sounded like she was filing her nails. "A work friend, you said?" Wolf asked.

"Party of three."

"Just gonna pick whichever one's more handsome to spend the night with?"

She stopped filing, privately thrilled, as she always was. "You're *jealous*." It came out as a hissing little rebuke.

"Maybe he'll offer to show you an impressive yardage of Greek steel?"

"Well ... you can't call a girl a fool just for hoping." While he laughed, she poked at him again with her tone. "You're jealous of *that*, too."

"I'm married!" he protested.

"Gives you *three* things to be jealous about, then!" She blew a kiss down the wire and whispered, "Mind you don't turn green, *mein Schatz*." The line clicked.

***

Finale Day, 1615h

"A full house," Sabine said proudly to herself, reviewing the list of confirmed invitees. It was the best possible sign. Significant figures were now making time in their schedules to visit with 'Sabine.' Many accepted the initial invitation out of curiosity, and at the urging of a close friend who would vouch for Sabine and her methods. Beyond that, each Fountain member had their own reasons, a mix of the personal, the professional and the aesthetic.

Sabine's very special brand of 'life coaching' had brought remarkable change to many of her clients. Leaders and Investors liked to return often to her home, parting with a small fortune in 'administrative fees' to do so, but their loyalty was scant reward; Sabine had transformed their careers. Everyone here, tonight and every other night, owed Sabine a debt of some kind, or soon would, but a little networking and influencing on her behalf was a trivial price for the Elixir.

There were some, naturally, who took square and determined aim at Sabine's bedroom door, and more often than not, tripped on the way there. She remained both single and, somehow, too classy (or too resourceful) to have become embarrassed by a tittle-tattle. Any resentful ex-lovers were reminded of her thoroughness in matters of security, a tactic which maintained her relatively blameless reputation. There were no tapes, that much was certain; these days it seemed there was a 'tape' about everyone.

Sabine achieved all of this by being stylish —she was constantly reevaluating her look—but never ostentatious. She was, in the eyes of key people in Hollywood, a genuinely interesting figure, a worldly and graceful host who promised sophistication amid very select company. And all from behind a many-layered veil of secrecy, which precluded public fame. She did no press, never advertised, and was rarely photographed. To Sabine's muscular ego—that of an exhibitionist, a rope-master, an enslaver—the subservience of Hollywood's elites was ecstasy. The blanket secrecy they themselves imposed on each other only redoubled her enjoyment.

And if ever her self-esteem needed a pick-me-up, she could point out one of the growing display of 'historical curios' in her home. "There's the couch where Lytton and Lyle came up with the original idea for *High Noon at Clear Lake.*" The western was a huge 1950 hit for the director-producer partnership. "And out on that terrace, Tony

Rasmussen proposed to Princess Barbara. He told me in advance," she said, confiding, "he was nervous as a cat. But that gave me time to ask our groundskeeper, Mr. Preiss, to set off some fireworks." Hardly impromptu, the ten-minute display marking the royal engagement had led the weekend's *Hollywood Gazette.*

Tonight's guests, including Sabine's newcomers, would share specific traits. Seniority was an important part of Sabine's selection criteria; older men and women were wealthier, and more prone to the ravages of aging than their younger colleagues. Both attributes made one an excellent candidate for Fountain.

Second in Sabine's mind—and of growing in importance, as Fountain expanded—came her guests' networking potential. They were, after all, to be members of a society rooted in mutual assistance and trust. A director had a huge variety of phone numbers in his Rolodex; jobbing actors, on the other hand, had to wait for the phone to ring. Producers knew other people with money, which usually meant more people in the right age bracket. A surprising number of clients were coming from the creative trades, among them an Oscar-winning lighting designer.

Tonight's meeting would hopefully yield others, three or four accomplished script writers who might be, she suspected, of the right means and disposition to Participate. After all, as she reminded them, time waits for no one, nor can anybody smoke and drink heavily for decades without cost. As a backdrop to her sales pitch, Sabine was planning a commodiously small event, calculated to produce more than the sum of its parts. Or, what was that modern word Keck used to say, just to confuse everyone? Not *synchronous*, or *gingery*, but it sounded like both. He knew so many *words*. And so much else.

Once their initial fee went through, Participants could request access to Fountain's proprietary concoctions: The Classified Inventory. A single dose was all an entry-level member was guaranteed. Beyond that, they'd quickly be talking *real* money. Investor-level members had sold Manhattan condominiums, and in one case, forty-two feet of sleek, ocean-going perfection, to gain access to this second level. In return, they received six doses, and four visits a year with Sabine, who remained, to them "Dr. Ehrlinger." Investors liked to remark, especially in front of lowly Participants, that they'd been moved from Coach to First Class.

To reach the level of Associate, which provided a personal nurse-trainer-nutritionist, and round-the-clock pharmaceutical services, was to have all of First Class to oneself. Sabine would send couriers with tailor made concoctions, "fresh from our laboratories," never revealing that they'd been delivered under parachute by Wolf and *Big Boy* at ever-growing risk.

But some way beyond the Participants, Investors and even Associates, there existed another level, that of Fountain Head.

Informally, they were called The Leaders, an 'extremely select group,' according to Sabine, which was something of an understatement. In 1951, Joe Average pulled down $3,200 a year, after taxes. If Joe saved hard, he could walk off with the keys to an American-made car for around $2,000. When the wife and four kids came along, a comfortable home would run twelve Gs, maybe more with a big yard.

By the time Karl Dietrich achieved the rank of Leader, he'd given Sabine Ehrlinger and Fountain Inc. well over a million.

Karl had ascended alongside six other, equally affluent, donors and so, as she put it candidly—and drunkenly—to a starstruck Helmut Wolf one night, Sabine was, "raking it in like a bent croupier." These elite Fountain Heads spent more time with Sabine and her staff than with their own families and became her every waking concern. "When it comes to Leaders, we have only one rule," she'd announced to Karin the night they'd inducted Dietrich. "Leaders can never, *ever*, die."

"Everyone ever born will die, *Lieber*," Karin warned sensibly.

"Well, Fountain's Leader-donors *can't*, or they'll completely fuck up my business model. People won't buy a billion-dollar immortality drug if past customers are too dead to tell their friends about it."

Karin was polishing the bulbous, brass orb of a huge soup tureen. It already shone. "I think you should be straight with people, when it comes to their health," she said.

"I think," Sabine said, checking her date book and running a brush through her hair, "you should shut your ugly mouth." She stopped to growl at the brush for snagging her locks. "Or I'll gas you and shove you in a boiling oven." She set down the brush and turned. "I've done it before, you know."

"Congratulations on the achievement." *Deadpan.*

"Hundreds of times. We were getting better with practice. Like a string quartet."

"You're a heartless, soulless bitch," Karin said, quite matter-of-fact.

"The apple of my mother's eye."

"And mine, too," the old widow had added, earning her a kiss on the forehead.

The pitch itself was well-drilled and honed. Immortality was not only scientifically possible, she claimed, it was available *now*. It had always been Keck's plan, she read in his Future Files, to "leverage the Unique Selling Point of Fountain membership."

The whole thing was a ruse, of course. The drug cocktails offered a temporary reprieve for most, and a useless expense for some. The dream was powerful, but Sabine's claim to have mastered the secrets of eternal life rested only on terribly fragile supports; a tragedy among the Leaders could be dismissed as random ill-fortune—or, in a pinch, made to look convincingly like it. But multiple casualties among the Leaders would be terminal for their burgeoning, and already highly profitable business.

For now, those profits were Sabine's primary responsibility to Bonehouse, and to Keck. He would see her success spreading like a secret infection as each member gained that critical level of certainty in her medications and began counseling their friends to become Participants. There could be no inoculation against the desire for Eternal Youth, for Endless Happiness, or Whatever They Chose to Call It. The scent of that desire—a *fear*, if they'd ever be honest about it—hung around them all like an alluring, fragrant mist. She had watched it condense into thousands of droplets, each forming around particles of this elusive 'confidence.'

With carefully screened recommendations now comprising a full third of the group, Sabine knew it had begun finally to rain.

***

Yanis & Jillian's apartment, 2 weeks before Finale Day

In their apartment, as evening approached, Yanis looked over the private briefing documents that had been delivered by armed courier.

"Movement of the craft has been completed and everything is now secure," read Sam's tilted penmanship. "Groom Lake's salt flat provides an excellent parcel for storage. There are two unpaved runways, each spanning 5,000 feet. I hear the Air Force is interested in acquiring this property, but it will serve our purpose for now. Surprised the USAF would want the attention, being in such proximity to the big tourism destination they're building about 80 miles southeast of here.

"But I assure you, the craft is secure. I have been inside and am currently mapping the layout and analyzing the systems. I will continue to perform testing as requested to discover how everything works and then report my findings."

When he was finished, he set the document in the fireplace, and ignited it. He looked at the clock. Time to get ready for this shindig. A practice run, of sorts.

He was standing in front of the bedroom mirror, nervously asking questions. None of them were about tonight's gathering with Willy Leitz and his singular wife, Ramona. The dazzling singer-actress was almost forgotten. Their minds were on another invitation, two weeks away still, one they'd labored long and hard to secure.

"Do you think Dearborn will be there?" was Yanis' latest question.

"He's a super-patron, a Leader, so I assume so," Jillian said. She was well into the lengthy process of selecting an outfit from the wardrobe provided by Prophet. They had spared some expense, but not much, and she had only two more weeks to make herself look like she belonged among Californian royalty. Her hair still needed work, but even when she was being honest with herself, the rest was, as Yanis reminded her often, "to die for."

"And Courtley? Wouldn't it be a gas for you to meet him, after watching all of his movies with your grandmother?" asked Yanis.

But she was thoughtful. "Would it truly be Courtley? I mean, he's so completely changed."

Yanis was still practicing with his tie. "Reminds me of the plot of *Cocoon*," he said, then caught the idea in mid-air. "Hey, you know what? We could spin that! Do a script about aliens who are giving people secret injections to prolong their lives ..."

She appeared in the doorway, looking distinctly unimpressed. "A little too close to the bone, all things considered, wouldn't you say?"

"Hm?"

"Aliens rescuing humans? Remind you of any recent events?"

"Ah, yeah."

"And secret elixirs? I seem to remember some mention of them and this woman, Sabine ... what was her name?" she said sarcastically.

"They do say, 'write what you know,'" Yanis told her.

"Yes, but what you write is still supposed to be fiction. Come to think of it, this whole crazy story would make a good movie, one day."

He'd assembled the tie, but it was crooked. "No lie."

"A movie, so far," Jillian said, adjusting it for him, "without an ending."

"But, nevertheless, approaching the start of an interesting scene?"

She laughed easily, surprising herself as she retreated to the tiny half bath to check her makeup. "If it's *not* interesting," she said, "we'll have wasted a lot of time and effort for nothing."

"Relax. Dearborn's vouched for us. Said we were younger than the average Participants, but that wasn't a problem."

"Provided we have the right, um, *beliefs*. And lots of money."

He shrugged. "We don't make the rules. Maybe they're just looking for some new blood."

She appeared again at the doorway, just as horrified as before. "New blood? We really are trying to hit both feet at once with the shotgun, aren't we?"

He winced with regret, and then they were laughing about it, which was always a relief. But it couldn't last. "Come on, comrade and fellow exterminator of the Nazi scourge," she said, hauling off his ragged tie and helping him start again. "We're not playing dress-up, unfortunately. We're trying to look just different enough from ourselves so we're taken seriously as potential Nazis." She frowned at the asymmetrical tie, refusing to cooperate. "Potential *Participants*," she clarified. "The Nazi stuff seems mostly optional, if public reporting is any guide." Very few Fountain members had made political waves, and only one had recently fallen afoul the law, via the IRS.

"When obtaining something truly priceless, like these elixirs," said Yanis, undoing the tie altogether, "the exchange might have to include your soul."

"Only as collateral for the juniors," speculated Jillian, "but for the higher-ups, the Leaders, it's got to be a permanent deal. This business of tithing, like Fountain is just an innocent church for fringe believers." Raised Anglican by her parents, Jillian retained a respect for The Word, and found Inge's borrowing flatly distasteful. "But if she's really buying these expensive industrial parts ..."

There was a mountain of evidence, despite Fountain's best efforts. Gifted CIA and FBI veterans found little trouble in penetrating the shield of shell companies and dodgy mailing addresses which protected the enterprise. *Sabine Ehrlinger* had created elements of a legitimate trail for herself, but the gaps were too big to explain. And then, after sustained diplomatic pressure behind the scenes, Prophet had obtained transfer records from two small, regional German banks who were anxious to help in what David Walcott told them was a "routine IRS investigation."

Instead, the documents detailed over a hundred million dollars of illegal transactions. Where cash had to flow unseen, there would be risks and expenses—residual paperwork, disloyal partners, and the inevitable bribes. "The only thing that makes sense is that Keck's equipping at least one major laboratory," Yanis said, repeating a conclusion he'd reached on first seeing the list of purchases. "Centrifuges, professional-level glassware, forty or fifty different substances, some of them pretty unusual, and you remember that *bovine vaccine?* What on earth?"

Jillian twirled briefly in the mirror; the cream and burgundy dress was a good fit around the middle, but a fraction too long. "Everything is nefarious. We don't have to wonder about it. Once we get all the facts, every single element of that list will prove to be detrimental to humanity."

The only question would be: could Prophet, its resources stretched, possibly find Bonehouse before some new evil crawled out to infect the world?

Yanis shuddered. "Okay, watch me get this right, finally," he said, grabbing the loose tie with determination and then measuring its position by eye before having another try at the knot. He felt a hapless subject to almost everything else that was going on, but his appearance was one of the simple ways he'd found to exercise a little control.

Jillian watched him, lips parted as he fiddled with the necktie. She'd never known a man to be so dedicated, so intelligent, and yet so earnest and endearing. Her breath hitched as she stepped forward, unbuttoning his shirt.

"What?" Yanis asked, as if he didn't know.

A kiss followed. The stroke of her hand down his torso. A soft moan from her lips.

Moments later, the tie, the shirt, and her dress, were piled on the bedroom floor.

***

Boeing Superfortress B-29-F13A, 'Slim Jim,' 72nd Reconnaissance Squadron, 45 miles NNE of Curacao, Caribbean Sea, 12 days before Finale Day

"Before we head off into the unknown, are we absolutely sure that's him?" Gibbs asked his pilot.

It wasn't a difficult question to answer, but Major Speight worked through the evidence out loud. "Well, the target aircraft is indeed gigantic, has indeed got six engines, and our guys at the docks heard the pilot speaking German on the phone." He turned to the younger pilot with a patient smile; they'd been airborne for seven hours, already. "I'm convinced. You?"

"Yeah. Let's tag along, see where he's going."

The other guys at Prophet, the ones flying long recon missions trying to find Bonehouse, or ferrying strange people around, had doubted that the fabled *Big Boy* was even real. Once Speight and Gibbs spotted the monstrous seaplane during a pass of the harbor at Curacao, its vast wing acreage glinting in the sun like a beacon, the question changed. Now, more than anything, they needed to know where Wolf went in *Big Boy* once he'd finished propping up a bar on the harbor.

"Where are you going, Wolf Man?" asked Garcia, his tone husky and predatory as they watched the rising blip on the screen. "Where does that big bastard plane set down without anyone knowing?" The plane's betting pool was up to $450, with Speight's money on the Amazon rain forest, and Gibbs imagining a secret beach redoubt on a tropical island.

"Now remember, this guy's real good," Speight reminded his copilot and the six other crewmen, listening on headsets from their stations in the rear of the huge, converted bomber. "He's snuck in and out of all kinds of places. But we've got his number, right, fellas?"

He barely needed the intercom to hear their answer; his men were loudly enthusiastic about finding Wolf.

"This motherfucker thinks he can give Nazis a first-class ride into the States? Fuck that," the aircraft's navigator opined. He'd be tracking Wolf's route, helped by two electronics specialists who would read *Big Boy's* infrared and heat signatures. They might only have one more chance, and every tool aboard the Superfortress would be in play. "He's heading almost due south, bearing one-seven-seven, leveling out now at ... sixteen thousand."

Speight brought the B-29 into a very steady turn to follow Wolf south and passed over a cloud-enshrouded coast just as a thunderstorm broke to their east.

***

Tyndall AFB, Panama City, Florida, 18 hours later

Sam was shaking his head again. "Can't be."

"I'm telling you what we saw," Speight insisted.

"What your instruments saw, you mean," argued Alistair Wheeler. "We needed a visual confirmation, an actual sighting."

"Visibility was for shit. He landed on a gradually sloping hillside, as far as we could tell, but then the sun went down faster than a bank teller's shutter," he explained.

Sam had pointed to the illustration countless times already. "But this is a seaplane! With the floats on, *Big Boy* would be way too heavy ..."

"I'm telling you, they must have strengthened the fuselage."

"And the landing roll would be huge, at least two thousand feet, maybe four—"

"What you do," he proposed, "is slam all six of those big fuckers into reverse as soon as the wheels touch down, then deploy a braking parachute out of the back. It can be done."

Of course it could, Sam knew. Wolf was a legend, an invisible sprite who lived in the air and came down only to further confuse those looking for him. "Alright. The location is ... well, it's awful." If

Big Boy had indeed come in to land at the semi-mythical Bonehouse, then anyone with violent intentions toward Keck and his men would be forced to think twice. "Mountains to the north, crappy weather a lot of the time, steep hills on either side, very remote and easily defended." It sounded hopeless, but to Menzies, Walcott, and the others back at Tempsford in 1944, so had Operation Asphodel.

"Yeah, it's a doozy" Speight sighed. He was exhausted, and his men were already catching up on Z's while he had to persuade this egghead that the Nazis had truly built a tiny airbase in the Argentine pampas. "But that's someone else's problem, right?"

***

3 hours later

It wouldn't be long before tempers started to flare. Six different missions had been proposed, with four still on the table. None were ideal, two were terribly risky, and the lack of detailed reconnaissance made everything harder.

"We've got a problem with intel," Sam tried to explain, "because of the orbits."

But only Keller and Clavel were following. "The wrong inclination to the equator," the German officer told the others. "They're tasked with observing not South America, but your potential future enemies in Russia."

"And those in Germany," Sam added, "just so you don't feel left out."

"You do so love to be at the center of things," joked the more junior French officer, Clavel.

"I don't suppose your government could launch a new one?" Keller asked.

Already aware of his superiors' concerns, Sam said, "The Germans see everything with their radar, and can determine the orbit of every satellite. A launch specifically tasked to photograph Keck's region might tip them off."

The dearth of intel would remain, Keller saw. "Then, all we can do is parachute in an advanced recon team."

"How long ahead?"

"Up to ten days," he said. "Time to view the camp from both of these mountain ranges, if necessary." He slid three different sketches of the camp into view.

"Wait, where did these come from?"

"A local informer. We never saw him again," Sam told him. "And a rough drawing, made near dusk while trying not to be seen, from the windows of *Slim Jim*, our B-29."

Setting out the basics of the raid, Keller talked them through the recon phase. "We'll need time to travel, detouring these few villages and any road intersections. All on foot, moving only after sunset." The more Keller described it, the more perfect to him it seemed; crawling around in the dark of night, hunting actual living Nazis, right where they lived. The rising battle-lust brought a sweet, anticipatory tightening of his throat.

"Then, Lieutenant Keller," said Sam, "I suggest you pack your gear."

"Now?"

"You said you need ten days?"

"I do."

"That's perfect. Because the raid's in twelve."

9

Bombshells

Yanis and Jillian's Apartment, Los Angeles, Finale Day, early evening

Caan met them in their lobby. He pulled a folded rectangle of paper from his jacket pocket and handed it to Yanis. "This is for you. Don't ask how I got it."

Yanis spread the paper flat and scanned it. "Well, well," he said, noting the familiar scrawl of Sam Clark. "The eagle has landed."

"The what now?" Caan asked.

"Just an expression," Yanis quipped, ripping the paper in half and then setting it in the large stone ashtray next to the mailboxes and igniting it with a Zippo lighter he'd picked up at the five and dime. Caan's brows raised, but he said nothing.

"Looking sharp," observed Jillian with a smile as she joined them.

"I got to make my impression quickly, don't I? You high-fliers have got all night." He'd be there just for the cocktail party; no one had yet extended him an invitation to Participate. "You think it's because I'm paying alimony, and I'm poor as a church mouse?"

The issue had always bothered Jillian. "Kinda hurts to be giving Nazis that kind of money."

"*Suspected* Nazis," Caan felt the need to say. "And only temporarily."

"You can suspect all you want," Yanis said, "but tonight we're going to see some proof."

"You're going to see a lot more than I am," Caan said. "What am I supposed to be doing, while you're all getting inducted or injected or whatever?"

"No one's injecting me with jack shit," Yanis insisted.

"Ditto," said Jillian.

"Just have yourself a cocktail, walk around the place and take things in," Yanis said, figuring that was Caan's plan all along. This was hardly his first rodeo, after all. "We know little enough about the place, as it is."

"Yeah," Caan scowled, "kinda hard to do surveillance when her people patrol the place like it's a prison camp," a security policy which was revealing in itself. "The stuff we were able to get with cameras and those experimental microphones ... well, I don't know. Wouldn't stand up in a court of law, that much is true."

"We know," Jillian recited, having thought about little else for many months now, "that she's been receiving and making large payments." Money had left the accounts of confirmed Fountain members, and then become all but lost in a maze of shell companies. "She's renovated the house so much she'd have been better off demolishing it and starting again, but other than that, she's not spending money on herself." Following the money had brought them this far; their success, if Fountain was indeed to be destroyed, would owe a great deal to Prophet's own version of The Few: a handful of hard-working, largely female forensic accountants.

"The Germans are famous savers," he said, "but for a newly rich lady with a popular brand, the lack of conspicuous outlay is suspicious. Where's the money going?" Caan asked, half-rhetorically.

"Can we think," Yanis said, interrogating yet again information which had already yielded its conclusions, "of an activity which might require lots of secret money? Maybe a political slush fund?"

"Nah," Caan said. "These are Hollywood types, not suits from The Hill." Only Chandler had political aspirations, and at only thirty-six, they remained nascent.

"A stock portfolio, then," Yanis said next. "To take advantage of the new technologies."

"No evidence of that, either," Jillian said. "Unless she's buying and selling through discreet proxies."

"Possible," Caan admitted, "but there's no record of a steady income from financial investments. Still doesn't seem to fit."

"Only one thing does, really," Yanis said.

"Yeah," Jillian said. "*Bonehouse.*"

***

Same time, Finale Day

"The Elixir of Life," Karin scoffed. "Only a charlatan claims to cheat the Grim Reaper."

Sabine had preparations to make for the evening induction and chose to shrug off Karin's latest needling. It was true, of course, but Sabine had at least studied part of the question, completing courses in nutrition assembled by Keck 'back' in 2014. The unfamiliar foods contrasted strongly with her own mother's cooking—they tasted of something and were good for you—necessitating Karin's assistance in the kitchen. Once Fountain was up and running, Participants received recipes, while Investors could order direct. Leaders were given a chef who prepared their meals on site.

Caloric restriction, gut health, and quitting booze and cigarettes were the obvious places to start, but Sabine soon found her mind opening to ideas which offered surprising, untapped value. A sequence of mysterious, robed Asians visited Redwood Rise throughout 1950, spending time with Sabine and a tiny, fascinated cohort of Leaders and Investors.

Karin turned up her nose at the pungent green tea she was obliged to make, and remained suspicious of this, and everything else. With her haughty derision, she inadvertently showed Sabine a potential stumbling block for many potential Fountain members: their traditional conservatism might lead them to echo Karin in dismissing the proceedings as, "jungle temple hokum." But more than once, even Karin became a little more calm and tolerant amid the fragrant curls of Nepalese incense, and Sabine had learned to win them over with a splash of ceremony. To herself, she called it, The Secret Order Gloss.

Beyond simple meditative techniques, Sabine had employed chemists to synthesize something Keck called MDMA. If ever the mystery and ritual of Fountain were insufficient to draw in a potential Participant, she reasoned, a potent back-up plan would be needed. At least, the idea began that way.

"They're impressionable," she explained while Karin made them both an informal lunch of soup and rolls in the mansion's kitchen, one mercifully quiet Sunday a week before the induction ceremony. "The drug just helps make them more so."

"Well, I've been laying down and breathing in and out for years. If it's supposed to make me impressionable, why do I still never listen to a word you say?"

"It's not just the breathing," she said, reading from Keck's binder on the topic. "By inducting them into a culturally spacious and peaceable behavior-paradigm, we can lower their heart rate, metabolism, and prevailing cortisol levels."

"Speak the People's *German*, girl. And be sparing with science. I was taken out of *Gymnasium* early, to tend to my aunt, remember."

It hardly took a medical degree to see it. "Laying down with your eyes closed, breathing deep, is relaxing. It helps relieve stress."

"Good God!" Karin stopped and set down her chef's knife. "People need to know about this! Order the scientists to study it at once!"

"If you're relaxed," she pressed on, long since padded against the barbed wire of Karin's skepticism, "I mean *really* relaxed, then your daily worries are gone. Your back doesn't ache. No one's bothering you for anything."

Karin leaned against the wall as if falling asleep and began snoring.

"Listen, you salty old ham hock."

She chuckled to herself, returned to her chopping. "So, all your millionaires and their trophy wives are there, laying happily like well-fed newborns. What of it?"

"I need things from them."

"Separate and apart from the *millions of dollars* they've given you?"

"I need them connected, indebted, *dependent* on each other's discretion. I need them in thrall to Fountain, and to me. And I need them *hopeful*," she said, "more than anything. Keck, he's a lunatic, but this research is solid and conclusive: being hopeful and positive helps you live longer."

She stopped, dropped the knife again, and announced, "I know that! My mother knew that, too! My *great-grandmother* knew, and so did *her* great-grandmother." She resumed chopping, but soon stopped. "I tell you, these 'future folk!' They're jetting around and walking on the moon, but they need an army of scientists to tell them the simplest truths of life!"

"Will you get on and make some fucking lunch before my stomach initiates a *coup d'état?*"

"Soup's almost done. But *was in der Teuffel* is this other stuff you're having me make?" She peered at the recipe book, absent her reading glasses. "sprouted bean kin-ky po-key?"

"Sounds like one of Jeremy's cocktails for Orgy Night. And it's *kimchee*, woman. The pickled vegetable from Korea."

"Ugh!" She stepped back, despite being nowhere near any kimchee.

"It's just spicy sauerkraut, Karin, for the love of Christ."

Swift, stout, instantly embarrassing, the slap landed like a snowball. "I choose to stay blind to whatever happens in the basement," Karin intoned, "but Jesus is Lord in this kitchen, and you'll respect His name."

"Sorry."

"Good. Now, you're obviously trying to tell me something."

"If you'll stop interrupting for long enough."

"Get the hell on with it, then!" Bonded by circumstance and an immediate, mutual respect, the two had begun exchanging 'old couple' barbs almost from the beginning. The staff loved the way the two leading ladies carried on, reassured despite the clamor that they fought only with plastic knives. "I'm trying to make lunch, here. Hurry up."

Sabine encapsulated the rest of the research, patiently and convincingly enough that Karin allowed the potential effectiveness of 'mindfulness,' whatever the hell that was. "Back home, at the School for Girls," Karin summarized, "they'd have called it paying attention and doing what you should." In other words, she thought to herself, being European and female at the turn of the 1920s. "So, you say a few minutes' lay-down is going to transform their mental outlook?"

The urge to strike Karin repeatedly with a large, metal soup ladle receded, with patience. "It takes time to work, but it helps with stress and mental focus. Also maybe addresses some diseases, we think."

"Taking it easy for a while makes you feel better," Karin summed up. "Years of study. What a waste."

"It makes their lives run more smoothly, including some really difficult stuff, and I don't really care how or why. If it means they're less likely to die, I'm fine with it. Besides," she concluded honestly, "it relaxes me, too."

"Relax when the job is *finished*, and the Reich restored, *Lieber*."

"Go slit your own throat, wizened old broomstick."

"And the devil bugger you in your sleep." She began serving the soup in steaming ladles of pea-green dotted with pork and herbs. "So, that's it? Ten minutes' nap on the floor, and they're all just eating from your hand?"

"Not quite. Once they're completely calm and entering a tranquil state of mental equanimity and peace, I hit them with," she remembered from the Files, "a Schedule-A rave drug."

Karin tutted at this, though the last word was the only one she understood. "You should be straight with people about their health," she said. "Strange new concoctions with only letters for names."

"It's a useful tool for our work. Some people," Sabine said pointedly, "lack the imagination to use the whole toolbox."

"I've plenty of imagination, whippersnapper."

"Crap. You've not conjured a fresh thought since the reign of the Kaiser."

"I'll mend your tongue with a scouring pad, I swear it."

"Got to catch me first, decrepit pensioner!"

"Oh, yes," Karin remembered with a snap of her fingers, "while we're speaking of tools and imagination, I'm never *ever* going into your room to clean again. What in the name of the Fuhrer, God rest him, are all those, those … *rubber* things?"

Once she'd spent a gleeful minute imagining the look on Karin's face, Sabine said, "Oh, give it a rest, you sexless old crone. You're just jealous that mine still works."

"Works? *Works?*" she hooted. "What a *fascinating* choice of verb!"

Sabine growled like a frustrated teenager. "I'm changing my mind. The gas oven would be too good for you."

"Oh, go boil a ham in your crotch."

"Unfuckable hag," Sabine countered.

"Torrid little slut."

They took a moment to taste the soup together. "Good amount of herbs. But, more salt?"

"*Ja.* Just a touch."

***

McDonnell F2H Banshee of squadron VF-11, USS Kearsage (CV-33), the same time, in flight, 125 miles NE of Chaco, Argentina

Captain Christopher King kept radio silence. There was nothing new in this high-altitude blackness anyway. Outside, there were distant lights, but mostly he saw only great swathes of black which could have been water as easily as fields or forests. The only point of interest was a tiny green blip on the pilot's radar screen, nice and steady some thirty-two miles distant. It told him that the great Wolfman was airborne again, right on schedule.

King's long-winged Banshee emitted no electronic energy. The wily old German likely carried passive electronics gear, and would detect King easily, but the giant plane generated all the thermal signatures his pursuer would need.

"This thing," he whispered to himself, amazed at the power of the modified Banshee's Night Vision system "is straight from the funny pages."

He could keep his throttle back, conserving fuel while easily matching the behemoth's steady cruise speed. King's refueling hookup was due to rendezvous in an hour, and with luck, he'd be able to track both planes through the new system. Really, it was close to magical.

But there was no rush to refuel. Wherever Wolf was going, he was taking it slow.

***

Observation Post (OP) Hector, 1200 yards NW of Bonehouse, the same time

It wasn't like the movies, Keller had time to reflect. In Hollywood, recon teams somehow gained a perfect overview, secure from attack. In reality, dealing with Kristock Keck, you were lucky to get a decent view of the place from halfway up a tree, with your ass around your ankles. Surely, the devious Nazi had designed the place that way; he was the kind of man who'd invest a week's surveying to create a decent map.

It was infuriating. "Motherfucker," said Keller of his opponent. He seldom called him anything else.

Mercifully, two giant tufts of grass, their bases immune to the gusting mid-afternoon wind on the eighth day, bent apart to create an unobservable gap just wide enough for his binoculars. Ninety percent of the place was laid out in front of him, with only Keck's own hut—of course—tucked away behind other buildings and a small rise.

Bonehouse was a bit ramshackle, smaller than he'd imagined, and weather-beaten from several winters. But then, its people were visionaries, off-the-grid freelancers, earning their own money, out to change the world. Hardship could be expected, though Keller would have been delighted at how much of it they'd been experiencing.

"It's just three accommodation buildings," he'd reported on the bulbous 1950s field radio. 'Control' was an impatient Eli Caan, transcribing every word but always wanting more. "Keck's own hut, four labs, two little warehouses, a canteen, and a shitty, miniscule joke-of-an-airstrip. One AA gun west of the strip, but I don't know if it's operational. Hit that with a rocket. Then, a single fighter-bomber pass with six cluster bombs, and the whole evil experiment will be over."

The Argentine government, though helpful, wasn't about to let Uncle Sam nuke the pampas. They did, at length, relent on a raid; Keller was told to be ready for two 'sticks' of airborne friends, and to watch for 'fireworks northeast of the airbase,' both around midnight-forty.

And once that operation was confirmed as a go, Cann would be ready to launch another, simultaneous raid. This one nestled in the Hollywood Hills. But instead of dropping bombs, its target was a bombshell.

***

1855 Redwood Rise, 1815h, Finale Day

As soon as they arrived, pulling up to the front steps in Caan's Buick, uniformed functionaries were there to open the door and welcome them. At the door was a woman, not especially tall, perhaps five-six, but wearing the most eye-catching silver satin dress. To Jillian's envious eyes, the dress didn't so much flatter Sabine as redefine her; with her tall heels and glittering diamonds, she was Monte Carlo in Hollywood, a welcome breeze from Europe, effortlessly dispelling the humidity of Los Angeles.

"*I could tell you,*" she quoted as she descended the steps, hand already outstretched, "*but then, I'd have to kill you.* What a line, what a treat!" she trilled, allowing Yanis to take her hand.

Petrified, Yanis was able to move only because Jillian made him rehearse the gesture seventeen times in their apartment. "We'd like to think we've got other good ones in us," he said, smiling gratefully. "George Tower," he said, "a real pleasure to finally meet you. And may I present my creative partner, Jean Davidoff." She had not aimed to outshine Sabine tonight—*who could, possibly, on her very own stage*—but felt quite sure she could outthink her.

"We're so very grateful for the invitation," 'Jean' told the host, who clearly enjoyed these moments of initial obsequiousness while new guests were still bowled over by the renovated grounds. "Your home is remarkable," was the only remark she chose to make.

"It needed *so* much work!" Sabine said, as though sorry for the place, rather than angry at its former owners. "But it's coming to life now, I think." She greeted Caan, who almost stumbled over the basics, tongue-tied by this woman. She smiled like a stalking spider, then turned.

They followed her up five stone steps and into an entryway which opened directly into the living room, where picture windows framed a huge swath of the Pacific. A movement attracted the eye, waves striking rocks in the far distance. "Good heavens," Jean said, the emotion genuine. "You can see to the edge of the world from here."

Sabine gave a strange chuckle. "I thought we were already standing on it. For me, California is as far from home as Japan."

"You must miss Germany," Jean tried.

"It's been a long time," was all Sabine said, perhaps only a little homesick. "But tell me about *Total Memory*, your new film. It's released, when, next month?"

"That's right," George told her, trying to be concise; their films were a means to an end, but from what they'd already witnessed, that end *was* Sabine. "A man dreams of a vacation to an island, but can't afford it, so scientists implant memories of his having been there."

"Pretty soon, he's not sure whether it's true or not," Jillian added, "or even who he is."

"Sounds like a psychological one," Sabine grinned. "I love those. Something for the mind to chew on." She excused herself to greet some other guests, promising she'd hear more later.

"Much rather we listened than talked," Jillian muttered in Yanis' ear.

"Good reason to keep our ears open. Where's Caan?"

He was mingling, Yanis saw, with a knot of actors, all old friends who were surprised but pleased to find him in Sabine's home. "Dearborn's here," Yanis noted as a maid offered him a tray with a glass of expensive scotch. Jillian watched him take a small, precise sip, as though measuring it as part of an experiment. "Not looking to get shitfaced, despite the temptation." Across the sunken living room, Dearborn laughed, loud and boomy, at something Caan said.

"Now," Sabine said behind them in a conspiratorial tone, "you won't let Mr. Dearborn loiter around the drinks cabinet, will you?" She gestured the issue with a drunkard's tilting wrist.

"Oh, he won't be any trouble," said Yanis, entirely unsure. Dearborn was given to high spirits and spontaneous antics, especially when the booze flowed freely.

Sabine's comment was icy. "He doesn't need another episode on his record."

Blanching slightly, Jillian noted another famous face. "And you invited Chandler," she marveled. Blond, still-eligible, Lt. Col. Charlie, or Charles—*but never, ever Chuck*—Chandler (USAF, Ret.) was maturing into an honest-to-God American hero.

"Why don't I introduce you?" Sabine offered. She wafted over to the little cluster of men, which parted and formed a horseshoe around her as though they'd practiced it. "Are people still placing bets concerning you, Mr. Chandler?"

He grimaced, but he was used to all this. "That stuff's just nonsense. Made up by the papers." Still, once he'd very quickly met 'George' and 'Jean,' he seemed ready to head over to another small group which included the evergreen Rupert St. Martin, and the ravishing Amelie Dearborn.

"What kind of bets?" Sabine wanted to know, halting the famed pilot's departure.

"It's just nonsense," he was saying again.

"People are trying to figure out," Caan explained, "whether he'll become President of the United States *before* walking on the moon, or *after.*" The group laughed together while Chandler, always good-natured, extricated himself to speak with a friend. Sabine permitted it, already moving in another direction, a responsive hostess with a very light touch.

Once they'd gone, Caan was more comfortable with Tim Courtley and the two new young stars, and chose to let his jealous side show. "Son'bitch made more dough from two lousy movies than we all did busting our asses for a decade," he complained.

"*Wings of Paradise* wasn't as terrible as it should have been," Yanis said, justifiably.

"True, true!" Courtley agreed, miming a banking fighter jet with his hands. Some of the flying sequences had been way ahead of their time, thanks in part to the 'cinematographic genius' of a certain someone.

"But," Caan said, "come on, *Dwight's Angels?* I mean ..."

"A complete and utter piece of shit," Dearborn pronounced as he reappeared. "Going to the bar is faster than waiting for the girl," he confided, as though relating vital intelligence. "Plus, I read old Chuck Chandler got some makeup girl pregnant in Cincinnati." Courtley accepted a cocktail from his friend with lip-smacking relish.

"Go easy on Chandler," Jillian said, sensing the aging actor was already half in the bag. His wife was across the room with the pilot and some others, giving Dearborn more leash than usual.

"What, go easy on a shitty movie because its Big Star got hammered at breakfast and crashed his stunt plane?" said Dearborn.

"The man was seriously injured, and that's after earning himself God-knows-how-many medals in the Second One, so have a little heart, huh?" Caan said.

"Sure, sure."

"And if you believe everything in the *Weekly Confidential*, you'll tell us the Germans have landed on the moon already, and built a ... I don't know, a nuclear missile base, or something," said Caan.

"Nope. But they're headed that way. You watch 'em. Chandler will have to get his skates on if he wants to be first," Dearborn warned.

"I'd rather watch Sabine. The way she fits into those slinky dresses ..." leered Tim Courtley.

"I hear she works out." Jillian hoped to drop some speculation, and receive more in return, in case it was more than that. "Special routines. Developed by the Army."

"I think someone told me it was calisthenics," said Dearborn, trying to remember. "Or was it yoga?"

"Veganism, I heard," said Tim Courtley.

"What's that?" asked Dearborn.

"Special diet. No meat, only vegetables and nuts," Yanis said.

"Sounds terrible," Dearborn decided.

"To look like *her*, I'd eat as much kale and 'heart-healthy grains' as they told me to eat," said Jillian.

"But how do people stay alive, without meat?" Dearborn asked, apparently genuinely.

"Go back to your high school in Wisconsin," Courtley told him.

"I'm from Iowa, you jackass."

"And tell them that they failed in their responsibility to educate you."

"Educate me about this, genius. How the hell does Sabine get all these people in the same room?"

Courtley was as used to star-studded events as any actor in the world. "Charm, I suppose. And that fabulous, umm, how shall we say ..."

"Unforgettable," chuckled Dearborn.

"Tastefully framed," Courtley added.

"Rack."

"I said *tastefully*," Courtley objected.

"Décolletage?" tried Dearborn. His drunkenness was rapidly advancing toward 'tottering,' with plans to tack toward 'oblivion.' But he regrettably still had things to say. "I like mine," he chose to explain, "the same way I like my cocktails: foreign, fruity, and *luxurious*."

Sabine brought over a middle-aged couple, movie investors of some kind or another. "Mr. and Mrs. Joseph von Techt, it's my ... sort-of-pleasure to introduce, far more drunk than he should be on this *particular* evening, the esteemed Nathan Dearborn," she coughed, "*formerly* of the Royal Shake—"

"Legal action pending!" Dearborn objected, entirely too loud for the space.

"—speare Company, and," Inge made to continue.

"And, one of the finest actors," Courtley said, determined to pull things back on track even as he fought his own growing intoxication, "one of the finest actors ever to grace the Old Vic." He grabbed Dearborn's hand; several things had spilled over it, one of them sticky. "A bloody good Lear, and an equally good friend of mine, God help me," he laughed. "Dignified only by his beautiful, long-suffering, bloody amazing wife, Amelie," he said finally as the lady in question detached herself from the nearly constant, nearly all-male huddle around her.

"*Enchanté.*" She was impossibly thin, a Modigliani cast before its proper time, and two-thirds of the reason Chandler reappeared to join the group.

"*Ma petite crème de menthe,*" Dearborn drooled, "you know the esteemed Captain Chandler."

"Lieutenant Colonel," whispered Jillian. She'd hated this kind of lazy disrespect for the military, even before Asphodel; it was like Dearborn had called a respected CEO a middle manager.

Dearborn plowed on. "And I've been telling you for *weeks* about George and Jean, haven't I? These two," he enthused, "are script writers, and set designers, and they produce features, and—"

"And they're able to recite their own resumes," Caan reminded him, glancing around at the others for a little help. Thankfully, 'Sir Tim' chose to step up.

"Mr. Tower," said Courtley, "what say you and I bring Mr. Dearborn out to the terrace, grab a little fresh air, and talk movies?" One of Sabine's staff, a slender blonde in a brilliant white blouse, deftly handed Courtley something and he ushered the others toward the French doors. "Do me a favor, Nathan? Knock that back, there's a good chap."

"What's in it?"

"It's not like you to ask."

"Fair enough."

"It'll help sober you up, and tomorrow morning won't be so entirely shit," he promised, un-stopping the bottle and obliging his friend to drink it down. He complained at the bitterness, and was still a little wobbly for a while, but within minutes, his eyes were clear, and his back had begun to straighten. Back at the party, Amelie put it as bluntly to these friends as to her others. "I was on the edge of leaving Nathan. The *very* edge. But Sabine did the things that she does, and ... he's a new man. Well," she laughed, "*re*-newed, anyway. I suppose underneath, he's the same as ever, the incorrigible man!"

While Yanis gave the potentially useful Dearborn time to catch his breath, Jillian made a beeline for anyone who might advance her knowledge. "There's serious money being earned here, but she's not spending all of it," 'Jean' reminded 'George,' off to one side. As she sashayed from one brief social moment to another, she stuck to her maxim for the evening: Ears open, ask a few questions, share everything we find.

Jillian found a good spot, around a corner, where she could loiter for a moment as though waiting for the ladies' room. Within earshot were a group of five women, all close friends to each other, and all Associate level or higher.

"It's no good simply hearing about it from someone," one woman said. "The invitation has to be personal. Isn't that something? Everything else is mass-marketed, but this is *individual.*"

"And I don't even know why you'd *tell* anyone else, what with two hundred members already."

"Yes," agreed another. "It's an *incredibly* precious resource."

"She wanted to *know* all of us, as though we're adopting her daughter, not buying her products."

"Who'd ever call it just a *product?*" another woman said.

"Nobody knows what's in it. I asked her if I could have it lab tested, and ..."

The others were completely horrified. "You didn't! Tell me you're not stupid enough to—"

"I didn't give any to anyone," she promised them. "It would have been at my brother-in-law's lab, in Reno."

"Remember what she said? Patents, honey bunny, patents! Worth *billions*, with a B!"

"I guess that's why everyone is sworn to secrecy about their doses. About whatever instructions she gives."

"She told me, on my first day, that there was no point in swapping medications or diets with someone or borrowing one. 'What works for one may not work for another,' she said."

"But, I mean, my brother-in-law said there had to be a good amount of crossover, maybe some nutrients which are in everybody's doses. Mineral salts and vitamins, he said."

"You want to start guessing what's in there, and formulating some crazy knock-off, be my guest. But I'll bet you a thousand bucks your idiot brother-in-law blows himself to smithereens before he discovers the secrets of immortality."

The others delivered similar warnings. "Plus, it seems kinda ... *distasteful*. After all the trouble she goes through, for us. I'd never dream of trying to rip her off."

"No way! I'll need her to keep all my grey-haired friends going!"

As they laughed together, a very 'Hollywood' sound to Jillian's ears, the timber of entitlement, Jillian noticed that Sabine had sent staff through the room. They stood among the Participants and Candidates, their presence quieting the group.

"Friends," Sabine began, "it's not quite time to begin, but I wanted to draw your attention to the sunset. We'll be able to enjoy it for a few more moments before the blinds are drawn." The group turned, almost unanimously, to see the Pacific, lit by a waning star. The fabric of its atmosphere was scattering the last of the day's light, exposing the entire visible spectrum as a riot of oranges and reds.

"And with a free bar, I can only guess that everyone has a glass full of something?" Sabine inquired of the group. Two maids finished circulating with an ice bucket and champagne, and another with scotch and a soda bottle. "Well, I'm sorry. That must wait for a moment. Please set your drinks aside, there, and find your name on the wall chart." Experienced members led the way, reassuring those who found the instructions jarring, or just unexpected: *Lay down on your back and relax.*

Dearborn caught Jillian's elbow and quipped, "My first time, I couldn't tell if this was summer camp, or some crazy head-shrinking exercise, or just an orgy!"

His wife gave Jillian an apologetic smile. Next to her, Karl Dietrich, a Fountain veteran, gave the actor only a stony silence. Four times a year, they were called to Sabine's residence; each was a solemn and memorable occasion, unfit for idle chatter. "Nathan?" Amelie said. "Shut up."

"Right."

"And lay the other way. Your feet are at the wrong end."

Thirty-two people made their own space in the broad, sunken living room; through the windows, the sun was trying to scorch away the atmosphere, leaving it reddened and sore.

The group found plentiful cushions, rugs, and mats to lay on, and got themselves situated. Yanis felt decidedly vulnerable as Sabine issued the first instructions. "Lay back. Breathe deep," Sabine told them. "Slow and steady. You're in my home, but you should feel as though it's yours."

She led them into ten minutes of increasingly deep breaths. Around halfway through, she asked that each person reach out to at least one other, so that a web of human connections began spanning the room. "As you breathe and metabolize the oxygen, send some of that nourishment to your partner." There were some giggles, but then a more serene, focused aura descended on the room. Parts of the group seemed to breathe as a unit, so that a gentle rhythm emerged. "Consider only the breath, and the touch of your partner. Feel it in your nose, down into your chest, lifting your belly. Feel every *atom* of it."

The quiet exercise sustained itself. Sabine began kneeling by each of the prostrated members, most of them in evening dress, speaking very quietly with them as they held hands. Each was a luminary, famed or respected or both, and all were her senior. It took every ounce of self-possession and worldly grace to elevate herself so that she could become their trusted guide in this unfamiliar terrain.

There was no rush, she reminded them often, conscious that haste would threaten this sophisticated calm, an atmosphere which took planning and great care to sustain.

She held the hand of Delia Whitman, whose mezzo-contralto could no longer fill an auditorium as once it had. She also pressed one of the little white pills into the ample palm of Peter Prendergast, whose worsening palsy left him looking ever more diminished and beaten. The drug would not help Whitman to sing, or Prendergast to regain motor control; none of what happened tonight could, despite the sophisticated sales technique, Sabine's enticing blend of cultish secrets and hypnotic serenity.

She shrugged; Prendergast had spent seven years lying about *Der Fuhrer* in the pages of the *'Jew York Times.'* Sabine would continue to take, and spend, his dirty money, all while cursing him to further illness.

But to make sure he spent as wildly as Sabine wanted him to, she had to persuade Prendergast, and a hundred others like him, to level up. Time itself was the enemy, and so, Sabine decided, the ideas of 'immortality' and 'eternity' would appear early and often. Feeling creative one night, after her evening's date had already left in the cab she'd decided to call for him, Sabine penned a kind of ritual. From its first experimental performance, it proved wildly popular, a quick way to come together and create that rarefied, febrile atmosphere Sabine needed.

This evening's iteration would be the fourth, so the Participants, Investors, Associates (and, to be sure, the Leaders) already knew the short sunset liturgy by heart. Candidates, like Jillian and Yanis, would observe. In their case, with enormous interest.

One by one, she released the members from their breathing practice, and handed them something too small for others to see. Staff then reunited the guests with their champagne glasses and ushered them into the dining room, where a first course of fresh oysters was ready.

They ate in companionable quiet, watching the sunset or reveling in the piquant, saltwater delights of the oysters. Then, calmed and alert, the group silently and collectively faced the setting sun as it appeared to slide under the glass-topped ocean. With everything still, the ritual could begin.

"I am Sabine Ehrlinger," said their founder.

"*We are Fountain,*" everyone replied together.

"I am Karl Heinrich Dietrich."

"*We are Fountain.*"

A woman's voice, another of the Leaders. "I am Ulrike Langer."

"*We are Fountain.*"

"I am Dennis Ellory-Maintz," said an elderly man.

"*We are Fountain.*"

Twenty-two names were heard, asserted first as an individual, then again as part of an intrinsic whole. Finally, the group bowed with grave respect toward the setting sun, and there was an anticipation, a clearing of throats. Sabine began and they were all with her:

"I am come to the Fountain,

To drink the pure light of Forever.

To dance in endless song,

Untripped by meddlesome time.

I will drink of the Fountain,

Deaf to the stern clock's rebuke.

I will serenade the numberless sunsets,

And rest in certainty of the morning.

I will laugh by the Fountain,

At the dull and credulous fools,

Who see impermanence as their defeat,

And hasten to yield, meek and futile.

I am come to the Fountain,
To dine on a speck of star-fall,
To be ignited, a beacon in the human dark,
Deathless, ever reborn, boundless."

***

11 miles NNW of Bonehouse

"Alright, this is definitely it." The square-edged pattern of a classic landing approach was easy for King to spot. "Crosswind leg. He's going to land somewhere ... about ..." King glanced down at his map, but dared not flick on the light, lest Wolf see him in the darkness. "I mean, it's in the middle of nowhere, but he's laying it out exactly."

Six minutes later, Wolf turned again, leveling out another ninety degrees to port. "Alright, there you go. Downwind leg." King copied the trajectory in a slow, broad turn. "Got to be ready to lower your landing gear about now. Maybe ask your buddies to light things up?" Whatever Wolf was carrying, it was worth the risk of a landing on a strip hacked from a wooded hillside in the Argentine highlands. At night.

Six lights formed a dim row between the two ranges of bulging, uneven hills. They definitely hadn't been there a second before.

"I got you now, big old piece o' shit."

***

1855 Redwood Rise

Fizzing with energy, the group embraced and then held hands. The formality peaked, like the high point of a Catholic Mass, and then fell away as canapes were served and the members began circulating once more. "The food here is always just *excellent*," thrilled Amelie Dearborn. "Her chef must be a magician or something."

Dietrich had actually spent the war as a *sous chef* in Hitler's own kitchens at Berchtesgarten, but 'Sabine' wouldn't be revealing that to anyone. As the generous buffet meal commenced, she was speaking on the phone. On returning to circulate among her most valued customers, Sabine made a point of standing where she could see George and Jean.

Especially George. There was something about him, more worrying still than the phone call she'd just received concerning the contents of his apartment; Fountain's professional spies were both quick and thorough, and she'd have the incriminating objects in her possession soon.

No, it was his appearance.

Was it that he looked familiar? Could he have been at an LA party she'd attended, or a premiere?

She searched her memory, finding that aspects of many different faces seemed to suit that of 'George Tower.' It was what connected all those faces that she found particularly interesting.

All of them were Jewish.

She looked for Chandler. There would need to be a phone call, and she couldn't deprive her guests of her company at this stage in the evening. When she found him, he already looked worried.

***

Between bites, unaware of the crisis developing behind the scenes, the members of Fountain naturally grouped with others of the same level, though as Candidates, Yanis and Jillian were mostly concerned with calculating the scope of the required 'donation' for new Participants.

Amelie Dearborn told her, "It doesn't have to be massive, especially if you can offer attractive sales avenues through your friends."

"But most of them could never afford something like this," said Jean.

"It's remarkable," Amelie replied from her own experience, "what a person can afford when they must."

"Hey, shouldn't Jean and George get a discount?" Dearborn suggested. "You know, as friends of existing members?"

"Sabine has her own expenses to consider," Amelie pointed out, clearly impressed by a woman with such business savvy and quite taken by the way Sabine effortlessly wielded her feminine power. The men in the room tracked her, calculating their maximum bid as though she were a spectacular figurine being sold at auction. "A lot of the raw materials come from abroad, I think."

"Really?" asked Jean, who then sipped her champagne, subtly and nonchalant, as though the answer might not matter to her.

"She's forever telling me about her pilot." She leaned in close, her expressive face warning of a looming indiscretion. "A war hero and an absolute *stud*, apparently. Why else would she and everyone call him King Banana?" she laughed.

"To get a 'peel' of laughter from everyone?" said Yanis. It was a joke born of nervousness, but it worked, and he got the appropriate groan from the group. Then, as they continued, their conversation packed with details he knew Jillian was memorizing, Yanis returned to scanning the room. He played it cool, surveying the scene while sipping his drink, just people-watching.

Definitely not spying.

All manner of small exchanges were taking place. Most were in the currency of social cache—an offered introduction, an admiring remark, a compliment on an outfit—but some were literal. A dozen times, he saw members of Sabine's staff give something to a Participant. Once the room became rife with it, the open trading and gifting of illicit drugs was quickly accepted.

"Safrole oil," explained a chemist whose attempts to sound less German only made him sound more so. "It comes only in small amounts by courier from our friends in Japan. Down in my lab," he said of the basement, "fractional freezing gradually isolates the isosafrole." He continued with a smile, "You know it's worked when the whole lab smells of licorice." There were other steps in the process that Yanis missed, and a couple of chemical acronyms. "The resulting yellow-green liquid can then be dried out to a salt and purified before being shaped into MDMA tablets."

"Hard to 'Just Say No,'" Yanis reflected to himself a moment later, "when literally the *coolest kids in the world* are doing it."

Envelopes were transacted. Some were thin—travel tickets? A false passport? Or just an address for a location shoot, or an upcoming party?

Caan found him, sliding in next to Yanis beside his chosen pillar. "If you could get all the autographs in this room, and take them back to 2014, could you buy a Ferrari and retire?"

"They wouldn't recognize about ten percent of the names at all," Yanis said. "Reality shifts so easily when timelines are disturbed. It's crazy, really. The ripples, heading out, touching everything."

"Speaking of which," Caan made triply sure they couldn't be overheard, "has Inge, um, done anything physical with you, yet?"

A very puzzled look. "You mean, injected me with the stuff you were talking about?"

"No, I mean ... being tactile, you know, pawing you and such. Tim Courtley over there is on that drug she's been handing around, and he's talking eighteen-to-the-dozen. Says she likes to begin with new male Participants by gaining their trust."

Sabine was at the back of the room, perhaps returning from upstairs, and began circulating again with ease.

"I think by trust you mean *loyalty*."

"Yeah, I think so, too. Okay," he said, "here's Jean."

She was wide-eyed, still processing. "Do I ever talk as much as that, when I've been drinking?"

"Let's just be glad of 'unguarded moments.' What did they say?" asked Caan.

She passed on the broad strokes, adding details about the affluent woman with the chemist brother-in-law. "Said he might be able to analyze the Elixir."

"He isn't," Caan said, well ahead of the game. "His lab's too simple, and so is he. That includes his security setup. Easiest burglary Prophet has done all year."

"You didn't tell us?" Jillian asked, offended at only learning this now.

"You didn't need to know. I wanted you focused on the social whirl, not the chemistry of the Elixir. Besides, it had all the features Yanis and yourself guessed it would. Our lab guys said the genetic components were freshly encoded with something called 'Crispy.' I didn't even understand the introductory paragraph."

She took a moment to chuckle. "Crispr," she said. "An amazing technology from 2014."

"Not so amazing," Caan reported, "when it's being used to breed the perfect Nazi."

"Say," Yanis offered after a sip of the drinks they'd been handed, "these are tasty. Got a little kick."

"I thought she said it was like a Shirley Temple," Jillian said, closing her eyes and giving her head a quick shake as the third sip settled in her throat.

"More like a Shirley MacLaine," quipped Yanis.

"Hm?"

"I feel a bit 'out on a limb,' if you get my drift," he said, wriggling his arms to mimic a balloon in the breeze.

"Oh right," she said, blinking herself to attention. "All that transcendental mumbo jumbo."

"I think that's the idea," Yanis smiled.

"Proper bit of rubbish, if you ask me."

"Om ... my God, don't look now, but here comes our gracious hostess, slinking up and looking like Ginger Rogers' alt-kink cousin."

As though teleported, 'Sabine' was now by Yanis' side. "You've been neglecting me," she said. "Let me show you around a bit." She made no eye contact with Jillian, as though Sabine had simply forgotten Yanis was attending with a plus-one. Instead, she took Yanis' arm like the rudder of a small vessel, and began steering him from group to group, making quick introductions and pointing out some of the expensively assembled paintings.

"The fuck is going on?" Caan asked Jillian by her pillar, genuinely puzzled at the behavior. "She just walks off with your date, without even a *by your leave?*"

But Jillian wasn't lost in bitterness, at least, not on the outside. "Cover me, Eli." She set off, shadowing Sabine and Yanis, who was never physically beyond the German woman's clutches. She would lean into him and whisper something, and then giggle before pawing his shoulder. It seemed almost submissive, but that was a ruse; there was actual danger here, and Jillian worried that Yanis might not see it until it was too late.

Her fear was realized almost immediately, when he cheerfully knocked back a pill Sabine had given him. "Jesus, boy, what are you *doing?*" On reflection, she supposed he was just doing his best to fit in, the way they'd been trained.

Then Jillian had to watch Yanis being steered away from the party, with 'Sabine' playing the cute hanger-on, even while planning their every move and encounter. She moved him along quicker to escape Chandler, who seemed determined to speak to her. Jillian saw him pout with frustration and was able to follow him to one of the hallway telephones. He loitered impatiently, as though waiting to hear from someone.

By then, Sabine was handing Yanis a drink, which he quaffed after clinking glasses with hers. Next, she succeeded in whisking Yanis upstairs, past where Jillian could easily follow. Across the room, Caan made an odd face and headed in her direction, a finger to his lips. Chandler's phone call came through, and he turned away to listen; it seemed significant, even vital.

Air Force hero being weird and worried. Prophet handler looking concerned and maybe confused. Partner upstairs with only a sadistic bitch for company.

As the thought crossed Jillian's mind, Sabine peered down the staircase, now intently making eye contact. The hostess' glamorous, party-ready smile briefly morphed into a callous scowl. Jillian's stomach tensed, aware that this display had been reserved for her alone. At the top of the stairs, Yanis appeared to wobble. Sabine turned her gaze to him. But this was not a look of concern. This was a confident acknowledgment of satisfaction, like a spider luring a helpless fly into its meticulously woven web. Sliding her hand onto Yanis' back, Sabine guided him to a door.

She nodded to a pair of goons at the end of the hallway before ushering him inside. The door closed and locked with a swift click.

Every one of Jillian's alarm bells went off at once.

Operation or not, Yanis is in trouble. Like a lamb being led to slaughter.

***

450 yards from Bonehouse

They heard it, then saw it. "Clavel, call up Nemo," Keller asked of the Frenchman, the only other survivor from the NATO team which had accompanied Jillian Qualmes into the mine. It felt a thousand years ago, the last time he'd prepared to fire a weapon in anger.

"*Big Boy* is on final," Clavel said into the radio mike. Over the shared secure network, he heard King key his 'OK.' The next button he pressed had a very different outcome.

Orange-yellow flame burst from the Banshee's nose, and two seconds later the rapid-fire twenty-millimeter canon could be heard down in the valley. At first, the assault seemed ineffective, like a nail gun against a cathedral, but when King closed and fired a second burst, even as Wolf tried to jink right and avoid, the US Navy veteran smashed open two of *Big Boy's* engines in a cloud of steam and smoke and hot debris. Immediately aflame and quickly losing speed, the giant struggled to climb, but the fire in its engines worsened and spread. The plane was now a huge raft of debris-in-waiting, a temporary roof for the valley, already on fire. The aerial blaze became too bright for the eyes as more of the plane's cavernous bulk was overwhelmed. "Coming down!" warned Keller.

Wolf's last roll of the dice had been to drop his wing, selling height to buy enough speed to bring control to a belly-landing on the scrubland, somewhere up on the valley wall. It failed when the giant completely stalled out, standing on its tail to form an absurd vision, a roaring bonfire in the sky, visible for a hundred miles. Then it tipped over, gave up, and tumbled helpless into the forest. The explosion made day of night, with booms and crackles following the fatal moment. Keller saw the panic through his scope, the central square of Bonehouse suddenly filling with the half-awake and the half-dressed. Keck had his Luger drawn, yelling orders. Even at this distance, the plane's funeral pyre illuminated their faces.

"Velociraptor," Keller said into his jungle uniform's lapel microphone. It would mean nothing to those who'd built Bonehouse, should they somehow eavesdrop on Prophet's secure communications. But the twelve heavily armed operatives waiting nearby all recognized the code word as a unique invitation: *Go. Kill Nazis.*

***

1855 Redwood Rise

The thrill of it made Jillian's legs shake for just a few seconds, and then deep breaths helped her regain control. "Velociraptor," was their 'Go' code word, and Caan reinforced the point by discreetly pressing a .22 automatic into her hand when he got close.

"Anyone asks, you're looking for Yanis."

"You're sure it has to be—"

"Yes. I can't go up there, I'm too official, it'll start a fucking war. It must be you. I'm sorry."

She looked down, shielded from the others by a large potted plant and Caan's figure; to the outside, he was drunkenly making a play for her affections, not an uncommon proposition at these parties. The automatic was loaded, with a round in the chamber and the safety on. No need to disturb the party with an errant shot.

"Anything happens, I'm calling the cavalry."

"The cops?" she asked, checking her route to the stairs.

"No, I'm talking about Barksdale Air Force Base. Gonna call in an airstrike and wipe out all these Nazi-sympathizer motherfuckers."

"They're going to have bigger problems than just dying," she said, tucking the pistol into her handbag. "Wait 'til the press—" But there was no time. "Anyway. I'm off."

The first challenge was to look innocent and devil-may-care, all while feeling supremely stressed. And potentially murderous. She made it to the stairs without looking up, checking the placement of her rings and her nail polish, enacting just a little of everyone's ignorable, backstage routine, the things they do when they're unobserved. The stairs themselves spiraled around, so a completely discreet ascent was impossible, but her checkered dress pattern partially hid her against the white marble and black railing. Thus, slightly chameleon-like, but nervous as the animal's next meal, she reached the landing.

The CIA knew which Sabine's room would be: third on the right. According to their audio recordings, it was both the master bedroom, and the bedroom of The Master. She'd heard enough to know that Yanis shouldn't be in there for a second longer than necessary.

The door was locked, and she felt in her purse for the automatic, preparing to blow the lock off and burst in like the FBI, shouting like a maniac. But there was a voice behind her, and she froze.

***

Yanis felt his body totter into the room, his head lagging a half-step behind. His eyes scanned the trim, tidy space. A monochrome palette featuring an eclectic mix of glamorous Art Deco shapes paired with functional, German restraint.

No, he realized upon closer inspection. Not Art Deco. *Bauhaus.* Perhaps that Intro to Modern Art course he'd had to take in college wasn't as useless as he'd thought.

Stretched across a corner was a stunning Le Corbusier chaise. Just beyond it, a pair of velvet drapes, the color of a moonless night. An evenly spaced collection of abstract expressionism paintings centered around what Yanis was certain was an authentic Jackson Pollock. Curated chaos surrounded by mid-century, geometric forms along the dove grey linen walls. Black silk sheets tucked neatly into the corners of the mattress. Atop them, a simple duvet in the same dove grey, and a luxurious blanket that appeared to be made of real mink. Warm light came from an elegant crystal fixture that hung from an ornate ceiling medallion and two matching sconces on either side of the bed. A plush, tufted, charcoal grey velvet headboard emerged like a monolith from behind the row of pillows.

It didn't take much to imagine Sabine indelicately reclined here, giving or receiving libidinous service. After all, that seemed to be her preferred currency. Whether the headboard was intended to muffle lustful cries of carnal gratification or provide a solid grip for those in the throes of hedonistic pleasure was unclear. But like everything else in the room, it seemed to have been chosen for functionality as well as aesthetic value.

The sleek lines of a black leather and chrome Barcelona chair at the end of the bed caught his eye. "Wow, is that an original?" he fumbled, still reeling from the second drink.

"Updated," she clarified, leading him toward it. "Ludwig redesigned it in 1950 to use stainless steel. No bolts."

As he leaned to get a better look, she gave him a firm, playful shove, depositing him on the seat. His head dropped back, heavy and swirling with intoxication. Sabine slanted herself over him, offering a generous peek at what clods like Nathan Dearborn referred to as her 'unforgettable rack.'

"George," her voice arrived in multiple shadowy syllables as Yanis tried to shift his focus upward to at least her collarbone, "I'm so impressed with the work you and your ... *business partner* are doing."

Jillian. Shit. She's going to be pissed when she finds out about this. But I know she'd want me to go along with whatever Sabine has in mind, especially if it means bringing down this whole charade.

"Well, thank you very much," he managed without slurring too much.

In a move as fluid as that satiny silver column draped over her body, she slipped off her shoes and straddled him.

"I hope you don't mind me pulling you away from Jean," she said, "but I've had my eye on you all evening."

Yanis felt his quadriceps tense as she slid her parting legs over his.

"You have?" he stammered, trying to catch his breath.

She took a firm grip on the half Windsor knot of his necktie and gave it a yank, unraveling it as she whispered in his ear.

"Yes," she purred. "And I was hoping for the opportunity to ... get to know you better."

Without hesitation, she began trailing kisses along his neck. Simultaneously, she wound his now removed necktie around her hand until it formed a neat roll. As she worked her way toward his earlobe, her kisses evolved into aggressive nibbles.

Yanis felt his eyelids droop. He blinked rapidly, hoping to shake whatever had been in that pill and those drinks. By now she was unbuttoning his shirt, her petite hands slipping inside as she continued to nip at his neck from her laptop perch.

"Well, it appears you're getting your wish," Yanis said, his wits somewhat returning as she unbuckled his belt.

"Lucky me," she said, pausing to look him in the eye as she unbuttoned his pants. Her fingers glided down his zipper. "Perhaps we should continue this elsewhere?"

She stood and walked toward the chaise. With a flick of her diamond-wrapped wrist, she parted the heavy black drapes. But instead of a window, Yanis saw a massive wrought iron gate fitted into an archway. Sabine reached through the bars and flipped a switch. Slowly, a whitish glow began to illuminate the space.

"Come," she said, motioning to him with fluttering fingers. "Let's get to know each other."

Just play along. Hopefully, Jillian will forgive me for what I'm about to do.

Yanis stood. With leaden legs, his feet somehow crossed the floor without tripping over his loosened trousers. He took Sabine's outstretched hand. "What's this, your lair?" he half-joked as he lifted it to his lips.

Her Hollywood laugh, well-rehearsed, rang out as she turned a key in the gate's lock. As she led him through the arched opening, the lights grew stronger. Yanis noticed a small metal table ahead of him. On it were a variety of shiny objects, as if a handyman had emptied a toolbox and laid its contents out in neat rows. Beyond the table was another bed, sparsely appointed with only a set of stark white sheets and a headboard made of wrought iron like the gate. Over it was a candelabra, constructed of industrial pipes and cables. Lipstick red walls surrounded the bed. Ornate, carved silver frames housed various collections of leather goods. Collars, riding crops, masks, harnesses, and several items Yanis couldn't easily identify. His breath slowed and his stomach turned as he took it all in.

The clank of the wrought iron gate snapping closed behind him jarred Yanis from his bewilderment. Sabine hung the key on a filigree hook affixed to the wall. Then an icy smile crossed her perfectly painted lips.

"When I bought this property," she began graciously, "this gate had been at the driveway. I had it replaced, to ensure confidentiality for myself and my guests. Fountain guards its privacy with the utmost discretion, George. But it seemed a shame to waste it. Such beautiful craftsmanship. So, I had it re-installed here, in my … *personal retreat.* Only to be appreciated by selected guests."

She ran her cupped hand slowly up and down the length of the thick iron bar. As she did, she stared at Yanis. The twinge in his groin made clear he understood the implication. "Forged steel is rather alluring, seductive. I adore the feeling of something so strong and solid in my hand."

With that, she released the bar and walked straight to Yanis. Reaching into his pants, she accessed her target without delay.

"See what I mean?" she said playfully as she gave him a firm squeeze.

Droplets of sweat beaded on Yanis' brow and he began to tilt.

"Oh darling, aren't you feeling well? Come," she said, leading him to the bed, "let's make you more comfortable."

She laid him back on the thin white linens, centering him below the industrial candelabra. The scent of bleach, no doubt from the crisp sheets below him, filled his nostrils. He looked up, eyes fogging, as she finished undressing him. She was saying something about how attractive she found him but to Yanis, the words were jumbled. Besides, he was fixated on the object hanging from the ceiling. With the bright white lights at full strength, now he could see that it wasn't a candelabra after all. At least not entirely. This was an elaborate pulley system.

Sweating and panicked, he started to rise from the bed. That's when he realized she had handcuffed him to the headboard.

"Oh, don't worry, darling," she cooed as her liquid silver gown slipped to the floor. Only her glittering diamond jewelry remained. Her body, lithe and sinewy, was as appealing sans clothing as it had been draped in satin. "I'll take good care of you."

Yanis struggled against his restraints as she began attaching a variety of apparatuses to his naked body. "Don't do that," she clucked, shaking her head. "It's better if you don't fight it."

She stood back and gazed at him, shackled and splayed, sizing him up. Then she removed something from the wall and climbed onto the bed, straddling him again.

"I must admit, though," she said, fitting a leather collar over his neck, "I'm a bit cross with you."

Barely able to speak, Yanis grunted. "Why's that?"

A second, icier smile curled the corners of her mouth. "You've not been honest with me."

"Oh?" he tried, perspiration flooding his back.

"Kristock told me all about you, Professor Yanis Miller," she growled, tightening his collar with a yank of the strap.

***

"White Crane?" It was an older woman, maybe sixty, with glasses and an imploring expression. "You are to meet me here, yes?" She seemed anxious, but an arrangement had clearly been made, one about which Jillian was entirely ignorant. A moment later, though, her memory provided a match for the pleading, saintly grandmother's face. It was that of Sabine's housekeeper, Karin Horváth, the hard-boiled Hungarian who ran the place.

But what the fuck was Karin talking about, and why was she expecting someone called White Crane?

Jillian stalled. "How do I know it's really you?" she asked, then glanced down at the pistol in her evening bag, its grip ready.

"In the hills above Lake Balaton," Karin replied, almost as though reciting a poem, "there is a house with a little orchard and a stream running through it. Once we are finished, you have promised the governments will meet, and they will agree I can make my home there."

Confused but intrigued, Jillian weighed the value of this mystery against the unknown dangers facing Yanis. "Would it be alright," she asked, "if we talked in a few moments?" Jillian was still focused on accessing the locked bedroom, though this bizarre, unscripted encounter needed an explanation.

"You mean … after?" the woman said, suddenly disappointed. "Then, what would be the use of my report? Without an *interrogation*, I mean?" She said the word in a whisper, adding yet more to the prevailing wreak of 'spook-craft.'

"Do you think the interrogation would be a better idea?" Jillian asked. The drip of information needed to grow into a flood, and fast.

"Well, it's not really for me to say. As far as I'm concerned," Karin was saying as Jillian noted movement on the stairs, "they could all hang."

It was a man in his forties, apparently looking for the bathroom. He saw the two women who had paused rather oddly outside Sabine's bedroom door and approached with a cordial smile. "Quite a party!" he said, keeping his voice down. "Is our mistress," he asked politely, "perhaps too exhausted from all the socializing?"

Karin was studying the man's face with intent. "Perhaps," she said.

Then, another figure could be seen climbing the stairs, and Jillian found herself watching her hasty but workable plan wantonly unravel according to the Law of Random Fuckups. "I don't think Sabine is ..." she said, "um, ready to be disturbed quite yet."

"Is she alone?" asked the first man, then turned to find the second approaching. "Ah, my friend, it is a little crowded already. If you'd be good enough to—" He stopped, then extended a hand in recognition.

It was Eli Caan. "Colonel, good to see you." He shook the officer's hand.

"And you, Eli. Our meeting like this seems to happen, just by chance, every now and again, no?"

"Better for everyone that it does." Then the two men regarded the two women.

"Red Stork, I am White Crane, and this is a friend."

She looked at them both, then back to Jillian. "And her?"

"Also a friend," said White Crane. He pointed to the key ring in Karin's hand. "We'd like you to open the door for her, and then quickly leave with us. You won't have to come back here ever again."

Jillian ground her teeth with impatience and fiddled with the dainty strap on her bag as the vacillating old woman made up her mind. There were so many keys on the ring that it was worth enlisting her help, despite this delay.

***

Bonehouse, the same time

They began the assault simultaneously. From his overview, Clavel killed all the armed personnel he saw. Some were locals, hired mercenaries to bolster Keck's defenses. The rest were skinny, sunburned Krauts; stupid idealists and marooned submariners. He put a very satisfying bullet through each one.

Either side of the sniper fire that began coming in, breaching charges and mortar rounds went off, wrecking the side walls of two buildings and causing more casualties in the square. The mess hall was shredded by a long burst of MG fire and screams in the watchtower told Keck his observers were gone.

"Protect the lab!" he was yelling, but the crewman who turned to listen was immediately hit—through one side of his jaw and out the other—and dropped to the dust in agony. "The escape route! The motorcycles! Get the lab samples and go!" he yelled to another, who hurried in that direction.

Keck was close to panic, surrounded by a well-prepared enemy. People were shouting, falling, trying to encourage others but everything was being cut short. A loud bang, more a pressure wave than a sound, thumped him in the chest, and he was knocked flat, winded, gasping.

Down in the dust, part of his mind broke off from the rest, and began calculating how likely it was that Inge had betrayed him.

She has no need of me now, anyway, with all her money and fame.

Bullets raked the ground in short lines near the main guard post, chasing the defenders away from their posts. On the other side, Keck saw that Neumann was blackened and alone, sprawled under the awning of the mess tent. He wasn't moving.

And if the samples get away, spirited out on a charter plane, if they can survive the perilous journey long enough to be appreciated by my supporters in Berlin, then my work would still yield something.

At least a part of this brazen, desperate enterprise would be saved.

Another of the buildings caught fire, the smoke already billowing around the corrugated tin roof. They'd built the hut for Inge. God only knows what she got up to in there, the treacherous bitch.

Or perhaps the Americans had figured it out. Put all the evidence and sightings and photographs together and made a plan. It'd have taken someone as smart as that Jewish mathematician, the one from the future.

The one I poisoned to death and then watched get buried under a whole fucking mountain for daring to steal what was rightfully mine.

Someone was talking to him. For the first time in many months, it was a white face, a westerner, that he didn't recognize.

***

1855 Redwood Rise

Yanis shuddered as Inge pronounced his name. She'd no doubt spent as much time rehearsing that phony Hollywood laugh as she had ditching her thick German accent. But now—intentional and harsh—it resurfaced, spitting out the name bestowed upon him to honor his ancestors. He knew all too well what Inge and her type did to Jews. With the collar cinched around his neck, he felt his lungs collapsing.

"That's right," Inge said, dragging her fingernails over the collar before aggressively pinching the sides of his mouth, forcing him to pucker up. *"Der Sturmbannfuhrer* sends his regards."

Eyes white with terror, Yanis felt Inge's lips force themselves onto his. The kiss was rough and furious, like a fireman battling a blaze, ending with a thick wad of spit propelled into Yanis' mouth. He gurgled, the collar too tight to allow for a proper cough.

"You see, when Fountain conducted a membership background check on *George,* his description reminded me of what Herr Keck had told me about you. So, I had your photograph taken by one of those cheap paparazzi types who frequent the places where pathetic degenerates like Willy Leitz have lunch hoping to make the next big deal in this town. Those vultures will work for pennies. Anyway, Kristock confirmed your identity immediately."

She traced his face with a singular, sharp nail, "What are you doing here, Yanis?"

He twitched as her fingers fluttered over his skin. His face began to flush, and he struggled to maintain a steady breath.

"He also told me to have some fun with you," she said, wrapping his tie around his feet and then his belt, effectively binding his legs. Yanis groaned, unable to move and his pulse weakening. "And I intend to do exactly that."

Fully nude except the diamonds at her neck, ears, and wrist, Inge reached back to the metal table and picked up a capsule, taking a long sniff and closing her eyes. She exhaled fervently, then unclasped one of Yanis' arms from the headboard. But instead of releasing him, she shackled it to a pulley hanging from the candelabra above the bed. Then she did the same with his other arm, discarding the looped restraints on the bleached white sheets. She stood at the side of the bed, mere feet away from him. Slowly, she tugged at the pulley, raising Yanis' body a few inches above the mattress. As he ascended, she took another hit off her capsule, her smile widening.

"You sick, depraved Nazi bitch," Yanis growled with what little voice he had left.

But Inge, feeling the effects of the inhalant, only smiled. "You've not seen depraved yet," she cackled as she pushed Yanis, bound and helpless, back onto the mattress and climbed on top of him. Then she fastened another collar, this one with a metal knob on it, around her own neck.

"We're going to enjoy this," she murmured, forcing him inside of her, "together, Professor Miller. You see, good playmates know how to share. These collars will constrict alternately. When one tightens, the other loosens. Do you understand?"

The red walls blurred as Yanis gagged, his neck chafed against the collar. He tried to speak, but only a low moan escaped his lips.

"I will take you to the edge of ecstasy, in exchange for your agony," Inge continued. She inhaled again, her eyes closed in pleasure as she began to grind her hips. "I am in control here," she said as she flipped the switch on her collar.

Yanis felt his collar loosen slightly and he gulped like a toddler learning to swim. His goal was to take in as much air as possible while he could still breathe.

"Ahh," Inge exhaled, her taut, diamond-accented body rippling with fulfillment as she increased her pace. With waning strength, Yanis rubbed his feet together, trying to free himself from the tie and belt restraints. Unwieldy at first, and then more controlled. But Inge matched his movements, undulating like a cresting wave atop the bleached sheets.

He moaned again as he struggled beneath her muscular thighs. The collar had already taken his voice, and now it was threatening to take his strength and consciousness, too.

"It's no use, Professor Miller," she rasped, dragging her fingernails over his naked, tortured body. "As I said, I am in control." Then she flicked the switch on her collar again.

His lungs full of air, Yanis screeched when the collar squeezed his neck.

***

Jillian had never heard that sound before, but she recognized Yanis' voice inside the bedroom. His muffled cries and moans were familiar to her. But this was an indicator of severe pain.

"Alright, that's it. Back up," she said. She shoved Karin away from the door, inadvertently into the arms of her handler, Colonel Yevchenko of the KGB. On cue, the two goons at the end of the hallway rushed forward, knotting together with Karin, Caan, and Yevchenko. The men exchanged punches as a panicked Karin screamed, and the five of them tumbled to the floor.

Seeing her opportunity, Jillian pushed hard on the curved, brass handle. She snatched the key as she slipped inside, barely maintaining her balance in her high heels. Her evening bag dashed to the dove grey carpet. With her hand still on the doorknob to keep herself upright, she felt a fist slam against the other side, but she quickly secured the door with a twist of the deadbolt.

Focusing her investigative skills, she scanned the setting. The immediate space was deserted except for a pair of nearly empty champagne flutes near the metal legs of a black chair. But between dark velvet curtains, framing red walls and wrought iron scrolls, came a harsh, fluorescent glow. Punctuated by deep, feminine moans.

A chill descended Jillian's spine. "George?" she called, unsure if it was necessary to maintain cover as she hurried to the gate and peered through the bars.

Sabine, stripped bare except for a thick black collar and glittering diamond jewelry, was astride Yanis, rhythmically rising and falling. He turned his head, framed by a wide leather collar. Restrained at his wrists and ankles, he caught a glimpse of Jillian, whose breath escaped in a jagged burst at the shocking sight. His eyes broadened momentarily, then fluttered closed.

Alerted to the presence of an uninvited guest, Sabine swung her head toward Jillian, her neat blonde waves swishing to a stop. It was a leering look, one that made Jillian frantically anxious. The perfect intersection of loathing and ecstasy.

"You're too late, Inspector Qualmes," Sabine sighed through sputtering rasps, her diamond earrings bobbing as she edged toward her climax. As she began to shudder, her manicured fingertips came to rest on a button in the middle of her collar. "He's giving me his last breath."

Yanis' skin was the color of berry stains, his face bloated, mouth contorted.

Consumed with rage, Jillian threw herself at the gate, desperately searching for the latch.

Sabine let out a hearty laugh. "It's locked," she scoffed. "And I have the key, Jillian. Like I said, you're too late. Outsmarted by the master race."

A loud thud against the door reminded Jillian that her purse was still on the floor. She sprinted over and grabbed it, pulling out the automatic.

"We'll see about that, Inge," she said, pushing the pistol between the bars and taking aim.

Inge's eyes, half-closed in rapture, now grew wide. Jillian fired a single shot into Inge's shapely, shuddering figure. The round pierced her liver, expelling a deep, nearly black stream of blood. It flowed down her pale side, soaking the crisp white linens. As she fell, Yanis' body went slack.

"Yanis!" Jillian screamed. She could see the key hanging on the wall inside the gate, but there was no way to reach it. She stepped back and emptied her magazine into the gate, blasting the lock. As she did, a bullet ricocheted into her wrist while another grazed her cheek. With adrenaline surging, she pushed against the gate, its lock now giving way. Jillian raced to Yanis, scrambling to tear the collar from his neck. As she unlatched him, Inge fell to the floor. Her eyes remained open, but, like the blood flowing from her liver, the life inside them had drained away.

"Yanis," she sobbed, cradling him against her, "don't leave me. Come back to me, Yanis."

She wrapped the sheet over his nude body, red with ligature marks from his restraints. His chest rose slightly, pressing out a weak, wheezing breath. Eyes focused on hers, he shook his head slowly.

"Shh," Jillian said.

"POLICE!"

A group of uniformed officers and plain-clothes investigators crashed into the first bedroom. A team of medics and an assortment of officials from various agencies followed closely behind.

"Ma'am," said a young paramedic, "let me look at that."

"What? Oh, sure," Jillian said. Then she turned to Yanis. "Don't go anywhere."

He closed his eyes and offered a weak smile as she walked back to the other room. Numb, she sat on the Barcelona chair, holding her blood-spattered wrist. She looked toward the red room. Through the assembled crowd, Jillian could see that a forensic team was already photographing Sabine's corpse. Another medic was trying to make his way to Yanis, blocked by the photographer.

"I'm going to need your statement," an officer told Jillian.

She nodded, still mentally reviewing what had happened. "Can you give me a few minutes?"

"Of course," the officer replied. "Take your time. We've got lots of arrests to process. I'll come back up in a bit. You want some coffee or something?"

She shook her head, which felt dizzy and hot. Sabine Ehrlinger/Inge Weber was more twisted than Jillian had previously thought. And that Nazi had nearly gotten the best of her. And Yanis.

Desperate to see him, she stood, despite the protests of the paramedic tending to her wrist. He laid there in the red room, a low moan coming from his throat.

"Yanis," she called softly, intending to comfort him.

But before he could answer, Jillian watched as his form faded away. Only the white sheet, stained with Inge's blood, remained. Rumpled and empty.

"These Hollywood types," an officer in the red room said as he pored over the items on the table. "Bunch a freaks."

"Thought you said there were two of them. Hey, where's the guy?" another officer asked as he pushed past Jillian and entered the red room.

She started quivering like a foreshock along the San Andreas fault.

This can't be happening. All this time and effort.

Time. What was that anymore, anyway?

So many calculated risks and fluid events and moveable parts. It couldn't end like this.

In the distance, a chorus of air raid signals rang out.

"Would you look at that?" said the first cop standing at the window. Two officers stood behind him, looking up at the sky. As the moon crossed toward the San Gabriel Mountains, it revealed a massive obstruction. An enormous spaceship hovering above the city, backlit by the moon's golden glow.

"Hey, Miss, I brought you some—" said the cop coming back to the room. "Where'd she go?"

***

Caan called the cavalry. None of the Fountain members or their guests were allowed to leave, and all would face lengthy questioning. There were no blue lights, just tint-windowed cars and dark-suited agents with guns. Everyone did as they were told.

"Karin," said Caan to the distressed housekeeper, "this is an unbelievably awkward time to reveal this, but White Crane here isn't with Allied intelligence. He's actually KGB."

She was aghast. "He's ... a ... a *communist!?*"

"You'd never have talked to us if you'd known," Colonel Yevchenko explained. "And the only difference between this outcome, and the one Karin planned with me, was that Inspector Qualmes pulled the trigger, and not someone from the *Spetsnaz*, our counter-terrorism unit."

"But ... all those films you wanted," Karin said. "Those strange little silver records. I made more and more copies, from every camera in the house, but you demanded new ones every week."

Yevchenko coughed slightly and leaned in to Caan. "*Kompromat,*" he explained simply. "The only high-quality luxury that ages best in a metal safe."

Caan laughed a most terribly awkward laugh. "Alright, well, we'll have to talk about all that. I see some complex negotiations on the horizon."

The only member of Fountain who was permitted upstairs, to his own surprise, was Chandler. He'd heard the gunshot and come running, only to be stopped by Eli Caan and warned that Sabine, "may have tried to take her own life. We're helping her now."

"But she'd never do anything like that, it's ..."

"Guess we'll find out. No, no, you really shouldn't go in there," Caan advised, "it's not pretty. In fact, you're looking a little pale and peaky yourself."

"Huh? What?" Chandler asked distractedly, still angling for the bedroom door but finding some guy he didn't recognize in the way. "Hey, fella, shift it along, okay? I need to see what the—"

"My wife," Yevchenko said, "laughed so hard when I told her about you."

Angry and already offended, Chandler was poised to be physical with this guy, whoever he was. "I said shift it, buddy. I don't care about your wife right now. There's serious things going on here, ya know?"

Yevchenko kept the same amenable tone. "She thought it was just so very cute. That's right, she called it 'cute,' how much you enjoy singing show tunes when you're cruising along at Mach 1."

His anger suddenly a frozen wave, Chandler blanched.

"The other guys in the locker room know about that, perchance?"

He forced the words out. "How do you ..."

"What can I say? We like to listen," he chuckled. "But don't worry. We only keep the interesting parts," he said, and leaned in to add, "future 'Mr. President Chandler.'"

A medical team arrived—not one from a local hospital—and entered the bedroom. At the end of the hallway, fretting between the prospect of facing reporters at the gate, and the developing hurricane of startling embarrassments unfolding behind him, was Chandler. He shrank a little as Caan passed him on his way to the stairs, out of this protracted nightmare. "What's up there, Chuck?" Eli asked, clapping the humiliated airman on the back. "You get some bad news on the phone, or something?"

A few moments later, a doctor emerged from the bedroom.

"Caan," he called. "Where are they?"

***

Bonehouse, Argentina

The same unfamiliar westerner had given Keck a cigarette, and he mostly remembered how to smoke it. Hands together, he cupped the offered flame. "This would be going very differently," the man told Keck, "if you'd trained your men properly, and led them well."

He almost spat out the cigarette with a derisory sound. "Submariners." Then, a deep and necessary drag before explaining. "It was like hoping that a limpet might one day win a sprint," he said, wincing as he braced a cheekbone which felt fractured. "Who are you? You speak German like a native."

"We're natives of very different Germanys, Kris," said Keller. "Yours was supposed to be defeated after an Allied triumph at Normandy. That way, mine was spared any more of your experiments and nightmarish visions of racial perfection."

Offended, Keck forgot about the cigarette; his hands were chained together, so it was hardly convenient to smoke, anyway. "You don't like it?" he asked, disappointed. "The remarkable 'Third Germany' I have created?"

"Created by tinkering with reality," said Keller, angry as he admonished this putrid relic of the SS. "Created through chaos by an incompetent trainee God."

"Created by forcing through some radical solutions."

"Radical and chemical," he pointed out.

"The war was over in ten days!" he shrieked. "I brought peace to Europe with a single decision."

This time, of course, Keller had him. "*You* did no such thing, you disingenuous parasite. Whatever name you give your doppelganger, it should be inscribed in history as that of history's greatest schmuck." The Yiddish was calculated to offend.

"No, that award goes to Professor Miller," he said. "A man who deluded himself he could crawl, terribly wounded, from his own grave to defy the SS. I wonder which got him first, hm? Tabun or Tallboys?" He glanced up, and then again, in anger, when he realized Keller was speaking with another man and ignoring Keck. "Am I not entertaining enough, Herr Keller?"

"Just receiving an inventory of the items our team has found so far," he said, bringing out a tablet device of the kind Keck hadn't seen since 'back' in 2014. "Which was supposed to happen first?" he asked, scanning the list with alarm. "The three-stage ballistic missile, the atomic bomb, the perfect blond-and-blue German? Or just," he said, wrapping his head around a live image being broadcast from Clavel's helmet camera, "the biggest fuckin' cow, ever?"

"I'm glad the aurochs survived your rather heavy-handed assault."

"Blame the French," he joked. "Those enormous breach charges were Clavel's idea."

"Were there any other survivors?" Keck asked. "My men?"

Keller pocketed the tablet and knelt down where Keck had taken a knee by the square's water standpipe. He'd been chained to it at first, but Keller relented. "Listen. This is the speech where I say, 'You've had a good run, but you knew would end eventually,' and things like that."

"I demand a military tribunal," Keck said.

"You could demand a slap in the face right now, and I might not bother to give it to you. I don't think you realize the situation."

"Enlighten me," he said.

"Your operation in California, 'Fountain' or whatever it's called, that's being wrapped up, right now. We have your contacts in custody, including the trio of morons who used to drive up into the hills to receive your para-drops from *Big Boy*. Oh," he said, palms to his chest, "my condolences on her loss. She was a unique specimen of man's hubris in the air. And Wolf, they tell me, was an original."

"So, you expect me to cooperate?" Keck said. "Explain all of the cutting-edge research we've been doing?"

Keller stood and stole one of Keck's cigarettes from the man's top pocket. "Jesus, these things are hard as bullets. Have the same effect on your lungs, too." He tossed it away. "Alive and kicking, you're a walking embarrassment to Germany. You think they want to admit that establishment bigwigs like Brennau and the others were secretly funding a Nazi research base?"

"They should be proud," he retorted.

"How would do you think Berlin's going to react when the world finds the truth about Fountain?"

"I'd imagine," Keck said, sounding brash, "that Hollywood will be crippled with shame. They'll learn the true loyalty of so many of their luminaries. A true shock, in the 'Home of the Brave.' There'll be calls for a vengeful new war against Germany."

"You hope!" he said. "A big split in the Atlantic alliance only serves fascists and thugs. As does another war. Just another chapter in the Wagnerian cycle."

"Such limited vision," Keck said. But Keller had turned away again, given a long string of details by three of his troopers, after which he made an extensive note on his tablet.

"Forgive me, this is less elegant than we'd prefer," he said to Keck when he was done, "but I've literally been asked to give you a choice. You ready?"

To reply would have been an acquiesce to his enemies' system of justice.

"One: Clavel kills you, in thirty seconds from now, with a bullet to the brain. You may have a blindfold if you wish."

He remained impassive, even took a smoke, and then said, "I'm waiting for two."

"Two: You step into what remains of your hut over there and end it yourself."

"Cowardice," he said quietly.

"Or Three: We fly you back to the Kearsage, and then to Florida, and then to an undisclosed location, for one last sit-down chat. I'm told that a group consisting of," he read from the notes, "Menzies,

Walcott, Wheeler, Thompson, Miller, Qualmes, and several dozen others wish to question you."

"Understandable. I'm a unique and fascinating figure, after all," he said, warming to the attention. "The only man ever to—"

"You're not letting me finish. Following their interrogations, the group will draw lots to decide which one of them gets to pull the lever, and you'll be ushered cordially to the gallows."

"Ah. So, you do have a backbone."

"There's no way out for you, Kris." One more update from his screen told him his men were ready to depart. One killed in action, three more injured, all expected to recover. Though they'd taken Keck's camp by surprise, his men waged a strong counterattack just before surrender. Keller was pissed but not surprised. "This must be a familiar feeling for a Nazi. No matter where you traveled in time, it'd be the same. You must know that by now."

Keck tossed the cigarette with as much nonchalance as the chains allowed. "How's that?"

Keller knelt by him once more, although bodily repelled by the disgraced officer. "I suppose you skipped '45, didn't you? These resonances with the Fuhrer's death will sound familiar only from history books, then."

"For that," he laughed, "we'd need Inge to play the hapless Eva Braun. And then I'd need to oblige you all with my suicide. I see no such resonances."

"You don't?" asked Keller. "The doomed last stand? The loyal subordinates sacrificed for some asshole's monstrous, grandiose dreams?" Then he stood and turned, signaling to Clavel that he was ready to get moving. He'd been eager to inform Keck of his fate, the same as that of every Nazi. "Those are the signs of history casting you out," rasped Keller, nodding once to Clavel before turning around, "and leaving you to die."

But he spoke only to a smoldering cigarette and an empty set of chains, strewn on the ground. Keller drew his pistol and spun around.

"Where did he go?" Keller barked to a shrugging Clavel as a large, dark shadow crossed the sky. They looked up at the enormous vessel blacking out the stars.

Keller kicked the dirt. "Motherfucker!"

***

1855 Redwood Rise

"I see," Caan said, stepping away from the group of suited agents and blowing out a heavy breath from his tightening chest.

Yanis. Then Jillian. And now Keck. All gone. So close to pulling this off and it had all gone tits up in an instant.

Yevchenko had detached himself from the arguing, investigating huddle in the living room, and was smoking quietly in the darker area of the terrace. Now he approached Caan. They stood side by side, wrists resting on the railing, gazing unfocused on the dimming lights of Los Angeles.

"The colonel might be prepared to work out a deal which spares the Participants some blushes," Caan offered.

"Look forward to the negotiations," Yevchenko replied.

"Keller and his men found Bonehouse. Inge is gone. Fountain is gonna collapse. And I got a sample of the Elixir."

"Whose ventilation shaft did you crawl down to get *that*?" asked Yevchenko.

"Oh, just old-fashioned fieldwork. Preliminary lab work says it's packed full of complex shit our guys don't understand."

Yevchenko nodded and took another drag on his cigarette. "What else?"

"US Navy shot down *Big Boy*. So, exit Wolf Man, whoever he was."

Yevchenko stubbed out his cigarette, exhaling a voluminous cloud. "Speaking of departures, I'm afraid my source chose not to participate further in the investigation."

"The housekeeper?" Caan probed, amazed. "She had a whole plan, the house on the lake ..."

"The betrayal was too much for her."

"Lying and stealing to protect the Allies, who offered peace and tolerance, was one thing. But being conned into supplying the dreaded Soviet KGB with information, that was too much?" Caan surmised.

"She chose a *'cyanide sayonara.'* They found her alone in her room."

Caan raked his hands through his thinning hair. The geopolitical cost would be awful, but worth it when the alternative would be a giant, ugly rip in the fabric of America, one from which the Republic might struggle to recover.

"Jesus," he said. "It's really true, isn't it? When it comes to the Nazis, choosing the wrong side means death."

| 10 |

Forever

Within visual range of Saturn's rings, Date: Engarian Time, Prime

The *Adjudicarus* zoomed faster than light from Engarian-controlled space, the long journey mitigated by the ship's internal time dilation. Slow by Engarian standards, the movement of the massive ship was more methodical than anything else. Rips in the timeline and respective waves of disruption, distortion, revision, and loop made for a reverberating kaleidoscope of different colors as perceived by the Engarian craft's sensors. This was uncharted territory with significant risk. Seeing the deep manifestations of the time stream, the alien inside stopped the ship.

"Ship, engage a waypoint here. We may need it to navigate."

"Confirmed," the ship responded. "Waypoint set."

Immediately, a momentary pulse of energy emanated from the ship, spreading in all directions and fading into space. Next, a tiny probe no larger than a fist was ejected. This would be the anchor in space, time, and dimension. Satisfied that this was done, the alien inside had the ship continue its cautious journey toward Earth, where he intended to study the criminals and these humans using his sensors.

***

Aboard the *Adjudicarus*, somewhere above Earth, immediately following raids at Redwood Rise and Bonehouse

An ethereal golden haze enveloped the noiseless space, as if replicating the dawn of creation. Still naked, Yanis floated freely, his limbs gently adrift in the tepid fluid encapsulated within the gleaming silver and glass tube. Beyond his confinement, the black void was punctuated by flickering blue and green lights. He sensed a dark presence, a slender figure observing from the shadows. Lashes fluttering, Yanis scanned his odd surroundings, trying to comprehend. His eyes came to rest on a tube identical to his own. As his vision came into focus, he recognized the toned figure floating tranquilly within it.

Kristock Keck.

At once, Yanis felt the ligature marks on his neck, wrists, and legs. Bruises had already begun to form after his sadistic encounter with Inge. He turned his head the other way, the after-effects of whatever drugs she'd plied him with still lingering. He wavered somewhere between woozy and coherent, a dull throb at his temples. But otherwise, serene and calm, even with Keck in such proximity. Seeing him contained—and, as far as Yanis could tell, asleep—was a comforting reassurance.

Yanis wondered where he was. Was he even alive? Perhaps Inge had succeeded in killing him, and he was in Gehenna, deep below the earth's surface. If so, here he would receive his reproach for all his mortal sins, and his soul would be cleansed and purified before he could ascend to the World to Come. If he remembered the teachings of his family's rabbi, it was possible he could be in this space for up to a year. But then, time had come to mean nothing to Professor Yanis Miller at this point.

As these thoughts bubbled to the surface from the murky depths of his awakening mind, another interrupted.

Jillian.

His last visions of her surged in rapid flashes. First, she was spilling into the doorway, a look of stunned surprise on her face as she discovered Yanis shackled in bed with a blonde Nazi bombshell astride him. Next, she fixed her pistol on Inge, ready to fire. And then, his head was cradled gently in her lap. The warm notes of her perfume washed over him, eroding his fear as she sobbed his name. Her delicate fingers raked his dark curls, comforting him before he drifted away.

He searched his surroundings as best he could, hindered by the lack of light. But it was futile. Jillian wasn't there; he could sense it. Only the mysterious, skeletal figure lurking in the shadows. A random symphony of twinkling lights speckling the black space. And the devil himself, Kristock Keck, who was now beginning to stir.

***

Keck stretched his hands outward, as if still bound by chains and holding the cigarette Keller had shared. But those things did not exist. Only the vaguely familiar sensation of floating in this amniotic spring. Weightless and unburdened. Another chance to reset the timeline and get it right. Irreversibly right. A final solution, indeed.

He looked around, sensing a slight motion beyond his tube. From the void emerged a shape, one much like the corpse of the alien that had crashed at Bonehouse. And this shape was now slowly, intently, approaching Keck's life-sustaining tube. Following a series of beeps, a blue light undulated over the tube's length, a result of the alien's scan. Keck's nerves bristled as the light passed over, inch by inch, eliciting sharp pain that disappeared as quickly as it erupted. He flailed in the antigravity chamber, ricocheting spasmodically into one of the walls before floating back to the center.

The next sensation was a jumble of voices—speaking different languages from around the world—filling his ears. Pieced together and overlapped like scraps on a quilt. Some French, some German, some English, some Japanese, and some he couldn't recognize.

But they all made the same demand: Identify yourself.

Keck straightened himself, the pain induced by the scan evaporated by now. "I am Kristock Keck, the leader of the human race," he proudly announced in English. "King of all humanity in the united human collective."

A momentary silence stilled the void. All beeps and whirrs ceased at his proclamation. Then he watched as Yanis' tube received the same, blue-lit scan. He saw the professor flinch and recoil as the pain washed over his naked form. Keck smiled at the thought of this nosy, meddling Jew experiencing even a brief dosage of the torture he deserved.

A single voice called out in rough, robotic English: Identify yourself.

"My name is Yanis Miller. I am a mathematician and cryptologist from the United States of America, and a professor at Jerusalem Polytechnic," he acknowledged, shifting in his tube. "And is there any chance I could get some clothes?"

Behind the skeletal figure, a flurry of lights, sounds, and signals erupted. As if an entire universe's radio communications were being intercepted at once. Keck understood that every language was being dissected, all methodologies being captured. Decoding 101. As elementary as the original Enigma system the Reich had used, just like the one that interfering professor happened upon, tucked away in an ice cave. The one that led him to *Der Dom*.

Seconds later, a deep voice spoke to the floating pair. "Both of you are in violation of this universe's laws and regulations regarding time dilation and time manipulation. You have caused significant distress in the timeline, multiple timelines, multiple time loops. There are several fissures and fractures; unresolved technology contamination in no less than four different timelines."

Keck and Yanis did their best to focus on the bony creature speaking to them.

It continued, "I have been called here to punish you, and to attempt to resolve the contamination of the timelines—which you have caused. Additionally, your race has not been set and protected at a level of understanding which allows you to manipulate time. However, failure to understand the law does not save you from its repercussions or punishments."

"So, I take it that's a no on the clothes, then? Okay, fine. But if I may, what is your name?" asked Yanis, fear edging the tones of his voice.

"Not that it is any consequence to you, but I am Arhegus, an Engarian, and the captain of this ship, the *Adjudicarus*," the voice said as the creature emerged from the shadows. "I came into your solar system eons ago."

The Engarian glided into the light surrounding Keck's tube and inspected him with the row of eyes beneath his hardened, crablike exoskeleton. Wispy grey and green hairs emerged from the connections between his bony plates. As it made its observations, writing of some type appeared in the air next to Keck's tube.

The robotic voice spoke again. But as each word was pronounced, it grew more refined and less robotic, now annunciating smoothly.

"You are a genetic match to the human that first traveled, and first used the sterling technology," the Engarian explained, "but you are not the same human that traveled in time."

Keck tilted his head, confused.

"By that," the alien continued, "I mean, you are genetically identical to another version of yourself, who later traveled. A copy. And in your current version, Kristock Keck, you have also been known as Joseph Taschner, Jose-Luis Cabrera, as well as other aliases. Some of your previous versions are privy to memories this version of you is not. But as I said, you, in the form which you present yourself today, are not the same human that traveled in time."

Wary and still processing the Engarian's explanation, Keck heard his words replay in the background, proclaiming himself the king of all humanity. Those words were then repeated in what he presumed to be the Engarian's home language. The being leaned closer, carefully inspecting Keck's face.

"So, you believe you are the leader of the humans, and this technology has propelled you to the focal point of your species," it said, the slightest hint of breath fogging Keck's tube as it spoke. "I can see that your species is ... *allergic* to my presence and is trying to take dramatic steps against the ship. Interesting."

With that, video screens appeared behind Arhegus, showing what looked to be a series of rocket launches. Imposing ICBM missiles bearing the flags of different countries, firing from various platforms. Some looked advanced and top secret, while others looked like they were part of a space program.

"These humans have just launched what looks to be projectiles with atomic weapons attached in order to destroy this ship," Arhegus noted. "Does your species not know who I am? And even if they don't, is this how you treat guests?"

After a momentary flash of light, each of the incoming missiles' payloads was vaporized, making it clear that any attempts to shoot at or damage the spacecraft would be futile.

Keck responded coolly, "My people are no doubt frustrated at my abduction. They interpreted it as an act of war. Please let me speak to my people and I will tell them to stand down. As we continue to communicate with each other, I freely welcome our dialogue and discussion between my species and yours. Please allow me the opportunity to welcome you to Earth."

He waited, unsure of what to expect from his Engarian host. But a moment of consideration was all it took before the word "granted" appeared in the air alongside his tube. Then with the motion of a long, spindly digit he said, "Proceed to tell them. They will hear you."

Keck straightened his spine and began. "People of Earth, this is Kristock Keck, your emperor. I am onboard the alien ship that you see hovering in the sky. Cease firing any missiles or making any attacks on this craft. I am currently in discussion with the aliens onboard, representing all of humanity. Stand down and wait for further instructions. Any attempts to damage the ship will be met with a frightful response."

Then with a flurry, the communication was sent back to Earth. All in Keck's voice, but in multiple languages.

The alien's attention now turned to Yanis.

***

As it had previously, a display of alien text appeared next to Yanis' tube. The Engarian's numerous eyes raised with surprise as he reviewed the readout.

"You have traveled multiple journeys, in both time and dimension, Yanis Miller. Additionally, your body contains genetic material from the Engarian species. How is that possible?"

Yanis's mind raced. He couldn't think of any reason his genetic code might include alien DNA.

"I ... huh ..."

Suddenly, he remembered that he'd tried to confront the original Keck on the alien ship—the crystal cathedral veiled deep beneath *Der Dom*. He'd followed the Steigers into the mountain tunnel. After discovering their corpses within the tunnel, among many others, Yanis noticed Keck up ahead. Clandestine, he crept farther into *Der Dom*, eager to see where Keck might lead him. Yanis watched Keck use the panel that allowed access the ship, then repeated his motions so that Yanis, too, could enter. Once Yanis was inside the ship, Keck turned and fired his Luger without warning. Yanis was shot in the jaw, mortally wounded. He recalled the sight of his blood dripping onto the sparkling white floors of the ship. Convinced he'd shot a random prisoner and presuming him dead, Keck continued. But for a brief time, as Yanis lay on the floor, his jaw gushing blood and his strength nearly gone, the ship itself had partly healed him. From that point on, he had some special connection with the ship, and could hear and feel some of the things that the ship wanted to do.

"I was near death's door," Yanis recollected. "I was injured, and the ship helped me, saving my life. I don't know what happened or how it healed me. There's no way I can explain it. But I believe it must have been during that time that my genetics were altered and fused with the alien species you speak of."

Arhegus drew back his skeletal frame and placed a bony digit at the tip of his chin. "Very interesting that humans and Engarians have some compatibility," he said. "This changes my thinking as to how to deal with you."

Yanis turned to Keck. "I hope you'll change your thinking on this man as well. He is not the leader of the human race. In fact, far from it. He is a monster, and one of the main reasons for the contamination of the timeline. He is directly and indirectly responsible for so many deaths on Earth. It's hard for me to even state the level of evil this man represents. Please do not believe what he says. He is lying to you, as he has lied to so many others. His only goal is to destroy humanity, not protect it."

The translation was prolonged. But once it was complete, the Engarian's attention was divided between the two men afloat in their respective tubes.

Suddenly, lights flashed to the left and right of them. An open space, like a large room, appeared and in it, several people materialized. The first was Jillian, followed by many of those from the German and UN team that had traveled back with her, Thompson, Keller, Walcott, Sam Clark, even Eli Caan, as well as several men from the last squad that had transported out from under the mountain.

Yanis and Jillian shared an unspoken moment of recognition. Overjoyed that they were together again, and at once petrified by the realization of what was happening.

"I am calling all humans who are out of the time sequence and out of the dimensional domain sequence here," Arhegus clarified. "And now we shall determine the appropriate response to correct the timeline and fix the fissures in the dimensions."

With his bony digits clasped together behind his exoskeleton, he paced as he continued. "This court will not stand for lies. Be advised your pathetic human attempts to deceive me will not be successful. I can see the past, the present, and the future, in multiple dimensions. Do not dare lie to me."

An ominous tone came over the last words he spoke. As he said them, gravity was gradually restored to the two tubes and Yanis and Keck touched gently to the floor. The others remained behind some sort of force field. While transparent, it gave off a golden hue. Then, in a blink, the tubes around Keck and Yanis disappeared.

"So, still no clo—" Yanis began, only to have Arhegus hold up his hand, silencing him.

A bright blue laser scanned all the humans in the open space. As the pain hit them, an alert blared. Texts appeared next to the golden field, all pointed toward Jillian.

"This is quite interesting," Arhegus said as he approached, reading and rereading the text. It had morphed into bright red now, with several blinking elements. Much different than the readout that appeared next to the two men in their tubes.

"This information changes everything," Arhegus announced as movement occurred behind Jillian. Everyone there, including Jim Thompson and those who had been on the original ship, froze.

"Come with me," the Engarian instructed, extending a skeletal hand through the golden screen. Jillian instinctively grabbed it and walked into the area that held Keck and Yanis. "This humanity you speak of has done an amazing job of contaminating the genetics as well as the timeline and dimensions. I see now that you three are tentatively but genetically tied. You also have alien genetics within you. Worse yet, your offspring will be the originators of the first temporal distortion of humanity."

Yanis and Jillian exchanged a confused glance.

The Engarian's long finger pointed toward Jillian's abdomen. "You carry within you a child that has Engarian genetics. And this child will be the first to discover temporal displacement."

Jillian's face fell in shock as Yanis filled with pride. While they had made love just a few weeks before Inge's soiree, it was too soon to know she was pregnant.

"We have deep treaties, as part of our rules for time displacement, that prevent us from tampering with the direct history of the creators of a species' time displacement capability," Arhegus explained, seeming troubled. "This technology is the limiting and qualifying technology which allows you access into a loose organization of alien species, all of which have the capability to do time interaction. However, because we are capable of time interaction, critical measures to limit and destroy a species' ability to generate this discovery have been specifically restricted."

A stunned silence had enveloped all onboard. In the unsuspecting stillness, Keck took advantage of the distraction. He grabbed the Engarian's arm and brutally hyperextended it in a shocking act of barbarism. Keck attacked with such severity that the alien's ligaments and exoskeleton cracked and popped. His time at Bonehouse, fortifying himself with genetically derived serums, had been spent in preparation for this moment. He pushed Arhegus to the ground, continuing to hyperextend his arm. Then he threw his knee into the alien's neck, cracking it in several places. A gooey, white ooze seeped out and Arhegus screamed in pain.

At once, Jillian and Yanis tried to jump to the rescue. Still reeling from Inge's drugs, Yanis was a few beats behind. His speed and coordination akilter. Jillian, meanwhile, threw herself at Keck, who met her attack with a brisk forearm, stunning her momentarily. Then he punched her directly in the face, sending her reeling backwards.

"That's no way to treat a lady, and the mother of my child, you piece of Nazi shit," Yanis yelled. Staggering, he lunged at Keck. But Keck easily dismissed him, flicking him away like a moth around the campfire at Bonehouse. Keck pressed his full weight into the alien's back and neck. Yanis charged again, but Keck pitched him to the floor. As Yanis managed to grasp the hem of Keck's shirt, it tore. Yanis slid across the floor, his naked body rolling in various directions.

Keck's deeply carved muscles rippled with power. As Jillian's eyes welled up with tears of pain, blood streamed from her nose in a torrent. The others, still behind the golden field, could do nothing but watch in horror. Keck then turned and stomped his foot into the alien's shoulder, severing it from Arhegus' twitching body.

"Professor Miller!" Sam Clark yelled from within the glowing area. "There's sure to be a way—"

But Keck's menacing roar drowned out the mathematician's voice as he spun away from Arhegus.

"A way? A way for what?" Yanis pondered from his position on the floor.

Undeterred, Jillian gave it another go, arms up in a boxing stance. "So, you like to hit women, huh?" she challenged, standing firm, and trying to divert Keck's attention. Meanwhile, Yanis climbed to his feet, charging Keck from behind.

"Again, you try to stop me, but you can't," Keck yelled, a bit of spittle glistening at the side of his mouth as he wrenched the last remaining ligament off the alien's shoulder. "Look at you, naked and pathetic. Weak and inferior as you'll always be. I've had years to enhance my own body at Bonehouse. Don't you see? I have transcended beyond the upper echelon of human capabilities. I am a supreme being, as our Fuhrer intended. And now you will die, for the last time, worthless Jew."

Jillian's punches landed hard, rippling Keck's skin. But with a sweeping uppercut of the alien arm that Keck was now using as a club, he lifted her off the ground. Yanis jumped on his back and struggled to keep hold of Keck as his augmented body arced. Ineffectual, Yanis went into a primal mode and bit at Keck's right ear. With a horrendous yell of pain, Keck drove his elbow into Yanis' solar plexus, knocking the breath completely out of the professor. Keck slipped back onto the hard ground, blood spurting out of his ear, or at least the stub that remained of it. And just like that day in the crystal cathedral, a red stream dripped from Yanis' face.

Keck again wielded the Engarian's arm, striking Yanis repeatedly in the head. Then he followed with a kick to his chest. Yanis lay motionless. Jillian screamed and then Keck, dropping the arm, turned and grabbed her by the throat. With a panicked expression in her eyes, Keck's large, veiny hands squeezed. Her eyes bulged, capillaries bursting as he choked the life out of her. Then he tossed her to the floor, discarded like a spent cigarette in an alley. Smiling with satisfaction at her elimination, he turned toward the captives in the open space.

Jim Thompson and the others shouted from behind the golden force field. Yanis was still as Keck caught his breath. He wiped away some of the blood from his ear, then looked at the men in the open space.

"Alien ship ... can you hear me?" Keck asked between deep breaths.

After a moment, a response came, in the Engarian tongue.

"Respond in my language," Keck commanded.

"This is the ship," came a disembodied voice, "what is your order?"

"Is there a way to let the humans behind this field free?"

The group of Allies shifted nervously, muttering quietly among themselves. Keck smirked, pleased that he had rattled them all to a man.

"Yes," said the ship, "we can return them to the surface via transport."

"Can you transport them directly outside the ship?" Keck asked, wiping again at his ear stub to staunch the flow of blood.

"Query received," the ship responded. "Yes, however, due to life safety protocol, it is reasonable to assume this would terminate all transported."

"Computer, transport all humans behind that field directly into space," Keck ordered.

"This will surely terminate these life forms—"

"Understood. Life safety, override," Keck sneered.

One by one, the men behind the golden barrier were transported outside the ship. And one by one, without ceremony, their bodies fell. When it was Sergeant Jim Thompson's turn, he stood defiant. Never backing down, shoulders straight, eyes forward as he accepted his tragic fate. The altitude guaranteed that each of the Ally men suffocated in their spiraling descent before crashing into the earth's inflexible surface. But Keck took little solace in their demise. He had made it his mission to cleanse the human race of inferiors and cause suffering to all who opposed his nefarious plan. And he wasn't done yet.

Besides, now that Keck had the power of this alien ship, every citizen of the world would become his subject. This was the moment to manifest his new world order. The dawn of an entirely new age, with Kristock Keck as the unquestioned Emperor Supreme. His long-awaited moment in the sun. Deeply satisfied with his achievement, he paused to look into the dark vastness of space and gaze down upon the earth.

It was over. The struggle that had marked his lifetime was finally finished. Domination of this world, and all others, awaited. At long last.

...

...

...

***

Aboard the *Adjudicarus*, moments later

With a gasp and a crackle, Arhegus began to twitch again. Keck approached, stepping over Jillian's corpse to get a closer look. The twitching began to slow, and with a final gurgling wheeze, Arhegus stopped moving.

As he did, the ship suddenly accelerated, throwing Keck backwards.

"Ship," he called out, "where are we headed?"

An electronic voice crackled over the speakers. "To the waypoint."

Keck struggled to get to his feet. The ship rocked violently as if being hit by unseen waves buffeted by invisible waters. He tried to peer into space, grasping at the controls. His frustration mounting, he yelled, "Ship, stop what you are doing!"

"Movement commands locked out. Waypoint protocol engaged."

Ignorant of the shadow creeping toward his back, Keck shouted, "Ship, I am in control now!"

"Think again," came the raspy voice behind him.

Keck spun around, greeted by Arhegus' arm throttling his bloody ear stump.

With Inge's drugs finally worn off, Yanis hammered away at Keck's head, knowing the loss of his ear would affect his equilibrium. Off balance, Keck reeled back, falling onto a control panel near his tube. The panel sparked and flashed, electrocuting Keck, who then went limp.

Yanis' eyes flashed. "Ship," he called out, "encapsulate this prisoner."

At once, the tube reformed around Keck, who was still convulsing.

Bloodied and naked, Yanis looked at Jillian, sprawled out along the ship's floor in death's final, rigid form.

"Ship," he said through a series of sobs, "can you teach me your ways? I need to learn everything there is to know about dimensional and time shifting."

"Affirmative," the ship responded, "Professor Miller."

He wiped a stream of snot and tears from his face, his breath coming in jagged gulps. Jillian and Arhegus were dead. Jim and the others, too. He looked at Keck, twitching in the tube as the current continued to surge through his overly developed body. They continued to feel the thrust, the deep acceleration, of the ship as it hurtled through space.

It would take time to learn what he needed to learn, but that didn't bother him. He had work to do. And it would be worth the wait. After all, time had come to mean nothing to Yanis Miller.

His injuries severe and his heartbreak more so, he collapsed on the floor near the controls. Completely overwhelmed, all went dark.

***

Yanis would never know how long he was unconscious. All he remembered was waking up to the cool surface of the metal floor. In the dim and blinking light, he could see her limp body. Distraught, he went over and cradled it in his arms. Jillian was his everything, and she was gone.

The massive Engarian ship slowed violently, rocking him as he held her corpse.

"Waypoint reached," the ship announced. "Resetting in 3, 2, 1 …"

At zero, the outside of the ship touched the tiny probe it had previously launched just beyond Saturn's rings. As it had previously, a blinding light emanated in all directions. Beyond weary, Yanis wondered if he was in a dream or a deep sleep. He had the sense of someone talking with him. But the words were just beyond the reach of his understanding.

Then the feeling deep within him—the alien part of him—called out, assuring him everything would be fine. As his eyes opened, he was in mid-conversation.

"… and in doing so, I made a waypoint," Arhegus explained.

"That's what Sam Clark was trying to tell me! A *way*-point. Like a set point where everything jumps back to if the timeline is disrupted?" Yanis offered, sounding more confident now within his tube.

"Precisely," Arhegus said. "Even if something happens to me, this ship will return to that point. All aboard this ship will have a memory of their being here, though it may not make sense as they enter new timelines."

"Like déjà vu," Keck said smugly as he offered Yanis a penetrating stare from the interior of his tube. "The feeling that you've exterminated this worthless scum before."

Yanis responded with an icy glare of his own.

"That is not for me to say," Arhegus offered. "But you would do well to hold your tongue for now."

***

Aboard the *Adjudicarus*, 3 years later

With its massive girth and rotund, funnel-like shape, the *Adjudicarus* seemed to defy the laws of gravity. It loomed in the sky as if incapable of hovering. But this cargo vessel's trans-dimensional capabilities and incomprehensible size had proven useful for transporting weapons, tanks, and other vehicles from 2014 to 1940s Germany.

In contrast, the *Granum*, its seed ship, was sleek and angular. After being attacked, the aerodynamic craft had crashed deep within the heart of the German mountains. It had lain, veiled in privacy for millions of years before a humble, doddering miner had accidentally discovered it in 1943.

And now, the *Granum* had been raised to the surface, ready to be turned over to its new pilot.

Arhegus stood and vacated the cockpit's seat. "I believe you are ready."

Yanis tugged at his sweater as he sat at the controls. This ship had been his home for three years, but he still hadn't adjusted to the internal temperature. Occasional forays into earthly dimensions to pick up supplies and test his knowledge had proven helpful, and he was confident that he could now fulfill his destiny.

"I can't say enough how much I appreciate you trusting me," Yanis explained.

"I trusted you because you tried to help me when Keck attacked. The regenerated Keck destroyed my timeline. The original Keck will be more vulnerable. Now everything is up to you, Professor. I will call up the original Engarian seed ship. You will transfer to that. I will return to my home. You will fix the timeline and let everything resolve, as we have discussed."

Yanis exhaled. The Engarian scroll, now familiar to him, popped up alongside him and read his vitals.

"You're nervous," Arhegus chided.

"Wouldn't you be?" Yanis replied.

"I do not have emotions. But if I did, I would tell you that there's no need to be nervous if you're prepared," Arhegus said as the seed ship appeared alongside their craft. "You know what you have to do. I have faith in you."

Yanis thought about Jillian, and their future family, assuming he didn't mess this up. "Alright," he said, "let's do it."

***

Redwood Rise, Finale Day

Sabine laid Yanis back on the thin white linens, centering him below the industrial candelabra. But this time, he recognized it as a pulley system. And he knew its intended use.

As she reached up to cuff his wrists to the headboard, Yanis spit out the pill he'd tucked into his cheek instead of swallowing. Then he pivoted, rolling on top of her like an Olympic wrestler pulling a switch.

"Oh, do you think you're going to gain control?" she oozed, wriggling with delight beneath him in her silver gown.

He tore the cuffs from her manicured hand and harshly clamped one over her wrist.

"Ooh!" she growled, "I like it rough, you know."

Without pause, he looped the chain through the curlicued headboard.

"Good," he said, yanking up her other arm and cuffing that wrist as well. "Then you'll love this."

Her eyes, lit with passion and craven lust, abruptly narrowed.

He leaned over and whispered in her diamond-draped ear, *"Der Sturmbannfuhrer* sends his regards."

Sabine's eyes, now widening with terror, flashed toward the door as it burst open. Jillian bolted in, keys in one hand, a drawn pistol in the other. Sabine began to curse in English and German as Yanis hopped off his captive and pulled up his pants.

Jillian's lip crinkled as he caught her relieved gaze from between the bars. Then he unlocked the wrought iron gate, where she fell into his arms.

"You're alright?" she whispered.

"Yes," he said, pulling her back and clasping his hands on either side of her face. "You remember the ship? And what happened up there?"

She nodded as Sabine continued her profane, bilingual tirade. "Keck killed us."

He pulled her close again and kissed her. "It's almost time." He glanced over at Sabine, arms stretched behind her head as she writhed on the stark white sheets. Then he turned back to Jillian and stroked her cheek. "You know what to do?"

"Mmhmm," she managed, her eyes locked on him as he walked to the other side of the room. A shadow loomed outside the tiny window. Yanis inhaled and closed his eyes.

Jillian's breath hitched as he disappeared. Now it was up to her.

"Inspector Qualmes," Sabine pleaded, arms stretched behind her head as she writhed on the stark white sheets. "This changes nothing, you know."

A wry smile lifted the corner of Jillian's lips as she turned toward Sabine. "I'm not so sure about that, Inge," she said.

"You can't hurt me," she teased.

"Thought you liked pain, *Fraulein Weber*," Jillian said in flawless German, passed down from her grandmother. She calmly walked toward her target, pistol raised. *"Der Schmerz ist Vergnugen, richtig?"*

Inge glared at her, but Jillian returned the steely gaze with exponential disdain and continued to advance. It occurred to Inge that she hadn't seen that level of determination in a long time.

Desperation seeping into her voice, Inge rasped, "Keck … will still eliminate you, Inspector Qualmes. Aren't you worried about that?"

Her reply came in the form of a single shot to Inge's liver. "Maybe," Jillian said as the gun reverberated in her hand. Dark, almost black blood began to flow, staining the silver satin gown and white sheets as Inge went limp. In a reluctant act of mercy, Jillian tossed a blanket over Inge's body as it transitioned to a corpse. "I guess we'll find out."

She tucked her pistol back into her evening bag and waited just inside the wrought iron gate, near where Yanis had stood. She let out a deep sigh. Almost immediately, a series of loud raps came at the door. But as Caan and the men from Prophet burst in, Jillian vanished.

***

Bonehouse, the same time

They began the assault simultaneously. But Clavel was stunned to find that Keck was well prepared. He'd forfeited his skinny, sunburned

Krauts, putting them upfront to absorb the first wave of gunfire while he hunkered down.

"Get to the lab!" Clavel shouted. "Don't let them escape!"

But around him, his men fell, targeted by snipers. Keck, protected by Neumann and a phalanx of armed guards, trotted toward Inge's tin-roofed hut.

"Mach schnell!" he yelled. He was grateful to Inge, depraved as she was. Thanks to her early warning, as well as his time aboard the alien ship, he'd already learned of this little visit. And he was ready for a very different battle. Once he realized that Jewish mathematician and British inspector had infiltrated Fountain, the rest was obvious.

A shame about Inge. Maybe her insatiable nymphomania can finally rest. But she was a necessary sacrifice to ensure that my work, my life's mission, would continue.

Despite the early warning, Keck still wanted to give Clavel the false impression that the Allies had a chance. It would make his defeat that much more humiliating. He ducked into the hut where another dozen of his sacrificial soldiers laid in wait, intending to lure Clavel's troops nearer. Their footfalls echoed closer now. On his order, Keck's men took aim.

"Jetzt!" he commanded.

The young soldiers burst from the hut, spraying Clavel's men with bullets and driving up the casualty count on both sides. Even Neumann. But it was enough to ensure an unimpeded path to the lab. Even as the mortars hit their target, shaking the hut, there was no need to rush now.

Calmly, Keck emerged as it began to incinerate. A few hundred meters to freedom, and he would walk, not run, in confidence. A smile curled his lips as he envisioned his escape.

He hit the ground with a thud, raising a cloud of dust.

"Going somewhere?" said the pale-faced westerner standing above him. He lowered the pistol he was holding. Keck recognized the sting at the back of his head and understood the pistol's handle to be the source. Woozy, he tried to raise his head, but couldn't. He fell back with a groan, his eyes drifting toward the lab as he struggled to keep them open.

"Cuffs," the westerner ordered, and two guards set to work. He lit a cigarette and observed with satisfaction. When they were done, they sat Keck upright.

"Name's Keller. *Kippe?*" the man offered, extending a second cigarette.

Keck nodded, and took it awkwardly, his chained hands restricting his movement as he leaned forward and brought it to his lips.

"There's no way out for you, Kris," Keller said. "Your fate is the same as every Nazi ..."

But Keck never heard the end of the soliloquy Keller had no doubt rehearsed like a B-list actor trying to break out of the interesting sidekick roles. By the time Keller had launched into his moral lesson about the Third Reich, Keck had vanished.

***

Aboard the *Adjudicarus,* immediately afterward

The Engarian tapped a long, bony digit on the ship's console. The final guest, still rubbing the back of his head and stinking of nicotine, had arrived. Jillian and Yanis huddled together. Keck's very presence, even in this environment, inspired an eerie chill of dread.

"You have compromised the plan," the Engarian said, wasting no time.

"I make my own plans," Keck smirked.

The Engarian rose from its seat and stalked toward Keck. Its crab-like exoskeleton flexed at sharp angles as it walked. "You have already been warned about violating the laws of the universe, and regulations about time dilation and manipulation. I told you before, I am well within my authority to erase you from time entirely for this transgression."

Keck's smirk softened slightly, like a poker player searching for a tell in a smoke-filled casino. But none came. Jillian glanced at Yanis, who tightened his grip on the small of her back.

"*Your authority?* I have no duty to recognize any authority other than my own," Keck sneered as the Engarian approached. "Your laws do not apply to me."

"Failure to recognize or understand the law does not protect you from repercussions or punishments. I have been called here to resolve the contamination you've caused in the timelines," said the Engarian, peering into Keck's smug eyes.

"I am the leader of the human race," Keck affirmed. "You cannot punish or erase me. I have fortified myself with a series of elixirs that have made me invincible—"

Yanis felt Jillian tremble as Keck confirmed what they had suspected but hadn't been able to prove.

"Fountain," Yanis blurted out. "That's what they were peddling, human DNA."

"Only the highest quality specimens, Professor Miller," Keck mocked. "Extracted at my ranch in Argentina."

"From?" Yanis fought the wave of nausea ascending his esophagus as the realization solidified in his mind.

It was Jillian who now tightened her grip, keeping Yanis steady. "You bloody monster," she scowled.

"Oh, Inspector Qualmes, you have no idea," Keck offered. "You see—"

He paused but continued to smile defiantly, seeming to relish this exposure of the plan he'd masterfully concealed for so long. All the aliases, all the locations, assets, and sacrifices. Every strategic chess maneuver, regardless of the moral expense. Even the child he'd given up in Hamburg. Every effort worthwhile to enjoy this righteous moment of victory. Jillian buried her face in Yanis' shoulder and exhaled rapidly.

"You are despicable," Yanis chimed in. "The idea of a genetically engineered master race is appalling."

"And yet, so satisfying now that I have succeeded," Keck retorted.

"Enough!" the Engarian ordered, raising a skeletal hand. Its eyes narrowed in rows, peering at Keck and then shifting toward Jillian and Yanis. "Silence as I determine your punishment."

Keck let out a breath, indifferent.

The Engarian returned to the console. Without hesitation, it placed its bony finger on a green button and pressed. Yanis' eyes widened as he watched Keck dissolve before him. But as he turned to watch Jillian's reaction, he felt her form dematerialize.

"What the fuck?" he exclaimed, a cocktail of rage and shock. "Where is she? Why did you—"

The Engarian again raised its hand. "Professor Miller," it said, "erasing Kristock Keck was a necessity."

"Yeah, I get that," Yanis huffed, his pulse surging, "but why Jill? What did she do?"

The Engarian focused its gaze on Yanis, pushing its hands downward in a calming motion. "You really don't know, do you?"

"Know what?"

"Inspector Qualmes was Kristock Keck's granddaughter," the Engarian explained.

"What? I've met her grandparents. How can that—" he scratched his head, slowly putting things together. "She never mentioned ... well, her mother's parents, anyway. Her father ... oh my God."

"What did she tell you about her father, Professor Miller?"

"That he was raised by a single mother," Yanis said, the truth absorbing like water to a sponge, "in Germany. Brilliant man. He went to Oxford and became a chemist."

"Is that all she said?"

Yanis racked his memory. "He ... she said he went to Oxford and I thought it was interesting because it seemed he'd come from such humble beginnings. I was surprised that a single mother could afford to send him there. Just assumed he had some type of scholarship."

"Did you ever meet him, Professor?"

Yanis shook his head. "No, and I wish I had," he admitted. "He sounded like a wonderful man, and I imagine we would've had a lot to talk about. But he died when Jillian was 20, several years before I met her. Brain aneurysm, I think."

The Engarain nodded. "I hope you understand that erasing Kristock Keck meant erasing her, too."

Yanis' heart balled up in his chest and his lungs felt tight. "So, I'll never see her again? It's as if she never existed?"

Shaking its head, the Engarian said, "I'm afraid not."

Yanis exhaled. His sorrow morphed into anger and he felt something melting down within his soul. "Then what the fuck did I even go through all of this for? All these ... *years?* Shit, I don't even know what time *is* anymore. All I know is that none of it is worth it if I don't have her."

"Erasing Kristock Keck means preserving the future of humanity," the Engarian calmly offered. "That's a very worthy objective. And you are a very worthy being. You've proven that time and again with your efforts to defeat Keck. You should be satisfied that he's finally gone."

Yanis recalled his time aboard the Engarian ship, following Keck just before being shot in the jaw and left for dead. The ship had healed him. There was a restorative energy there. Maybe this was for the best.

Except, it wasn't.

"Wait. If Jillian is gone, so is our child, and any other children we might have. You said yourself that our child would be an originator of the first temporal distortion of humanity," Yanis said. "So, if that's true, erasing Keck—and in turn, Jillian, and our children—is a violation of the time laws you previously mentioned."

Arhegus was silent as Yanis looked around, taking in the various buttons, switches, and blinking lights. The glowing blue stream that surrounded the chambers fizzled and pulsed.

"What can you teach me about all of this?" he said, motioning to the instruments, "about time dilation and manipulation?"

"I can teach you anything you like," the Engarian countered, "but I don't know that I want to. Why do you ask?"

"You just said I'm a very worthy being."

The Engarian nodded. "That I did. What's your point?"

Yanis set his jaw. "I have an idea."

***

October 1943, Bad Tölz, Germany

Yanis stood in the nook of the bed and breakfast's suite and checked the backpack. Diapers, wipes, blanket, a change of clothes, and one very heavy bar of gold bullion. He zipped it closed and set it on the corner of the desk with a thud.

Jillian emerged from the bedroom, her hair piled up in rollers and little Jim propped on her hip. "Have you seen his bottle?" she managed around a yawn.

Yanis smiled, walking over to take the infant from her arms. Then he kissed her cheek. "On the writing desk, Mama. The innkeeper, Hanna, was kind enough to warm it for us in the kitchen. I suspect she may be Miriam's grandmother."

"Miriam?"

"The woman who ran this place when I was here in 2014, after I discovered the Enigma machine in the ice cave. Anyway, she sent up some breakfast, too." He gestured to a plate of muffins and fruit. "Why don't you finish getting ready? I'll feed him."

She grabbed a muffin and took a bite. "You sure?"

"Yes," Yanis said as his son began to bob in his arms and reach for his glasses. "We have a long drive to the *Zitternberg* mine. Take your time."

She pulled the baby's chubby fingers away from Yanis' glasses and kissed them. "I'm still not sure it was wise to bring him along," she said.

"He'll be fine," Yanis replied. "Besides, what were we going to do? Hire a sitter and say, 'Can you watch our baby? We have to travel back to 1943 Germany and defeat the Nazis. Not sure how long it'll take, but here's an extra $25 for pizza.' Who would agree to that?"

"They don't even have proper car seats," Jillian protested.

"Sweetheart," Yanis said, placing a hand on her shoulder, "for the last time, he'll be fine. Our parents and grandparents survived this era, didn't they?"

Jillian sighed, her curler-topped head sagging to one side. "Suppose you're right," she resigned with a frown. "Gonna take a while to brush out my hair."

Yanis sat at the desk and raised the bottle for Jim, whose tiny hands pulled it closer to his mouth. "It'll be worth it. I love that Hedy Lamarr look you've got going. Maybe after this you can work out the technology for Bluetooth."

Jillian rolled her eyes and disappeared back in the bedroom. Yanis settled into the chair and rested his elbow on the desk.

Shortly, a knock came at the door. With Jim still taking his bottle, Yanis rose awkwardly, afraid of disturbing his son's feeding. When a second knock followed, he called out, "Just a minute," and tucked the bottle under his chin.

Opening the door, he saw Hanna, holding a tray with a coffee service. "I thought you might like some coffee as well," she announced. "I'm sorry it wasn't ready earlier."

Being careful not to disturb Jim's bottle, Yanis nodded toward the desk. "That's very thoughtful, thank you. Would you mind setting it down over there? I've got my hands full."

"Of course," she said as she entered the room. "Are you and your wife going into town today?"

"Uh, not really," Yanis said. "We're going to the *Zitternberg*."

Hanna reached for the backpack and tried to push it away to clear some space for the coffee service, but it wouldn't budge. "Oh my," she said, "you seem to have packed well."

"Well, we wanted to be prepared," Yanis said, grateful the backpack hadn't dropped to the floor. Gold bricks are anything but subtle.

Jim had finished the bottle, and Yanis bounced him on his shoulder, patting until he let out a loud burp. Then he began to coo at Hanna, whose eyes lit up with delight.

"Oh, you're such a sweet boy," she said, clapping her hands. "I bet you'll enjoy your adventure today. Climbing, I assume?"

"Yanis," Jillian called from the bedroom, "are you sure we've gone back far enough? Before Hitler—"

She stopped as she entered the nook and saw Hanna standing there.

"Good morning, Mrs. Miller," Hanna said, playing with Jim's toes.

"Oh, good morning," Jillian replied, shooting Yanis an awkward glance. "I'm sorry, I didn't realize anyone else was here. Thank you so much for warming the bottle and sending up breakfast. That was so thoughtful of you."

"Being a new parent can be frantic," Hanna said. "I thought it might be helpful. Besides, looks like you have a big day of climbing ahead."

Yanis raised his brows and nodded toward the backpack so that Jillian could follow along.

"Oh ... yes, *climbing,*" she said. "Yes. Big day."

They stood in silence for a moment, just verging on the edge of awkwardness.

"Well," Hanna said, giving Jim one last pat on the cheek, "I need to get back to the kitchen and begin working on lunch. I suppose I'll see you sometime this evening?"

Yanis escorted her to the door. "Yes, I'm sure you will," he said with zero confidence. "Definitely."

As the door closed, he turned to Jillian, who was letting out a relieved sigh. "Sorry," she offered. "I had no idea she was here. Do you think—"

Yanis shook his head. He poured a cup of coffee, then handed it to her. "No, I don't think she understood. She'd have no way to know. But even if she did, I'm sure she'd keep quiet."

She sipped her coffee and nodded. "I hope you're right. Well, I'm nearly ready. Give me ten minutes?"

Yanis offered Jim a pacifier as he began to fuss. "Sounds good. We're ready when you are." Jillian went back to the bedroom and Yanis turned to their son.

"Big day for Mommy and Daddy," he said as Jim's eyes grew heavy. "And an even bigger day for humanity."

***

October 1943, Berlin, Germany

Keck pulled up his collar and lit a cigarette, looking at the map in the dim light of the Berlin train station. Rail was a convenient way to travel, but the train had many stops between here and his destination. And he had no intention of pausing before completing his mission. His finger traced the lines until it centered on its target. The *Zitternberg* mine.

Alpine air seemed like a welcome departure from the putrid metropolitan stench. Piss and vomit, and the cheap perfume of the pale, lumpy *nutten* who targeted the area, rife with willing customers.

A thin-legged whore approached him, her tattered coat barely secured by a loose, hanging button. She caught his gaze and parted her lips, but he waved his hand, dismissing her.

"*Nein, hure,*" he spat, brushing past her, unwilling to compromise his singular focus.

He'd left Professor Hans Steiger behind in history, where he couldn't screw up anything else. This time around, he wanted the pleasure of offing this tippling lush of a miner for himself. He patted his pocket, feeling the Luger, and proceeded to the street.

Emerging in the faint light, he looked up and down the sidewalk. The workday was beginning. He could see the light on in the *backerei*, and soon a waft of yeasty dough greeted him. He walked silently, around the back of the building. In the alley, two men in aprons leaned against a sedan, smoking cigarettes and engaged in a spirited conversation. The chubby one opened the driver's door, reaching into the back for a coat.

Keck moved quickly.

"*Die autoschlussel,*" he ordered, pointing his Luger in the fat man's back. When his victim froze, Keck pushed the Luger's barrel deeper in the man's vertebrae. "*Jetzt!*"

Without hesitation, the man handed over the keys. Keck tossed him to the ground, then pointed the Luger at the other man as he shimmied into the driver's seat. With a squeal of rubber, he was gone.

Once on the *Autobahn*, Keck checked his watch. It would be afternoon by the time he arrived. By then, Steffan should be boozed up on the swill served at the *Bierhaus Bayerisch,* letting out spicy burps and leering at the homely barmaids.

An easy mark.

"Time to secure my future," Keck said, settling in for the drive south.

***

Bad Tölz

Hands on the steering wheel, Yanis looked over at Jillian, staring at the *Zitternberg* looming in the distance. "What are you thinking about?"

She shook her head. "When we were at the inn, and you were talking about Hanna, how she must be Miriam's grandmother. I think it's fascinating to go back and learn about our ancestors, see them when they were young, what hopes and dreams they had. What their daily lives were like. I don't know. Maybe it's just hormones, after having Jim. I just... I wish I'd known my grandfather. On my father's side."

"What do you know about him?" Yanis asked.

"Not much," she said. "He's always been a mystery. My father rarely spoke of his real father. His mother, my Oma, she raised him by herself for many years. She eventually married a man who was an accountant. I think my father was 12 by then. They were quite poor, apparently. But soon after, his real father left an inheritance for him."

"Really? I never knew that."

Jillian nodded. "He didn't like to talk about it. I think he was ashamed of not having a father. But that money allowed him to go to Oxford and become a chemist. I don't think he really wanted to take the money. But I suspect that in the end, he realized it might as well go to good use. And," she said with a sigh, "if I'm being honest, that helped me join MI6. I doubt I would've had that opportunity had he not been so well-respected."

"Way to go, Dad," Yanis said.

"Mm," Jillian mused, the smile of pleasant memories warming her face in the early day's light. "I do miss him, though."

"I wish I'd met him," said Yanis, laying his hand over Jillian's. Jim let out a soft snore from his carrier in the back seat. "He sounds like a smart guy."

"Brilliant," Jillian corrected.

"Like his daughter. Tell me, did he have a great sense of humor, too?"

She shook her head. "When he wanted, I suppose," she said. "But he was the quiet type. Always observing. Witty, but reserved. He only chimed in when he felt he had something to add to the conversation."

"I see," Yanis said. "I wish more people had that trait."

"Mm," she said again, the Zitternberg growing larger outside the car window. "Almost there, huh?"

Yanis looked ahead at the road's curlicued path. A few more twists and turns and they should be at the base of *Der Dom*.

***

Keck pulled over and checked the map. He looked out the sedan's window, wondering where he'd made a wrong turn.

"Shit," he hissed, realizing his mistake. He'd gone back in time so often that he'd been looking for a bridge that hadn't been built yet. Now he'd have to double back, costing him at least an hour.

He crumpled the map in disgust, sending it to the floorboards. Then he lit another cigarette and spun the tires as he jerked the sedan out of the gravel and headed back north.

***

Yanis slid the gold brick toward Steffan, hoping his end of this patchwork English-German conversation was being understood. "Then we have a deal?"

"*Ja, ja,*" the miner said. "The mine is yours. Although I don't know why you'd want it. All these years, it's brought me little more than salt and hardship."

Jillian beamed as Jim played with a stuffed elephant.

Yanis leaned across the table and shook Steffan's hand. "Thank you, sir. You have no idea what this means to me. To our family."

"I think we should celebrate," Steffan said, standing up and going to the hallway by the door. He grabbed his coat and hat. "To the *Bierhaus Bayerish,*" he said. "Drinks are on me."

Jillian looked at Yanis, noting the time. "The ... *Bierhaus?* Uhh, so early in the day?"

"Oh, we can sit outside," Steffan assured, motioning to Jim. "It will be fine, I assure you."

Yanis looked at Jillian, who shrugged. "Well, what are we waiting for? Let's go and celebrate."

"OH! One moment," Steffan added. He lugged the gold brick off the table and then went to the hall closet. There, he pulled up two floorboards and brought forth a box. He rummaged in his right pants pocket, and then the left, finally producing a key. "Ahh," he said, opening the box. He set the gold bar inside, locked the box, and put everything back in place.

They started for the door and Steffan stopped again. "Oh, I'm so sorry. In my enthusiasm, I'm not thinking straight. I'll need my wallet, and one other thing. If you'll excuse me for just a moment," he said, then disappeared to the bedroom.

"So, what's the plan now?" Jillian whispered.

"Go have some drinks," Yanis said.

"No, I mean, after?"

Yanis checked behind him. Hearing Steffan's celebratory humming from the bedroom, Yanis said, "We call in Keller and his squad and they work their magic with the explosives to make sure the entrance to this mine is completely sealed off."

"Are we ready?" Steffan called, gliding back into the room. "Again, I apologize for the delay."

"Let's go," Yanis said. "To the *Bierhaus!*"

***

Keck circled the block, trying to remember where this tavern was located. Women walked with their dinner groceries, huddled in groups, while a few men in business suits talked on a corner. He slowed and waited for an old woman crossing the sidewalk.

"*Mach schnell, alte Hexe,*" he growled. He thought about laying on the horn, but decided it was best not to attract attention. As he waited, his eyes drifted to a group of people dining outside. He squinted into the sun, trying to focus.

"*Heureka!*"

There was Steffan, the pudgy, hulking miner, facing the sidewalk. He sat with a young couple, the woman holding a baby in her lap. Keck looked up to see the old woman finally shuffling onto the curb and pulled the sedan into the closest parking space he could find.

"Only for deliveries, sir," called a voice from inside a butcher shop as Keck got out of the car. "You can't park here."

Keck pulled the Luger from his pocket and glared at the shopkeeper. "Sure about that?"

The man nodded. "*Jawohl,*" he said, retreating into his shop, smelling of stale blood and beef.

Keck walked along the sidewalk, scoping out the best angle on Steffan. Then he realized who was sitting with him.

"Son of a bitch," he muttered. "It's my lucky day."

He looked over his shoulder and crossed the street, approaching Steffan from behind. The three of them were laughing, a candid moment of frivolity, even in this grey-stained landscape. As he neared the doorway of the *Bierhaus Bayerisch,* a barmaid came out with a large round tray thick with steins, forcing Keck to stop and wait. She unloaded several drinks onto a table as Keck jostled his way around her. She nearly lost her balance.

"Hey!" she protested, but Keck persevered, never looking back. At last, Steffan's table was in sight. He pulled the Luger from his pocket and advanced.

It was that Jewish mathematician who saw him first. He stood up, arms raised, as he moved in front of the woman and the baby.

Keck aimed the Luger, his hand steady on the trigger. "It's over," he said. "You'll never seize *Der Dom.*"

"NO!" the professor yelled, shielding the others.

But Keck had already fired a shot, dropping the mathematician to the ground. The woman curled herself around the infant, but Keck's second shot ripped through both of them. She slumped over the table, dropping the baby on the concrete with a sickening thud.

Steffan turned around, facing Keck who was now stepping over the bleeding baby.

"What in the—"

But as Keck squeezed the trigger a third time, he was struck in the chest. A bullet launched from Steffan's own pistol.

After the exchange, Keck plunged to the sidewalk. The barmaid and other patrons screamed. Blood spilled from the back of Keck's head and his chest, while Steffan fell in his chair.

Yanis, severely wounded in his forearm, struggled to pull himself up from the ground. He checked Steffan's pulse. Weak, and then, nothing.

Then he moved over to Keck, his eyes open but lifeless. Keck gurgled momentarily, then stopped. Finally getting to his feet, he stumbled toward Jillian and young Jim.

Both dead.

Yanis ran his hands through his dark curls. A colossal fuckup he hadn't counted on.

"NO!"

***

Yanis sat in Steffan's cabin and scratched his head, taking it in as the sun began its weary ascent over the *Zitternberg*. He'd spent the entire night sobbing and angry. Bereft. Keck was gone, but his disappearance meant Jillian and young Jim went with him. If Keck didn't exist, neither would they. How could he have let this happen? Everything in life he cherished, gone in an instant. He was a mathematician, after all, and had been thorough in his calculations while aboard the *Adjudicarus*. Three years learning how to manipulate time, going back to marry Jillian and start a life of happiness together ... all to lose his most precious treasure: his family.

Yes, having Keck gone meant that humanity would be rid of his Nazi ideologies and cruel eugenics experiments. Forever. But at what cost? He was sure that returning to 1943 to buy the mine and implode it would've eliminated the possibility of Keck accessing the portal.

Unless...

He walked out to the salt mine's entrance and inhaled the morning dew, knowing exactly what he had to do next.

***

Hamburg, October 21, 1944

Keck zipped his trousers as Anna stared out the hotel window. It was dark, almost eerie, in these moments before sunrise. And rain had been falling throughout the night. All those months aboard the *Kriegsmarine* U-boat with nothing to look at but forbidden fruit Inge Weber had taken their toll. He found himself beginning to question this decision—the first in ages—made solely with his libido, not his usual, calculating frontal lobe.

He worked his hands over Anna's bony shoulders, noting her fragility, even through the barrier of his coat. In this adaptation of himself—now as Joseph Taschner—he seemed to have a deeper connection to his emotions. Something he thought he'd neutralized long ago. And yet, he felt an emptiness, despite their lovemaking only hours before.

"How will you spend your day, *liebschen?*"

"I'm supposed to meet my brother at two," she said, his hands working their way down her narrow torso. "He wants me to meet a friend of his."

He bent to kiss the side of her neck, briefly lit by a pair of passing headlights. Soon, they were entangled in the bed again.

***

The tires splashed through a puddle as Yanis pulled into an empty space at the far end of the hotel's lot. As the windshield wipers moaned against the glass, he checked his watch. Barely 5 a.m. It wouldn't be much longer. He sat back and thought about what had brought him here, a soft rain splashing against the roof of his sedan. While aboard the *Adjudicarus*, after watching Jillian and Jim die outside the *Bierhaus*, he'd pored over every bit of data regarding Keck's movements. In doing so, he was able to reconstruct a timeline, one he was confident would prove accurate. He understood his mistake now. What had Jillian called it, back in the woods? *Someone else's 1943. Not the one you started in.*

Betrayed by his confidence, Yanis eventually realized he needed to get back to R-Zero. The default reality.

He particularly focused on Keck's days while reinvented as Joseph Taschner. And what he uncovered was the game changer.

Jillian's Oma, Anna, had kept a secret literally borne of shame. As far as anyone knew, Jillian's father, Josef, had arrived in July 1943, when Anna was working in Munich. Her cousin, Sophie, had led a resistance movement against the Nazi party. Distributing leaflets and calling for an end to the mass murder of Jews, Sophie attended the University and studied biology. She had encouraged Anna to visit and helped her find a job waiting tables in a tavern. Barely 16, Anna looked older than she was, and had enjoyed the worldly environment a city rich in academia offered to one so under-educated. She fit in with Sophie's college-aged associates, often joining them for *bier* and sausages at one of the local taverns. No one ever asked how old she was; it was assumed she and Sophie were the same age.

Munich was rife with culture in the form of museums, opera, and Romanesque architecture. Anna would spend early evenings strolling the *Ludwigstrasse*, ducking into the *Bayerische Staatsbibliothek* to be among the volumes of books and maps, until the librarian announced they were about to close. She'd often wind up at the *Odeonsplatz*, people watching and wishing she could afford a higher education as she gazed toward the twin steeples of the *Ludwigskirche* and the Baroque grandeur of the neighboring *Theatinerkirche St. Kajetan.*

Munich's air of intelligentsia, provided by its teeming student and faculty populations, made it that much more stimulating to a woman-child who'd decided she needed to escape parental supervision. All to live her best life, *ihr bestes Lehben*, she'd convinced herself. When Sophie wrote that she should come for a visit, Anna embarked by rail the next day.

But as Sophie and her colleagues drummed up support for the resistance, Anna grew fearful. The Reich had taken notice of Sophie's group, White Rose. They'd already torn down the Herzog Max-Palais years before, and built the drab, ugly Bavarian Department of Agriculture. A massive, soulless box that stretched for blocks, punctuated only by endless rows of symmetrical windows. Clearly, the Reich intended to remove as much joy and personality as possible.

One night, as Anna returned from her promenade on the *Ludwigstrasse*, she discovered that Sophie was gone. Her brother, Hans, who lived nearby, had also disappeared. Fear gripped Anna's stomach as she tossed fitfully through the wee hours. It was in the morning that someone gave her the news. Sophie and Hans had been taken by the Gestapo, along with a friend, Christoph Probst. Three days later, the trio was beheaded by guillotine in Stadleheim Prison, retribution for their 'crimes' against the Reich.

Anna lingered in Munich for a while, but as the Nazis' presence grew, she feared her association with her cousins had made her a target. Each day, she peered over her shoulder, afraid of what she might find. A face. A uniform. A Luger plowed into her back. Scared witless, she gathered her few possessions and took the train to Hamburg in late June 1943. No one would know her there. Now approaching 17, she still had her life ahead of her, and she intended to keep it that way. The move meant her parents would lose contact, but that suited her.

She quickly found work in another tavern and then in one of Hamburg's many factories. A month later, the Allies bombed it all to shit in Operation Gomorrah. Anna was fortunate; her factory and the tavern had survived, so she still had reliable income. But from that point forward, her distrust of the Allied forces grew. More and more, the Reich seemed to make sense. After all, they had preached a stronger, better Germany, for Germans. And, hopefully, an end to this goddamn bombing.

So, it was no surprise that Anna found herself attracted to the working parts of the SS. They'd come by the tavern some nights and she'd practice her coy, flirtatious *tete-a-tetes*. Even without Sophie there as a buffer, everyone assumed she was much older. But her efforts were largely unreciprocated. No matter. Hamburg wasn't as intellectually stimulating as Munich had been, but Anna was determined to make the best of it, however long she was stuck there.

One late October morning, realizing she'd been granted time off from both the factory and the tavern, she planned an outing to nearby Luebeck. A chance to escape the dreariness of Hamburg's grey streets and downturned faces. At least Anna would have the cool air of the Baltic Sea and Luebeck's beautiful architecture to provide distraction. She set out by rail, dressed in a neat blue frock and floral hat. Intending only to stay a few hours, it was nearly evening when she boarded the train back to Hamburg.

As so often seems to happen in situations such as this, a handsome stranger caught Anna's eye. Reserved and jotting in a notebook, he stole an occasional glance at her comely, though still immature, form. His attention failed to go unnoticed. When the train pulled into the station at Hamburg, he smiled and offered his hand to help her down the platform. Her arm tucked inside his, he escorted her past the harbor to a serene little hotel.

Few words were exchanged, according to the account Yanis had read in Anna's diary, discovered decades later while Jillian cleaned out Anna's room in the nursing home. Jillian had kept the journal tucked in a desk drawer. But she never brought herself to read it, preferring to allow her grandmother's oral history to provide the chosen narrative.

But Yanis, able to access the journal, had discovered Anna's greatest confidence. Josef hadn't been born in Munich, as Anna had implied when she eventually reconciled with her parents, lugging a toddler in 1947. He'd been conceived in Hamburg in October 1944 and born the following July. Barely 18 at the time of his birth, Anna hid her shame of being an unwed mother. She made up a story to placate her parents, saying that she'd married Josef's father in Munich, with Sophie and Hans as witnesses. But he'd joined the Army and never returned. Even though she was underage, at least that implied that

Josef's birth was legitimate, something her parents were more likely to forgive. Besides, she knew full well that Sophie's and Hans' beheadings would prevent them from contradicting her. And all that time, her parents had assumed she'd stayed in Munich. No sense in giving them any reason to investigate Josef's paternity.

"He's just small for his age, *Mutter*," she'd claim. "All that rationing kept him from growing." A mother, grateful to have her child home again, will believe anything. A lie fills the belly like a warm, hearty spaetzle if she's been starving to hear it for years.

Over time, Josef's real father arranged financial assistance for him, which he eventually accepted. Oma Anna married a quiet English accountant, Wendell Qualmes, who adopted young Josef. And the rest, Yanis knew, was Qualmes family history.

He peered at the rising sun, just fracturing the drizzly horizon on this late October morning. He reached into the passenger seat and winced as he hoisted the backpack. That gunshot wound had never healed properly. He unzipped the backpack and eyed the stack of gold bricks and the letter he'd written, pleading with Anna to provide an education for the child she would soon bear. Then he patted his pocket, confirming the presence of the special instrument he'd procured for this occasion. After a series of quick exhales, he opened the car door and stepped into the dew-kissed dawn.

***

"*Liebchen*," Keck said, holding Anna one last time. He would be back at sea soon enough, and he wanted this moment to last. "I'm afraid I must go. Thank you for ... your hospitality."

She was wrapped in a blanket, hair disheveled, face flushed. He'd left a stack of *Reichsmarks* on the nightstand, enough to cover the room, breakfast, and cab fare. His purpose here had ended. He craned his neck downward, kissing her tender lips. With a hand on her cheek, he pulled away.

"*Mein Herr!*" she called out, causing Keck to turn around and raise a brow.

Her face was creased with worry, perhaps hiding a deeper concern in this moment. But she stood straight. "*Heil* Hitler!"

"*Heil* Hitler," Keck replied, then turned the doorknob and walked out. Deep in his thoughts, he didn't notice the rain-spotted backpack resting against the doorway, waiting to be discovered.

***

Outside the hotel room, Keck stepped onto the sidewalk. In the pale shadows, he lit a cigarette and walked toward the alley. He brought the filter to his lips and closed his eyes just long enough to picture Anna's warm body. He was sure to cherish that memory on long nights aboard the submarine and wanted to preserve it in his mind. A comfort of what once was and perhaps a hope of what might be again. But before he could open his eyes, a harsh right cross crashed into his face, knocking him back.

His skull bounced on the cobbled ground, scrambling his vision. When he looked up, a man with dark curly hair stood over him. A familiar face he hadn't expected.

"Damn, that felt good," the man said, a smile stretching across his lips in the dawning light, as if recalling a distant memory. "That was for my friend, Sergeant Jim Thompson."

Keck grabbed his forehead, a thick curtain of pain descending like a waterfall as he tried to steady himself and stagger to his feet. But Yanis kicked him in the face, slashing open his lip. Not yet genetically enhanced from the elixirs derived at his Argentine ranch, he was still a mere mortal in this timeline. Subject to pain like every other human. And Yanis wasn't about to show him any mercy. The time for that had long passed.

A deep groan came from Keck, who reeled and swayed, propped up on an elbow. Yanis stomped on Keck's chest, knocking him back to the ground. "And that was for my wife and son."

Keck sprawled on the sidewalk, choking on his unbalanced breath.

The past three years had robbed Yanis of his compassion. Absent of doubt, he removed the Luger from his pocket. Thompson had confiscated it during the battle for *Der Dom,* one of the more notable spoils of war. With a swastika embedded in the grip, it had been lifted from an SS officer long forgotten where he'd fallen at the base of the *Zitternberg*. Yanis could've opted for a high-powered Glock, or any compact, tactical weapon from the 2000s, a testament to technology's contribution to destruction. But the Luger—the Reich's preferred firearm—seemed like the most appropriate choice for the task that befell him. The narrow barrel glinted in the sun's first rays as he stepped closer.

"Life is indeed strange sometimes, isn't it, *Sturmbannfuhrer* Kristock Keck? You call yourself a king. The King Under the Mountain. The king of all humanity. Nothing could be further from the truth," he smirked, raising the Luger and taking aim. "As is the fate of all kings, your time to rule has come to an end."

Bleeding and dizzy, Keck gurgled, fluid filling his lungs. His eyes widened, indicating he knew he was severely compromised.

"Professor Miller," he pleaded between gasps, his stomach tightening like a wrench. "Don't—"

"Save it. I've waited three lifetimes for this moment, maybe four. I've lost count," Yanis said, cocking the Luger. "I'll have my future now, but that future won't include you. Because your time has run out."

Without hesitation, he fired, instantly neutralizing his target. As Keck laid there, the last of his lifeblood oozing out and his brains splattered on the cobblestones, Yanis calmly slid the Luger back into his pocket. Then he turned and walked away, letting the rising sun warm him as his shoes sank into the fresh puddles. Their fates now sealed, forever.

ABOUT THE AUTHOR

J. Channing is a dynamic and versatile author known for his thrilling and action-packed novels. Over his prolific career, he has penned thirteen captivating books under several different names, including the critically acclaimed *Atlas' Last Stand,* the quirky *Time Travelers' Rally Point,* and the intriguing *Murder at the Benbow Inn.* Channing's work spans multiple genres, often delving into science fiction, AI technology, and mystery, with intricate plots that keep readers on the edge of their seats. His series, Forever, explores a riveting narrative about an alien spaceship crash-landing in Germany thousands of years ago, forever altering human history.

In addition to his literary achievements, Channing has had a remarkable career as an entrepreneur and consultant. He has owned, run, or managed twenty-one different companies, leveraging his expertise to grow these businesses successfully. This extensive experience in the business world adds depth and realism to the high-tech elements often found in his stories.

Based in Boise, Idaho, Channing is also an accomplished engineer and manager. His technical expertise and innovative thinking frequently influence his writing, providing a solid foundation for his complex narratives. Moreover, Channing's adventurous spirit has taken him to twenty-six different countries. These global experiences enrich his storytelling, providing authentic and vivid settings for his novels.

J. Channing's unique blend of technical knowledge, creative writing, and global experiences makes him a standout author in the contemporary literary scene. His books continue to captivate and inspire readers around the world. For more information, visit his profiles on the Red Team Ink website, www.redteamink.com/our-authors.

www.ingramcontent.com/pod-product-compliance
Lightning Source LLC
LaVergne TN
LVHW021756060526
838201LV00058B/3120

9798330348589